PROMISED LANDS

PROMISED LANDS

A NOVEL

JANE ROGERS

THE OVERLOOK PRESS

WOODSTOCK • NEW YORK

First published in the United States in 1997 by
The Overlook Press
Lewis Hollow Road
Woodstock, New York 12498

Library of Congress Cataloging-in-Publication Data

Rogers, Jane
  Promised lands / Jane Rogers
p. cm.
1. Dawes, William, 1762-1836—Fiction. 2. Biography as a literary form—
Fiction. 3. Australia—History—1788-1851—Fiction. 4. Botany Bay
(N.S.W.)—History—Fiction. 5. History teachers—Australia—Fiction.
6. Penal colonies—Australia—Fiction. 7. Astronomers—Australia—
Fiction. 8. Biographers—Australia—Fiction. I. Title.
PR6068.0346P76 1997
823'.914—dc20

ISBN 0-87951-753-0
Originally published in Great Britain by Faber and Faber Ltd.
Manufactured in the United States of America
First American Edition
9 8 7 6 5 4 3 2 1

Contents

CHAPTER ONE

To Botany Bay

On 2 January 1788 the first ship of the First Fleet sighted Terra Australis. The fleet was fifty landless days from the Cape, eight months from England. With a fair to stiff wind behind them, the *Supply*, the *Alexander*, the *Friendship* and the *Scarborough* moved towards the coast at a good speed; the *Friendship* had broken her own record that day, making 191 miles. Cloud raced overhead, petrels rode or fought the wind, lumps of spume broke from the choppy sea and flew about the ships. By the last lunar observation Captain John Hunter and Lieutenant William Dawes had made, the position of Van Diemen's Land recorded in Cook's journal was entirely accurate.

William stood on deck with a glass, checking the distant shoreline as it gradually gained depth, colour, shape, solidity. It was not the end of the journey, but it was the sailors' first sighting of the continent they had come to settle. And after the voyage from the Cape, through the most inhospitable seas William had ever encountered, its appearance here – in just the spot recorded and predicted – had the quality of a miracle; or rather, of a figment which their collective desire for an end to their journey had willed into being.

A chart was a magical document. William had thought so on his very first voyage, aboard the *Merlin*, sailing from Portsmouth for North American waters. Magical, to find that precisely shaped coast materializing at the other side of the Atlantic. It was a whole stage better than learning to read, because what you read and imagined was also allowed to be physically real.

The voyage from the Cape had brought them across the southernmost parts of the Indian Ocean, almost into the Antarctic circle, and east to the southern coast of Van Diemen's Land. The line of their progress could be drawn on a chart; indeed, *was* recorded daily, the ship's position by latitude and longitude, verified by use of the sextant in lunar observation (on the fleeting occasions when the moon was visible) in conjunction with Maskeylene's lunar tables, and the readings of the Timekeeper. But for all its precision, William had a sense

1

that this record was pure fantasy; fantasy and almost incredible audaciousness of the intellect, to force into factual existence a direct journey across unknown seas, out of mental calculations and crosses on a piece of paper. For the reality of the voyage – the last stage of the voyage – was wilderness and chaos.

Not another ship had been sighted; it was not human territory. For days the fleet had rolled in a heavy sea with no wind, the ships swinging about with their heads different ways, chickens and goats washed overboard, and whales in the water all around them. Then strong easterlies had sprung up, driving them off-course, with rain, and albatross and petrels riding above the masts like sails broke loose; and huge seas that swamped the decks and wet everything below – clothes, bedding, and worst of all Maskeylene's tables that William had wrapped in canvas and locked in his chest; even they were wetted, so that the pages stuck together and tore easily, and brown stains blotted the fine figures and made them harder to decipher.

The ship's crew began to show symptoms of scurvy. The Timekeeper itself, which provided the basis for all their calculations and had been kept faithfully wound, with attendant rituals, at every midday since departure from England, was unaccountably let down: for which William knew he must blame himself above all others, and which omission of memory argued that his very mind was overwhelmed by wet black chaos. Sheep and hogs died nightly. For six days a gale kept the *Supply* almost constantly under water, shuddering, battling, moving up towards the air; then dumped on by the next great wave, pouring down the masts and deck, running between decks, into food and bedding, eyes, mouths, nostrils – over and over and over again. Men's flesh was pitted, shrivelled with wet, and white as lard with cold.

But it grew colder still. Bitter weather, dark with hail and snow, low clouds that met a rising, filthy sea: black fog and no visibility from ship to ship, the lamps muffled in brief halos of flurrying illumined snowflakes, so they had to sound their guns to avoid running foul of one another or drifting off into infinite blackness. In the ice-grey daylight the lookout on the *Supply* called out rocks under the bows, at which the helm was put alee – but instead of rocks the men on deck made out, humping out of the white froth, two huge black whales, so close to the ship men could have stepped from the gunwale on to their backs, and men below felt the beasts' tails beneath the wood as the ship moved over them. That wet, that darkness, that roaring of waves and

2

heave of non-human life and creaking of the labouring ship and snap and crack of canvas, shouts of sailors, cries of sea birds, and endless tearing howl of wind: William knew that was the reality of where they were, tumbled about by elements that could as easily send them five hundred fathoms down to the glassy black world at the bottom, or five hundred fathoms south towards waters infested with ice-floes and freezing stillness, as five hundred fathoms east along their projected course.

How could they dare to imagine that on a plane between the heaving sea and the whipping twirling howling sky, they, in their brittle wooden shells, could choose to move so many miles south, so many miles east, and arrive at a place determined by themselves, where the sea would end and a land begin, where they might shelter in an already imagined harbour (the outward rocks charted in Cook's journal, whose flimsy pages had twice made this impossible journey), and set foot on an unknown land which was ordained by their government, 12,000 miles away, to be their home?

On such a voyage, so far from England, the dots on paper, the lines and numbers on a chart, were blind faith. And so when you came in to land, like this, and found it where it should be, at the other side of the sea's incalculable wildness, faith was substantiated; the imagined made real; like proof of the existence of God (which indeed it was – proof of His eternal bounty and kind guardianship of their voyage).

William, turning from the blotted, faded chart, the diagram, the dream of land, to the physical, rocky, spray-crested shoreline, the regular land crash of waves beating huge and slow in his ears, felt his stomach convulse with an elation he had ascribed to and envied in seabirds: felt inside that moment when, in a high wind, a gull suddenly lifts from the topsail yard-arm, hangs weightless in the gale, then plummets sheer to its prey. Without a breath. Without a doubt. Motion.

*

STEPHEN
I wrote 'motion' then bracketed it, and inserted 'action'. On a read through, crossed out the brackets and 'action', leaving 'motion'. But now prefer 'action'. Of course. Action. What William does: go forth, conquer, explore – boys-own stories, action. As opposed to my – inaction.
The problem with 'action', though, is its military connotation, which I can't pretend he wouldn't think of. As a marine, he has seen action in

North American waters against the French; on the high seas against Malaysian pirates. 'Action' – an engagement, a grappling, a fight. Guns, bayonets, blood. That's action. Killing people is action. I can't imagine he would have enjoyed it or found it thrilling; he's too burdened with conscience to be elated by a fight. I may be wrong, but at the moment I don't see him relishing 'action' of that kind; and so, with regret, must forgo the word.

*

Hunter, ever wary of running on to a lee shore, gave the signal for the ships to lay to well before dark. This was as close to land as they would go for now; their voyage lay to the east, following the coast round, then north for Botany Bay. As far as William could make out, the land, which was high and rocky, was covered in scrubby bushes. In the distance were hills where the green was interrupted by odd patches of white, like snow. The darkness of the overcast sky deepened to night, and fires began to be visible on the land. How many natives around each one? Using Governor Phillip's glass, William counted twenty-six fires dotting the black land mass.

When he came on deck after dinner the wind had blown itself out, taking the clouds with it. Fires still glinted and twinkled from the land; overhead, closer-seeming than the fires, the southern sky's heavy crop of stars dangled almost close enough to pluck. The new moon, show-ing only a pared and delicate crescent of light, seemed to stand back from competition, allowing first place to the brilliance of the stars. Using the sextant, William took a careful reading of the moon's posi-tion at 1 p.m. Greenwich time, by the Timekeeper; then sat back with the charts he had obtained at the Cape to try again to make sense of the southern stars. The constellations were familiar shapes, but upside-down. His concentration was blurred by tiredness.

Next morning Van Diemen's Land had gone, melted away in the night. The sea was grey with a queasy irregular swell, and they were battling on to the north-east, against a gusty head wind.

They must be within a week, even if this wind kept up – say ten days at most – of Botany Bay. But even ten days would be too long for the sheep, because all the hay was finished. There was nothing on board for them to eat; the sailors mixed up a paste from flour and water, but it was too fine for the animals' stomachs and passed straight through. There was no wood left, and only a week's supply of coal. They had been on a three pints per day water ration for weeks, but now even that

4

must be reduced. Some bundles of wood were brought over in the long boat from the *Alexander* – Governor Phillip was determined not to put ashore before Botany Bay, and William sympathized entirely with his view. They were all, from time to time, looking over their shoulders to see the *Sirius* and the rest of the fleet catching up; their own time had been so bad, the others could not be far behind – and yet the plan had been for the flying squadron to land early at the Bay, and prepare accommodation so that the convicts could be landed straight away.

He was glad to be running ahead of the fleet. More than glad; he thought that if the Governor had not picked him to be one of the advance party, his heart would have dried up. If he had not been of the first party who would set foot in the new colony . . . He thought of Cook with envy; a ship of scientifically knowledgeable men, free to follow their own inclinations in putting in to land, charting, exploring, voyaging on – without the leaden cargo of convicts which determined and hobbled the First Fleet's movements.

And yet – and yet, he reminded himself, it may be that more good would be achieved through the efforts of the First Fleet, than through twenty voyages of scientific discovery. They were bringing this sad cargo as seed to plant in a new world; might the convicts not grow and flourish and produce a harvest better than their own poor selves? This is, William reminded himself, a very great social experiment and may lead to real improvements in the happiness of humanity – both by removing these unfortunate parasites from England, where at best they are confined in prison to plan new crimes, and at worst let loose to perpetrate them upon an undeserving public; and by bringing them to a new land where, if they choose to raise themselves by their own exertions, their pasts may be forgotten. It is a kind of rebirth, he thought with satisfaction, this long and difficult voyage is the labour that delivers them, fresh-hatched as it were, on to a new shore.

He hoped they would be reborn. Ralph Clark's stories of the women on the *Friendship* showed that they needed it. Ralph had described to him their abominable sluttishness, their swarming up to the seamen's quarters if ever opportunity arose, their mocking, cackling calls to the men.

'And worse,' Ralph had added. 'Much worse.'

'Worse? How?'

Ralph leaned closer to him. 'They *show*,' he whispered. 'They lift their skirts and show themselves – they *touch* themselves, to taunt the men. It is the most nauseating, depraved spectacle . . .'

A hot shudder of revulsion ran through William. These convict women were below. In the decks below the officers' mess; these women with their hot, sweating bodies, with their private parts that they made public display of – and *touched*. He got up quickly from the little table, and so far forgot himself as to give his head a real crack on the beam, although it was in exactly the same position here as in the *Sirius*, which he was used to. He wished Ralph would not speak, but Ralph was warming to his subject. 'In that week after we crossed the Line – you recall, when it was so hot and close – such numbers of them fainted down there in the hold that Master Gilbert sent for Surgeon White to take a look at 'em. And he said they were sick for lack of air and we must leave the gratings off. But do you know, then, in heat which made it an effort to stand, to sit, to raise a drink to your parched lips, they gathered themselves up from swooning on the floor and came up through the open gratings like monkeys hot for the sailors, and were found going at it in every corner of the ship. I came upon one myself with two sailors, up against the water-butt, and one had his – ' William put out his hand, to say enough. And Ralph paused, then nodded, and sank his head on to his hands. 'I wonder such creatures can be dignified by the name of women. They are animals, worse. I never thought to be so sickened. I wish to God I had never left dear Alicia and England.'

Ralph was a sensitive man; William did not wish himself back in England, but he did sorrow in his heart for the degraded appetites and lost souls of these poor, forsaken women. He did pray that they might be reborn.

The journey up the coast was wretchedly slow, battling against the same stiff north-easterly and with a constant stream of clouds overhead. The air was warm and moist, almost steamy. They could not see the land, away to the west; but knew when they were drawing near to Botany Bay not only by calculations of latitude and longitude, but also by the strength of the current opposing them, which had been recorded in this place by Cook.

Then on the seventeenth the skies cleared and the sun rose yellow in the east, and land rose green in the west. As the ship tacked forward against the current, every man with a glass strained to peer at the land, making out at last trees, rocks, low hills, and the heads and entrance to Botany Bay – and small stick-like figures ranged along the shore. Phillip commandeered his own telescope, so William was obliged to use the Board of Longitude's eighteen-inch glass; it became clearer and clearer, as they approached, that these dark figures were unwelcoming. They appeared naked, and were waving sticks or spears in gestures of defiance. At last the ship was near enough for the shrill sound of their voices to be heard over the creak and flap of the rigging and the slap of the waves against the prow.

'Warra! Warra! Warra!'

William listened again, then took his notebook out of his pocket. He opened it at the back and, turning it upside-down, wrote the heading 'Language of the Indians of New South Wales', and made the following entry:

'Warra warra = Go away.'

OLLA

I have a child. Who will be remarkable. He will change the world.

Faith is the key to miracles. Though he seems weak, he is strong. Though he cannot speak, he knows all tongues. Though his eyes are closed, he sees into men's hearts. He is small, but mighty.

I am his mother. I bore him, I will raise him. Feed and clothe him, shelter and defend him, answer his every need. All the energy of my being is his; he will take and use it.

And when he has taken every scrap of me, when I am transformed into him, as water is sucked up and absorbed by the roots of a growing tree, as wood is consumed and transformed by the fire it feeds; then he will stand alone, and they will see. Everyone will see then, what Daniel is. His power will melt wickedness, rage blazing through corruption and darkness, he will conquer and purify the world back to its innocent beginnings. All the shady stagnant places where light cannot break through the canopy – he will burn. Prisoners will spring from dungeons, and the sick from their confining beds. The face of the earth will be razed, and then new. Tender green shoots, tender and soft as the down on a child's head, downy new growth will flourish, covering the naked earth with its extraordinarily brilliant green. He is gentle but he will be pitiless, in the destruction of evil.

Because Daniel is powerful, I must be cunning. There are many who would wish him dead. Of course, because he would destroy them, wipe out their crimes and the sources and profits of those crimes. War and sickness would be finished, and those parasites who batten and grow on their pelts would be crushed, like so many insects.

That is why he has come in this form, appearing most weak, most unable, most powerless: so as not to arouse their suspicions. I am the custodian of his secret.

It's true, if they knew, Daniel would have more enemies than anyone on earth. The evil, naturally. But also the good. The good even more than the evil. The good are as selfish, as hungry for power as the others. Stephen, my good husband. Married me out of pity, to show his goodness. Taught the children in his school, trying to impart his goodness. He wanted them to be as he thought they should be. He fought to impose his vision on them. They fought back for their identities, for their lives. As he will, when Daniel comes to power.

He will not be able to see the greater good that Daniel brings to earth, nor will he see that purifying fire is needed, for the green shoots to grow. His vision is circumscribed. Violence is outside it. He cannot destroy. And therefore, he cannot create.

The new world will grow from the ashes of the old, as the phoenix rises from the flames that consume her. And even the good, if their minds cannot embrace that huge transformation, if their hopes and goodness are petty, like Stephen's, even they must burn. Only the innocent good – who remain open as the naked earth to all weathers, who do not struggle – only the innocent good will be spared.

I cannot answer everything that will happen, that is not my role. My role is to deliver a saviour: to prepare, to nurture, to guard. He is more than what I put into him. He enlightens me, not I him.

From the moment of his birth a hundred things have become clear to me. All doctors and medical experts are destroyers of life. Everything is the opposite of what it seems; once that key is applied the world springs forth translated, no longer puzzling to understand. Doctors destroy life through grim materialism. Through their belief that all flesh is tissue; that a human being is a skeleton, two hundred bones, a few organs and eight pints of blood. We are meat, and they carve.

Daniel, they said ('Oh, have you named him already? That's nice') is severely handicapped. Brain-damaged. Possibly blind. He may never walk, or perform co-ordinated movements. Damaged meat.

What is alive – the spirit, the miracle – they do not see. 'His quality of life will never amount to much, Mrs Beech. I'm sorry, that is very harsh, but you and your husband have to face it now and decide whether you want us to operate or whether you think it would be kinder, really, just to let him . . . slip away. I can promise you he won't feel any pain.'
'Slip away?'
'Normally it is our practice, in those cases where there is very little – no hope – of the child ever enjoying – to the smallest degree – a normal life; usually it is our practice not to sustain life artificially.' He frowns at me. 'Your English – it seems very good – you do understand?' I watch him. He chooses his words. 'Yes. It is usual, in

9

such a case, to abstain from medical intervention, and let nature take her course.'

'Let him die?'

'Exactly.'

'When you could keep him alive?'

'Yes, but the point I'm making Mrs Beech, is that even if we perform the operation – which he may not survive, incidentally, the statistics are in the region of 65 per cent, I believe – if we perform the operation, we cannot reverse or diminish the level of handicap he has been born with. And it would be very unusual indeed for a child with this type of problem to – to live beyond the age of five. I'm very sorry, Mrs Beech, to have to tell you this. But you need to have all the facts before you. Sometimes I'm afraid we just have to accept that certain things are not meant to be . . .'

'Thank you.'

'What I would like to do is to talk this through fully with your husband and yourself together – '

'Thank you.'

'If you could ask him to be here at three this afternoon?'

'Thank you. He'll be at work.'

'But surely he would want to be involved in a decis – '

'Thank you. I understand.'

'Mrs Beech – '

'Where's Daniel?'

'He's in the nursery, he's in good hands.'

'I want to see him.'

'Now that would be very silly, you need to rest, you've got twelve stitches that must heal up nicely – '

'I want to see him.'

'Well I'll see what sister says – ' making for the door.

'*I want to see him!*'

'You mustn't get excited, Mrs Beech. I'll send sister in – '

And then I make myself be cunning and calm because they would use their needle again, put me to sleep. So calmly quietly smiling I say to sister, 'I would so much like to see my baby, sister. I'm sure I would sleep, if only I could see him. It would put my mind at rest.' And she smiles at me, and sends a little girl in green with a wheelchair to fetch me, and they wheel me to the babies' room. They lie tiny and naked, red, in plastic boxes, like the vegetable compartment in the fridge. Daniel lies outstretched, peaceful, with those dreadful tubes in his nose and arm. He sleeps.

'He's very calm,' the nurse tells me, but she looks frightened. I sense that she can tell, she can guess who he is. I stare at him, and I can see the minute shudder of his heart beneath his ribs. He is wound, he ticks. Nothing on earth will stop him now. Unless I make a mistake.

Stephen is back within half an hour, with flowers, fruit, juice and chocolates.

'How is he? Have you seen the consultant? How are you feeling – oh my poor Olla.' He puts his arms around me, he is crying. He buries his face in my shoulder and sobs. Now he can pity not only me but also himself, and the child. There should be satisfactions for him in that. I meanwhile, am calm. At last he lifts up his head, and wipes his eyes and nose.

'The consultant hasn't been, has he? Sister told me between nine and ten – ' He glances at his watch, it is 8.50.

'Yes, he came early. He explained it all to me.'

'What? What did he say?'

'There is damage. They can't say exactly – of course, it would be dangerous to do tests on a new baby. But there is an operation which they must do immediately, to give him a chance. This is routine, many babies have this operation. Then we must wait and hope, they can tell us more as he gets older.'

'But – will he be – normal? I mean, is his brain – ?'

'How can they tell, Stephen? You want them to open his head? He is alive, I have just seen him, he sleeps peacefully, he wants to live. He cannot live without this operation, so he must have the operation and we will see.'

'Is he . . . deformed?' He is crying again.

'No. Go and see him. Ask the nurse to take you.' He is afraid but he goes, like a man to his punishment.

At 2.30 I send Stephen out with a shopping list of baby clothes, and ask him to choose me new library books. He will be gone for a couple of hours. When I see the consultant I tell him we have discussed the matter fully; my husband and I want everything possible done to save the child.

He opens his mouth to argue with me but I smile calmly. I have such reserves of strength now; such calm, cunning strength. I am a vixen and they will kill me a thousand times before they harm my child.

11

'Do you know what happened to my other children, doctor?'
He looks embarrassed, flustered, makes to reach for the notes in the envelope at the end of the bed, then thinks better of it.
'The miscarriages? Well often an early miscarriage is nature's way of disposing of an unviable – a damaged – foetus.' He gives in and does check the notes. 'Of course – you have had one full-term normal baby, there's no reason at all why you should not try – '
'You know my son Timothy died?'
He pauses, blinks. He does not know; why should he? Timothy was not even born in this hospital. It was nine years ago.
'I – yes – '
'He was normal,' I say. 'Perfectly healthy. For seven weeks. Then he stopped breathing. The 'cot death' as you call it. So I believe – don't you? – that while there's life, there's hope.'
He stares at his hands.
'We are not afraid of looking after Daniel. I will look after him, my husband has work. We want you to do everything in your power – I beg you, everything – to keep our son alive.'
He nods, he is ashamed now and I am glad of it. He nods and leaves my room.

And from now on my task at every turn, at every move of theirs, is to defend him. Conceal their death-mongering tales from Stephen, who would believe them; select from their armoury of skills those that will help my son, and reject those that degrade and stultify.

I know my role and what I can do. I do not take the tablets to suppress my milk. I ask the kindly little nurse for a breast pump and extract it. In the nursery he is being fed intravenously. But soon he will need my milk; it will nourish him better, give him more protection from disease.

*

After his operation, he makes a good recovery. On the third day they let me hold him. On the fourth day the sister says she's going to try him with a bottle.
'I will breast-feed him.'
'But – '
I show her my large milky udders. The little green-uniformed nurse will get into trouble, sister's nose is very out of joint. 'When you are given medication, it is in your own best interests to take it. You need to build up your strength.'

12

I do not reply.

'Have you breast-fed before?' she asks callously.

'Yes.'

'Well it won't be the same with a baby like this. He won't have the normal reflexes; he may have no sucking reflex at all. We'll need to feed him with a teat with a very large hole in it, that's the way to encourage him to suck. And the difficulty is, he won't have the same responses as a normal baby, he won't know when he's had enough. We feed them with a bottle so we know how much they've had, there's no telling with breast is there?'

Well yes, of course there is. My breasts are tight and hard as drums; when he has fed they will be soft and slack and empty. Surely I can be expected to tell as much, from my own breasts, as a farmer who milks a cow. He can tell at a glance if her udder is empty. Does she think me stupider than that? But I do not answer, cunning is important. I simply say, 'Let me try. It can't do any harm.' She plonks herself on the end of the bed to watch. But Stephen arrives, thank goodness, so I can ask her to go away.

I hold Daniel's mouth to my nipple but his mouth does not close. Stephen watches us intently. I am afraid I might begin to cry, when I should be cunning, cunning as a vixen. Suddenly the prickling at the top of my nose and in my eyes reminds me of that moment when the flow of milk is triggered – yes, it is the moment you are about to burst into tears, or sneeze, it is that same moment – of – of – . If the milk begins to flow into his mouth he will suck. He will swallow. I am sure of it. If I started the flow with the breast pump – or – ?

'Stephen – can you – it's because he's been on that beastly tube, he doesn't know what to do – if you would just suck, for a moment, to make the milk come – ?'

He looks at me then kneels on the chair beside the bed and takes my nipple in his mouth.

'Suck!' I say. 'Harder! Harder!' Suddenly I feel the rush of milk and blissful release, and see Stephen's startled eyes. He moves away and I replace his head with Daniel's, the milk squirts over his chin and into his mouth, I press his head up against my breast. Milk runs out of the corners of his mouth, I plug it with my nipple. We watch. We wait. He swallows.

He does not suck, but he swallows. That is a beginning.

13

CHAPTER TWO

Woolwich and the stars

Botany Bay was not the place for a settlement. Cook had promised open meadows, with lush grass and stately trees, well watered. But the land was marshy, unsuitable for building, infested with mosquitoes and dotted with tufts of coarse grass. The sailors, gathering armfuls for the starving sheep, cursed as it cut their leathery hands. Despite the sunshine there were no fruits or nuts or even edible greens to be seen – only a barren sameness of vegetation. The sparse trees were ragged with strips of peeling bark, and lacked proper fullness of shape in their branches. The wood was hard as iron and the wood-gathering party had little to show for their labour. No decent-sized watercourse was found; they had filled their barrels at small streams, but there was insufficient water to support a town. Added to which, the sea level in Botany Bay had sunk alarmingly at low tide; it would only be possible to enter or leave the harbour near high tide, and the openness of the entrance meant that it was poorly sheltered. Even on a calm day the swell inside the Bay was significant.

The rest of the fleet arrived only one day behind them, and Phillip set off immediately with a party to explore the coastline to the north. They returned with good news. Port Jackson, only a few hours' journey up the coast, was an eminently more suitable site.

It was impossible to sleep during the night before the voyage to Port Jackson; partly for excitement at the knowledge that the final harbour was so close at hand, and partly because of the constant comings and goings. Phillip had decided that the *Supply* should set sail at first light, ahead of the others, taking a company of marines and forty convicts – but these had to be transferred from the *Lady Penrhyn*, and arrived with much shouting and hallooing in the middle of the night.

Dawn revealed the almost incredible sight of two large sailing ships outside the harbour. At first they were thought to be Dutch, come to contest the British claim to New Holland; their sudden appearance in these distant, empty waters seemed an omen of ill luck. But then they were recognized as French, and Governor Phillip remembered hearing news, back in England, that a French expedition of scientific discovery was in the Southern Seas. He determined, nevertheless, to sail for Port Jackson without delay, and raise the standard there before paying respects to the French. It must be made clear to them that this was an English colony.

At daylight the *Supply* weighed anchor, but the strength of the wind forced her sailors to drop it again within minutes. A real gale was blowing in from the sea, from the south, making it impossible for the ship to approach the mouth of the Bay. It was a wind for the French, should they wish to enter – but they had dropped back out of sight, and the Governor's anxiety over their intentions increased.

The strength of the gusting wind showed no sign of dropping, but when the tide turned they weighed again and set out on the ebb, with loosened topsails, into the teeth of the gale. William, on deck, watched the men in the rigging struggling to obey the bosun's orders as ropes and sailcloth became violent, thrashing weapons in the wind, and the little brig slapped against and lurched over the huge rollers coming in from the sea. It felt as if the force of them would shiver her apart. It would be too ridiculous to have made such a journey, only to founder in Botany Bay itself. He noted with relief that though the *Sirius* had made the signal for all ships to weigh, they had all anchored again and were making no move to follow the *Supply*. He feared greatly for the astronomical glasses and instruments on the *Sirius*; he had packed them in rags, and their boxes were securely lashed, but to wilfully subject them to such a battering by the ocean was foolishness. It only needed the *Supply* to hoist English colours at Port Jackson; the other ships, surely, could wait for calmer weather.

When they were at last out of the Bay they ran north along the coast, the sky above them full of wheeling sea-birds riding the winds. The land began to rise and become more rocky, the cliffs were flanked by sandy beaches at the base. The rollers coming in were high but even, and the air cloudy with the mist of their spray. The regular crash as they broke on the shore was amplified back to sea by the cliffs, and seemed almost a drum roll of expectation. Finally, the steep bluff heads of Port Jackson came into sight and they rounded into the harbour. The report from Phillip's advance party was accurate: sheltered, wooded bays stretched out to both left and right, the way divided by a rocky outcrop facing the port entrance. Taking the southerly channel, they sailed for several miles into a landscape of extraordinary beauty. Up ahead the sun was dropping towards the horizon behind banks of

15

swiftly moving cloud, and casting stray beams of strong yellow light across the densely wooded hills. The trees grew thick and luxuriant as a jungle over the land, ending, before the deep blue waters' edge, in curves and crescents of pale gold sand. Any number of bays and inlets and landing places offered themselves, both to left and right, and the depth – as they moved on down the channel taking soundings – remained sufficient to take the largest ship afloat. Along some of the bays groups of natives stood by their canoes, waving and shouting. It was hard to believe they had paths and homes in the dense, closed foliage behind them. The crashing rollers of the open sea were here no more than a gentle swell with a little surface wrinkling of waves running lightly before the breeze.

Phillip had chosen a deep, narrow cove on the south side of the harbour, about six miles in from the sea. The water was four to five fathoms, enabling ships to come close in to the rocky shore to unload. He named it Sydney Cove in honour of Baron Sydney, the Secretary of State for the Home Department, the man responsible for this prison-colony. It felt more protected, and also more mysterious, than Botany Bay. The steep cliffs and valleys, the darkness of the woodlands, promised secrets; the distance from the sea's noise made the rustles and squawks in the undergrowth sound louder. There was a scent of eucalyptus in the air. They would not go ashore till daylight now. On deck after dinner, William heard strange cries and calls from the forest – monkeys? Birds? Jackals? He could not tell. The sky was completely obscured by clouds and after a while the darkness seemed to William to be more intense than any he had known. It seemed to flow towards them from the dark woods and to rise up to them from the black watery depths, and to descend on to them from the pitchy skies. It was a calm darkness, a safe, warm, enfolding darkness. There was no danger from wind or wave. William cradled his optimism, glad to be in the place, glad of a night's slow initiation before landing; a dark vigil of hearing and smelling what would become also visible, tangible, in daylight. He wanted to pace and control his reactions, to come at it, as it were, in readiness.

The twenty-sixth dawned clear and bright. Phillip and the officers made the first landing. Dividing the centre, at the heart of the bay, ran a fresh stream. They pulled up the boats on the strip of sand near this stream, and walked a little way up it. It ran fast and silent through the thick woods. William, like several of the others, crouched to cup his hands and drink the sweet water. Underfoot the ground was rocky; it sloped up gently from the water's edge into the darkness of the trees. Phillip did not give them time to explore.

'We will commence clearing the woodland from the shore upwards. The first party of convicts and marines can be landed immediately. A flagstaff will be erected here where I stand to commemorate the landing place. I want guards posting to prevent the convicts escaping into the woods, where they may annoy the natives.'

Each officer was given detailed instructions and the knot of men broke up to follow them.

William was to select a spot for the construction of a saw-pit and set a gang to work on it, then examine the surrounding area to discover the best sites for particular accommodation and tents. A limit was also to be set to the initial clearance, a perimeter that soldiers could patrol.

Once he had fulfilled the first order, William set off to examine the area and mark a perimeter. Sergeant Knight, detailed to accompany him, he left in charge of the saw-pit. It was such a luxury to be alone – to be walking, alone, on dry land – that he wanted to savour it. He automatically counted his paces as he walked, heading inland (due west) for the first half-mile, then south (parallel with the stream) for half a mile, then east to rejoin the course of the stream higher up. There was patchy scrub between the big trees, but it was not difficult to make his way through. At the end of the half-mile south he notched three tree trunks with his knife, and squatted with his back against one, for a drink. It was mid-morning, and very warm. The voices of the men labouring on the shore were muffled by the trees now; the vast land silence was emphasized by little, close noises. Odd rustles and a cracking twig; the irregular repeated patter of something small (a type of seed, he guessed) falling from a high tree to the ground; the sudden whine of insects closing in. There was no wind, no bird-song, no sound of water. For a moment he closed his eyes, leaning his head back against the peeling, papery bark; through his absorption in sound and silence and solitude came a little tug of memory, which he momentarily resisted, then allowed himself to be pulled along by . . .

He was back in the empty dormitory at Woolwich, squatting with his back pressed against the chimney-breast for such dregs of warmth as he might glean from the fire downstairs, his ears cocked for any change in the level of raucous chatter and laughter from below. The yelping, breaking voices of his fellow cadets made him think of dogs. While they stayed in the dining-room he was safe. In the evening darkness of the dormitory he was protected, invisible. His alert eyes

17

knew the shapes of shadows in the room, the lighter rectangles cast by the unshuttered windows; moved up to seek the tiny consoling pricks of starlight which sometimes showed through the higher panes. On overcast nights there was no hope, no distant stars, nothing else in the universe but himself and the darkness and the yelping dogs who would at any moment come pounding up the stairs and into the dormitory in a storm of light and noise. The terror before they burst in was always worse than anything they did. Knowing this, he forced himself to remain still through it, his bowels loose, his breath short and fluttery, eyes fixed on the window. Once they were in the room they were only boys; could only jeer, insult, torment, in so many ways. They liked to make him cry or talk, and sometimes he did, when they twisted his arms up his back or stood on his hands. But it was not *him* that talked or cried, he himself was still leaning against the chimney-breast, away from them, untouched by them. It was a little better since he had stopped trying to sleep on a bed; they had stopped putting filth in it, and Henry Abbott who shared it (all the younger cadets sleeping two to a bed) had stopped kicking him for that. Now he curled on the floor underneath it, and they sometimes forgot he was there.

He was not the only one, he knew that. Some boys came and left within weeks. They had broken John Fletcher's wrist and his father had named four of the ringleaders. He was told they would be flogged, but everyone knew the masters were afraid to punish them. God saw them. God saw their behaviour, and one day they would suffer for it.

God tested his chosen ones – as Christ himself was tested by suffering – to prove their strength and love. It was important to remember that the tormentors were weaker, that they had given in to the Devil's temptations to be vicious. They were weaker, their victims stronger. It was important to remember.

The chaplain, Mr Curzon, held a meeting on a Sunday afternoon for those boys who wanted to attend. The majority sneered at them for mealy-mouthed Methodists, but were not willing to waste their Sunday afternoon freedom on disrupting the meeting, so it continued in peace. Sunday morning service was obligatory, but the afternoon meeting was different. It was a small gathering of selected and self-selected outcasts; Mr Curzon talked to them about Christ's life, and read the latest pamphlet of John Wesley's sermons, or passages from *The Pilgrim's Progress*. He talked about the responsibility of each man for his individual soul, about the joy and suffering which sprang from that accountability to God. He showed that conscience was man's greatest friend, and to do right *in spite of all*, the true Christian's joyful duty. Sunday afternoon was the place to draw strength for the week.

There was no point in telling Benjamin, his father, about the bullying. Either Benjamin would have thought William a coward and told him to stick up for himself, or else he would have complained to the headmaster, making William's situation ten times worse. Benjamin knew Lieutenant-Colonel Patterson, and four members of the Board of Ordnance – that was how William had got into the Academy. William understood the inflexibility of his father's ambitions for him – and, indeed, the gratitude and obedience he was owed in return. As Clerk of the Works in the Portsmouth Ordnance Office, Benjamin wanted his son to be a high-ranking officer. The Royal Academy – 'the Shop' – at Woolwich was the obvious route to a commission in the Royal Engineers, and thence to a military career that Benjamin himself would be able to influence and advance, through his Ordnance Office contacts. There were a number of favours he could call in, on William's behalf.

But to stay at Woolwich – to endure three or four years of it, and then to be in the Royal Engineers with these same louts as fellow officers – was an appalling prospect. The only way out would be to suggest to Benjamin a more ambitious and glittering career path; to display a special talent, to seduce his paternal pride with the notion that William was destined for greater things in some other arena. When he was fifteen, William returned to Portsmouth for the summer holidays obsessed with not going back to Woolwich. He spent the first week pacing round the docks, imagining himself into a position aboard one of the naval vessels there.

It was possible to slip past the gangs of sailors and dockers manhandling stores, the knots of drunken young midshipmen returning from the Blue Posts, the dockside molls looking for custom, the men and chests and supplies and weapons loading and unloading, the hawkers, the bum-boat women, and the beggars, unnoticed; to be more anonymous in that crowd than sitting alone in his father's house. And he was consequently very startled when a tall young man who bumped into him glanced into his face and said, 'William Dawes!'

It was William Bradley, four years his senior. Bradley's last year at Portsmouth Grammar had overlapped with William's first, and Bradley had taken William's class for music while the master was away. They looked at each other warily, noting the changes time had made. Bradley's face was more closed, more defensive; he wore his black hair in a pigtail, like a seaman, and he was deeply tanned. He had been in

19

the navy three years. William admitted he was at the Royal Academy at Woolwich, and Bradley laughed sympathetically. 'It can't be as bad as the Naval Academy here – my father says that for thieving and gambling they put the prisoners on the hulks to shame.'

'Is that why he let you go to sea?'

To go to sea himself, William knew he would have to run away. Benjamin would simply never consent to him beginning as a second lieutenant's boy or whatever it was Bradley was working his way up from.

'He certainly wouldn't have wanted me at the college – he teaches there. Maths and astronomy. You can imagine, how they would treat a master's son – '

William nodded.

'He teaches me himself when I'm home,' Bradley volunteered. 'Astronomy. He's got a reputation for that. He teaches a few private pupils.'

Before any plan had formed in William's mind, he was groping after a glimmering – a glimmering of light at the top of a dark window. Stars. Might stars become the hard currency of a career bright enough to dazzle Benjamin?

He discovered from Bradley that his father was nephew to the great James Bradley, late Astronomer Royal. That he had worked as James Bradley's assistant at the Royal Greenwich Observatory, and that his knowledge of the science was as up-to-date as any man's in England. Astronomy was not part of the studies at Woolwich.

Over the following days William borrowed and read several books on astronomy, understanding maybe a quarter of them; and nursed a seed of hope, examining it and tending it to see how it might grow and yield him an escape route. In his attic bedroom at night he opened the thick opaque skylight and stood on a chair to look out at the stars. Fixed in glittering and dispassionate silence, they looked down equally on the noisy taverns and dockyards, on the Royal Academies at Woolwich and Portsmouth, on silent hills and fields, and on the empty rolling sea. They were farther away than anything. They were a way out.

When he had finished the astronomy books, he read them over again. Benjamin, innocently delighted by his son's new interest, borrowed an old telescope from a retired captain he knew, and William studied and drew maps of those sections of the night sky which were visible from the two attic windows. In August, terrified but determined, William called to see Mr John Bradley. He was mellower and more gentle than his son, but similarly tall, and with the same piercing, bright eyes. William asked if it was possible to come for private tuition in astronomy. When he told Benjamin, he had already spent a morning and an evening with John Bradley, and been introduced to the astronomical quadrant, a reflecting and a refracting telescope, and a range of detailed charts.

He told Benjamin carefully, circumspectly. Firstly, the news that would please him: that William was learning astronomy from the master at the Royal Naval College, who was formerly assistant to the Astronomer Royal. Secondly, that in order to continue his studies in astronomy, it would be necessary for him to remain in Portsmouth and not return to Woolwich.

Benjamin was appalled that William wanted to abandon engineering. His studies in gunnery and fortification and bridge-building, in mining and magazine techniques, in the setting up and supplying of trains of artillery – was all this knowledge, and the career that should follow it, to be thrown away? Where on earth else was it useful, but in the Royal Engineers? William would be ready for a commission by and by, where else would he get one without needing to spend a farthing, but in Engineers or Artillery?

Quietly, respectfully and persistently William answered that a commission in Engineers was nothing to the honours that might await him if he could pursue studies in astronomy. Astronomers were highly valued by the navy; they made discoveries which were useful in navigation. They were on the way to solving the riddle of how to measure longitude at sea. They were revered as scientists, explorers, men of learning. A captain of Engineers was nothing next to an astronomer. Benjamin capitulated.

Standing on the chair in his bedroom and staring through the propped-open skylight at the constellations he could now name and draw, William offered up a prayer of thanks, and a vow to be worthy of the freedom he was being given. He would work. He would learn. He would do something great. He would never go back to Woolwich.

And so he had studied under John Bradley for eighteen months, while Benjamin discussed his future prospects with everyone who crossed his path at the Ordnance Office. Once William was seventeen, he and Benjamin reached a compromise. It was agreed that he should take up the offer of a commission as second lieutenant in the Marines. His engineering and fortification skills would prove useful on land

– and his knowledge of astronomy would be an asset, in terms of navigational skills, at sea. He would pursue his interest in astronomy as and when he could, and would hope that one day he might be given some astronomical observation duties as part of his marine service.

And now, he was here. Astronomer by appointment of the Board of Longitude to the Botany Bay expedition. Unpaid astronomer, true; still on no more than the pay of the other second lieutenants. But with specific duties to establish an observatory, and responsibility for Board of Longitude astronomical instruments worth £500 and more. This was where he would make his name, God willing. God's design was becoming apparent, bringing him from the wretchedness of Woolwich, via his meeting with William Bradley, to astronomical studies, the commission in the Marines, and his present duties. As if proof of a designing Hand were needed, William Bradley was here in New South Wales as well, serving as first lieutenant on the *Sirius*. Mutual respect and liking, as well as the Portsmouth connection, drew them together.

He shifted his position, taking the weight off his aching ankles, and knelt on the dry ground. Silently he offered up a prayer for the success of his observatory, adding the hope that all his work in New South Wales might prove pleasing to God. Then he got to his feet, took a careful compass reading, and set off due east.

When William arrived back at the landing spot, men were toiling like ants. The boats had made several journeys now and piles of crates, boxes and barrels stood on the sand. Groups of men were at work tree-felling, and their axes and shouts made a constant clamour. Others were dragging branches and trunks to the saw-pit, which was being lined with ready-cut logs from the *Supply*. Others were piling branches of grey-green leaves on to a high smoking fire. Four men were unrolling the bundled canvasses of the tents, and counting out poles, pegs and strings in even heaps. The Governor was in discussion with a couple of men who supported a drunkenly tilted flagstaff; as William approached them he realized that they must have struck rock, and could not find a spot deep enough to plant the flag. In all there were fifty men on shore. By early afternoon the heat was so extreme that the Governor gave them an hour's rest, and they retreated into the shade of the trees with bottles of rum and water.

In leaving Botany Bay, they had moved from one extreme to the other – from sand to rock, from open land to a site where each yard of ground had to be cleared by main force, with grunting labour and sweat. The wise man builds his house on rock, William reflected, willing his imagination to conjure and see, here in this wooded cove, a neat English settlement: hospital, storehouses, quays, a timber church crowned with a cross, grey smoke rising contentedly from chimneys. The vision wavered, then disintegrated into the air like smoke itself. Would they come to this stream every morning to fill their water casks? Would they wake every day to this view across the harbour to the dense woods on the opposite side? Would the sites of tree stumps, of particular rocks, become familiar markers on daily paths? Yes. They had crossed the world to reach this spot. Now they would make it into what they wanted. Yes, he told himself firmly.

By late afternoon it was clear that not one of the tents would be erected that night. The flagstaff was up, and straight, on its third proposed site. Men were exclaiming in astonishment at the rockiness of the ground, demanding how such large trees could find nourishment in it. Maybe the thin soil was unusually fertile. When the *Sirius*, followed by all the rest of the fleet, came sailing proudly down the harbour, the men on shore downed tools with relief and ran to the point of the cove to wave and cheer.

And then, in the last light of the setting sun, Phillip and all the officers gathered around the flagstaff to watch the Union raised. After a roll by two drummers, the marines fired several volleys and His Majesty was toasted by all. Only the officers had come off the other ships; next day the marines would be disembarked, but the majority of the convicts would stay aboard until their accommodation could be rigged up.

'We need to clear 'em off the transports within the week,' Surgeon White confided to William and Bradley, when the Governor had finished his instructions. 'Or scurvy and dysentery will clear them for us.'

'They must be impatient to come ashore,' responded William. 'After eight unbroken months aboard – '

Bradley smiled sardonically. 'Not for them the shore delights of Rio and the Cape, eh?'

White chose to ignore him. 'Eight months nothing. The lags off the hulks at Portsmouth haven't set foot on land for three or four years. What they'll be capable of doing in the way of labour, God alone knows.'

After the toasts the boats plied back and forth to the ships and all men ate and slept aboard that night. They had not seen a single native all day. The stores that had been landed were covered with canvas and left.

*

STEPHEN

Olla has not even asked what this one is about. Which is fair enough, I suppose; there's no obligation on her part to feel or feign an interest. We remain discrete. Discreetly self-contained.

William Dawes. A man with choices. An educated, conscientious man in a new world. Clean slate, new stick of chalk. What will he do with the burden (gift, Stephen, at that stage; gift, they call it), do with the gift of his life?

He has (believes he has – does it come to the same thing? For a while:) power. Thinks it his duty to influence events and shape the course of history.

Alright then. Let him run. Give him his head, and let him run with it.

Outside the sealed and inescapable bubble of this present, admit other worlds.

This is the present. I am Stephen Beech. I circle quietly around the tiny stagnant backwater of the office, harmlessly processing names numbers ages and sexes from one educational institution to the next. Safe, neutral work. I cannot do any more damage. I'm not a teacher, or a socialist, or an activist. I'm not a player.

But allow me. Allow me, at least, to imagine.

CHAPTER THREE

Like an offering

Next day was warm but cloudy, with fitful, erratic wind. Now more groups of convicts were landed, with detachments of marines to guard them, and a watch was set at the boundaries of the area William had marked. The convicts were warned not to straggle – more for fear of how they might annoy the natives than for any chance of their making an escape, since there was nowhere for them to run to in the whole continent. The Governor gave strict orders not to fire on the natives, even if they stole.

William was set to surveying now, using Knight and a private as his assistants. He took pegs, cord, sextant, rule, and marked out (between trees notched for felling) where the women's tents must be erected. Two new saw-pits were dug, and in the afternoon the Governor's temporary house, prefabricated from wood and canvas in England, was landed on the eastern side of the stream. Phillip indicated the slight prominence where he wished it to stand, and while a group of men struggled to unfold it and understand its plans, William set six others to clearing and levelling the spot.

The day passed in a blur of heat and labour. It was only when he was being rowed out that evening to the ship, among the last to leave the land, that William could look up and notice the progress a day had made. Nothing was finished, but the forest edge was greatly scarred. Five little tents stood incongruously amongst the undergrowth. Smoke plumed into the air from a half-dozen fires, and raw earth and pale stumps lay exposed to the air, as if a great set of teeth had taken a bite at the coastal forest here, tearing it from the land.

But the convicts were weak and dazed. He had kept his eye on a couple who were assigned to clearing a path to the site of the Governor's house, and they had done no more than remove one sapling all afternoon. He noted the slowness of their movements and ghostly pallor of their skin. One had no teeth in his head and his gums were red and swollen. Surgeon White was right; if scurvy had not actually broken out among them, it was not far off. No plants that were recognizably edible had been discovered yet. Governor Phillip had announced that, as a priority, ground for a vegetable garden was to be cleared, and had selected an area adjoining his house; but they had done no more than mark it off today.

Looking back again at the land, from the ship's quarterdeck, the size of the impression they had made upon the coast was brought into proportion. They had barely scratched it. The coastline was endless; the woods and hills and cliffs extended limitlessly on all sides. This land was vast, its true extent not even known on charts. How could they hope to tackle it, to tame it, to make it theirs?

There was a mood of hilarity in the wardroom which jarred on William. The Governor was dining with Captain Hunter on the *Sirius*, and Captain Campbell and a few other marine officers had come as visitors to the *Supply*. They were exchanging stories about the natives at Botany Bay; Philip Gidley-King had led a wood-gathering party there.

'When they saw our men begin to cut down the trees, they leapt about like creatures on hot coals – ' he pushed back his chair and danced from foot to foot, imitating – 'jabbing with their fingers – see? – and babbling loud, angry as you like!' He pranced and jabbered, lips turned out, eyebrows drawn down in a puzzled scowl, while the other officers banged the table with their fists and laughed.

'They will take anything they can get – hats – clothes – '

'Tools – '

'They did not know – ' Ralph Clark's laughing, incredulous voice rose above the others – 'what sex we were!' A couple of the young second lieutenants began a slow hand-clap. 'They were pointing at our breeches and at their own parts – ' Ralph could hardly speak for laughing.

'The clothes are a complete mystery to them,' Watkin Tench interrupted. 'They cannot tell where we end and our outer coverings begin. Add to that our lack of beards – ' His reasonable tone took a little of the hysteria out of the atmosphere, and Captain Campbell concluded the tale: 'I asked for a volunteer to undeceive them, and Baines dropped his breeches. I daresay the man has never given so much pleasure by the act before – ' laughter. 'Then they began to point to each of us, and to Baines' member, as if to say, we might all be pleasantly surprised if we looked inside our own breeches!'

More laughter, in which William joined, but with a sense of unease.

'They have erected the miserablest wigwams you ever saw, out of a couple of strips of bark apiece, along by that northern shore – they will fall down each time the wind blows – '

'And their canoes are just as pitiful, made of a bit of bark tied at the ends with string, like a purse – easier to upset, less sea-worthy, than a milkmaid's bucket – '

'And the women go as naked as the men! They do not even – '

William rose quietly and left the mess. It would take time to understand the natives' nakedness, their flimsy canoes, their anger at the chopping down of trees. Phillip had been right to suggest that only officers should have intercourse with them; and a code of conduct should be laid down for officers themselves. How could natives respect men who dropped their breeches and pointed, roaring with laughter, at their private parts? Or who sniggered and winked after innocent native girls, who perhaps knew no more than Eve before the apple, why they should cover themselves?

His mood oppressed him and he wandered the ship looking for Bradley, who usually avoided the more rowdy sessions in the wardroom. It would be a relief to land and have more choice of company. Some of the officers were very irreligious. It would be a comfort to make proper acquaintance with Reverend Johnson, who'd travelled on the *Golden Grove*.

William spent the next morning on board, packing up his charts and the portable instruments. As he was rolling his clothes and bedding ready to be taken ashore, he was called on deck. It took him a minute to recognize the fat sweating figure leaning against the rail. Augustus Alt. The surveyor. He'd sailed in the *Prince of Wales* and William had met him ashore at Rio, at a dinner given by the Viceroy. Alt had drunk himself insensible. As William approached, Alt flapped his hand at him and swung round to lean over the rail again. There was the unmistakable sound of retching. William walked to the opposite side of the deck and saw the *Prince of Wales'* boat pulling for the shore; it was piled high with baggage. Three other boats were pulled up at the side of the creek, and the shore was seething with people. Nearly all the marines must be landed by now – and their wives and children. He remembered hearing that Alt was ill at the Cape. He turned back to him; Alt was wiping his large face with a dirty handkerchief.

'Let's get out of this damned heat.'

'Shall we go to the wardroom?'

'Aye, anywhere, lad.' Alt followed him heavily down the companion ladder and it crossed William's mind that if the surveyor lost his footing, he would crush William like an egg.

They sat either side of the long officers' table, and William was unpleasantly struck by Alt's smell: a rotten, sweet smell, mixed with the acidity of recent vomit. He tried not to wrinkle his nose, then hit on the expedient of sitting forward with his chin resting on his hand, and his bent forefinger pressed across his nostrils.

'I've been sick,' said Alt unnecessarily.

'I'm sorry. Is there a lot of sickness on the *Prince of Wales*?'

'Christ knows. I wish I'd never set foot on her. It's a poor thing for a man to travel across the world to find his grave.'

For a moment William couldn't find any reply. Alt laughed. 'Don't look so frightened, laddie, I'm sure you've as good a chance as any. Now, look here, you've been ashore – you've been surveying, they tell me?' The large white face was gleaming with sweat again, and William could not find any trace of a smile on it.

'Well sir, Captain Phillip – Governor Phillip – asked me to pace out a boundary, and find some flattish sites for the tents – so as not to need so much levelling – '

Alt nodded. 'Aye, I know what flattish is.'

'I'm sorry, I – and so I – I have done that – although obviously the sites are only for the moment, temporary, subject to your – '

'He's asked me to draw a plan,' said Alt surprisingly.

'A plan?'

'For the settlement. A proper plan – you know, streets, barracks, storehouse, church – so that permanent constructions can be started.'

'There is a lot of wood to clear.'

Alt shrugged. 'He sent me orders at dawn. He's settling the convicts and marines on the west side of the stream, and himself and his staff, with a smaller batch of convicts, on the east; and he wants a plan of streets and necessary sites – a hospital and, oh, a burial ground, he wants a spot for that – and a quay for loading stores – '

'I see.' William had thought that Alt was angry with him for doing his job. Now he was at a loss – was it Phillip the man was angry with? He made the suggestion of a town plan sound like idiocy – the last thing any man of sense would want. But he was the surveyor, wasn't he? Why did he think he'd been included on the expedition? For his drinking abilities?

'So you've walked over it, lad. And you've some experience at surveying?'

28

'Well – I have experience of measuring accurately – distance, gradient, angles – '

'You'll be fine, then. You'll be fine, lad.' Alt pulled a small bottle from his clothing, took a long swig, corked it and stood up. William stood too.

'I'm sorry, I don't understand – '

'You'll be fine,' repeated Alt.

'Are you going ashore? Would you like me to walk the area with you?'

Alt laughed. 'As ye can see, I'm in no fit state.' He heaved himself up the ladder. William followed at a safe distance.

'Shall I make some drawings – a map of ground levels?'

At the top of the ladder Alt turned and looked down on him, considering. 'Aye. If ye wish. Aye.' He turned and called. 'Bosun! A boat for the *Prince of Wales*, now.'

William went back down to finish clearing his things, completely confused by the incident. Why had Alt come to see him? And why had he offered to do drawings for Alt? Wouldn't there be enough to do in building an observatory and setting up the instruments, without offering to do that fat drunk's work for him?

He got ashore that afternoon, to a scene of chaos. A group of children were playing tag through the growing heaps of unloaded stores, which by now included a forge and anvil, and all the smith's stores, besides more bales of tents and boxes of tools. Hens, a dozen or more, were flapping and pecking around the stores and getting underfoot. A party of marines was struggling to erect a marquee, which collapsed on them twice, to loud cries and curses. One of the marine's wives was crying shamelessly, while her husband argued with her, attempting to shield the sight of her from his fellows. When he asked her a question repeatedly and she did not reply, he lost his temper and stamped away, shouting, 'Get back to the ship, then. Spend the night in comfort, eh?' Men were dragging logs and branches to a number of fires, and the sound of axes rang through the air. Captain Campbell appeared out of the crowd and tapped William on the shoulder.

'Get someone to take your stuff up to that end tent – you're with Watkin Tench, for the time being – then see about where the latrines should go, would you? Governor's already told 'em to keep well away from the stream, but the sooner we have an appointed spot the better. One for the women too. I'll send you a half-dozen men to dig a trench. Have you seen these lorikeets? Hutchins managed to catch one, a very fine specimen – in my tent. Come and have a look when you've a moment to spare.'

That night, William couldn't sleep. They had not yet rigged the poles to hang their cots from; spread on the hard ground the sheet of canvas in its wooden frame was no protection. The ground seemed to bruise him and shrug him off each time he turned over. And when he did manage to drop off, its unyielding stillness permeated his body and woke him in a sweat. He felt his own heart would stop beating. Its motion was too alien, stillness would overwhelm it. He could not remember feeling like this after other long voyages. Now the lack of the waves' motion was an absence, as if a mother who gently rocked his cradle had withdrawn herself. There was a chill in the night air, too, gusting in through the tent flap, and a tinge of smoke, and the smell of land – distance – instead of the warm, soothing fug of quarters aboard ship.

After the third waking he lay with his eyes open, listening to night-sounds, telling himself there was nothing to be afraid of. Watkin's breathing was soft and regular, he was sound asleep. From outside the tent, the same fitful breeze that brought the drifts of smoke carried snatches of distant voices – or maybe that murmuring talk was the wind in the leaves, not human at all. He told himself that outside there would be stars; a skyful, now, at quarter moon. The sight of them would calm him, as it always did. But his stare remained fixed on the side of the tent, and his body did not move. It had become as still and unresponsive as the ground it lay on. He was afraid.

He lay so rigidly still that tingling pains began to shoot through his left arm and shoulder. He made himself sit up, bowing his head to his pulled-up knees, clasping his arms around them. What was there to fear? The size, the stillness of the land? Land cannot hurt you. Attack from the natives? A watch was posted. Besides, he was not afraid of a skirmish, he was not afraid of danger. No, he was afraid – perhaps . . . of what would happen. Not in its minutiae – not the hard work of measuring and drawing and raising his observatory; not the disagreements with other officers, or the discomforts of insect bites or working in the heat; not homesickness or hunger, or mutiny from the convicts, not the physical danger . . .

He was afraid in spirit. Afraid of this place. Afraid of presuming to act, presuming to have meaning – afraid, ludicrously, of being made nothing.

He *was* afraid; he checked his breathing and forced himself to inhale more slowly, deeply, and to exhale in the same slow rhythm. His heart was racing. It was foolishness. The future was plain; having arrived safely, for which they must continue to thank God, they would carve a home in this wilderness. The convicts would be reclaimed as worthful human beings, able to cultivate and enjoy the fruits of their own honest toil. He would build an observatory and chart these new skies, and watch for Maskeylene's comet – and other unknown heavenly bodies – night by night. In so doing he would add to the sum of human knowledge, and to the safety of all who sailed the southern seas. He would do his duty as a marine officer, guarding the settlement from attack by natives without and from rebellious convicts within. And he would observe and learn from this new land, cataloguing its strange array of flora and fauna, making friendly contact with the innocent savages who roamed the bush, and discovering the secret of their language and religion. This would enable him and others to spread the word of Christ among them. He would explore, build, observe, record, enlighten. He would be instrumental in the establishment of this new world, and he would try, from the bottom of his heart, to make it such a new world as God might approve.

Well then. How could such an enterprise be worthless? If *that* was worthless, what was there of value in the world? Wouldn't other men – men in England – give their eye-teeth for such an adventure?

But the adventure's challenge and meaning, though he could articulate and itemize it, was, tonight, ethereal. While the land, the stony hard ground, was all too real beneath him, his purposes seemed wafer-thin: painted scenery to this hard rock; a frippery thing that might be blown away in the next gust of wind. He might be, simply, nothing. A leaf on a tree. A speck in the dark. Nothing. And in the end it might be as if he had never existed. This land might obliterate him: obliterate them all.

His tensed buttocks ached where they pressed on the stony ground; he could feel the bony imprint of his knees on his forehead, through the thin layer of blanket. And in this uneasy position he slumped into sleep at last, waking again with a jerk as the first rays of the rising sun penetrated the tent flap.

His heart lifted at the light. Watkin was still snoring peacefully. Dawn meant it was nearing five-thirty; soon they would beat reveille. He shuffled stiffly from his blankets and crawled out, taking his rolled-up breeches with him. The camp was completely still, strangely lit by the horizontal rays of a sun just emerging from the rim of the Pacific.

31

He pulled on his breeches and boots, and turned away from the sun and the dazzling water of the harbour. The tents he passed were silent, empty boots stationed near each flap. He was surprised not to see the look-outs pacing, but then noticed them down away to his left, crouched over a kettle on a small smoky fire. He saluted them silently and they jumped up belatedly and returned the salute.

His shadow was a stripe of darkness preceding him into the woods. Nothing moved – nothing – only he. In the sharp early light colours were very bright against the dark backgrounds of their shadows. The grey foreign plants were almost an English green in this light; there was a rich, luminous edge to everything – a kind of perfection. He noted with surprise the lack of dew. Two brilliant blue butterflies, their wings like the eyes on a peacock's tail, danced before him, plaiting the air with colour. The silence was broken by a sudden racket of bird noise: a fast, repetitive, single-note call which he traced to a gum tree ahead. In silhouette against the pale sky the bird was the shape of a kingfisher, only too big. It had the same sharp dart of a beak. It did not fly off as he drew nearer; the call, which had been alarming at first, now began to seem more like laughter. It was answered by a faint, distant, copy-cat call. The trackless space became territory, the territory of a pair of laughing birds.

Suddenly he felt less like a trespasser, not minding so much the crunches and crackles of his own footfalls, now the silence was broken. Almost imperceptibly the land had been rising, and he now found himself on the crest of a gentle slope, able to look out over a great expanse of scrub ahead, which melted away into a lavender-blue distance.

As he stopped to take in the view he had the curious impression that the bushes in the middle distance were shifting – were moving. Staring more intently, then, he made out that they were not bushes at all, but animals – quite large animals, with the bulk of their bodies upright like a man's -- tall animals, who moved hesitantly then froze. He took a step forward. And suddenly, they were off – moving in great leaping bounds, through the bushes they so exactly resembled – bouncing over the ground, large ones, small ones. All suddenly in motion – and, as suddenly, gone. It must be the creature Banks had drawn: that strange marsupial kangaroo. The sudden exhilaration of their movement had made him catch his breath. He let it go now, slowly, eyes straining across the still grey landscape for any further motion.

The sun was already hot on his neck; hot in earnest, like a banked-up fire. He turned to look back the way he had come: the same still trees and bushes, the pale trunks of the gum trees, with their long, irregular branches and glitter of leaves; the sudden dart of a red and green parrot from one bush to another. He noticed that the bush itself was red and green, with small red flowers whose thin petals stood up like hairs.

Quite suddenly, he had a sense that it would resolve. This dreadful, huge stillness would resolve – into moving creatures; moments of beauty; sudden brilliant flashes of sound and colour; unknown beasts and flowers. There were squawks overhead and he looked up to see a great flock of birds passing over. Their plumage was grey, or maybe pinkish – the size of pigeons, he judged – but as they flapped their wings they concealed and revealed a patch of dark glowing pink on the inside of each wing – in their armpits, as it were – a hot, pulsing pink against the clear blue sky. He stared until distance swallowed them, and the huge blue arc of the heavens, and all the golden heat that was in it, made his head swim and float. God had made this world and brought them to it. The black night, with its pitiful tatters of fear, dropped away. He breathed in deeply and the strange smell of euca-lypt was a pleasure, and the flies that were settling on his chest and upper arms were a wonderful detail – enough to set him laughing aloud – for they seemed to want no more than to be carried upon his clothes, like sailors on a ship, and offered him no harm whatsoever.

He heard the drummers beat reveille while he was still making his way back. It sounded right. The drums belonged in this landscape, heralding civilization, order – the gifts they could bring to a wild but peaceful land; a land which lay spread open wide before them like an offering.

STEPHEN

Something so reassuring about civilization and order; you know where you are. With order. Civilization. The rich man in his castle, the poor man at his gate. And all the proper divisions of class and wealth between.

Yes, they're tricky old things to attack, civilization and order. Especially since we didn't even realize we were doing it, when Robert and I were cast as THE CAMPFIELD COMP REVOLUTIONARIES. What headlines.

ANARCHY RULES AT SCHOOL. CHILDREN RUN AMOK!
'ANTISOCIAL AND UNCIVILISED' CLAIMS PARENT.

We just thought we were progress. Not the antithesis of civilization and order. Robert and I actually thought it was progress. Which meant we were ill-prepared for the counter-attack. If we'd known it was revolution, perhaps we'd have geared up to wage a more respectable fight. To defend our vision.

'Vision'?

Yes, you bastard, vision. Like Martin Luther King. 'I have a dream.' OK? Limited, maybe; geographically, financially and philosophically circumscribed – but nevertheless a vision. Out of little visions, you wanker, giant oak trees grow.

A vision of a school. Where kids would learn self-respect, and respect for others. Where no one would be beaten or punished or bullied, either by staff or children. Where human equality would find expression in the abolition of hierarchies; where a twelve-year-old's voice would be seen to carry equal weight with an adult's. Where sexism and racism were eradicated. Where discrimination on the basis of intellectual ability was abolished, and an equal opportunity to learn was offered to all; no swotty top bands, no sink bottom streams. Where life and the world were objects of study, so that car mechanics and ballet dancers and chefs and poets all came in to talk about their work. Where the school was part of the community, with facilities and books – and lessons too – for parents and grandparents. Where subjects that matter were not swept into a taboo-ridden corner; where children could learn freely about sex, politics, religion, death; and where freedom of thought and belief was sacrosanct. Where institutionalizing them with uniforms, and

34

militarizing them in rallies called assemblies, was rightly seen as dehumanizing. Where justice was learnt in practice through debate, and social responsibility fostered through every individual's obligation to maintain the school environment for the sake of all. Where finances were discussed openly, and choices about the future made together. Where privilege and inequality had no place. And where a new generation, reared with this knowledge, would one day be able to change the world. Isn't that a vision?

A vision of heaven. It brings tears to my eyes. It had as much chance of surviving in 1980 as a naked new-born baby on the Siberian steppes in winter.

That's not true. Now, OK. Now it wouldn't last a day. But not then. Other schools survived. Comprehensive community schools – some of them were ten years old by then, more than ten years old. That's the fucking joke. We weren't even trail-blazers, Robert and I.

No. We were two clever young men who'd begun in the right place at the right time – zapping up the promotion ladder in enlightened Leicestershire where the bad old days of the eleven-plus were already long forgotten; not dry enough behind the ears to know what we were up against at Campfield. When a backward Labour Local Education Authority decides to take the plunge and go comprehensive, and the Director of Education wants a flagship, of course he brings in a head and deputy with comprehensive experience – bright young outsiders with all the new ideas. To run the brave new school which used to be Pithills Secondary Modern. And of course the bright young things have even more radical ideas than they let on at interview. Which they are confident they will achieve by sleight of hand, for the good of all.

They would have hated us whatever we'd done, the aging staff of Campfield Comprehensive. And the redeployed staff from the grammar (second-raters, the ones the old head wanted rid of) hated us even more. Not that we went out of our way to be liked. We hadn't the nous to realize that was necessary. We thought they'd be *glad* to move out of the dark ages. And wasn't the climate already changing by then? The swing against the sixties gathering momentum?

Oh, many and various are the reasons for the complete collapse of

Campfield Comprehensive. Nevertheless I must admit the final straw was of my own making, I broke the camel's back. Publicly. And privately. I broke it.

OLLA

He feeds at the breast, Daniel. There is no doubt that he feeds, and
gets some goodness from it. It is very slow, of course. He will suck a
little, swallow a mouthful. He seems to like having the nipple in his
mouth. But then he forgets – is thinking of something else. I prompt
him, stroke his cheek, joggle him. Sometimes he will suck again. At
other times – not. I am sure he will learn. He wants to live, I know that,
I can tell he wants to live. When hunger drives him he will suck. But
they keep us in hospital a long time, 'stabilizing', as they call it. And
they weigh him every day, and they watch me feed him. The sister
brings the bottle with the special teat and says he must have it. I
refuse. She argues with me but I do not enter in. Just smile and say
no.
'Do you want him to starve to death?'
I reply, 'No.'
She brings in the consultant, who studies Daniel's weight chart and
asks about his nappies. He also says I must give him the bottle.
'Hunger won't drive him to suck, Mrs Beech. He hasn't got the
proper reflex. He doesn't know how to feed himself. By withholding
food, you cause him to lose strength. I'm afraid he must be given the
bottle. Let sister take him and feed him – '
I have no choice. I have to agree.
Stephen says to me, 'The consultant asked me if I thought you were
depressed. You're not, are you?'
'No. Not in the least.'
'That's what I thought. He says you may suffer from post-natal
depression. I told him you are tougher than you look.' He laughs.
He thinks I am too tough. He would like me to cry and need
comforting, he would like to look after me, perhaps, and save me
from myself. But he knows perfectly well that is not necessary, I am
stronger than he.

They are looking for ways to gain control over Daniel, though. And
their best card is to dismiss me. Say I am depressed, unable to act for
the best, not good to look after my baby. I must be cunning. I must
never give them grounds for taking him away. Where necessary I
must obey them, at least while they are watching. I must show them
what a good girl I am.

So I agree. I feed him with the wretched bottle. He gasps and chokes
as the flood pours down his throat, but he also swallows some. He

swallows more, I admit, than he has taken from me. He is colluding with me, doing this to placate them. What he took from me alone was enough – but now they are watching, he gulps this down to please them and deflect their critical eyes. He knows what is happening. He helps me to protect himself.

I am remembering Maria's baby. Why? I haven't thought of that place for years. The forest, rows of pines on all sides. In the middle of nowhere I walked into their camp. They were living in two beat-up vans and a tent. Maria was sitting on a log outside the tent, she was holding and cuddling that little baby like a doll. It was only a few days old.
She was a simpleton, Maria, with a broad grinning child's face and big fat breasts. Fat! How could anyone be fat living like that? The others were all skinny as skeletons. She watched her baby sucking and sucking on those big fat breasts, it could have all it wanted, plenty. She laughed and nodded while I watched, saying, 'Good, good, good.'

They were foreign – hippies – I understood only a little. I think they were lost, or maybe hiding from the police. They were American and Dutch, they had been everywhere. To India, they told me, to Africa. 'Marrakesh!' they shouted, and laughed. 'Algeria! Morocco! Best shit in the world!'
They were all sick. Two of the women used to drive to town in the evenings. When they came back in the morning they brought food. They spent the day in bed. There were three scrawny children who ran wild in the forest, killing and eating squirrel, rabbit, birds. They said they were going to Geneva, they had some stuff to sell in Geneva that would make them rich. But one of the vans was broken and they could not fix it; the men did nothing, only sat round the fire smoking and nodding and smiling. They asked me about mushrooms and I showed them which were safe to eat. I cooked mushrooms for them on their fire, and they told me I could stay with them and ride to Geneva.

Fat Maria did not sit with them, or smoke. She was strong, she gathered firewood and tied it in bundles; the women took it away in the van to sell. I helped her get it, she tied her plump baby to her back and worked all afternoon, stopping only to feed the baby.

One morning when the women came back there were raised voices and tears. One of them had been beaten, the side of her face was all bloody. They did not go into town again that week, and we ran out of food. They sent me and the children out hunting for mushrooms. They boiled some twigs in a pot, trying to make them soft, and chewed them; a couple of them vomited after that. The men were taking the whole engine of the broken van to pieces.

When I watched Maria's baby sucking and guzzling I ached with hunger, I had to swallow the saliva that sprang to my mouth. The baby seemed to grow each day, its face rounding out like a waxing moon; and Maria's breasts began to wane. One day I noticed with surprise that the breast was smaller than the child's head.

We collected more firewood but they kicked it and said, no good. They would not go into town. Some of the men went off in the night and came back with sacks of vegetables which they had stolen. They said no one was to go into town any more, we must get back on the road. We had to make the vegetables last until the van was ready. I was hungry, I thought of leaving, but I wanted a ride to Geneva.

Maria's baby was growing, but Maria was getting thin. Her bulk began to disappear, just like the moon when it wanes from full. Her puffy flesh seemed to be collapsing into sagging creases, bags of skin that dangled from her frame. Her large round baby began to cry. I watched her putting the nipple into the baby's mouth, and the way the baby seemed to leap on to it like a soldier coming to attention, and Maria staring at the baby's face in astonishment. Its face puckered with disappointment – it spat out the empty teat, and screamed. She lifted her breasts, envelopes of yellow skin, and flapped them at me. 'Empty! Empty! Milk all gone.'

The other women were arguing and shouting at the men. One boiled some vegetables and mashed them and gave it to Maria to feed the baby, but the baby only screamed. It screamed with rage, scraping the nerves like a saw, screaming all through the night until one of the men shouted at her to take it farther away. You could see even from a distance how quickly the baby waned, how its fat dropped off to skin and bones.

The woman who had been beaten asked me, would I go into town and earn some money? I would not be recognized as one of them. Then they could buy milk for Maria's baby. I went to say goodbye to Maria, her baby had stopped crying. I saw that it had waned from round to concave, it was a sliver of a baby now, thin and bent.

In the evening the hippy woman drove me to the edge of the town and told me to walk in, to the railway station. I should wait on the corner opposite the station, and when a man passed by, catch his eye and smile. I should take him under the arches at the back of the station. She said there's lots of other girls there, you'll be all right. He'll pay you. She said she would wait for me in the van, but she couldn't come out because they knew her.

I walked the way she told me, until I was out of sight of the van. Then I turned off down a different street, stopping myself from running, because that would attract attention. I walked all night, till I came out of town at the other side and I passed a boarded-up house with a derelict garage. I squeezed in between loose planks and slept on a sledge in there. It was from there that I got my bicycle.
But Maria. Fat Maria. I never thought of her again until this day. Now I see her big nodding grinning face, and the baby fastened to her full moon of a breast, she is saying, 'Good! Good! Good!'

*

Now I have Daniel at home. I have won the first round. I have him at home, alone with me, away from all their interfering and questioning. Away from the medicine and injections, away from the fish-eyed sister and the worried consultant. I have him here and Stephen has gone back to work.

I have a list I will obey: I will be here for the health visitor, the social worker, the midwife, the physiotherapist. I will agree to have him weighed, measured, monitored, examined, because they must know I am an ideal and responsible mother. The house will be clean, and Stephen's tea on the table. By conforming to their requests, I buy Daniel's and my own freedom. He is mine, and I will help him to be most great.

When he is sleeping I sit and stare into his cot. When I look at his face, I know. This is a new land, a new world – a different kind of person. His vision will not be mine; his hearing, his touching, his smelling – not like ours. The world reforms, transforms, undergoes metamorphosis. Into what? Maybe black will shine and light will be dark, music sounding as glowing pulses of colour, voices tumbling as solid shapes. Maybe a finger stroking his cheek will twang and ripple as a harp. The world's hard edges will dissolve, its essences will flow to him. The world must come to him, and because it will offer itself, he will know. He will understand what the millions who blunder about searching have never found. Secrets, like lovers, will offer themselves up, to the one who does not pursue them.

This is the focus of the world, now; it is realigned, its purpose and centre are here and the one who will understand them – who understands all – is here.

I am not young, or a fool. I am not besotted. This boy is different. When I was carrying him he was still. Suddenly I would be afraid – he was too still, not moving, was he dead? I would hold myself quite silent, listening for him. And then I would find him. His stillness would come into focus. A note, in all the cacophony, reached me. A sure, sustained sound, already within other sounds; a steadily burning flame, a pilot-light. I knew his stillness was strength, purpose. Unlike other babies who flail and thrash like boughs in the wind, he grew in stillness, with purpose, his energy concentrated. For what? I longed to see him. More than any other person. Yes, even Tadek, my brother.

He knows Tadek. Before – beyond – the fact of his flesh, my womb, the umbilical cord, he brings with him the – what is it? Taste, I want to say – he brings the taste of my homeland. When you lift your face out of doors, to the wind, and you know in your mouth the land you are in – taste, he brings the taste of the marshes. He knows where Tadek is buried. The silver-birches, the thin slippy light, the flash on water, the pale marsh grass – water, wind, light, space. He is from my country. He knows what I know.

The language. Thick slippery words like dead fish. Opaque and clumsy. He does not need. This English is not his language any more than mine. It interposes itself between my meaning and hearers' ears like blubber. He does not need language. He understands all languages, and he needs none. His communication is pure. His understanding, instant. The barrier of language collapses under the ray of his attention.

People are always afraid of what they do not know. They must give it a label. This makes it safe. Most especially if what is not known appears contrary – such as, a powerful child. Which surpasses them in intelligence. And understands the universe in ways they do not.

If a child is not ordinary, if it does not have ordinary eyes and ordinary ears and ordinary hands fit for seeing and hearing and touching the ordinary dead old world, the chairs and tables and cups and saucers and knives and forks of numb familiarity; then it is strange. And there is only one way to be strange, and that way is bad. Daniel is badly strange. Handicapped. A cripple. A loony. If a child is strange it is feared; as much as if we still lived in caves with bearskins on our backs, and believed cross-eyes and harelips to be marks of the devil.

*

Seven weeks. Yesterday it was seven weeks since Daniel's birth. He has lived now one day longer than Timothy. He has passed that hurdle. I thought it unlikely that Stephen would remember; and he did not. This morning when he had gone to work, I took down the suitcase of Timothy's things from the top of the wardrobe, and showed them to Daniel as he lay in his cot. I showed him the photographs: Timothy's round bald face with the beginning of a smile in the corners of his mouth; me clutching him like a bundle; Stephen holding him up in the air and laughing. The shawl Stephen's mother made for him, fine wool crotchet. His soft cotton baby clothes, the two sets of little blue leggings, jacket and hat that I knitted, his terry nappies, the little bootees threaded with satin ribbon. I showed his birth certificate:
Timothy Stephen Beech, male, Twelfth April 1982, mother Olla Beech, father Stephen Henry Beech, certified to be a true copy of an entry in a register in my custody . . .
The cards of congratulation, from Stephen's colleagues, family and friends – 'A baby boy! How wonderful!'; bunnies and flowers and butterflies and teddies and balls and toy trains. I showed him the basket with the half-used Johnson's baby bath, the talc, the Vaseline, the baby oil, the nappy pins. I showed him the tub of baby wipes, the packet of breast pads I had been using, the changing mat with dancing teddies on it; the three towels with embroidered corners, made into a hood to keep his damp little head warm after the bath. The plastic see-through bracelet they put on him in the hospital, 'child of Olla Beech'. His weight card from the clinic. The list of breast feeds, how long he fed on each side, and at what hour, in my own writing and a

variety of colours of ink. The baby book recording baby's first year of achievements, unused, given me by Stephen's sister. The book of advice on baby care and products that came with the free pack of disposable nappies at the hospital. His new dummy still in its packet. The tub of cotton buds on stems, for cleaning the delicate whorls of his ears. The half-used pack of cotton wool. The two cot-quilt covers I made for him, embroidered with his name. His presents: the yellow and white teddy bears, the blue rabbit, the set of colourful baby-gros still in their cellophane packet, the Beatrix Potter plate, bowl and mug set, and the rattle that floats in the bath. The china plaque for his bedroom door with 'Timothy's room' and blue birds painted on it. The little soft white hairbrush I never used on him, because he had no hair. Lastly I show him the pop-up picture book that Stephen bought, which is bright and lovely. He has not bought a book for Daniel.

I show Daniel each of these belongings of Timothy, and he sees and remembers and understands. He takes Timothy's life and death into himself. He has lived longer than Timothy, he takes it in. I brush his hand with the teddies, the rabbit. I take the lid off the Vaseline so he can smell its waxy oily smell. He doesn't have Vaseline, there is a softer cream now with a gentle perfume. I brush the golden down on his head with Timothy's little unused hairbrush.

When he has seen it all, I pack it in the suitcase again, and I wrap Daniel up and put him in his pram. We take the suitcase into the garden. I leave Daniel near the house because smoke would be bad for his lungs. I take the suitcase to Stephen's bonfire site. He keeps a can of paraffin in the shed. I pour it over Timothy's case, and light a match. The stiffened canvas material of the suitcase flares and burns brightly; I move back beside Daniel to watch. After a while the flame dies down, there is some kind of plastic lining to the case which melts and does not burn. Using the clothes prop I poke and beat the case, to break it up, and pour more paraffin over the insides. Now it burns well, the nappies and photos and cards and picture book are blazing brightly; the cellophane packaging of the baby-gros shrivels and peels back, the woollen shawl hisses and glows. We watch from a safe distance. Timothy is gone now, he is erased. Daniel is the survivor.

In the afternoon, while Daniel is asleep, before Stephen comes home,

I take a bucket and gather up the solid remains: the half-melted plastic containers, the name plate and pottery set, the charred remains of the changing mat and the blackened back of the little white hairbrush. I rake the ashes for all the solid lumps, gather them in my bucket, wrap them in newspaper, and put them in the dustbin. We will never think of Timothy again, Daniel and I. He is finished. Daniel lives longer.

*

He is ill. His temperature is high and his breathing congested. I hold him beside a bowl of steam and Vick but there is no change. He does not cough, but each breath is a labour. It is a chest infection of course, the doctor knows less than I do. I squirt the antibiotics down his throat with a syringe but he vomits it up, together with the phlegm his stomach is full of. It is thick and slippery, milk comes straight up with more of it, he cannot digest through that layer of slime. He has kept down almost nothing for three days. I know there is something I must do, but what? He is exhausted with all this, with all of us. It is too difficult, too much, what he must do and be. He lets the disease in, and turns the pain into a battle within himself. He says, it is easier to fight himself than this – this – blind dumb idiot world.

He knows what he is doing. He will not die. He will not.

CHAPTER FOUR

The Indians

William met his first Indians later that day. His orders from the Governor were to prepare a map of Sydney cove and its environs; Captain Hunter and Lieutenant Bradley were charting the harbour, and he went out with them in the *Sirius'* longboat to take sightings and measurements.

They passed a number of tiny native canoes close in by the opposite shore. William's attention was attracted by a sudden flash of silver as one of the Indians raised his spear with a good-sized fish thrashing on the end of it. But the fishermen took no notice of the longboat. In the next cove there was a whole party of men waving and gesticulating on the beach.

Bradley shook his head. 'I don't know where Mr Banks got the idea that the place is sparsely populated. We see more each time we come out.'

'I think we'll try landing,' said Hunter. 'If you can get out along that promontory, you'll be able to measure and sketch the whole Sydney side of the harbour. And I can ask about water. We'll keep the boat in the shallows in case they're unfriendly – '

As the boat moved in towards the crescent of white beach, the Indians became still – a line of men holding their spears upright. Hunter stood and held out his arms, to show he had no weapons, then Henry Waterhouse, the mid, helped the three officers out of the boat. The line of blacks moved back a little as the white men came on to the beach. William looked up at the semicircle of faces. It was very quiet – no sound but the squeaking of the rowlocks as the men dipped their oars lightly to keep the boat in position. The Indians' eyes were flicking from Hunter to Bradley to himself and back again; they stood poised, tensed for action, ready – he guessed – either to throw the spears or to run away, or maybe to do both.

It was a shock to be facing them, across ten feet of sand – those little black stick figures who had comically pranced and waved spears in the distance; the natives, the Indians, the Ab-Origines, as Cook had called them, the poor, naked heathens of New Holland. They were not like any men he had ever seen before. Not like the silent, elegantly clad, powdered footman Negro at his godfather's house, whose warm, coppery skin, slender height and nervous, intelligent eyes put William in mind of a thoroughbred horse; the man would not speak, no one knew if he had been dumb from birth or since some later accident, but William's uncle declared him the best, most trustworthy manservant he had ever had. Not like the destitute Negroes who had fought in America, and still wore the ragged remains of their uniforms, who begged and hawked and portered in the streets and were as much a part of London as knife-grinders or flower-girls. Not like the two black sailors on the *Sirius*, whose strength and agility in the rigging had made them celebrated figures amongst the men, and whose dancing – when the fiddle or the pipe was played of an evening – evoked whistles, clapping, stamping of admiration. Not even like huge Black Caesar, the convict black, whose superhuman strength and singleness of mind made him as dangerous as a gigantic baby; whose appetite demanded that he eat his week's ration at a sitting, and steal for the next six days, and who had cried when he snapped a fellow convict's arm. Not like the exotic Indians at Rio, nor the silent, oppressed slaves with their cast-down eyes at the Cape.

No. These were stark naked. Their jet-black skins glinted with grease. A foul, rank smell of fish-oil hung around them. Their lank hair and beards dangled to their shoulders; objects – feathers, teeth, small bones – were tied into the hair. Their chests were scarred with long livid welts across the ribs, wounds which must have been deliberately inflicted – symmetrical, evenly spaced. The one nearest William had a hole bored through the central cartilage of his nose, and a long white bone sticking through it. His eyebrows were drawn down and his eyes narrowed in a grimace as fixed as a mask. The spear he held was taller than himself, tipped with a barbed sliver of shell that flashed in the light. He was a figure from a child's terrors, from a nightmare. He was a savage.

William felt the contents of his bowels become liquid, as if he had swallowed a dose of fear which dropped straight through him.

'We come in friendship,' Hunter said evenly. 'We will not harm you. We are looking for a river. Water?' He paused then made a gesture of drinking, and repeated the word 'water'.

The Indians did not react.

Suddenly William's eye was caught by a movement behind them, and he glimpsed the outline of a naked woman who stepped back quickly into the trees. The Indian nearest William followed his look, and then met William's eye with a flash of warning.

'We have gifts for you,' said Hunter in the same even, gentle tone. He set down on the sand the sack Henry had passed to him. Moving slowly and keeping his eyes on the Indians, he bent to draw out of the sack a handful of trinkets – some beads, some strips of cloth, a couple of little round mirrors. Glancing back to his opposite, William saw that the native was watching Hunter's every move. The Indian's chest, William realized suddenly, was rising and falling rapidly, with short, fluttering breaths; his wiry legs quivered, and so did the arm that held the spear. The toes of his right foot clenched down into the sand and William felt his own clammy toes inside the wetness of his boots mimicking the movement, curling, wanting the feel of the soft dry sand. We are the same, he thought.

The Indian glanced back at him, assessing the distance between them. William saw how he was torn between his fear of Hunter's sack, his need to keep William covered, and his desire to run away. When Hunter slowly stood upright again, with his hands full of trinkets, and took a step towards them, they fell back a step, lifting their spears from the ground. Hunter froze. William noted the new dark triangle of sweat marking Hunter's jacket between the shoulder-blades, spreading to meet the older stains around his armpits. A stinging trickle of sweat ran into his own left eye, and he blinked hard, not wanting to attract attention by raising his hand to rub it away. The seven marines in the boat had muskets and orders not to shoot; he prayed they would not panic. Then Hunter took another step forward. The black before him held his ground, reached out an arm that was visibly trembling, and grasped the beads and ribbons. Hunter nodded at William and Bradley and the three of them fell back a couple of paces. The line of blacks broke and they clustered round the one who held the gifts, talking and exclaiming in quick, musical voices. A couple took strips of cloth and tied them round their heads. William watched others hold the mirrors up to the light and turn them so they flashed in the sun. The man who had stood near him was sniffing at a string of beads – he held it out to a fellow who also sniffed it and made a dismissive gesture. The man who had taken the gifts from Hunter dropped the mirror he was holding, and they all turned to face the whites again.

Hunter nodded and smiled. 'We are looking for a river to fill our

47

water barrels. Is there water near here?' He made his gesture of drinking again.

'Bado,' one of the Indians said. A couple of others repeated it, and then they pointed east, stabbing at the air as if to indicate a distance – pointing and stabbing. 'Bado, bado.' They were still holding their spears.

'Thank you,' said Hunter calmly. 'Water is bado? We will go over there and find it.' He copied their pointing gesture. William saw his native glance at another with a quick flash of smile, and both of them pointed as Hunter had done – self-consciously, a little theatrically – to the east. Hunter bowed and William and Bradley quickly copied him.

'Goodbye. I'll wait here while you two get into the boat,' he said, in the same loud, pleasant tone, 'and when you're in will you stand up and call out 'Goodbye' to distract them as I follow you.'

As he was helped into the boat William turned and saw that the Indians had moved a few steps down, closer to Hunter. Hunter was a brave man.

'Goodbye!' he called loudly, and as Hunter turned to wade through the shallows the Indians came right down to the water's edge. When Hunter reached the boat one of them let out a cry. Waterhouse steadied Hunter as he stepped in and immediately gave the order to pull away. The knot of figures on the shore suddenly broke into exuberant, extravagant motion – dancing, stamping, shouting, leaping in the air and waving their spears, letting out howls and yells and hoots.

There was silence in the English boat until they were out of range. Then Hunter turned to William and Bradley with a quizzical expression on his face, and everyone in the boat burst out laughing.

'What are they doing? What's their game?' The men stopped rowing and there was a buzz of relieved chatter and speculation.

'They're glad we're gone,' Bradley said quietly. 'They're celebrating our departure. They think they've driven us away.'

Watching the prancing figures, who had again, with distance, become comic, William slowly nodded his agreement.

'We'll take readings and soundings farther along,' Hunter said. 'It wasn't worth attempting then and there. But isn't it curious – ' he turned to Bradley – 'how each party's reaction to us differs?'

Bradley narrowed his eyes to squint across the bay, then reached for his telescope.

'Don't you think they may be different tribes, sir? If each tribe inhabits one particular area of woodland – well, news of our arrival may not have reached them all.' He raised the glass to his eye. 'There's quite a large gathering on the southern shore down there.'

'We'll stick to the north for now,' replied Hunter. 'I want to be done by nightfall.'

'Watkin told me the Indians he met at Botany Bay were friendly,' William said.

Bradley nodded. 'We've met five or six groups now, in the course of exploring the harbour, and some have been welcoming, completely unafraid – even dangerously curious, wanting to touch our clothes and weapons and see inside the boat. But others – ' He shrugged.

There was a silence as the men pulled steadily over the little choppy waves.

'They were terrified,' William said.

Hunter passed the telescope back to Bradley. 'That's where the danger lies. I don't think any of them are malicious – Cook's reports certainly make them out to be fairly peaceable. But if we frighten them, I imagine they may well be driven to attack us. That's the Governor's concern – that we do nothing to provoke an attack. Now, Henry, you see that island? I want to pass between that and the rocks, we'll pull in there – ' He turned to give his directions. William glanced at Bradley.

'They were terrified of what we were going to do,' he repeated quietly.

Bradley nodded. 'Yes. Of what we had in the sack.'

'But their fear – ' William struggled to pin the exact thing. 'We didn't deserve so much fear.'

'How d'you mean?'

'It was silly. They thought the sack contained something dreadful – or powerful – and it was – '

'Nothing but trinkets.'

'Exactly. It meant nothing. Told them nothing.'

'But what *could* it tell them?

'Well something about us. I mean, something that matters. They had to screw themselves up to a desperate pitch of courage; us too, on both sides, we risked our lives. What for? To give them some mirrors they've already thrown away, and a few coloured rags.'

'It's a calculated move. We meet them, we show ourselves to be peaceable and generous, we allay their fears. Next time they meet us they won't be so afraid.'

'But they think we've gone away – you said, they were doing a victory dance. They think they've driven us off.'

Bradley smiled wryly. 'Well they may continue to think we'll go away. They may hold off attacking us *because* they think we'll go away. If we seem to go away once, we may seem to do so again.'

'But – ' William gazed at Bradley. 'You make it sound as if – '

'They won't attack us anyway,' Bradley interrupted briskly. 'Care has been taken to show most of the groups we've met our superior fire-power. Just in passing – you know – firing at a bird, or a target – just so's they know it would be dangerous to take us on. So they'll know their place.'

'What are you trying to say?'

Bradley grinned and lowered his voice. 'You're an innocent, William. They need to be peacefully subdued. Our lives in the settlement would be wretched if they mounted attacks from the wilderness. We need to . . . trick them into friendship.'

'Trick. Trick. Why trick?'

'Because why *should* they be friends with us?' Bradley hissed. 'We are invaders.'

'Oh no. No. Think what we can offer them. Religion, the salvation of their souls, the comfort of God's love. We can teach them to build shelters and make clothes, we can teach them to grow crops so their food supply is secure – '

Bradley shrugged and unrolled the harbour sketches he'd brought with him. 'If they want these things. We don't know that they do.'

'They are men – with souls. They must want some higher form of life than – than roaming the woods like animals.'

Bradley raised his eyebrows. 'I shan't argue with you about souls. But I am in good company. Captain Cook called these people the happiest on earth. I am not the first to think they may not want our civilization foisted on them.'

William had read and reread Cook's journal on the voyage out. He knew the passage Bradley referred to:

> The natives of New Holland may appear to some to be the most wretched people upon the earth; but in reality they are far happier than we Europeans; being wholly unacquainted not only with the superfluous but the necessary Conveniences so much sought after in Europe, they are happy in not knowing the use of them. They live in a Tranquillity which is not disturbed by the Inequality of Condition; the earth and sea of their own accord furnish them with all things necessary for life; they covet not magnificent Houses, Household stuff, etc. and they live in a warm and fine climate and enjoy a very wholesome Air . . .

But Cook was speaking only of material things. Not of souls that wandered, lost in darkness, ignorant of the promised bliss of heaven. Not of souls that hungered to know God, or of minds that would find joy in intellectual exploration, in reading, in scientific knowledge, in philosophy. Cook belittled them, imagining that they could be happy without spiritual or intellectual fulfilment.

It was noon and very hot in the boat, and Cook and images of 'household stuff' – great boat-loads of chairs and tables and carpets and china and beds – tumbled heavily through William's mind, weighing him down in an uneasy, sweating doze. They piled unwanted around the country, making dark mountains and obscuring views, and the Governor and Captain Cook were arguing over them, complaining that they must be shifted, but not by the convicts, who knew too well the value of such things, for they were thieves. No, the value must be taught to the heathen Indians who must learn to prize them.

He woke with a start to find Bradley gently shaking his arm – his head was on Bradley's shoulder.

'Sorry – sorry – ' He sat up straight.

Bradley smiled. He looked happy. 'It's all right. You can stay here. I'll do the readings with Waterhouse.'

Belatedly William realized that they were anchored close in to the rocky shoreline, and that Bradley and two others were exchanging places with seamen in the small boat. This part of the coast seemed deserted. There were no natives, and no vessels in sight; only the moving sea, the wooded shores and the rocky outcrops above.

After his dream it seemed extraordinarily empty – he stared across the glittering water to the huge stillness of the opposite shore. No natives, no dancing figures, only a flock of large birds flapping their way slowly along the coastline. And on the nearside, nothing but rocks, blank, barren, empty. Were there tracts of this country where *no one* lived? Desert, like the moon, unpeopled?

He watched Bradley and Waterhouse scramble over the rocks in a business-like fashion and set up the tripod for the sextant on a flat stone. He was pleased by their practicality. An unpeopled land was a terrible thought: the pointlessness, the waste of it. The sheer vegetable stupidity of the seasons circling over an uninhabited land mass; of seeds germinating, growing, flowering, withering – all unseen and unharvested by man; of trees providing shade; of streams flowing; of pasture lands growing, of fruits rotting. No. The land was made to serve man, to be worked by him and to render back to him the fruits of

51

his labour. The land was man's backdrop, his setting. Land without man would be as futile as a stage with no actors; it would have no meaning.

*

STEPHEN

'Where man is not nature is barren.' There's a thought to conjure with. And Green wisdom now the opposite. Where man *is* nature is barren. The fight's on for Wilderness places; stop the logging/mining/tourism. Stop the lousy people, stop them breeding.

Does it make a difference? To confidence, say? To William's, knowing that his existence stops barrenness, that he is the lord the earth was made to serve and nourish; that only his presence gives it meaning?

Must do. How can we be confident, knowing we're exploiters, trashers of the planet? Devouring rainforest, puncturing the ozone layer, driving species after species to extinction? How can I like myself? Best thing I could do is to prevent further consumption by topping myself right now, specifying coffin-less burial with no headstone.

Unless of course you set a value on defiance. Watkin Tench's *Account of the Settlement at Port Jackson* describes the Aborigines' terror of thunder, and the way they dealt with it – by going out dancing and shaking their spears at the heavens. He honours them for it; superstitious terror does not make them cowardly, but heroic. So twentieth-century man? Heroic in the face of terror? Eat drink slash and burn, for tomorrow we die – not just us but the whole fucking planet. Consume while you can, because soon there'll be no one here to appreciate whatever scraps remain. Yes. Where man is not, nature is barren.

But *are* there societies whose be-all and end-all isn't consumption? Who don't make the earth barren? Yes. Who don't multiply like rabbits. Yes. For example, the Aborigines of Australia.

Good. So where does that leave William Dawes, faced with a sealed, self-sufficient, harmonious continent, a viable ecosystem, untouched by white men?

Well at a loss. What a fucking stupid question. The damn thing doesn't even exist for him. If a continent is in balance, if its

52

predators and preyed-upon all flourish, if its animal and vegetable occupants have evolved to survive its ferocious climactic extremes; if black humans live in it without disturbing these natural balances, without so much as scarring the face of the earth by building or farming, intervening only to burn off an area from time to time, which stimulates regeneration – then so what, as far as William is concerned. So what? Because that is in the absence of Europeans. White men are not there to witness it. And therefore *it doesn't exist*. It can't be acknowledged, or preserved, any more than a perfect eco-system on Uranus (or up it, mate) could be. It is *outside* the known. William cannot value it or lament the fact that it is under threat because it is not a thing he can know. All he can see is empty, going-to-waste land. With a scattering of poor savages who don't even have the wit to build proper shelters. He does not have the words – the ideological equipment – to deal with the notion that it might, in any way, be better not to build than to build. It would be nonsense; literally, unthinkable.

But William has a proper, counterbalancing sense of man's insignificance in the universe, despite being an eighteenth-century man; because he is a star-gazer. In gazing at the stars he can't help but know there are movements, and destinies, beyond the human scale, and that there are galaxies where man is not, and where he cannot get close enough to know if they are barren, but that it might be presumptuous to assume that so much and so many and so far are all entirely barren: it might be reasonable to give them the benefit of the doubt, as one would try also to give those poor noble savages the benefit, and assume – if necessary in the face of the evidence – that their lives were not entirely brutish and barren. Yes. William is innocent but not pompous; enlightened but not lacking in humility. He is on his way to being Romantic. He believes in freedom and equality, and is opposed to the slave trade. Although he worries about their souls, he's quite capable of believing in noble savages. And in the perfectibility of man. Here endeth the interruption.

CHAPTER FIVE

Better to marry

In the scramble to establish some kind of order in the wild woods of Sydney Cove, it seemed to William that every man found himself doing three men's jobs. His astronomical duties were nagging for his attention, but he was also called here there and everywhere to help with measuring and surveying. The Governor notified him of his opinion that the Board of Longitude's instruments were best kept safe aboard the *Sirius* until an observatory had been erected, with which William absolutely agreed. But the observatory must be begun as soon as possible. The *Sirius*, like the other boats, would need to be unloaded and made ready for other duties. He must find a site for the observatory!

Alt was onshore at last; William showed him his suggested sites for hospital, barracks and women's quarters, guiding him through the sweating work gangs and smoking fires along what had already become tracks – pathways where the sparse grass and undergrowth was worn and scraped clear to rock and dust, by boots marching, convicts' chains dragging, tents and barrels being pushed and rolled.

Alt smelt bad, and his attitude of exhausted contempt for the settlement grated on William. No doubt he was a good surveyor, but he seemed to find nothing good in the site, and kept up a steady stream of invective against the godforsaken country, the hellish heat, and the convict scum. He moved heavily, his jacket patterned with patches of sweat, and William forced himself to keep to his slow pace. After listening for longer than he felt was polite without responding, William murmured, 'I suppose it was not your first choice, to come to this country, sir?'

Alt stopped in his tracks and bellowed with laughter. 'Not my first choice!' he repeated. 'Not my first choice!'

William blushed, not knowing how to react.

As they passed the hospital tent (Alt declining William's offer to look inside) Reverend Johnson came out, with his bible and a half-empty bottle of wine in his hands. William had not seen the chaplain since the Cape. He was thinner now, his face, above his black cassock and high collar, scarlet with heat. The marines in their cut-off red coats were suffering badly enough in the New South Wales sunshine; the chaplain's clothes, William reflected, must be a torment.

Johnson nodded at them and asked Alt how he did; upon Alt replying that there was nothing wrong that a drink would not cure, Johnson tucked the wine bottle into the folds of his cassock.

'I have just been giving a little sip to a fellow who is dying. Surgeon White is complaining that there is no wine for the sick – nor any sickroom comforts to be had. This is from my own supplies, sir,' he added uncomfortably.

'Reverend Johnson – I'm sorry – ' William spoke before Alt could reply – 'I'm very sorry I missed your sermon on Sunday. I very much wished to be here for the first Sabbath service in this country, but Lieutenant King and I were delayed at the French ships.'

Johnson nodded.

'I heard from Captain Tench,' William continued, 'how fine a sermon you preached.'

Richard Johnson's querulous, anxious expression softened into a smile that made him look almost babyish. He was bareheaded, and his fine hair stuck to his head with sweat. At the Governor's dinner at the Cape, William recalled, it had been powdered and beautifully curled in a roll like a sausage around his head, just above the ears.

'I worked on that sermon – and several others, prepared for certain occasions – during the voyage, and my dear Mary heard me practise it. "What shall I render unto the Lord for all His goodness unto me?" Thanksgiving due for our safe and speedy voyage.'

'I am sorry I missed it,' William repeated. 'That sense of community in prayer will give us all the strength for our labours here – ' He was conscious of Alt staring at him rudely. On an impulse he reached out to shake Johnson's hand and the chaplain clasped his warmly in return.

'Come to supper and meet my wife, Lieutenant Dawes. Come tomorrow night.' He glanced warily at Alt. 'And – of course, Mr Alt, sir, if you would honour us – '

'No, thank you, thank you.' Alt brushed the suggestion from the air with a flabby hand. 'I am happier aboard ship than on land, till we get a few creature comforts here. I shall go back aboard tonight, Reverend, and make my drawings in civilized surroundings. Some of us were not built for camping, eh?'

As they moved on up the hill William heard him muttering to himself, 'What shall I render the Lord my arse.'

William spent the following day happily, alone, scouting for the most suitable spot for the observatory. There had been a thunderstorm during the night, and more rain threatened in the massed low grey cloud, under which the heat sat trapped. There was a close stillness in the air; when William checked the thermometer he found it hard to believe it was only seventy-four degrees Fahrenheit, so much did the humidity accentuate the heat. The convicts were working slowly, like figures in a dream where every movement is sluggish and oppressed through fear, though here it was only the heat that clung heavily to their limbs.

Leaving the working gangs behind, William explored the higher shoreline along both sides of the cove, starting with the easterly. He passed the Governor's prefabricated house on its levelled patch of raw ground, and the tents which had been erected nearby for the better type of women. A garden patch had been dug on this side, and some of the specimens from Rio and the Cape planted out here. He stopped to examine the plants, impressed by their health and vigour after so long at sea. The citrus saplings, in particular, with their glossy, deep green leaves, looked as if they had germinated here. Behind them, in the dug earth, he noticed that there were already several rows of pale green shoots sprouting: peas, and beans, planted only a few days ago! Of course, this hot, moist climate was ideal, like a green house. 'Let us render thanks' indeed; what a magical, fertile land they had come to. How soon all wants and deficiencies would be supplied. Soon they would be making their own wine, with the fruit of those Cape vines staked beside the lemon seedlings. A land of milk and honey.

Shouts and whoops from the harbour reached him as he made his way on through the close-growing trees to the shore. When he reached the land's end he turned left to follow the shore back towards the harbour. There was no spot that seemed to recommend itself particularly for an observatory, and he did not dawdle, having a sense that he would know it immediately when he found it. On rounding the head he got a clear view down the cove, and was reminded of the cause of the shouting. Today the women convicts were being disembarked. One of the longboats was at the landing spot already, and a crowd was seething around the bank by the flagstaff amongst the piles of unloaded stores. Three other boats were moving across the smooth water, and men's voices, bellowing rhythmically from the shore, urged them on.

How glad those poor women would be to set foot on land. William felt a small stab of guilt that he had not considered their situation before – knowing that they were arrived at last, they had been kept in their prison below decks for a full week. It was necessary, of course, since they could contribute nothing to the clearing of the site, and had no quarters to move into. He had heard Watkin giving orders for their tents to be erected today. What hopes and prayers of thanks must spring to their hearts as they neared the shore; their new home, with the faults of the past behind them, and everything to build anew. There was a roar from the shore as the second boat landed, and a flurry of movement among the crowd. He began to retrace his steps.

He found his observatory site later that afternoon, at the height of the opposite head; he knew it as soon as he saw it. The shape of the prominence called to mind Greenwich Observatory's funny little hillock, high and round like a child's drawing, above the flat banks of the Thames. The functions of two separate observation rooms at Greenwich would need to be combined into a single one here; at Greenwich the first-floor Octagon room with its thirteen-foot-high opening windows provided a good all-round horizon, while observation along the meridian line was carried out in the Quadrant room, where the big fixed transit telescope yielded a north-south view of the night sky through a roof shutter.

Here, lack of building materials and time determined a one-storey building, so a hill was even more important. This observatory would be octagonal in shape, because the whole sky must be scanned – not through windows (the only glass in the settlement was destined for the Governor's house) but through roof shutters that opened around the whole 360 degrees. The quadrant would then be fixed in a secure position, but the night glass could be moved around to observe any section of the sky.

What was best about this site was the great slab of rock jutting out of the hillside, which could be used as the foundation for the octagonal room. Not only would building time be saved, but there would be no movement whatsoever within the room. Secured to the rock with a bracket, the quadrant's readings would not suffer even the slightest discrepancies through the instrument's position shifting, and the astronomical clock, lashed to the rock, would keep regular time until the crack of doom. He climbed up on to the rock. It was already level with

57

the tops of many trees; a relatively small number would need felling, to provide a clear horizon. Below and beside the rock a larger room could be built where he would live and sleep, and keep the meteorological instruments. They could build a connecting staircase against the side of the rock.

The plans and drawings he had made during the voyage would need some modification; he had not foreseen anything as felicitous as this rocky outcrop. He turned slowly, looking down over the clumps of shimmering grey-green leaves, considering the best approach to clear for bringing up the instruments. There was a strange purplish tinge to the light. As he looked up at the sky he was startled to see a livid streak of forked lightening over the bay – followed almost immediately by an explosion of thunder. A curtain of rain moved in across the bay, transforming the colour of the sea. For a moment it was like being God, up there on the rock, the sky around his ears alive with rolling thunder and flickering streaks of light. Then the rain cut off the view, and he jumped down and ran for shelter in the trees.

Later, walking across the settlement to Reverend Johnson's tent, William became aware of the unusual stillness around him. Work was finished for the day but since the rain had stopped, he would have expected to see groups of convicts wandering about in search of vegetable leaves, or sticks for their fires, or fetching water from the stream to cook their suppers. The place was deserted. As he drew nearer to Reverend Johnson's he could hear an excited babble in the distance – whoops and calls and laughter, and music – yes, he strained after it – it was a fiddle. Were they dancing? The sounds came from the women's camp – of course, they must be dancing to celebrate their landing. What a delight it would be to them, after so many months cooped up below decks. How wonderful for their poor children, to be able to run about freely!

Richard and Mary Johnson's tent was similar to those of the marine officers. In the early twilight, intensified by heavy, dark clouds, the tent glowed pleasantly with the light of an oil lamp inside. There was a one-man tent pitched beside it to house their servant Samuel. Samuel was turning a good-sized fish on an improvised spit over a fire, watched anxiously by Richard through the tent flap, which he held closed beneath the point where his head poked out. He waved William to enter, and fussily closed the flap after him.

'The insects in the evening, mosquitoes and such, are very trouble-some to Mary. We try to keep them out.' William had not been intro-

58

duced to the chaplain's wife before. She greeted him kindly, and he took a seat beside her. She looked a little older than her husband – a thin woman, very plainly dressed, like a Methodist, with wide clear eyes and a sweet smile. Her pale complexion was marred by a number of dark blotches.

'I think they are attracted by the lamp,' she said. Following her glance William saw that there were indeed a number of insects dancing in the lamp's halo.

'No, those are moths,' Richard pronounced after a moment's inspection. 'The ones that bite are attracted by – well – by flesh.'

'I have covered every inch except my face; what more can I do? Get a veil like a bee-keeper?' She laughed ruefully, and William noticed that it was true – she wore gloves, the neck of her dark dress came up almost to her chin, and her bonnet was pulled down over her ears.

'Do they bite you, Mr Dawes?' she asked. 'Richard has the good fortune to be not at all to their taste.'

William observed a slightly pained expression cross her husband's face.

'Shall we change the subject, my dear?' he suggested, and, setting three glasses beside the lamp on the tiny table, he carefully filled them with wine.

William asked them about their voyage; they had travelled on the *Golden Grove*, and he had heard that they had both been quite ill at sea. Mary Johnson was the only officer's wife (the chaplain ranking as officer class) permitted to accompany her husband to New South Wales, and Richard expressed a fear that her health and comfort had not properly been taken into account. She contradicted him gently.

'I am well enough, Richard. Since the military officers' wives were forbidden to come here, I count myself fortunate indeed. What are the hardships of the voyage, or the bites of a few insects, against the unhappiness I should have felt at parting from you?'

They smiled at each other, and William found himself smiling too, a little foolishly, and with a keen sense of embarrassment. Richard turned to him.

'I owe her presence to a rather nice point of theology, you know.'

'How's that?'

As they spoke, Samuel brought in the fish and served it, setting out plates of rice, bread, pickled walnuts and wild spinach besides.

'Our table is still aboard the *Golden Grove*,' Richard apologized. 'I'm afraid we have to hold our plates as we eat. Yes. When Mr Wilberforce put forward my name as Chaplain to the Fleet, I was given a list of the chaplain's duties. One of them, you will not be surprised to hear, is to join men and women in holy matrimony. Now I was at that time a bachelor – and it occurred to me to wonder how I might proceed if I myself felt prompted to enter into the blessed state of marriage – '

There was a pause as he dealt with some fish bones; Mary took up the story.

'So he asked his bishop if he might marry *himself* in New South Wales, in the absence of any other clergyman – ' She glanced at Richard and smiled fondly; he nodded and continued, 'And the answer was no. Every other unmarried man in the colony could find a wife and, through my good offices, enter into wedded bliss; but I myself must remain unmarried until another clergyman could be found to tie the knot.'

'And so poor Richard was compelled to find a wife with unseemly haste,' Mary put in, 'and to marry her on the very eve of departure – '

A frown wrinkled Richard's forehead. 'You're teasing, Mary,' he said gently. 'And I know Mr Dawes listens as a friend. But we must be respected, as God's servants, to give our labours on His behalf the best chance of success. Let's not make light of our holy marriage vows, even in jest – '

'Richard – ' Mary's voice was indulgently warm. 'I don't make light of it, my dear. I thank Him for the vital work he asks us to perform together here – '

Richard patted her arm. 'Our courtship was short,' he told William, 'but I believe you will not find a happier man and wife on earth.'

William swallowed his mouthful of fish and smiled. The Johnsons' sincerity was beyond doubt, but their displays of mutual affection made him feel awkward. He tried for a change of subject.

'You mentioned Mr Wilberforce, sir – do you have the pleasure of his acquaintance personally?'

He was interrupted by the sound of a woman screaming close by the tent. He leapt to the tent flap and opened it. The sudden southern darkness had already fallen, and he could see nothing beyond the embers of Samuel's fire. There was the sound of running footsteps and panting breath, and the woman screamed again, then a male voice shouted, 'Now I've got you!' The thudding footsteps receded and disappeared amongst the trees. William glanced at Richard, who had come to his side.

'D'you think we should go after?'

Richard peered out uneasily, then called to Samuel, who answered that he had seen nothing.

'We won't find them in the dark,' he said. 'I think the screams may have been in jest, though why there is a woman out of the women's camp, I am not sure. The guards should be more vigilant.'

'It's only their first night ashore,' said Mary. 'They will be unsettled. I'm sure it's easy to get lost.' She looked at her husband. 'Do you think we should go up and pray with them?'

'No, Mary, it would not be appropriate now. Especially not in the dark. In the morning we'll visit and see what help we can give – ' He settled himself carefully on his chair again, and took a slow sip of wine. 'Yes,' he said. 'I do know Mr Wilberforce. I was introduced to him by Mr Newton, president of the Eclectic Society.'

William nodded. It was the most fervent evangelical and missionary body in England; he himself had attended their meetings in London a few times and come away feeling inspired.

'Mr Wilberforce was kind enough to suggest my name to the Admiralty and, when I accepted the position, to speak with me about what might be achieved.'

'You should see the books, Mr Dawes!' Mary interjected.

'Yes, we have a veritable library of Christian instruction, thanks to the archbishop and Mr Wilberforce. They applied to the Society for the Promotion of Christian Knowledge, and literature has been sent out for the reform of the convicts and the conversion of the natives – four thousand books in all!'

'It's on the *Golden Grove* still, till we have somewhere dry to store it,' Mary said.

'I occupied myself during part of the voyage, in cataloguing them. There are five hundred psalters, Bibles, children's stories, Woodward's *Caution to Swearers*, *Exhortations to Chastity*, *Dissuasions from Stealing*; one hundred copies apiece of *Exercises against Lying* and Osterwald's *Necessity for Reading the Scriptures* – '

'Oh Mr Dawes!' said Mary. 'There is the opportunity to do so much good here!'

'Yes.' His embarrassment left him, now he could catch on to their mood of optimism. 'It's true; we have the chance of making great – wonderful – changes in people's lives, of helping them to turn their backs on wickedness and start afresh – '

'I wanted to ask you, Mr Dawes – '

'William, please.'

61

Richard inclined his head politely. 'William. About our illustrious Governor.' He paused, frowning; carefully set down his empty plate and glanced at William. 'You are, I am sure, better acquainted with the Governor than I – having had the good fortune to sail with him on the *Sirius*. I know we should be thankful to have such an experienced man at our head in this new country – '

'But,' said Mary quietly and firmly, looking directly at her husband.

'I am coming to it, Mary, I am coming to it. From the evidence of your time on board *Sirius*, William, would you say the Governor was a religious man?'

'You know he is not!' Mary said softly; Richard raised a hand to forestall her, and she quietly set down her plate and folded her hands in her lap.

'To be honest, sir, no.' William reviewed the voyage in his mind. There were no regular ship's prayers aboard the *Sirius*, not even on a Sunday. And the conversation, on those occasions William had sat at captain's table, had never remotely touched on matters of religion. He himself had a few times felt out of step, most especially when they had first touched land at Botany Bay and he had yielded to the impulse to fall to his knees and thank God. The Governor had spoken of erecting a flagstaff, but not of thanking God.

Richard nodded unhappily, setting his palms together and balancing his chin upon the outstretched fingers, as if about to pray.

'I understand the pressing problems he has to consider. But worship is important. It is important that the convicts be shown, by the example of their betters, that God is honoured and – and – a part of their lives.'

'Has he put obstacles in your way?' asked William.

Richard Johnson sighed heavily. 'I had to make a number of representations – before he would permit me to hold the service of thanksgiving last Sunday. And I cannot get his ear to discuss the building of a church. I know he has ordered plans for a hospital, storehouse, courthouse and barracks – and for residences for himself and Major Ross – but there are no plans for a house of God – '

William nodded; he could confirm that. Beyond the church site marked on the city plans Alt had been asked to draw up, a church had never been mentioned.

'And for God's servant to be accorded proper respect by the convicts – ' Richard hesitated, his face was wretchedly anxious. 'Well, he must be – he must be – '

'Richard,' said Mary softly.

He glanced at her and gave a little helpless nod.

'He must be accorded respect by the Governor,' she said simply. 'The higher-ranking officers and the medical men have all been invited to dine with the Governor, and Richard has not.'

Richard grimaced. 'Surgeon White tells me the Governor has me down for an Enthusiast.'

A surge of angry energy prompted William to his feet; he paced to the tent flap and back again. 'I sometimes think that anyone who demonstrates faith, or makes even the slightest attempt to act in accordance with Scripture, is branded an Enthusiast so that others can feel more comfortable about ignoring religion.'

'It's true.' Mary turned to Richard. 'Isn't it? Easy to call anyone who cares about the Lord 'Enthusiast', and make them out to be a crank.'

'But if the Governor has this opinion of his chaplain,' Richard pointed out, 'my chances of achieving God's work are seriously handicapped. I have to find a way of proving to him that I can be as temperate as – '

'As any idle country vicar who leaves all the preaching to his curate?' broke in Mary fiercely. 'God comes before the Governor, surely.'

'But I need to work through the Governor, Mary, I need to work with the Governor. I have a much better chance of success if I can work *with* the temporal powers.'

William looked at Mary's hands twisting in her lap. He turned to Richard. 'Even if the Governor is himself irreligious, he must see the benefits religious conversion will bring to the convicts, in terms of their good behaviour, and the harmony in which they might live – '

Richard nodded. 'Of course. By their works shall ye know them. Of course he will see the importance of the role we have to play.' He went to the tent flap and called into the darkness for Samuel to clear their plates. When he glanced back at William his face was anxious again.

'You won't – I mean, our worries about the church and so on – are safe with you?'

'Of course. You don't know what a relief it is, after some of the company on board ship, to talk with people who have a real sense of God's purpose in bringing us here – ' William laughed, and Richard clasped his hand warmly. 'There is such scope for work, for hope, for change to a better way of living – '

He was interrupted by a deafening rolling crash overhead, which startled him so that he jumped to his feet, knocking his chair over backwards. In one movement Mary had flung herself at Richard and buried her face in his lap. The two men stared at each other wide-eyed, but before either could speak the explosions of sound began again. A battle – there must be a battle – the ship's great guns being fired . . . As William struggled to make sense of it, the tent sides suddenly billowed and sagged in a tremendous gust of wind, taking out their light, and an even closer sound, of torrential rain beating on the tent, pouring to the ground in streams, blotted out the gunfire.

'Another storm,' came Johnson's voice in the darkness. His wife was sobbing. 'Calm yourself, my dear. It is nothing more than a thunderstorm.'

This time the rolling crash of the thunder seemed to be inside William's own ears, inside his head, exploding and reverberating in pounding waves of sound. Suddenly brilliant lightning made the tent walls white, revealed the sparkling runnels of rain that had permeated the canvas, showed them each others' pale, shocked faces – and flickered out, leaving their startled eyes blind with darkness. The thunder was continuous, rolling, pounding overhead; a new gust of wind brought William's side of the tent flapping in, loose and collapsing.

'I'm going to try to get the pegs in again,' he bellowed to Richard, although it was impossible that Richard could have heard him above the noise. The loose canvas billowed and snapped like a sail; feeling his way blindly through the thick darkness to the tent flap, that sound and sense of living canvas brought back to William the terror of his first climb up the mast, the terrible, giddy height and the huge, powerful sheets of canvas that of their own volition seemed to swell or slacken or flap angrily back to knock a grown man to his death – huge, barely controlled servants, violent and pitiless in revenge. As he sensed he was nearing the flap he nearly stumbled over a large soft obstacle which hit him at shin level; patting it, he realized it was the servant Samuel, who lay crouched with his head buried between his arms, shivering like a dog.

In the instant that his searching hands found the tent flap and pulled it aside, he was drenched. He stood gasping for breath between the torrents of water running down his face, straining his eyes to make out anything in the darkness. When the next sheet of lightning came he moved off round the tent to where it was unpegged – and crouched, scrabbling in the mud, as darkness snapped down again, feeling for the pegs and rope ends. As the thunder rolled down to a brief silence he became aware of other sounds, dimly, through the hiss of the rain –

screams, panic-stricken shouts, voices calling for help. The next bout of lightning enabled him to secure two of the uprooted pegs; the third was split, and he bound the lashing rope end around a rock, futilely, knowing it would slip free in the next strong gust of wind. Standing and cupping his hands around his eyes to shield them from the driving rain, he saw that there were still lights in several other tents. The cries and curses must be from those whose canvas homes had blown down entirely – but farther away in the distance, women were screaming and screaming.

He poked his soaking head into the Johnsons' tent again.

'I'm going to see if I can help –' he shouted, and caught Richard's answering, 'I can't leave Mary!' and the whimpering of the servant. He closed the flap and made his way slowly, stumbling over the uneven ground, slipping in the dirt which had turned to sodden, treacherous mud, heading for the women's camp. The rain lessened to a normal downpour, and when there was a sudden glimmer of light he glanced up and found it was the moon, big and low, illuminating the outlines of clouds which rushed madly across its face, so that its light was as inconstant as the flickering lightning.

The noises from the women's camp were louder now: a cacophony of terror – women shrieking, men shouting, calling, cursing. As he gained the level of the campsite the cold moonlight suddenly revealed a scene from hell. All but two of the tents were down, and those remaining leaned drunkenly, half-dismantled, on their poles. On top of the collapsed canvas – and on the ground – on the rocks – in the filthy mud – bodies were writhing – struggling, rolling from side to side in frenzy.

His first thought was that somehow they had been struck by light-ning – injured, all of them, knocked to the ground. His second was that they were fighting, as men fought when their ship was boarded, rolling round the deck in the last desperate stages of hand-to-hand combat. Straining forward and wiping his eyes on his sodden sleeve, he looked again and the moonlight gleamed on muddy water and white buttocks – moving, struggling, heaving, pumping . . .

One figure reared up, with a terrified female scream, and another on the ground lunged at her and brought her thudding down – and the sounds in William's ears disentangled themselves into separate sobs and screams and grunts and oaths – 'Fucking whore – fucking whore' and gasps of – of pain, of pleasure? Of beastly animals rutting. The men, after eight months at sea and months, maybe years, before that

65

locked in the all-male hulks, had got to the women. As the thunder crashed and the rain lashed down with renewed vigour, they rolled in the dirt and took their pleasure.

William froze, unable to believe the evidence of his eyes and ears. Nearby, a woman was moaning and sobbing, 'No! No! No!' repeatedly. Another called in a drunken, singsong voice, 'Over 'ere lads – come on, Jenny's waitin' for yer, come to Jenny.'

To his right the searchlight moon suddenly illumined a woman's face, eyes closed, dark with blood at the mouth, sliding up and down in the mud like a rag with the frantic thrusts of the man astride her. There was a running scuffle and a couple landed almost at his feet – he grabbed at the man's shoulder to save himself from falling.

'Clear off! I got 'er first!' The man bellowed, lunged, and swung his fist at William. Overbalancing, William clutched at the standing figure's legs, and the man freed himself with a kick. William felt a sudden blinding pain, then dark.

When he opened his eyes it was nearly dawn, the storm was over and there was a thin grey light in the sky. His head ached horribly, and he was very cold. Struggling into a sitting position, and touching his head gingerly, he felt the sticky blood, and turned to look at the rock he'd fallen on. The place was quiet; in the tricksy, colourless beginnings of light he saw still rounds and lumps on the ground which he took for bodies. Attempting to stand, blackness swam into his eyes again and he fell to all fours; raised himself slowly, very slowly, and began to creep back to his tent. The animals – the obscene beasts of the night – had disappeared amongst the rocks and stones and trees. All that was left were the splayed, drooping, flattened canvases of the battered tents, and muddy straggles of dark clothing littering the ground. A woman's shoe right in his path – he suddenly remembered the couple who'd knocked him down, and looked back. But there was no one there. In between two blinding pulses of his headache he wondered if it had been a nightmare – terrible, but only imagined.

His tired mind skittered away from it, focusing on the simple problem of one step followed by the next, keeping balance, not falling again, covering the interminable swaying distance of a hundred-odd yards to his tent.

Mr Worgan, summoned by Watkin Tench to bathe and dress William's head, gave them the night's news. On the *Lady Penrhyn* the sailors had been given grog to celebrate the discharge of the women, and some had come ashore with it, against orders. They had shared it with the women. Later in the night the male convicts had run amok through the women's tents and, because of the wildness of the weather, the guards had been unable to enforce their authority. At midnight lightning had struck the big tree around which the pens for sheep and hogs had been built. The tree was split from top to bottom, five sheep and a hog killed. Fires had started in a couple of other trees struck by lightning but the rain had put them out.

William felt sick and weak. Today was to be the parade, and the reading of the Governor's commission before an assembly of every soul in the colony. Today was, officially, the beginning.

In his full-dress uniform, sweating like all the other marines in the heat, he turned himself into the required puppet. The marines welcomed the Governor with flying colours and a march from the band. Then they formed a circle around the whole body of male and female convicts, who were ordered to sit on the ground. The gentlemen present were called into the centre, to stand near the Governor, Lieutenant-Governor, Judge Advocate, and other dignitaries. William stared into the seated crowd, observing the skeletal thinness and obvious ill-health of numbers of them. Many had slack stupid faces, many were muddy, bloodied, barely clad in an assortment of stinking rags. Collins' words (as Judge Advocate, he was reading the Commissions) floated past him at a distance – the Governor's authority . . . the civil court . . . the discharge of the transports . . . the conciliation of the natives . . . on and on until it was the Governor's turn to speak.

Phillip addressed the convicts in a steely tone of anger, which William had not heard before. He had given them a degree of freedom, he said, to find out their natures; and they had revealed themselves to be, many of them, incorrigibly depraved. Therefore they would be treated with the greatest severity. The soldiers had positive orders to fire on any of them attempting to get into the women's quarters at night. Theft of any article of stock or provisions would be punished with death, because the theft of a chicken here, where stock was so scarce and could not be replaced, was an injury to the whole community. His humanity and feelings towards his fellow creatures might militate against such severity, but justice demanded that the laws be enforced rigidly, and justice would prevail over all. Their employment would be to construct houses, first for the officers, then for the marines, and last for themselves. William allowed his gaze to wander over the convicts as Phillip spoke. They were not taking in the Governor's words, but staring stupidly around at the trees and soldiers and the women, or blinking at the sky. His hot, aching head formed an impression of a horde of mangy, half-starved rats, flushed out of the bowels of the ships and contained here by the ring of soldiers, eyes glinting malevolently in the light, waiting for what their captors would do next. Phillip's description of them as 'fellow creatures' caused the spectacle of last night to rise before his eyes again; these were his fellows? No.

And did they have any sense that this was a new beginning for them, an opportunity to turn their backs on the bad old ways? No. No more than the stinking rats in the bilges.

Well then, why were they here, any of them? What on earth was the purpose of this venture, if the convicts were so incorrigibly evil that only lashes, punishment, incarceration could contain them?

One of the soldiers swayed in the sunshine and fell to his knees; a couple of his fellows dragged him into the shade of a tree, and splashed his face with water. The air was waving and wrinkling with heat. Phillip's hard, unvarying voice talked on; he was recommending marriage to the convicts, as the state best suited to the accomplishment of their desires and a decent Christian way of life. Marriage. Would such creatures marry?

William's mood wavered and shifted as the distance was doing through the haze of heat; the possibility of pity suddenly entering his heart and altering his perceptions. It is better to marry than to burn.

For how long had they burned, these poor, damned souls? For how long, cooped up with none but their own sex, subjected to the sound and spectacle of unnatural vices, deprived of even a moment's privacy, tormented by hungers that could not be satisfied? Fettered and stalled like beasts, was it surprising they had resorted to beastly behaviour? They were to be pitied rather than blamed for their terrible congress in the dirt; it was from this animal level that education and religion had raised mankind. To how little, then, of either of these civilizing influences, had these poor devils been exposed.

Shame flooded through him. May God forgive him for judging them so harshly. Christ's own example lit the way; love and pity for the sinners, and open-hearted forgiveness. Because they were weak, they must be helped, not punished. They must be guided into a better way.

And with a growing clarity now, as if he had inserted a more finely polished lens into his glass, he began in his own mind to examine the Governor's commands. Must the convicts be shot for going to the women? The sailors – free men – consorted with the women. As did some of the officers, and the ships' captains. For a man to go to a woman was not a crime. Because the convicts had abused their freedom, they must lose it. But would that teach them any better how to use it in future? And food. If they were hungry, they would steal. The officers would not steal, because the officers would not go hungry. Handy, dandy, sang his aching brain, handy, dandy, which is the justice and which the thief?

Phillip's speech was drawing to a close. William looked at the women, who sat clustered together with their children in the shade of a couple of huge gum trees. Some were surprisingly well turned-out, with neatly pinned hair and even a little rouge on their pale cheeks, looking about alertly to catch an eye among the soldiers. Others were the picture of despair, ragged, bruised, dishevelled, with pale, listless faces and sunken eyes. They had seen too much hardship. Swelling pity in his heart caused his eyes to brim with tears; may God help them and their children, may God help all of us, to find a way to live together in kindness here.

At the end of the official business the officers were all invited to a cold collation at the Governor's tent. William, head throbbing painfully around the fragile new vision of the past hour, made his excuses to Captain Campbell and retreated to his tent. He needed to be alone; to think; to pray; to assess how these new insights must guide and shape his actions from now on.

STEPHEN

Interesting how well those children grew. Everyone comments on it.
By 1800 those sickly infants who'd endured the rigours of the voyage,
and the crises of rationing of the early years, were bigger than their
parents. Runty cockney stock, taken out of the cramped cellars and
gin-palaces and thieves' dens – taken out of smoking stinking
London and set down in good fresh New Holland air – grows tall.
Runs wild, splashes in the sea and browns in the sun. In one
generation they were transformed; the children of stunted, sickly
criminals became like gods, tall, straight-limbed, healthy. Hardly any
children died – and the women bred like rabbits. Even women they
supposed to be past child-bearing age were spawning litters of
healthy brats. And all that on a restricted diet of rancid salt meat
and aged weevily flour. A wonderful instance of the effects of
environment on health and physique. Someone must have studied
an example they can monitor in recent history? There must be cases,
after wars – returning refugees – how about Israel, in the early days?
It's a pleasing image, in New South Wales: the seed of that seemingly
poor stock grew tall and straight and vigorous. While back in dear old
England, after another full century of filthy air and slum housing, the
army was reduced to recruiting whole battalions of Bantams to die for
King and Country in the trenches, and the height difference between
officers and men was an average what, six inches?

The test of a free country. That no matter what your social
background, you should have as much right as the next man or
woman to grow to a decent height. Achieved in the convict colony by
1800. And possibly not yet in Britain.

That image of golden girls and boys on the sands of Sydney cove –
there's a biological propensity there towards rude health, that
warms my heart. A simple correspondence between human beings
and say, turnips, flourishing in a richer soil.
And are you interested, Stephen – unusually interested, perhaps – in
rude health these days? Thanks to the feebleness of your own
offspring? Do your unviable children (oh, Tiny Tim! oh, Victorian
babies so loved of God he called them home untimely!) account for
your trespass into sentimentality? Do this one's multiple and
undeniable defects conjure up in you a maudlin obsession with
strength and vigour?

70

This is not the place.
Stephen, this is not the time or place for it. Come to the child later. Not today.

And there's no need to be sentimental about golden girls and boys. They eat and drink, they shit and fight and breed, their health *is* rude. Sentiment is applied to the weak, the sickly baby in its cot. Sentiment pretends there are other reasons for being alive. (To suffer. To be loved of God.) No. I have no sentiment. No more than does my wife.

Dry-eyed Olla. Unyielding, ungiving, unforgiving Olla. Olla who does not pretend that she does not despise me.

Who rightly chooses not to confer so much as a flicker of her attention on whatever it is keeps me shut in my study for hours on end. Silently makes felt her satisfaction in my absence.

Are you whining? You are. You're complaining, Stephen! What d'you want? Her dewy-eyed applause? Unstinting admiration?

No. Dry-eyed zero's what I want. Dewy admiration doesn't suit. Anna's eyes were always dewy. Wet and hopeful as a dog. Anna would have *loved* to know what I was writing. A flicker of interest? Spontaneous combustion, at the least. It would have been, 'Marvellous! Brilliant! *Clever* Stevie, tell me all about it.' Her effusions, her bright smiles, her endless understanding. Her dewy eyes and eager sympathy, nauseating me even as I burrowed into her. Her juicy surfeit of sympathy, enough to drown a man.

How could I respect a woman that respected me? I have earned Olla's contempt.

Wanted it. Even craved it? One of the strands in the fuse that set off the sexual fireworks? I think so, yes. From first sight. In her too-big black chambermaid's dress. Her skinny, fragile, tough-as-nails body. Her bony waif's face and contemptuous eyes. Skeletal, burning, tough as an old boot. *Real*. Ready to hate me. A knowing child-bride, fierce with pain and anger. Oh yes. A physical pang, I can feel the echoes still. Love/lust/love – at first sight.
Olla.

OLLA

Stephen watches me. It makes my flesh crawl. I can't help it – he makes me feel terrible. How is it? The day will pass quickly, too quickly. Daniel and I take our bath, I help him move his limbs in the water. He feels the power of arms and legs to swish through liquid; he hears the splashes movement makes, on the right side, right arm; left side, left arm. He learns the results of movement in sound, in change of temperature on his skin. He feels pleasure when restricting clothes are taken off and his body is supported by kind water. He will move a little of his own accord, smile, make low gurgling sounds. He is happy, I think, as much as ever will be possible in the prison of the flesh.

I dry him, dress him, give him breakfast. He is exhausted by now, it is eleven, I put him in the pram to sleep. I rinse his night-time nappies, put them to soak and the other clothes to wash. Then we walk down to the shops for food, he sleeps, when we are back I hang the wash. I prepare his lunch, and Stephen's and my dinner. I wake him, change him, feed him, play with him and do his exercises, and then I read to him. Afterwards I put on music and clean one room – this is the way I manage the house now there is so little time, one room each day in turn and round back to the beginning again: kitchen, dining-room, lounge, hall and stairs, his bedroom, ours, the study and bathroom together, one each day of the week so the whole place is cleaned weekly at the very least.

There are other things intruding upon many days, appointments for him all the time, at hospital or clinic, tests, inspections, injections, examinations; or the social worker comes to tell me her problems, or we must go to collect a new supporting pushchair or a special car seat. When my routine is spoiled I must fit in more next day. He has fresh-cooked food every lunch and dinner. If we have to go to the hospital I make his favourite puréed vegetables with chicken and take it in a jar. He eats less well away from home. It is distraction. His food is his strength. It was potatoes for Tadek, every day, potatoes, potatoes, potatoes, black bread, tinned corn beef. If a builder were to build only with mud; if a sculptor must make a statue out of chalk . . . Daniel I make and make to grow, I give tempting varied succulent tastes, cunningly mixed to contain every vitamin, mineral, protein, every chemical note of body-building goodness to make his cells divide and multiply. His appetite will never be jaded by cabbage soup, endless potato, he will never turn his sad face away from food as Tadek did. This help I can give, goodness in his mouth and belly.

By now it is maybe 5 p.m. I know from the knot in my stomach, Stephen will be coming home. Yes, he rattles his key in the door; opens it, enters. I am preparing Daniel's dinner. He comes into the kitchen.

'Hello love. Good day?' His voice grates, he looks at me but not at Daniel, he is empty and has nothing to say. I wish he will go into the dining-room with his cup of tea but no, he sits at the kitchen table and watches me.

'Yes, fine, thank you. And you?'

'The usual. You know.'

Indeed. I turn on the blender and purée Daniel's food, its noise mercifully fills the room. Silence when Daniel and I are here – our silence is sweet. Stephen's entrance makes it ugly, tense; he sits in the room like weight, and oppresses me with his not-talking, with my not-talking, with our not-talking. He wants me to look at him and speak to him, but I have nothing he wants to hear, and he has nothing he wants to say. 'The usual.' I will him to take his misery out of our room, out of the sunny kitchen I share with Daniel. Let him drag the corpse of his happiness across the hall and up the stairs to his study and shut the door, instead of demanding that I deliver him from it.

He thinks of things to say. 'What's that you're feeding him?'

'Poached salmon with asparagus and boiled potato.'

'It smells good. I can smell lemon.'

'Yes, a little.'

'I bet there aren't many babies with a diet like that!' He pretends to smile. What does he expect me to say? He is pitiful.

After a long silence now he drains his teacup and sets it down. 'I'll just take a look at the garden. The beans might be ready.'

Yes. Good, go out there and stay, find something new to plant and harvest, something that will take you hours.

When the door has closed behind him the room lightens, and Daniel blinks up at me and opens his mouth. Stephen is not good for him.

I used to wait for him to come home. I used to watch the clock, boil the kettle. Now I boil it also, but so he will not have to wait so long in the kitchen for it to boil – so he can make his tea quickly and go.

73

It is the opposite. When I waited for him to come home, he was often late. Why did I wait? It was my job, I was his wife. But I am still his wife, it is still my job . . . And now he is never late. Well then, I must have wanted to wait. Now I do not. That's all.

He is different. He was excited, had things to say, ideas to explain, friends, too many things to do. He brought that into the kitchen, it filled the room with life and light. Now he brings darkness, he is anti-matter. He will suck the energy from Daniel and me, he is destitute, a beggar. Now he is death. I think it is that simple. On the whole I do not think, I only wish him removed. He is entirely familiar and entirely alien. A bad combination. I would know better how to deal with a man like my father now, drunk, violent, maudlin. Stephen is worse than violent; he is void.

Perhaps I knew this when I met him, and made myself ignore it? He made life easier for me. He was a stroke of luck.
No. I did not see through him because it was not possible – he was alien but solid. It is time and failure that have eaten him away. He is the negative now, of the positive photograph then. I took my time believing in him, I was cautious enough to test the ice. I was destitute but not asking to be rescued, not crying for help, not slavishly grateful when it came. I was not trying to poach his life, or suck out the marrow from his bones.

*

Daniel must know the story, he must know all my life. Openly, from my lips; I must feed him my life as an albatross feeds her young, regurgitating her bellyful into his gaping beak. He will make sense of it, he will see the meaning of it. He will use it to grow.

The Crown Hotel, Buxton, is where I met Stephen. 1975, after London.
I run out of hospital before Mack comes for me. I am dizzied by the noise and traffic, crowds on the pavement. I must get out of London before Mack finds me. I must escape. It's filthy – Victoria coach station, hot dry wind of dust, a filthy one-footed pigeon scrabbling in the gutter, grey glaring light. I see a poster: COME TO LOVELY BUXTON, HEART OF DERBYSHIRE'S PEAK DISTRICT. Green hills fill the view. There is a fine clean building with pillars, a wide empty street. It is far from London.

OK, Buxton. Coach from Victoria 8 p.m. Arrive Buxton, midnight.

That first night I sleep on a railway platform bench. No one comes. Then round the hotels, the fourth is the Crown; yes, chambermaid – £9.50 a week with bed and board.
They give me a room of my own. High up under a sloping roof, with skylight window. Standing on the bed I see across roofs to green hills. Bed, chair, hanging rail for clothes. I can lock the door.

The job is for the season, ends September. Six weeks, £57. I need shoes, but still I can leave here after buying uniform, shoes, sanitary towels, with £40 or more. I will be cushioned. I will not be in dangerous places again, I will find other work and get more money. I will get a place of my own.

Two more girls work here. They speak fast with strong accents – I do not understand. They giggle. After work I go in my room, shut the door, sleep. I sleep and sleep. I lie and look at stars or clouds moving above my skylight. It is my room, no one comes in. No one bothers me. The work is easy: changing sheets, making beds, sweeping rooms, cleaning bathrooms; setting tables before breakfast, lunch, and dinner. Washing pots after lunch and dinner. From three to five is off.

The hotel is not full. All the smart rooms are full but there is a corridor on the third floor which is not smart, numbers forty to fifty-two. They must share the bathroom and toilet; the wallpaper is faded, the springs have popped out under the beds. The windows are nailed shut. These rooms are 'due for renovation', says the housekeeper who shows me round. They are sometimes used but never booked in advance. They are not reservation rooms.
They put late-night comers here, and ones who won't complain. Couples who don't want anyone to know where they are, and won't fuss about the springs because they think the broken bed is their own fault.

I am passing reception with a laundry basket when Clarrie calls me to show a couple to forty-two. They have rucksacks and are wearing shorts. As they follow me upstairs they congratulate each other on finding a room, it sounds as if they have tried some other places already. I unlock forty-two, give them the key, and go on with my basket. The girl shouts me when I am at the end of the corridor.
'Excuse me – how do we open the window?'
I return and examine the window; it is nailed shut, as I know.

'Sorry. This room will be decorated. I cannot open.'

'This is ridiculous,' she says, sitting on the bed. 'The beds are crap – listen – it'll do my back in.' She bounces, squeaking the springs.

'And no ventilation – what are they charging for this?'

The man – Stephen – smiles at me. 'It's not her fault. They can charge what they like if Buxton's full, can't they?' The girl pulls back the bedclothes angrily.

'Sheets are clean,' I say. 'I change sheets.'

'Thank you,' says Stephen. 'Thanks for your help.'

I go. I hear the girl complaining again as I shut the door.

They are cyclists, they leave early morning, after seven-thirty breakfast. I go to strip their room around eight-thirty. The first thing I see is a watch, lying on the bedside table. I listen to it – working. It looks a good one, leather strap, 'twenty-one jewels' written on the face. I put it in my pocket, strip the beds and make them up clean. I am putting out clean towels when the door suddenly opens and the man barges in. He is sweaty and panting, he stares around the room. 'I'm sorry – oh, you've cleaned already. My watch. I think I left my watch by the bed. Have you seen it?' He sits on the bed, still short of breath, smiles at me.

It may be worth £10. There is a jeweller's that sells second-hand watches on the high street. It may be worth more. The question is, will he tell the manager where he lost it? Might I be searched? He wants to be friendly, he keeps smiling.

'No. Sorry.'

He goes to the bedside table. 'I could have sworn I left it here – I have this kind of mental picture, putting my shoes on, of seeing it there and thinking, must put the watch on before we go. Then Cath said something, and I got distracted – '

'Perhaps it's on the floor,' I say. 'I haven't swept.' He kneels and peers under the bed, runs his hand along the inner edge of the bed-frame.

'No. D'you think it could've got wrapped up with the sheets when you pulled them off?'

'If it was on the table I would see – '

He looks unconvinced. I open the linen basket and begin to pull out dirty sheets.

'Has anyone else been in here? Before you?'

'No.' No point lying – if he asks anyone else they'll say the same. I continue to pull out dirty sheets – he comes and takes a corner, pulls too, we empty the basket and he checks the bottom.

'Damn,' he says. 'It was my uncle's. It was a good watch.' He goes over to the window and lifts the curtain as if it might be hidden there. I bend forward to pick up the linen again, and the watch slips out of my pocket, on to the white sheets. I cover it quickly with my hand, check to see if he noticed. No, he is staring out of the window. I think of saying, 'Here it is. I found it!' No. He's about to give up now. It's his own fault, he was careless. I stand up and slip it back in the pocket, then suddenly he's right beside me and I didn't hear him walking over.

'Let me put these back for you. I'm afraid I'm making extra work.'

'Is all right.'

'Where are you from?' he says, stuffing the sheets in. 'I love your accent.'

'Poland.'

'Been here long?'

'One year. In England.'

'Only a year? Your English is very good. Have you got English relatives?'

'No.' I want him to go now. I am afraid he might have seen me slide it into my pocket. I don't want to lose this job. It was a stupid thing to do.

He smiles. 'What's your name?' He is going to report me.

'Olla.'

'Well Olla. I've lost my watch. Serves me right for being so careless, I suppose. I'm going to have a coffee before I get on that bike again – would you like to join me?'

What is he playing at? Does he know I have it or not? Does he think I will admit for the price of a coffee?

'I have work.'

'Of course. When d'you finish?'

'Three.'

'Not till three? Don't you even get a lunch-break?'

He is playing tricks. 'Excuse. I must – go bathroom.'

'Sorry.' He smiles. I go to the toilet. I take the watch from my pocket and examine it. There is a name engraved on back: N. J. Beech. His uncle? If I try to sell it they can trace it by this name. I will give it back. I don't trust him, and I am behind with my work. I return to the room holding the watch in my hand.

'Look. I found it in my pocket. Maybe it slipped in from the sheets – '
'Goodness!' He smiles. 'It must have got caught up in something –
perhaps the pillowcase – '
'Yes.'
He stares at me. OK he suspects, but I have given it back, he can't
prove anything. 'Thank you.'
'OK. I get on.'
'Of course – ' he stands aside for me to take the laundry basket out.
'Goodbye. Thank you.'

I have to work hard to catch up before it's time for table laying. I am
angry, I should have kept my nerve, it was worth one week's work
and maybe more.

I want to look in the jeweller's window; at five-past-three I run down
the back steps and he is in the drive with his bicycle, smiling.
'You came out! I was afraid you might be sitting in your room writing
letters home or something.'
What does he want now?
'I'd like to buy you tea, to thank you for finding the watch. Do let me,
please – ' What has he done with the girlfriend? He is quite tall,
brown curly hair, light, blondish on top. Bright brown eyes. Bicycle,
rucksack, shorts. He is on holiday, he is not poor. Why not? Why not
have tea with him?

He takes me to the tea rooms opposite the spa. He orders ham
sandwiches, cream cakes, and tea. He asks me questions. How old
am I? Where do I live?
'Crown Hotel', I reply.
'But after the holidays?'
'I find another place in September.' He thinks this is strange. Where
are my parents? How did I come to England? What did I do in
London?
'No,' I say. 'This is like detectives.'
He laughs, he has good teeth. He tells me about himself: teacher of
history, unmarried, his parents live in Lancashire, he has a sister, he
is on a cycling holiday with another teacher, Cath; he is twenty-five. 'I
don't know what else. What else would you like to know?' He has a
good smile.
'Are you rich?'

He laughs. 'The watch,' he says. 'D'you want – I think maybe you should have it. It fell into your pocket; seems like fate or something.'
He is strange. But if he wants to give me his watch, why not?
'For nothing?' I ask.
Suddenly he blushes. 'Of course,' he says. 'No, not for nothing. For having tea with me. Thank you.'

I go back to my room with a full stomach and the watch in my hand. He goes away on his bike, fine. I sell the watch for £12, to the shop in the high street.

CHAPTER SIX

Clearing the land

Governor Phillip summoned William to his prefabricated residence the following day, to discuss his duties. On questioning the sentry, William discovered that Surgeon White was with His Excellency; he waited outside, watching the convicts assigned to the Governor's garden scratching ineffectually at the ground.

White came out looking flushed and angry. He nodded to William and strode off towards the hospital tent. When William entered the Governor did not look up from his writing. William felt awkward in his presence; despite sailing together on the *Sirius* and *Supply*, they had had very little communication. The Governor had given him permission to set up the instruments and make observations during their six-week stop at Rio, but had arbitrarily and, as William thought, curtly, refused permission at the Cape – giving as excuse that the instruments could not be moved without disturbing the cargo of bread which was stowed on top of them. William had a sense that the Governor disapproved of him – maybe he too had been branded as an Enthusiast.

Now Phillip set down his pen and fixed his gaze on William, still without speaking. His protuberant grey eyes and large curved nose reminded William of a sheep; but only while he remained silent. When he began to speak, his precise, toneless voice and cold authority made William feel confused and stupidly young.

'I have been speaking with Surgeon White. He tells me – amongst other things, amongst a litany of complaints concerning the inadequacy of hospital facilities, for which I have no remedy at present – he tells me Mr Alt is not fit to perform his duties as surveyor.'

There was a brief silence, William being unsure if a response was expected. At length he stammered,

'Not fit – ?'

'Unwell. Clearly, you are the person best suited to undertake his work, thanks to your knowledge of engineering. I intend to have you excused from all marine duties, to free you to set about a number of surveying and building projects. We need a gunpowder store very urgently; I have promised Surgeon White we will begin a hospital building this week; I am concerned that questions of drainage should be fully explored before any permanent erections are embarked upon – '

'But, sir – ' William could not hold back the interruption; the Governor raised his eyebrows and waited. 'I beg your pardon, sir. But the observatory – I have orders from the Board of Longitude to build an observatory to house their instruments, and direction from the Astronomer Royal to watch for a comet in August, which is only five months off – '

Phillip glanced at the clock. 'I am aware of all this, Mr Dawes. The Board of Longitude, for all their wisdom, were not in a position to foresee the illness of Mr Alt, nor the consequent difficulties. Regretfully, I must overrule their directions.'

'But the observatory – ' It was the only reason William was here. He was not even officially a member of the land detachment; he was extra to that detachment, thanks to negotiations between Royal Astronomer Maskeylene, the Board of Longitude, and Baron Sydney. He was here because accurate measurements of longitude on this coastline, and careful maps of the southern skies, were needed by all British ships intending to navigate the area. And the comet; sighting of the comet, which Maskeylene predicted should be visible from the southern hemisphere, would validate Halley's theory about comets' orbits, making a major contribution to scientific knowledge. Was he to be prevented from doing this, by questions of drainage?

'Lieutenant Dawes, in the Navy it is not the practice of young second lieutenants to argue with their commanding officer. I should be surprised if it were, in the Marines.'

'I beg your pardon – I – '

Phillip nodded wearily, cutting him short. 'There is no reason why you can't oversee the building of the observatory alongside your engineering duties. I will allocate a small party of convicts and marines specifically to work on clearing a site; but you must understand that the observatory is of less importance to the survival and well-being of the colony than your other work – and organize your time accordingly. You may go.'

As William stepped back out into the sunlight, he realized he must look exactly as Surgeon White had done, leaving the house ten minutes earlier – red-faced and miserably angry.

Wanting to be alone to digest the interview, he made for his tent, but was unpleasantly surprised to find Watkin Tench there. He was sitting on a water cask and using a wooden chair for a desk. He looked up as William entered.

'Ah! Caught me skulking!' he said.

'What are you writing?' William asked.

'A journal. You know – of the settlement's first year. Should sell like hot cakes back in London.'

William sat on his cot, since he could think of no excuse for leaving immediately.

'Have you seen the Governor?' Watkin straightened up. Even with his uniform creased and his hair standing on end, he looked solid and authoritative, the sort of man who inspires others with confidence. He was one of the most popular officers in the detachment. William knew he was lucky to be billeted with him, but his own inclination for privacy made any sharing of accommodation a trial.

'Tell.'

William shrugged. 'He has given me Alt's duties. Which he says are more important than building the observatory. I've got to find sites for drains.'

Watkin closed his diary and tucked it under his bedding.

'You know when we went up Table Mountain?' he said, rather surprisingly. William nodded. The scorching heat of the day of their climb came back to him; the smoke rising from the gullies where the runaway blacks hid; the odious sight, the terrible smell, of the bodies of recaptured slaves who'd been broken on the wheel and displayed publicly, as a warning to others. The barbarous precision of the Boers. 'We wanted to get to the top,' Watkin continued, 'for the view. For scientific interest in the mountain's formation. Most of all, to take readings of the early evening stars. But we forgot to take any water.'

It was true. They had sucked pebbles to try to bring some moisture to their parched mouths, and when they came across a brackish puddle in a crevice of the rock, they had both lain down full length to lap at the stagnant water. He had been afraid that Watkin, who was heavier than himself, and whose face had turned a dark puce, might collapse from the heat.

'Well His Ex is remembering the water. He's right, William. Basic supplies and functions have to be established before exploration and research and so on can begin. We made light of it at the time but you know as well as I how easily a man can fall from a stroke of the sun or lack of water in the heat – '

William stared at his knees. This was the last thing he needed to hear: Watkin defending the Governor and praising his good sense. Easy for Watkin to be reasonable, he had no special mission or instructions, he had all the time in the world.

Within William's irritation there was a flicker of contempt for Watkin, which he recognized and was ashamed of. Watkin was a solid officer, a captain – technically, William's superior. That insidious little flame of contempt sprang simultaneously from a sense that Watkin was too easy-going, too ready to accommodate and compromise, and from the knowledge (gained during the scramble up Table Mountain) that his father was a dancing master. He had been dancing master for a great family – the William Wynns, who had provided for Watkin's education and made him into the gentleman he undoubtedly was. Nevertheless, his father was a dancing master, and perhaps that accounted for his – superficiality – at times. Even as he thought this, William disliked himself for its mean-spirited snobbery.

'I'm sure you're right,' he said stiffly.

'It won't be long before the camp is running smoothly,' Watkin said kindly, almost paternally. 'You can't cure the sick in an observatory, or even store gunpowder in it. When it comes to observing, William, I'll give you every assistance within my power. When your instruments are set up, count on me as your apprentice.'

William could only smile and nod, blinking his eyes against the disappointment of Phillip's instructions, and in shame at his own spiteful view of Watkin, whose kindliness now cut him to the quick. Watkin stood up, his height making it necessary for him to stoop under the canvas, and attempted to smooth his uniform. He took out his watch and looked at it.

'I've had the summons from Major Ross,' he said. 'For eleven.'

'Must I go?'

Watkin shook his head. 'It's officers with responsibilities in the land detachment – you're still officially attached to the *Sirius*, aren't you?'

William nodded, then remembered what Phillip had said. 'I'm excused all marine duties anyway, to get on with the surveying.'

'You're well out of it, then. Rossie's stirring up trouble for the Governor – wants us to refuse any duties extra to our military ones. Contrary old toad. Seems to think he's been sent here to do nothing more than puff up his dignity.'

83

Watkin ducked through the flap and vanished. William allowed himself to wipe the smarting tears out of his eyes. Men and women lay sick on the ground in hot, airless tents, and he begrudged the building of a hospital because he wanted to hurry on to star-gazing. The chaplain wanted a church; Ross wanted barracks for his men. What right had he to put his own desires first? Clasping his hands he prayed for forgiveness, and for an escape from selfishness, into a more generous vision.

To assist in clearing the land and building the observatory, the Governor allocated William three convicts and four marines (who would each be paid a shilling a day). William realized that there had been no mention of any extra payment to himself for undertaking the surveyor's work, and that it would be impossible to raise the matter without creating more difficulties between himself and the Governor. He had deserved the unfairness of that; he put it out of his head. Work on the observatory must proceed steadily, but not at the cost of ignoring his other duties; no, to make time for the observatory he would get up earlier, finish later, take no dinner-time rest. There was no one looking over his shoulder, he could drive himself as hard as he liked. It would be a dereliction of duty to have travelled to this distance and then not be in a position to observe the comet when it came, even though the Governor's work clearly demanded the bulk of his energies. He set himself to achieve both in record time.

For the observatory, clearing the area around the big rock was the first task. The point was covered in trees and thick brushwood; hard physical labour was required. It was clear to William that the fastest way to get results was to be closely involved in the work himself. The marines he knew – four decent, hard-working men – the convicts he did not. All three were from the *Alexander*. On the first morning he brought the seven of them to the rock, the marines bearing tools he had been issued from the stores. He outlined his plans; the observatory would stand here, with the clock wedged on this immovable base. The slanting shuttered roof of the observatory would allow the sky to be examined in sections, and the setting and rising of the moon and even the lowest stars on the horizon should be visible from this spot, if the tree-line could be cleared back sufficiently. All trees between the rock and the cliffs must be cleared, and a good semicircle on the landward side. There must be a wide track down to the settlement, to allow passage for the instruments. As he spoke he watched the men. The

84

marines were listening, glancing round at the woods as he spoke, assessing the amount of work ahead of them. The youngest of the convicts, Barnes, sat slumped in complete apathy, never once looking up. He was a small, weak-looking youth, with livid blue-yellow bruising down one side of his face, and rotten teeth. The other two stared at William with contempt. They were both older than him, one tall and skinny, the other heavier, with thick black hair and a sly, knowing face. His name was Stokoe. William knew he would have to supervise their work personally; Major Ross had announced that supervision of convict labour was not a task for the marines (despite rumours that Governor Phillip had begged him to allow it, no overseers having been sent out with the convicts). Indeed, the marines were only persuaded to clearing and building work by the promise of extra payment, Major Ross arguing that all they were obliged to perform were guard and military duties.

William dispatched the marines to work on a half-dozen large trees he had already marked, and turned his attention to the convicts. 'I promise to treat you fairly in return for your hard labour; your past crimes are of no interest to me. It is only required that you should prove yourselves honest workmen alongside your fellows.' There was no response to this. Barnes continued to stare at the ground. There was something unfinished-looking and repulsive about his face. William turned quickly to the others and asked if they had any skills in this type of work. It turned out that the tall one, Clough, had been a chimney-sweep in his youth. Everything the man said was with an aggressive lifting of the chin, daring his listener to react or disbelieve, spoiling for a fight. Stokoe had worked as a waterman. All three had the same strange northern accent, but at least they did not speak in the incomprehensible canting tongue which nearly all the London convicts used, and which sometimes necessitated the use of an interpreter. Barnes had never been regularly employed – he had already spent four years in the hulks. William reflected that he could not have been more than twelve when he was sentenced.

'Well then,' he told the three, 'none of you has tried this kind of work before. But I am sure you will not find it difficult. I will ask the marines to tackle the larger trees, your tasks are to hack at the saplings and undergrowth, and to drag it to the fires.' He found himself talking quickly, uneasy before their indifference; the thing to do was to get them started. 'Follow me. We will have one fireplace here, right by the rock – and another on the seaward side of the trees. Drag your wood to the nearer of the two. The larger tree roots must be dug out, especially those along the route to the settlement. The others we may leave till later. I am not sure if the land around the observatory will be farmed or not . . .' Hurriedly he issued them an axe apiece, and pointed to where they should begin. Stokoe leaned on his axe.

'Shall Ah gan for watter, sir?'

'Water?'

'Thirsty work, this.' Stokoe grinned slyly at Clough. 'A man'll keel ower in this heat, wi' nowt to drink.' He was right. The marines carried their own canteens, but the convicts had nothing. The nearest water was the Tank Stream, down in the middle of the cove. If William let them get their own water he would lose half their day's labour. Supplies would have to be brought up each day.

'Very well. Stokoe, you go down to stores – here, take my belt to show I sent you; request two buckets, fill them at the stream and bring them up.' Flinging down his axe, Stokoe sauntered off through the trees. 'And look sharp!' William shouted after him, and was ignored.

Clough and Barnes stood before him, axes dangling from their hands. He realized that Barnes had no boots; the sole of a shoe was tied to one foot with a couple of strips of filthy rag, and the other was bound with sacking. Clough did have boots, but they were in the last stages of dilapidation.

'Barnes, where are your boots?'

The boy did not reply.

William repeated, more gently, 'What's happened to your boots? Were they stolen?'

Barnes nodded once.

'Did you report it?'

Another long silence then Barnes shook his head.

'Why not?' Even as he asked, William could see why not; because he would have suffered for it.

'What happened to your face? How did you get those bruises?'

No reply. Clough was grinning when William glanced at him; he nodded and tapped the side of his head significantly.

All right, William told himself, all right. This would need sorting out. Barnes was being bullied; he was weak and slow. But not now – not here. Now they must get to work, or the observatory would never be built.

Suddenly William heard the marines calling to each other as they threw ropes over a tree – and the sound of their axes, chopping. It was a ringing, inspiring sound. He nodded quickly at Clough. 'If you clear this brushwood first, it will be easier to drag logs – ' They stood staring at him stupidly, Clough with his eyes half-closed and his chin thrust forward. Then Barnes raised his axe with one hand and brought it down, dropping with its own weight, into the top of a small bush. William watched incredulously.

'D'you not know how to hold an axe, man?'

Barnes did not move.

'I'm speaking to you, Barnes. Answer me. Have you never used an axe before?'

Silence. Clough grinning.

'Have you never chopped wood?'

Barnes shook his head.

'Have you?' William asked Clough.

Clough shook his head too.

'Never chopped kindling – never – ' Well how should they have, William reminded himself quickly. Sweeps were generally orphans, they began at five or six years old – who would let one have an axe, or wood to chop? As he took Barnes' axe, his father leapt into his memory. His father had shown him how to hold an axe, gripping it firmly with right and left hand; taught him not to chop in towards himself; shown him how to swing a long-handled axe to make the most of the weight of the implement.

It was an incident which lingered painfully in William's mind – fraught with difficulty of explanation and understanding. He was home from Woolwich for Christmas. Benjamin had come back from the dockyards one evening in a rage. He had been dealing with a couple of army officers who'd come supposedly to inspect ordnance supplies and materials, and who (according to Benjamin) 'don't know a barrel of gunpowder from a fart, not even if it blew up in their face'. It had been impossible to persuade them of the need to shift out-of-date gunpowder from the yard, or even to get them to recognize which heaps of timber were rotten and unfit for use. Benjamin reserved a special hatred for officers who were ignorant of the practicalities of their duties – nearly always Army, where money alone (the buying of a commission) was sufficient to secure senior positions, without any training whatsoever. It was one of the reasons why he had chosen 'the Shop' at Woolwich for William – because he would be taught an engineer's business, he would not be an ignorant gentleman sipping port and admiring the shine on his boots while his defenceless troops marched to their deaths.

When Benjamin had finished vituperating against 'gentlemen who should never have come away from the card tables at Bath', he cross-questioned William about his knowledge of the constituents and storage of gunpowder, and the ways to judge the strength and soundness of timber.

Gunpowder was not a problem; the Woolwich cadets had learned to make it earlier in the year, in the one class they attended with industrious enthusiasm, and had used it in fireworks of their own design. These were useful, according to their instructor, either in celebration of a victory, or to cause alarm and confusion amongst the enemy. But William did not know enough about timber to satisfy Benjamin, who shouted angrily, 'You'll be telling me next you don't know how to chop wood!' Of course he didn't. It was a menial task; no officer would ever need to chop wood. But Benjamin had the bit between his teeth and insisted on dragging William out into the yard to demonstrate the chopping of wood.

'How can ye order men to work if ye don't know the meaning of it?' he demanded. 'How can ye tell good timber from bad if ye don't know how to chop it?'

William remembered with compound shame the sight of his portly, short-winded father raising and bringing down the axe; shame at the time for the impossibility of explaining to his father how it was at Woolwich, and shame at his father for subjecting them both to such a humiliating scene; shame now at his own young arrogance, because in a new country where the men were convicts and none of them knew how to chop wood, it was an officer's role to teach them. Benjamin had been right.

'Here. Hold it like this.' He demonstrated, as Benjamin had demonstrated to him. 'Now swing it so – not wildly, keep control over it all the time. Never aim towards your feet or legs – it may split the branch and come on to hit you – ' He demonstrated again. Clough was grinning with stupid malice. 'Chop down near the ground – then it won't need doing twice, there'll only be the stump to lift – see?' He took a couple of deep breaths and swung at a gum sapling, which bounced back only a little chipped from his blow. But he cracked it with his fourth stroke, hitting it six inches above the ground; dropped his axe and twisted the slender trunk round with his hands till it snapped.

'There,' he panted, straightening and dragging the sapling to the fire site. 'Like that. Barnes, you have a go.' As Barnes raised his axe William glanced down at his smarting hands and saw a dark red mark in the centre of each palm. After four or five trees both hands would be blistered. These men would be just as bad; no one but the seamen had done any manual labour for months, they were all soft. And the labour that was to be done . . . But they would succeed. They must, because there was no alternative.

'No!' Barnes was swinging wildly, randomly, at the trunk, making no impact.

'No. You must control it. Swing it slowly – take aim.' He took the axe from Barnes and demonstrated again. He noticed that the man's arms were trembling as he handed back the axe. 'Are you ill?'

'It's heavy,' whispered Barnes. Clough began to laugh in a high, false cackle.

'Clough, get to work!' William snapped. 'Here, it's not difficult – ' to Barnes, clasping his own hands around the axe handle beside Barnes' dirty fingers, raising and swinging the axe slowly with him. 'See, it's not difficult. Try again.'

Barnes tried again, five times, and each time either missed the tree trunk entirely, or dropped the axe nervelessly when the blade connected with wood.

'You're not trying!' William shouted. The man simply stood, head hanging, staring at the axe on the ground. Clough was tapping at the bark with his axe, barely denting it. When he saw William glaring at him he put a little more force into it, but the effect was still of a person play-acting a woodcutter. These men were perfectly useless.

William looked down at his feet, holding in his anger and trying to work out what to do. No one had deliberately given him the worst convicts; doubtless there were many others down there just as bad as these. And the few with skills – woodcutters, carpenters – well it was only right that they should be employed on the storehouse and hospital, two buildings which were absolutely vital to the life of the colony. But what was he to do with these men? Train them, help them, correct them – *and* build an observatory? Yes, he told himself firmly, and no point complaining about it. He forced himself to recall his mood of the day the Governor had read the commissions; his sympathy for the convicts. It was his duty to help them, to teach them the skills that would enable them to lead honest lives in this new world. It was his duty to help them rebuild themselves as decent characters, even more than it was his duty to make them build an observatory. He must speak to them as rational men.

He took a deep breath. 'Sit down.'

The convicts gawped at him.

'Sit!'

They sat.

'All right now. You are here to work. This land must be cleared. If you are ill, you will be excused. But otherwise you work. I do not intend to punish you, a flogging will not make you better workers. If you work well you will be treated well. More importantly, you will have the satisfaction of knowing you have worked well; the satisfaction before God of being able to say, 'Father, I have done my best.' If you think of your labour here as an offering to God, a token of repentance for the crimes you have committed, then as you labour, you earn forgiveness, you enter into righteousness.'

He stopped. Barnes seemed to be asleep, Clough was watching him vacantly. Forgiveness and righteousness were perhaps too difficult for them to grasp, in their present condition. The hungers of the body come first, he reminded himself; they need decent food and clothing. I will engage their interest in spiritual matters later.

'You need boots, both of you.'

Clough nodded, and Barnes stirred himself and scratched at his sacking-bound foot.

'I'll get you new boots from the stores. If you work.'

They both looked at him.

'Good. Now, if you really can't use the axes at the moment – well then – ' He stared at the scrubby undergrowth. Digging up roots? Sawing timber for the building, once there were some big trees felled? Sawing. Yes. 'To begin with, you can dig. You can dig a saw-pit where we can prepare the timber for the observatory.' He jumped up and paced round the rock. The pit may as well be close; why drag the logs twice? 'Here,' he said. 'Here, I'll just measure – I'll just mark the outline for you. There are only two spades, we'll have to hope Stokoe can use an axe – ' He gave them spades and went over to see how the marines were getting on.

The marines had a big gum chopped almost through, but it had fallen towards another, and was supported at a 45-degree angle by its branches entangled in the standing tree. Ropes attached to the original tree were now also tangled in the standing one. The men were arguing about what to do, one wanted to fell the second tree, a couple wanted to use more ropes and pull the first one free. They were big trees – over sixty-foot tall, each of them. There would be no possibility of the combined efforts of the five of them controlling how both trees fell.

'We must pull clear the one that has toppled,' he told them, and sent Munday back to the rock for more rope. The branches were wedged in such a way that the tree would need raising up, to move the main branch from its position to the right of the trunk of the upright tree, and allow it to fall down to the left, where there were no large impediments. He directed the throwing and fastening of the rope; Scott was the most accurate rope-thrower. Once the two main branches were roped around, three men on one side and two on the other began to heave. The tree did not budge. The angle, of course, was hopeless; they were trying to pull forward a weight above them. William called to them to stop, and they sprawled to the ground. It was very hot, William watched a couple of them take long draughts from their canteens and remembered that the convict had not returned with the bucket of water. The men were looking at him, to find out what to do next. He stared at the interlocked branches. Were they securely enough wedged to absolutely prevent the tree from falling? He judged so. Then a man could climb it, and saw through the interlocked branches. He asked for a volunteer. Munday and Scott both offered, which was better than one; they could use the big saw between them. And there were the ropes already in place to pull themselves up by, and to hang on to if they fell.

Munday went first, and he made a fine display of it, holding a fixed rope and walking up the inclined trunk, leaning his weight till he was sitting securely on a branch of the upright tree, before nodding to Scott. Scott began walking, but then lowered himself to straddle the trunk, leaning forward so his belly was against it, edging his way up more cautiously. When he was half-way, reaching forwards to pull himself another body-length up, the rope slipped from his grasp. He flattened himself against the trunk, clasping his arms round it. He was about thirty feet from the ground. William bit his nail. These marines had spent the whole voyage on or below decks, while the seamen ran up and down the masts like monkeys. He could do better than this himself. A couple of the men called out to Scott but he did not move, and William motioned to them to be quiet. He went and stood beneath the frightened man.

'Scott. Listen. You're nearly there. Look up to Munday – don't look down. Just inch your way along, you're perfectly safe.' No movement.

'Munday, can you throw him the other end of the rope again?' Munday coiled the fixed rope and threw it, accurately, so that it landed just in front of Scott's head on the trunk.

'Grab it, man!' Scott did not move, and the rope swiftly uncoiled itself and slipped from the branch.

'I'll get it, sir.' Munday had taken up the rope again, and began to lower himself down towards Scott. It was what William had wanted to avoid – the weight of both of them on that leaning trunk. He opened his mouth to object then shut it. The longer Scott stayed up there the more terrified and incapable of movement he would become. Munday was edging down backwards, astride the trunk, the rope grasped in his right hand.

'Munday!' William shouted. 'Fix that rope around your chest. And take the other one down with you, for Scott.' Munday glanced down and nodded. As he was making his way back up to get the second rope, there was a sudden cracking noise, and the fallen tree settled more heavily into the upright one, dropping three to four inches. Munday let out a curse, William saw him lose and regain his balance. Scott was still wrapped round the trunk like a sloth. William noticed, though, a dark wet patch spreading on the seat of Scott's breeches. Munday had regained his composure and was knotting one rope securely around his chest, holding the second in his teeth. He began to wriggle backwards down to Scott. When he reached him he passed the free rope behind him. Scott did not move. William stood directly beneath him, he could not see the man's face but he could see his hands, white with pressure, gripping the underside of the trunk.

'Scott, listen to me. Munday is right beside you. You're quite safe. I want you to sit up, slowly, and take the rope from him.' No movement. This was going to end badly, William was suddenly convinced of it. Their *first* tree. Someone was going to get killed. He wiped the stinging sweat out of his eyes.

'Scott. Sit up. That's an order.'

No movement. William took a deep breath, and bellowed,

'*Sit up, man!*'

Scott raised his head a couple of inches from the trunk.

'Take the rope in your right hand. I'm going to count. Take the rope on three. One, two, three.'

No movement.

'*Take the rope.*'

Scott's left hand shifted a couple of inches on the trunk, then reached forward and grasped the rope Munday was holding steady behind his back.

'Good. Well done, Scott. Now, you're going to sit up very slowly . . .' Movement by painful movement William directed him through passing the rope around his chest, tying it, grasping hold of Munday's belt, and inching slowly up behind him. In the middle of this Stokoe appeared. He affected not to understand William's angry sign to clear off back to work, and William did not want to shout to him for fear of distracting Scott, so he remained, gawping. William was aware, as he watched the two men move with agonizing slowness up the branch, of his own acute physical discomfort. He needed to empty his bladder, his clothes were soaked through with sweat.

They were approaching the intersection of trunk with branches now – the last difficult point. Noting this, William realized his own idiocy. What was to be done with Scott once he was in the other tree? How on earth was he to be got down? They should have come down to the ground, from the half-way point. William should have directed them down, not up. He watched Munday grasp the branch in front of him, and ask Scott to let him go for a moment. He watched Scott let go, and grab feverishly at his own rope; he watched the rope tauten across Munday's shoulder as Munday shifted his weight forwards on to the neighbouring branch – and he watched Munday, knocked off balance by Scott's rope, miss his branch. Munday had been coiling in his own rope around his hand and forearm as he inched upwards. As he fell the coiled rope pulled tight with a jolt. He screamed; they saw his feet flailing in the air for a moment and then he was up again, left arm over the branch, heaving his body weight up. He was sobbing and swearing.

'Munday! Munday! Are you all right?'

'My arm! My fucking arm!' He was trying to unwind the rope.

William took the trunk at a run – it was wider than a plank – and was up to Scott almost before he knew what he'd done. He lowered himself to all fours then straddled the branch behind Scott. Munday was watching him from an absolutely white face.

'Scott,' said William. 'We're going down. You're going to uncoil your rope steadily as you go. I'm behind you and I'm going to hang on to you by the belt and help you down. We're going now.' In a blur of exhausted heat and terror he got Scott to the ground. He was afraid Munday would faint but the man was still sitting in the same position when William got back to the top of the trunk, minutes, or hours, later.

Munday's hand was a livid red, and swollen. William rested his sweaty forehead against the trunk for a moment to work out how to get the injured man down. The rope was still around his chest.

'If I tie your arm in a sling, d'you think you can shuffle backwards with me holding on to you?' Munday nodded, his face was pale and slippery with sweat. William noticed that he had bitten his lip so it bled. He felt in his pockets; there was nothing but his little leather-bound notebook. He offered it to Munday's mouth. 'Here, bite on the leather.' William unbuttoned his shirt and pulled it off, tied the arms together and slung it around his own neck to test it. It needed refolding and retying several times before it was anything like – and then retying around Munday's neck. When William lifted the arm the man moaned and swayed with pain.

At last they had negotiated the transfer from branch to trunk – at last (William's balls were agonizingly sore from the last journey down the trunk) they were on their way down. On the ground William gave Munday a good dose of rum and instructed the two marines who had been watching to help him down to the hospital tent. 'And bring back my shirt,' he shouted after them. He hadn't got the money for a new one; and if that was left lying around at the hospital it would vanish. When he emptied his bladder he found that his breeches, between the legs, were worn threadbare. No wonder he was sore. The dinner-time bugle sounded. Stokoe had disappeared.

He left Scott leaning against a tree, still looking more dead than alive, and made his way back to the convicts. The three of them were sitting in the shade beside the saw-pit area. They had done no more than scratch away the surface of the patch. William's exhaustion was swamped by a surge of rage.

'Is that all you've done?'

Stokoe did not even look up. Clough insolently displayed his grimy hands; a large blister ballooned the skin of the right.

'Ground's too 'ard, sir. And we're needing watter.'

'Where is the water, Stokoe?'

'Broke his arm has 'e?' enquired Stokoe matily. 'He's not ganna be chopping so much now, eh?'

'Where is the water I asked you to fetch?'

Stokoe shrugged. 'There's nae buckets at store.'

'But I gave you my belt – '

'They lack buckets – ' he caught Clough's eye and laughed – 'and that's nae all they lack, they'll be finding shortly.'

'Where's my belt?'

Stokoe slowly pulled it from his pocket. 'You're lucky ter ge' it back, sir. Puckermouth there reckoned as I'd prigged it – tried to tek it off us, he did.'

William's anger ebbed away, leaving him reeling with weakness. 'Go down to the stream for a drink, all of you. Come back when they sound the afternoon bugle.' They shuffled off. Glancing round, William could not see the axes, he should have taken them in . . . He leant back against the rock, his head swimming. So much for the first morning. A man injured. A dangerously wedged tree. Convicts who could neither work nor even provide themselves with water. Missing tools.

He couldn't imagine how he had managed to run up that trunk. His body was as weak as a kitten's. When he brushed at the tickling on his back, and a couple of ants stung him, he nearly burst into tears.

CHAPTER SEVEN

We are all men

Next day William was controlled and determined. He could not spend more than the morning at the observatory site; work on the gunpowder store was to begin this afternoon. He sent the marines up ahead to start work. He had obtained three pairs of boots for the convicts. Clough complained that his were too small but when William offered to change them he refused to take them off. Two of the axes were missing, and when he questioned the convicts about them they simply shrugged. He was convinced Stokoe had taken them; the man did not even look away when questioned, but stared into William's face with an insolent half-grin, daring William to get angry.

'You are making your own work more difficult,' William said patiently. 'There are no more axes. You will have to use a spade.'

The three men made no reaction. He tried again.

'I have to account for these tools to the Governor. I shall have your tent searched.'

Clough and Stokoe glanced at each other and smirked.

'In fact we will search there now,' he said to Stokoe. 'Lead us to your tent.'

'We've got nae tent.'

'Well lead us to your sleeping quarters, man.'

Stokoe turned insolently and began to make his way slowly across the site. Clough followed him.

'Barnes. Come with us.' Barnes followed, stumbling as he walked, his eyes dazed and unfocused. He seemed ill.

'D'you want to report sick, Barnes?'

The man stopped and stared at William out of his bruised, swollen face, then shook his head.

'Have you been in a fight?'

Barnes did not reply, and William, looking ahead, realized that Stokoe and Clough were standing waiting for them beside a large tree. They made no move as William and Barnes caught up.

'Well?' said William impatiently.

Stokoe pointed sardonically at the tree – taking a step closer, William realized that it was hollow and that there was a large hole in the base of the trunk. He peered in.

'You sleep here? But where is your blanket – your things?'

'Hidden,' said Stokoe. 'Salted away. These lags'd lift the shirt off yer back, sir.'

'You sleep in a tree?' As William said it he realized it must be true. Not enough tents had been erected yet – not enough ground had been cleared – to accommodate all the convicts. If Stokoe had stolen the axes they would be in someone else's hands by now. He was wasting his time.

William had managed to get a bucket – one – from the stores. 'Clough. This is your water bucket. For the three of you. You're to fill it at the Tank Stream on the way up in the morning, carry it up to the site you're clearing, cover it and leave it in the shade, and bring it down in the evening. I will keep it overnight.'

Clough jerked his chin like a snapping dog.

'I'm making you responsible, Clough. If you lose this bucket – or this bucket is stolen while entrusted to you – I'll – ' he only paused momentarily – 'I'll have those boots back.' He passed the bucket to Clough and started up through the woods to the observatory. The convicts dragged behind. William had to shout at them to get a move on, and to shout again to Stokoe not to go with Clough for the water. They passed other working parties, all of whom were progressing at a pitiful rate. Overseers had been appointed from among the convicts themselves, and there was a system of punishments to support their authority, but a sad lack of skill or knowledge amongst them. Like the rest of the convicts, they preferred to sit and stare at the scene rather than to labour at forcing others to labour in the sun. The problem of lost (stolen) tools was endemic. And the tools were of the poorest quality to begin with; heads flew off axes, handles snapped, when the blades of spades struck rock they shattered.

But his party had boots now, and water, it was a start. He ordered Barnes and Clough to continue digging the saw-pit, Stokoe to chop down saplings. He himself measured and paced and took levels around the rock, calculating the dimensions the observatory would need to have. The rock, which extended on two sides just under the surface of the soil, would stand in stead of foundations. He'd told the marines to leave yesterday's disaster well alone. Perhaps a high wind would topple the tree. Or he would get a big party up here at some point to heave on the ropes – twenty men instead of five. At dinner time he was pleased to find they had felled three trees that morning, all of a goodly size. Stokoe, however, had done no more than fell one scrawny sapling.

That night after William had pulled off his boots and breeches and climbed into his cot, Watkin, who was already bedded down, asked him how the work was going.

'Pitifully slow. But I've realized today how to make the convicts work harder. I must work alongside them.'

Watkin did not reply. William leaned up on his elbow.

'At the moment they are treated as slaves, given orders – their labour is simply punishment. If they can be helped to see the productiveness of that labour, how it will bring good results for all, including themselves – then they may work with a better will. And how better can they be persuaded of the value of the work than by seeing free men *choosing* to do it?'

'You think that's best? For a lieutenant to roll up his sleeves and labour alongside convicts?'

'Yes! Precisely because it is not expected. They will see from that how urgent it is for the work to be done. I can set a pace for them and shame them into greater efforts, and my labour added to theirs will in any case accelerate the work.'

'William, there are other factors to consider.' Now Watkin also propped himself up in the darkness. 'Your position of authority over them – and over the marines – will be undermined, if you reduce yourself to their level. Organisation and peace within the camp depends upon the officers, who are the brain, giving orders to the convicts who are the labouring arms and legs. Our roles are different.'

'We are all men,' said William stubbornly.

'They are convicts. They have forfeited their freedom, by reason of their crimes. They must do as they are told.'

'But they can *avoid* that, as you well know, Watkin. They can be forced to go through all the motions of obedience and labour, and achieve *nothing*.'

'If they see that laziness is followed by punishment, that hard work is rewarded by decent treatment, they will work. You can't expect them to know more than that.'

William was silent; he disagreed absolutely with Watkin. If they could not become responsible men, what was the point of bringing them here to make new lives? If they were no more than slaves, who understood only punishments and rewards.

'Each of those men has a soul – ' he began. But Watkin laughed.

'Ah no. Don't start on that tack with me, William. I am content to leave souls to the church.' He lay down again.

After a moment William lay down too. Watkin broke the silence.

'Once you work alongside them, your rank and dignity – the very things that make it possible for you to direct them – are undermined.'

'No. Dignity is – is overrated. Christ did not stand on his dignity, he washed the feet of sinners.'

'But he was not a lieutenant of marines. Your action affects the rest of the battalion – you cannot act independently. If you reduce the authority of the officers in convicts' eyes – '

'Watkin – how am I going to do that, through working with three convicts up at Point Maskeylene? No one else will even *know* I work with them – '

'They have tongues in their heads.'

'Look; it's now mid-February. If the marines fell five trees a day – and if the convicts clear three square yards a day (which is ridiculous, since they have so far cleared no more than one sapling, and dug a saw-pit six inches deep between them), then there are felled trees to be sawn into sections, and roots to be grubbed up along the track – we're looking at five weeks', six weeks' work. Then the timber to be sawn for the building – then the construction and fitting out the interior, the instruments to be brought ashore and fixed in position – d'you think all this can be done by August?'

'I don't know.'

'More than half my time must be spent on other duties, thanks to Mr Alt; and I gave Maskeylene my word the observatory would be ready by August. What would you do?'

Watkin sighed. 'I'm just concerned that you don't make things harder for yourself.'

*

STEPHEN
'Each of those men has a soul.' Yes, William, all are equal before God. And should be equal before man. Not such a radical notion, is it? Until you apply it, of course.

To wealth, health, housing. Education.

Naïve, Stevie. Always have been. Who wants equality? When you can pay to give your child a leg up. Pay to secure the inequality of other children. Pay to send yours to a school from which children who cannot pay will be excluded.

If that simple evil is still permitted . . . why the devil did I expect to be able to abolish lesser ones? I should have gone out with a flaming torch in my hands. A torch and a gun, not motions and amendments for discussion.

I misjudged the old staff at Campfield. I thought they were being petty. I never acknowledged they were involved in a life-or-death struggle against equality, to preserve their own identities. That identity *is* power and position. Fighting for their right to sit at a segregated dinner table and be waited on by twelve-year-olds. Asserting that the girls (only girls!) who served them thought it a privilege. Claiming that the sight of their teachers in a dinner queue would wipe out kids' respect and bring on anarchy.

They believed that. When I abolished staff table, liberating them to queue like equals with the children, they brought sandwiches and hid in the staff room to eat. They were afraid. Which I didn't see. I saw they were afraid of the kids and despised them for that. But I didn't see they were afraid of equality, that the idea of it enraged them.

Would it have made any difference?
I'd have taken them more seriously. If I'd realized they were *the enemy*, instead of just a bunch of idle old buffers who didn't want to take their own dirty dishes back to the hatch.

That was the trouble. Robert and I thought our position only needed explaining to people for their enthusiasm for change to flow as naturally as ours. Which is actually as ridiculous as expecting William's poor old convicts to *want* to work hard to build his observatory. Teachers like Gough, who'd been dragging bored kids through geography CSE for decades; why the hell should they listen to a new upstart head, all starry-eyed about mixed ability, wanting to disrupt their painfully achieved equilibrium, and give a voice to the kids they beat and tyrannized – why the *hell* should they listen?

If we had realized how little there was in it for the older staff, would we have behaved differently? It would have been possible, I suppose, to be more politic. To look at it as a problem where some benefits for them must be part of the answer. Rather than assuming that their interest in universal good would overwhelm all scruples about personal discomfort and loss of leisure time. Which is why they were so vindictive; because they wouldn't align themselves with universal good, we – and they – knew they must be labelled evil.

Isn't it a mistake, if you want to change things, to be the ones in power? Isn't it only if you come up through the ranks, in opposition to the powerful ones, that you gain popular support? If Robert and I had been the newest scale-one teachers at Campfield, crusading from our classrooms for mixed-ability teaching; supervising our own tutor groups when they wanted to stay in at break; doing our own continuous assessment and termly reports to parents; running our own abolition of corporal punishment; if we had done all this, converts might have followed. I suppose. In practical terms it would have been impossible, since it would have impinged on the running of the school and undermined most of its values. The system would have broken down – although the kids would have coped perfectly well. As part of daily school life they go from one classroom where they sit and work in silence to the next where they riot and abuse the teacher; they know what is expected. They can read a teacher quicker than I could read his job application. The kids would have coped; kids generally do cope. It's the adults whose imaginations and capacity for hope dry up.

*

Next morning William had other duties to attend to and did not get up to Point Maskeylene till after dinner time. The convicts were arguing as he moved to join them. He heard Clough shout, 'Yer said yerself yer didna want the bitch!'

William paused, still concealed by the trees, for Stokoe's reply.

'I telled yer no.'

'Yer said she were scum – '

'Ah didna mean for yer to gan behind me back, bobtail!'

'She's nae thy bun!'

There was the sound of movement then Stokoe's voice, low. 'Oh aye?'

They were losing valuable time. William moved on towards them, and as they heard him approach Stokoe loosed Clough's arm and spat contemptuously at his feet.

'All right, you two. Back to work. And you Barnes.'

William took off his jacket and picked up the big saw.

'Stokoe. You will saw with me.' Stokoe came to his work mechanically. He does not think it at all strange that I am working with him, William noted with satisfaction. But it will force him to work more steadily. They began the slow, backbreaking task of severing the branches from the trunk of one of the newly felled trees, so that it could be dragged to the saw-pit. They worked in silence, until Stokoe stopped and raised his hands for William to see. Blisters were swelling on his palms. William wiped the sweat from his face. 'Wrap a rag around them.'

'What rag?'

'I don't know. Your shirt.'

'Ah've only the one to me back.'

'Well – here,' William tossed his handkerchief over. 'Come on.'

It took them nearly an hour to get through the thing. As it fell away, William slid into a sitting position with his back against the trunk, and flexed his sore aching hands. He heard Stokoe slump the other side of the trunk. William's arms and shoulders and neck and back all ached, and his shirt was stuck to him with sweat. The wood was as tough as iron – even when they got it to the saw-pit, how long would it take to cut it into building timber? They would have to use some other material. Maybe the cabbage trees would be easier to work. He took a swig of water, hesitated, then passed his canteen to Stokoe. The man took it without thanks, gulping greedily.

'Who were you talking about?'

'Sir?'

'A woman.'

'Oh, her. A whore – off the *Penrhyn*.'

'And she's your – ' William hesitated, hoping Stokoe would supply a word, but he didn't. 'You are attached to her,' he tried.

Stokoe spat and was silent.

'I mean,' persisted William, 'you said she was yours.'

'In a manner o' speakin'.' Stokoe suddenly sounded more cheerful. 'Are yer wantin' to dock, sir? She's a prime article.'

'Oh – no – no, thank you.'

After a long pause Stokoe said, 'Me hands are red raw, Ah canna do more today.'

William forced himself to his feet. 'We'll drag it to the saw-pit. You don't need your hands; we'll make a rope harness.' He had seen other men pulling logs in this way, but he and Stokoe strained against it, without it budging an inch. He called the three marines to help, and with the five of them heaving on their ropes, the trunk eventually began to move. All the time he was sweating and straining, his brain was calculating, considering: importance of clearing a track as they felled – wide enough to roll the trunks along; or using rollers, smaller logs cut from branches – yes, transport them lengthways then, feed a roller under the front – roll the trunk its length along it, yes; why was he able to *offer* the woman? Did Stokoe take money for her? What right did he have to dispose of her like that? William stopped, and raggedly, with a jolt as the extra weight hit them, the others stopped pulling too. 'Sorry. Sorry.' He counted to three and they heaved the log into motion again.

It was important, William told himself, that the convicts should understand what they were doing and why, so that they could share his enthusiasm for the project and feel that their labour was worthwhile. When they were sitting limply in the shade at the next dinner time he joined them, and described to them some of the differences between the sky here and the sky in England. Barnes simply sat, mouth half-open, eyes glazed. Clough and Stokoe listened. William suspected that they were letting his words wash over them, but Stokoe did ask why it was important to chart these stars and work out accurate latitude and longitude for Sydney Cove, and he seemed to understand when William explained how great an aid to navigation this would be. Then Stokoe suddenly said,

'You're wantin' this star-watching place up in a hurry, then?'

William nodded. His mouth was full of the dry sourish grey bread that the bakehouse was now providing twice a week. Some of the flour they had brought from England had got damp in the boats coming ashore; there was an unmistakeable tang of mould in the bread.

'Well if yer was to lay hands on some rum – ' Stokoe was leering ingratiatingly.

William forced himself to swallow. 'Rum?'

'Aye.' It was the only respect in which the convicts' rations differed from the marines'. They were served no allowance of rum. William looked at Clough, who was grinning at him. Even Barnes had turned his poor stupid head and was staring at William with a glimmer of intelligence in his eyes.

'For you?' William asked.

Stokoe nodded. 'That'll mek us work – give us heart, like.'

William hesitated. 'I'll see about it. It may not be possible.' He knew that Phillip's original intention had been to keep the convicts dry, and thus reduce violence and disputes among them. But sailors from the ships who came ashore at every opportunity brought rum and gave or sold it to the convicts. William had heard they gave it to the women for sex – and there was a trade in stolen native weapons as well which the sailors would take back to England for souvenirs.

To give them rum stank of bribery; and yet he needed to encourage them to work by every means at his disposal. Watkin had recommended rewarding hard work by 'decent treatment', and laziness by punishment. The punishments were none of them any use. William had no stomach for seeing men flogged; nor could he consent to deprivation of food, or seeing them tethered with a chain like animals. If they were paid for their labour with a regular tot of rum, then it could be withdrawn if they were lazy. They would feel that, they would feel the lack of it. It was a humane carrot and stick.

If it served to speed the progress of the observatory, he was justified, it seemed to him, in paying for the rum with Board of Longitude money. After all, if it had been possible to employ extra labour with money, he would have done so.

He handed out the ration himself, at dinner time, and saw them drink it. His main anxiety had been that they might store and sell it, which this prevented. Barnes now fell asleep regularly at dinner time, slumped snoring against a tree, oblivious of the insects that settled at the corners of his eyes and mouth, or crawled up his filthy clothes. The other two talked or argued quietly.

They were working more steadily, William assured himself; day by day the cleared area slowly increased. They had taken responsibility for their tools and water bucket, and when he arrived from marking out the road to the hospital, he found them busy. They did not work with any enthusiasm, but it would have been over-optimistic to expect so great a change overnight. Certainly it had not occurred to them to question his authority. He was pleased to have proved Watkin wrong; and it was unnecessary, after all, to mention the rum ration to Watkin, since as a superior officer it would place him in a slightly awkward position. William could quite happily shoulder the responsibility for that particular bending of the rules on his own.

It would be possible, he considered, maybe within the next fortnight, to raise the subject of religion with them. The quiet period of dinner time would be very suitable; maybe he would simply read short passages from the Bible to them, New Testament parables like the Prodigal Son, stories that they would find relevant to their own lives. If they could be reminded of God's forgiving love for all men, what hope and energy it would give them.

When the rum ration had been instituted just over a week, William was approached by Stokoe at the end of the dinner hour, and asked if he would spare a couple of tots 'out of Christian goodness' for someone who was suffering. It was precisely what William did not intend to encourage, and he refused immediately, enquiring, however, who the 'sufferer' was.

'It's Molly Hill, sir – the doxy you were askin' after. She 'as her bellyful, an' she'll be wantin' a drop for the pain – ' He smiled his horrible ingratiating smile.

'I am sure she will be given all the medical assistance she needs in childbirth.'

'Aye, but she canna stop fashin' ower the bairn she lost at sea – a spot o' rum'd ease her. Ah'll tek it to her safe – '

'There's no question of it, Stokoe. I can only give you your dram that you drink here. What happened to her baby?'

But Stokoe shrugged and turned away, losing interest in the subject now it was established that he would get no extra rum from it.

OLLA

My brother. Tadek.

I have lived this before. But now the shape of it is different. Now I have power. Now I can make what happens. Before, I was only a child, I could not save him.

Daniel has the look of Tadek. I watch his face, he has the look. His eyelids are blue and flutter as he sleeps. His breaths come quick and short, a little thick. Nothing is easy for him. His soft skin crusts quickly with sore patches, becomes rough, angry-coloured. Around his mouth . . . under his nose . . . in the corners of his eyes, the skin is red and distressed. I see Tadek's face. And his flabby little belly, his tiny cherub's penis like a bud where sores also come easily, his sad thin legs.

I am in charge now. No one can hurt you, my baby. I am the mother now.

Our stepmother makes him sweat. When she sees his face turn blue, and his lips gulping for air like a fish, she screams: 'As if I did not have enough to do – a dead weight, a boy no more use than a chicken. He cannot even bring in the wood!'

My brother. I lie awake at night, listening for the air going into your lungs. Often there is a pause or a choking sound, it seems it will not, cannot go. I lie awake, willing it. He will live. I will protect him. I will stop them hurting him.

Sometimes, yes. Sometimes, no. When *he* comes in from drinking I am afraid, and angry with myself, knowing that to show fear is the most dangerous thing. I tell Tadek to hide under the bed, and go to the kitchen myself as bait, so he does not have to look for us. Tadek is afraid of the dark but I tell him, listen to my voice. You will hear me talking to the father, in the kitchen. Listen to my voice, it will be saving you from the dark. Oh, my voice *will* save you, Daniel.
I get him bread and cheese, undo his boots, stoke up the fire, trying to guess before his fuddled brain knows itself what he wants next. He punches me once for just that –
'D'you think you know everything, you cheeky bitch? D'you think you can tell me what I want?' I can, but the mistake is seeming to. I am successful so many times in this that when it ends I have no plan up my sleeve.

'Where's the cripple?' I am unlacing his boot. 'Answer when you're spoken to.' He prods me with his foot.

'I – I don't know.'

'Liar. You bloody do know. You've hidden him, haven't you. Think you can fool me?' He pushes me away and rises, lunging at the corners and shadows, muttering to himself. Then into the bedroom. There is nowhere else to look – only under the bed. I have chosen the most obvious place.

He has to get down on his knees to drag Tadek out; he pulls him like a doll by the leg. 'Your big sister, eh? She puts you up to this, you haven't even the wit to hide, cripple. For this my Ailsa dies. For an idiot with a wide mouth to feed.'

Sometimes when he speaks of my mother he simply cries, maudlin self-pitying tears, and cries himself to sleep. I hope for this. But he looks up and sees me in the doorway; I should have slipped back out of sight but I was anxious for Tadek –

Seeing me reminds him, and makes his anger rise again. He pulls Tadek closer to him.

'Hiding him from me. Hiding my son?' He speaks with contempt, self-disgust. 'Afraid I'll hurt him, are you? Think you know better?' I do not reply; to agree, or to contradict, would only make it worse.

'Well?' I can hear the rage rising.

'No.'

'No? No – exactly, no. You don't know better. Because he'll be hurt now all right. I'll tell you why. *Because* you hid him. See. You think you can get it all your own way, eh? I'm not as stupid as you'd like to think.' He is shouting now, his face plum-coloured. I know at any moment he will –

'You play tricks on me, I'll play tricks on you. You want to hide the boy, I want to *find* the boy. D'you get it? Do you?' Turning suddenly and viciously he hits my brother in the chest, a sideways blow with the length of his forearm. My brother gasps and staggers. I hear him wheezing but the air is not going in.

'No!' I run forward. Worst mistake. The father smiles.

'Ah! Come to save him? Miss Valiant, come to the rescue. Why d'you want to rescue him, eh?' He kicks at Tadek's legs with his one booted foot, and Tadek pitches forwards to the floor. I throw myself over him, I am crying, sobbing, with the terrible helplessness of a child. My father takes a step closer then loses his balance and falls

107

back on the bed. I lie still, shielding Tadek as best I can. He is gasping and gurgling in the back of his throat but still not getting a good breath in. My father pulls himself up from the bed and staggers out, holding on to the wall for support. When he loses his balance he is no longer dangerous – he is puzzled and careful, he will sit himself down by the table and sleep with his head on his arms.

When he is gone I get up and close the door as quietly as I can; pull Tadek up to sit on the bed. His face is blue, his eyes staring, blood trickles from his lip. I begin to rub his back, up and down, round and round, breathing in and out slowly and deeply myself to remind him – to show him – oh, God, to do it for him if I can. At last a shuddering breath comes. As it does his thin body is jerked violently by a spasm of hiccoughs. They shake him, jerk him out of rhythm, make him glisten with sweat. But he is breathing again. He cut his lip when he fell, it bleeds for a long time, but does not seem to hurt him.

I do not hide him under the bed again. Next time I tell him, sit at table where he can see you when he comes in. Next time, go to bed, be asleep already. Next time, sewing by the fire so he can see how useful you are.
That is another mistake. He hits us both: I for making Tadek into a woman; Tadek for being as weak as a woman, doing woman's work.

Stephen suddenly jumps on an idea tonight. Watching me feed Daniel. 'Your brother who died – '
'Yes.'
'There was something wrong with him?'
'He was weak, yes. Sickly.'
'What exactly was it?'
'He is dead now. Does it matter?'
He leans forward, puts down his knife and fork. He is excited. 'Well it suddenly occurred to me, Olla. It may be a similar – condition. I mean, it's the sort of thing doctors look for when they ask your family history – it's – '
'I did not tell them about Tadek.'
'But maybe you should. Maybe it's some sort of genetic thing, you know, hereditary. Your brother, your son – one of those disorders that's passed through the female line.'
I do not speak. Daniel is not swallowing, the food dribbles from the

corner of his mouth and I catch it and spoon it back in and it dribbles out again. He has eaten very little tonight. I think it is Stephen's voice which disturbs him. I want to keep spooning and spooning but his soft chin is reddened by the spoon, as I gently scrape the spilling food to insert in his mouth again. I must stop or his chin will be sore.

'Look. If you can describe your brother's condition, properly, to a doctor – they may be able to see similarities between his case and Daniel. It may give them some clues – if they know what it is, some clues for treatment.'

'Tadek died.'

'Yes but look at medical advances since then. How old was he?'

'Seven.'

'We should have thought of it before. There may be a genetic disorder – the miscarriages . . .' His idea animates him. He finishes the broccoli and carrots, and cuts another slice of beef. 'Tell me your brother's symptoms.'

'I was a child, not a doctor.'

'What you remember – '

I wipe Daniel's face, and put my finger in his hand, curling his fingers round mine with my other hand.

'He was a bad colour. Dark red and blotchy, or bluish. He couldn't do anything energetic – if he moved fast, he couldn't breathe. He couldn't run.'

'But he could walk?' There is hope in his voice, he is looking at Daniel propped in his special seat. The padded wooden support holds him at chest level so he will not fall forward on to the tray; it holds him loosely pinned to the curved back of the chair.

'Oh yes. Walk, use his arms, talk.'

'Like a normal child.'

'Yes.' I washed him, dressed him, taught him to walk. Slowly, quietly, in long evenings of peace when my father was out; in days of sunshine when he and my stepmother went farm-working from first light till dusk, and all I had to do was clean the house and make a soup. Over a summer and autumn I taught him to walk. He was resting and waiting at every step, his eyes shining with tears of effort. I made him walk. When he said he could not, I pulled him up again and told him, try. You can. He walked for me, for me and no one else.

'But then as he grew older, he deteriorated?'

'I don't know. He died.'

'But was it an illness – you've never even told me, was it sudden?'
'He just – ' I see his face. Frightened, blue. 'Olla,' he whispers. 'I can't get up.'
'Of course you can,' I tell him. 'This is silliness, you must get up. I'll help you.' I help him but he is weak, he has to lean on me to get to the kitchen table; he is too tired even to eat. What is it? Suddenly he has no strength at all, as if he were a tree still growing and something has gnawed away the roots underground. No illness, no. Just weakness – suddenly, and increasing with terrible speed, over a few weeks in winter. He weakened while the snow was on the ground, and died just as it was melting.

Stephen watches me with his kind look of understanding patience, his careful look of 'I sympathize but do not want to intrude poor Olla,' which restores my anger to me. He does not even know what he sympathizes with. He is a fool.
'He got weak,' I tell him, 'and died. No illness. His strength left him, he gave up the ghost. He gave up. I don't know why.'
Stephen is still looking as if he would like to ask more questions. When I rise to clear the table he stands also, waving his hand over the dishes to show that he will take care of them. I begin to unstrap Daniel.
'But what – ?' Stephen begins again.
'He died of lack of breath at the end. He could not get his breath. You can imagine watching a person drown, perhaps, in no water. That was his death. I was with him.'
'On your own?' His voice is horrified. Fool. Of course. And better that way – how glad I am my father was not there, that would have been horror indeed. Brother, my throat and lungs ached with breathing for you; I wanted you to breathe, my chest was sore with it. But you held my hand and choked and gasped and then fell still. I held your hand but you left me.
'Oh Olla, I'm sorry – ' Stephen is moving around the table towards me, his voice is hot and disgusting with sympathy. I turn quickly away, surely not a tear?
'I'm all right. It's nothing. Something in my eye. I did not mind being on my own with Tadek, it was better that way. He died painlessly. Now I must change Daniel.'

I lift his weight to my breast and get from the room. Stephen's suffocating cloud is left behind. There will be no tears, no weakness.

There will be strength. I am in charge now. Tadek, Daniel will live, as you would have lived. I will make it happen, and there will be no more death.

*

Every evening after our dinner, and for most of the day at weekends, Stephen goes to his study. I am glad that he is out of the way. He is writing a book, he says. About what? The early settlement of Australia. History. Old, irrelevant things. The public library phone once or twice a week, usually as I am giving Daniel his tea, to inform Stephen that books he has ordered for research have arrived, or that they cannot be obtained. A waste of everybody's time. I have to take the messages.

When I clean his study I glance over the piles of books on his desk and on the floor: *The Founders of Australia; A Biographical Dictionary of the First Fleet; The Journals of Captain James Cook; A Complete Account of the Settlement at Port Jackson by Captain Watkin Tench; The Remote Garrison; Sydney Cove 1788; An Account of the English Colony in New South Wales, Captain David Collins; Birds and Flowers of New South Wales: The Hunter Sketchbook; Phillip of Australia; The Fatal Shore.* And other modern books. There appear to be more than enough books on the settlement of Australia. I doubt very much that Stephen will have anything to add to the wealth of knowledge on that subject. His papers are strewn about – handwritten, printed. I square them into a neat pile. I do not want to have to see what he has written. When I sit beside Daniel, lullabying him to sleep, I hear the erratic clatter of Stephen's wordprocessor. He makes a folly, like those towers in the grounds of stately homes – an erection that serves no purpose. Stephen builds a pile of words, an exercise in futility; a piece of masturbation.

He should go back to teaching. That is what he can do. What he could do, when he had enthusiasm. Not this office work, and burying himself in the past. The writing occupies him, but he would be better employed cleaning the car and pruning the roses when he is at home.

No, he is out of our way. Once he is securely shut in his study, the house belongs to Daniel and me, we can pretend he is not there. That is a positive.

I liked it better when he used to go out. His meetings and causes and campaigns. Now he does not try to change the world – he does not

111

even dip his toe in it. He retreats up the beach, to the dry sand, and peers into history. His behaviour parodies his life. He demonstrates his own impotence. Like a senile old woman who cannot see her visitors because she is poking about in her handbag for something she has forgotten and lost that might have once been useful; he rummages through his history books.

He does not see Daniel. This must be what was intended. Daniel is to have one guardian, one protector who *knows*; and that is me. Daniel is grieved at times by Stephen's rudeness and ignorance, but it is safer for him if only I know his secret. And what could Stephen give him? What has Stephen left to give to anyone? He is a dry leaf in autumn. He is a man's shadow.

*

I tell Daniel the early days. He will know it all.
Buxton, 1975. When Stephen turns up again on Saturday to the Crown Hotel, I am not expecting to see him. We have tea and cakes again; he asks me my day off. And I tell him. I do not know what he wants. He asks me to walk in the countryside. When I say no he puzzles and asks me what I like to do. I say I like to be on my own in a room, peaceful; I like to earn my money and keep it.
'But with me? What would you like to do with me?'
It seems like a trick. A lot of what he says. He takes me out to eat, and pays. To the cinema. To a pub. I ask where is his friend Cath?
'Gone home, the holiday is over.'
'But you do not go home?'
'School doesn't begin again until September.'
'They pay you?'
'For the summer? Well yes!'
I find it hard to believe. One of the giggling local girls at the hotel says, 'Your boyfriend's waiting outside.' My boyfriend. Is that what he is?

He wants to know about my life. I tell him a little; about running away from home. Some of the places I have been. He asks why I came to England, but I think I will not talk about that.
He talks. His school, his kids, his plans, his beliefs. He talks about the hotel, saying my hours and pay are terrible, I should complain. He wants to see me in the evening, I explain we do not finish till nine, and I must get up at six. I need to sleep. I *like* to sleep. At our fourth

112

meeting, because he is kind and pleasant – I can tell that much – and will not be angry, I ask him, 'What do you want?'

'What d'you mean?'

'What do you want, why do you wait for me?'

'I – I like you.'

'You want to kiss me?'

He laughs. 'Yes.'

'OK.'

He must not come to my room, I am sure it is forbidden and I cannot risk my job. But after he kisses me in the park, I want him very badly. I keep thinking of him while I am working, I try not to but I do. His skin is hot, glowing; he touches me lightly, almost as if he is afraid of hurting me. But the length of him is pressed hard against me. My skin runs out to him. His breath is hot on my cheek, my neck. He makes me giddy. We are standing amongst trees, we have raincoats on; it has been drizzling lightly all afternoon. He holds my arms at the top, by the shoulder, and steps back a little, so there is a space between us. He looks at me.

I almost feel I will be sick; the space between us yawns. I will lift up my face and sway, falling, towards him. The ground is tilting me to him. I cannot breathe. It is the middle of the afternoon. The park is full of children and dogs and old ladies. I can hear my own heart pounding. He still waits, holding me apart; I can hear his breath coming short, he is biting his lip.

'Yes,' I say. 'Yes.'

'Tonight?'

I nod. He smiles a quick tight smile and walks me back to the hotel. We do not speak. All evening my heart beats, my stomach lurches, the rooms swing and tilt around me as I work. Between my legs is so wet and slippery I am afraid of marking the chair when I sit. I am sick with longing.

In the park that night we are very quick. He has found a dry place under some bushes, he spreads his coat on the ground. I almost cannot bear for him to touch me, my skin has become so sensitive I have to stop him from kissing my throat and breasts, I have to ask him to come inside, quick. I help him with the condom and we both come the moment after he enters me. When I open my eyes he is biting his lip again. 'Did you – ?'

'Yes. Can't you tell?'

He flops down on top of me and we laugh.

I am not sure why I wanted him so much. I suppose I was taken by surprise. I had not lusted for a man, before.

One afternoon he said, 'Have you slept with a lot of men?'
'Yes.'
'I thought so.' He seemed sad, so I told him, 'But I like it better with you.'
'Did you do it for money?'
'No. A few times for food. Once, for a job.'
'Here – ?'
'No.'
'You don't want to talk about it?'
'I don't think there's anything to say.'

When his school term begins I have only two weeks left in Buxton. I miss fucking with him. I think about it all the time, my clothes seem to rub against my skin; at night I walk back and forth the six steps' length of my little room, I cannot sleep. I even think of going down to the park to see if there's another man. I want it so much, anyone would do.

He comes at the weekend and tells me I must move to Leicester. Yes. But he wants me to live with him and I say no. I am not walking into that again. He sends me the Leicester *Mercury* on Monday when he goes back there, and I telephone to apply for jobs; the one I get is residential care assistant, old people's home. I move in there the following Monday.

I have a job. A room of my own. A boyfriend. I have money which I am saving.

CHAPTER EIGHT

Worgan's piano recital

On Saturday evening William and a number of other officers were invited by George Worgan to hear his pianoforte. It had travelled with him on the *Sirius*, and he had played it for a select audience at Rio. Now it stood in a tent all of its own, with a tarpaulin spread beneath it, and wooden wedges under two feet, to compensate for the slope of the ground. The gleaming mahogany perfection of the instrument in these rough surroundings was as extraordinary as anything William had seen. Nagle, of the *Sirius*' boat crew, had told him it was the most difficult object they had been asked to bring ashore. 'Not for weight, sir, the forge n' anvil takes the biscuit on that score; but for sheer awkerdness of shape – and the weight all up above instead of down where you'd be happy to 'ave a spot of ballast – yer top 'eavy, like, and buggered by the least swell – '

Worgan, his linen immaculately white and crisp (I must ask him who he gives it to, William noted; his own had been returned grey and strange-smelling by a washerwoman Ralph Clark had recommended), stood by the raised lid of the piano with Captain Campbell, laughingly pointing out its intricacies to him. Reverend Johnson and his wife stood nearby, listening and nodding seriously.

William glanced about for Bradley; he hardly ever came on shore, but Worgan must have invited him to this. Surgeon White was suddenly at his elbow, nodding and raising his glass.

'I was worried for that chap of yours, Mr Dawes – '

'Of mine – ?'

'The arm injury.'

'Munday?'

White nodded. 'The swelling was so bad I was afraid of putrefaction; I had determined to amputate.'

'Amputate?' William was horrified. He had not even visited Munday, had simply assumed the arm was mending.

'I was forced to postpone the operation for a day – one of the marine

wives in a difficult childbirth – and by the time I got back to him – '
White shrugged – 'he was on the road to recovery.'

'I am very glad of it. Very glad indeed. Speaking of childbirth, Surgeon White – ' They looked up at the sound of the piano, but it was only Watkin picking out a tune with one finger, illustrating something to Worgan and Campbell.

'I wondered if you know – idle curiosity, really – what happened to the child of a, a convict woman – Molly Hill? I believe it was born on board ship.'

White drained his glass, and nodded. '*Lady Penrhyn?*' He looked round for someone to fill his glass. 'Worgan'd better get this business started soon, I need to be back at the hospital at ten – I've been trying red gum on these dysentery cases and it seems to be having the desired effect – '

'Yes,' said William, 'she sailed on the *Lady Penrhyn*.'

'Well she's one of Arthur's, then, Arthur Bowes-Smyth tended convicts and crew on that vessel; and kept a record of births and deaths which is about as accurate as – as – my assistant Balmain's knowledge of surgery.'

William was watching Worgan, who had begun to usher his friends to their seats; the recital was about to begin. White's long-windedness could not be blamed entirely on his Irishness, William thought, but rather on his specific character as a man – his prickly, aggrieved sense of his own worth, of which others must be continually reminded.

'Infanticide. Molly Hill,' White said suddenly, precisely as Worgan, with a bow, took his seat at the piano. William nodded hurriedly and sat, there was no time for further conversation. Smiling at his audience, Worgan thanked them for coming.

'Though I must beg your patience for my own poor skills as a pianist, and could for your sakes wish a better musician here in my place – yet I am sure you will join with me in celebrating the arrival, and playing, of the very first pianoforte in this antipodean world!'

His tone was a little mocking, gently mocking, of himself, of the event, maybe even of his hearers. Yet the notion of this 'first piano' was indeed strange enough to rather mute their laughter and applause. It felt entirely appropriate that he should solemnly strike up *The King*, to bring them to their feet. As the last note died he nodded pleasantly at them and a convict girl entered with a taper and lit the two candles in brass holders over the keyboard. It was a theatrical moment; the flames wavered, then flared steadily. All eyes were drawn to the single illumined face in the tent, as Worgan, eyes half-closed, a little smile on his lips, bent to the keys like a lover. He played a Scarlatti sonata that William had heard once before. The notes tripped and danced along, making a spell of motion that held them all. Worgan was leaning his body a little in to the piano with the music, its fluid movement communicating itself also through his suppleness, and the abstracted pleasure on his face.

It was well-known that Worgan's father was a doctor of music; William wondered what had brought Worgan to the sea, and surgery. Clearly not a desire to escape the piano, for he played it intimately, beautifully. Would those piano-playing fingers exert a similar skill and spell over the diseased flesh or broken bones of a patient, William wondered? It seemed possible that Worgan's light, delightful touch might be visited on anything to which he turned his attention. William could not imagine Worgan struggling to choose between the callings of musician and naval surgeon. A man like Worgan would simply fall in easily with whatever chances opened up before him – moving gracefully between life's obstacles, not confronting in his own person pain or sacrifice or error.

Worgan paused briefly then launched into some recent Variations by Mozart. The candle-lit spectacle of his absorbed face above the gleaming instrument – a focus for all eyes, in the centre of the tent's darkening shadows – was a little disrupted by the materialisation, around the candle flames, of a swarm of insects. They danced and agitated in the light, while the notes flew out from under Worgan's charmed fingers. At last a particularly huge moth, flapping into the left-hand flame, extinguished it. The remaining candle illumined Worgan's tiny accepting nod and half-smile, as he played on without a pause.

Infanticide is murder of a child.

Worgan's life is a treat, an excursion, a party of pleasure, William thought; and yet he, like White, is a surgeon. And a good enough one (and of a better background, more of a gentleman) to be appointed to the flagship *Sirius*. I have never seen him in anxiety over a patient, as White is; never even heard him speak of a case, beyond its being an amusing anecdote or curiosity. This again shows his good breeding, of course. He charms his patients back into health, I believe, while White worries them out of sickness like a dog at their heels.

Infanticide is a terrible crime.

He tried to still his thoughts and listen to the music, but the unlikeliness of their situation made it hard to embrace; he could not banish

117

from his mind infanticide, nor the insects, the wooden wedges, the tarpaulin, the flimsy tent; the way the delightful, civilized arabesques of music were floating out into the smoky muddy camp, where marines were swigging rum and convicts and sailors crawling cautiously into the women's tents, and the wild woods all around were full of the listening ears of strange beasts and men to whom this piano's sound was incomprehensible magic, a weird and terrible singing voice, perhaps a source of nightmares.

Worgan paused for some minor adjustment to his instrument before his next piece, and White turned to William. 'Molly Hill – Bowes came to me with her case – he was concerned she had murdered her child.'

'Why?'

'It's not a thing will ever be satisfactorily explained. When they left Portsmouth the child was robust, Bowes said. She seemed to care for it – then all of a sudden, one morning only a week or two out of port, the infant was dead. Thriving one day, dead the next. Bowes told me he examined the corse and found no marks of sickness – he believed it had been smothered. There was something in the woman's manner made him suspicious.'

'What did he do?'

White shrugged and stood up. 'He told me at Rio – months later. There's nothing I could have done before, anyway. Without proper records and a post-mortem. We do not even have the record of their crimes; for all we know, she had already murdered a litter of infants in England.' He snorted at the incompetence of the rest of the world, and called to Worgan. 'Thank you, George. I'm off to the hospital now. I wouldn't be averse to your assistance down there tomorrow, if you have time to spare from your music. We admitted our two-hundredth patient this afternoon, you know.'

Worgan smiled and waved. 'Go on, Mr White, your good deeds are noted. I have been conducting a little experiment of my own with the yellow gum – in powdered form! – which I shall let you into tomorrow.'

William watched as White's resigned, rather bitter face broke into a smile, and he nodded. Once he was decently gone, Campbell and Ross began disparaging him, but Worgan silenced them easily with, 'He is as fine a surgeon as I have ever met, gentlemen, and so I forgive him his Irish manners.' As they laughed, he went on, 'Shall I begin the second half?'

Why should a woman murder her child? Of all the crimes on the transports, this must be the worst. William puzzled the question up and down and in and out of the new Haydn keyboard sonata that followed, but found no answer in either the fast or slow movement, nor in major nor minor key. Was she afraid now of childbirth because she might be tempted to kill again? Might it be a thing beyond her control? Or had the child in reality died, and so she grieved and feared for the next?

When Worgan finished there was a hubbub of praise for player and piano – and loud, laughing regrets at the lack of a lady's voice which might be well set off by such fine playing. William watched the Johnsons get up and bow to Worgan. Major Ross, he noticed, was engaging officers individually in serious private conversation; he heard the Governor's name mentioned, and David Collins, the Judge Advocate. William slipped past him to thank Worgan and say goodnight. He did not want to be drawn into the squabble over whether marine officers should serve as members of the court; since Ross and Campbell seemed to have little or nothing to do, it was difficult to see why they should not serve – though for himself he would resent yet another claim on his hard-pressed time. Ducking out of the tent, he noted with pleasure that it was a fine night. He could do a couple of hours' observation with the field-glass before sleep. He would banish thoughts of infanticide.

Next day other duties kept William from the observatory site until late morning. As he climbed up through the trees he was surprised not to hear sounds of the convicts working. The marines had been sent down to the shore to cut cabbage trees for timber, but the convicts should be busy chopping and sawing. As the site came into view, the lack of sounds of work was explained. Stokoe and Clough were fighting in eerie silence. Stokoe had his hands around Clough's neck and Clough, purple-faced, was pummelling him desperately in the ribs. William took it in at a glance, noting also that Barnes was lying curled (asleep?) beneath a sapling, with a dirty rag over his face.

'Stokoe! Clough! Stop it!' William was relieved to see Barnes shift and scratch his neck. Stokoe let go of Clough with a contemptuous shove that sent him sprawling to the ground.

'What's this about?'

Clough scrambled to his feet, he was crying.

'He hit me,' said Stokoe.

'Shitsack!' Clough threw himself at Stokoe again, flailing at him with powerless rage until William's shout stopped him.

'See,' said Stokoe.

'Sit down, the pair of you. Clough, what's your grievance?'

Clough sat with his knees bent up in front of him. He blew his nose and wiped the snot on the ground.

'*Clough.*'

'He 'it *me.*'

'Why?'

No reply.

'Why?'

'Hit a woman an' all.'

'What woman?'

'Molly Hill. Given her a basting – '

Stokoe turned furiously. 'Nowt to do wi' thee if I kill the bitch.'

William interrupted. 'Stokoe, you've already forfeited today's rum. If I don't have a straight story now you'll forfeit tomorrow's as well.'

'All right.' Stokoe looked at him maliciously. 'Molly Hill. Where's he but in her tent – nekked as a babby – trying his damnedest, as far as he's able – '

'I gived her 'alf a loaf.' Clough was crying again. 'I gived her 'alf me bread and she said yes.'

'But it's not up to her, is it?' from Stokoe.

'It's no fair!' shouted Clough. 'It's no fair when a man's – '

Stokoe laughed. 'It's his pride's hurt, sir.'

William felt his face go hot with disgust and anger. 'You're not married to this woman, Stokoe.'

'No.'

'Or engaged.'

Stokoe laughed brutally.

'Well then, what she does with Clough is none of your business. Quite apart from the fact that *none* of the men may enter the women's camp, by Governor Phillip's order.'

Stokoe stared at him with unpleasant amusement. 'No, sir,' he said ironically.

'If you have hurt the woman, she can charge you with it. You'll be punished.'

'She's not ganna charge me. She's enough on her plate wi'out charging me.'

Clough had stopped crying. There was nothing obvious to do except punish them both; and he had stopped their rum already. 'Well then, get back to work, both of you – and if I hear another word about this Molly Hill, I'll – you'll be sorry. Barnes! Get up, man. Where have you left your spade?'

Later that night, as he lay awake in his cot with the rain drumming on the canvas and dripping in through the seams on to himself and a snoring Watkin Tench, William thought again about Stokoe asking for rum for her. She needed rum because she was having a baby.

If she was having a baby – wouldn't she be . . . with Clough, would she still be able . . . ? He didn't actually know. He knew they were crude and ill-behaved, the women on the transports; it was impossible not to know that, people like Clark talked of nothing else. But as to what they might actually *do*, or want to do, or be forced to do with their bodies – he did not really know. He did know that he disliked Stokoe intensely. What hold did he have over her? Even if she had murdered her child, until it was proved, she had her rights, as much as anyone else in the land. He determined he would go and tell her that laws existed to protect women – even convict women – from bullies like Stokoe. The strong had a duty to the weak. As a marine he had that duty to all civilians; as a man, to all women. He would see her tomorrow. His conscience demanded it.

CHAPTER NINE

Molly Hill

William had to muster all his courage to approach the women's camp. It was guarded by two privates who saluted but kept their eyes fixed firmly ahead, ostentatiously not identifying him. It was late afternoon and hot; most of the women were sprawled in the dust in the shade of their tents. Some were sewing, one was washing a screaming child in a bucket. As he walked past he was humiliated to feel the blush rising to his cheeks. Women stopped talking and watched him pass.

'Who're you after, young sir?' called one.

'Molly Hill. I've a – message for her.'

There was laughter, and he heard his words repeated. 'A message!' 'Molly Hill!'

'Last tent but one on yer left,' the woman called back. And someone else shouted, 'I'll show yer a better time than 'er!' and they laughed. He quickened his pace, noticing the swarms of flies hovering around the tent flaps. There were babies crying. Suddenly a pair of marine breeches, stretched over a large bottom, emerged backwards, on all fours, from a tent in front of him. Captain Campbell ducked his head out of the tent, scrambled to his feet, and put on the hat that was handed to him through the flap. He nodded at Dawes, brushed his coat and departed.

Oh well, thought William sourly, at least he puts himself to the effort of visiting a woman. The convict Ann Cowley was still aboard the *Penrhyn*, Watkin had told him. Captain Sever was keeping her there to save the trouble of coming ashore to her. The whole machine ran on hypocrisy – even here in a new land, where better things should be possible.

In his anger he walked too far and had to turn back. The flaps on the second-to-last tent were closed; William hesitated, then called in a low voice, 'Is Molly Hill here?'

'Who is it?' The voice was tired and frightened.

'Lieutenant William Dawes. With – a message.'

There was a silence.

'Can I come in?'

'If you must.'

She was alone, sitting on a blanket with her back resting against a tea-chest. Her belly was huge with child.

'Molly. I am Lieutenant Dawes. I – John Stokoe and Richard Clough are in my work gang.'

She stared at him without reacting, her hands clasped around her globe of a belly.

'I – I hope you are well,' William added awkwardly. 'When will your baby – ?'

'Has he sent you?' she asked suddenly.

'Who?'

'Stokoe.'

'No – oh, no. I am here because I heard them arguing – well I questioned them, and from what I heard – '

She frowned, rubbing her belly. She had long black hair which hung limply either side of her pale, sweat-beaded face.

William made himself start again. 'If Stokoe bullies you, you know you can complain? He can be punished for it.'

She continued to stare at him in a puzzled way, her hands caressing and rubbing her swollen belly.

'Did he hit you?' William asked.

'Oh. It doesn't matter,' she said. A ghost of a smile flickered in her eyes. 'He doesn't know everything that goes on.' She drew her breath in sharply and winced, and her moving hands froze.

'What is it? Are you all right?'

She closed her eyes and rolled her head back against the tea-chest. 'It kicks me. It's been kicking me all day.' She opened her eyes. 'It takes your breath away.'

'Oh. Will it be soon?'

'Sooner the better for me. Will you help me up?' He moved to put his arm under hers and she rose awkwardly, first to her knees and then to her feet, leaning heavily on him as she did so. He saw in her white face, only inches from his, the effort and concentration she had to put into the movement. The skin beneath her eyes was as blue as bruises. When she'd got her balance she disengaged her arm and moved slowly towards the tent flap. She was barefoot and he noticed that the skin of her ankles was shiny, stretched taut over puffy swollen flesh. She went out without speaking, so he followed her, and when she heard him behind her she turned with a half-smile and pointed through the scrub to where the latrines had been dug.

'That's where I'm going. You wouldn't have a drop of rum on you, would you?'

Silently he uncorked and handed her his bottle.

'Oh!' She was surprised. 'Ta.' She lifted it to her lips, tilted her head and took a long draught. He watched her throat jerking as she swallowed; her neck was white and grey and blue, he could see the beating of her pulse.

She handed him back the bottle. 'Ta.' Then she moved off, and he turned to leave the camp. He walked quickly back the way he'd come. He could still see her poor thin working neck, as if it was right in front of him. Suddenly he was distracted by a whispered, 'Hey!' Between two tents to his right stood a skeletal woman in a petticoat. When he looked at her she put a finger against her lips and beckoned him. He stared at her, confused, and she pulled up her petticoat coquettishly to reveal a bony knee.

'Oh! No! Thank you.' He broke from the spot at a run and made his escape as quickly as he could, ignoring the stolid sentries' salutes, and the ripple of women's laughter behind him.

Over the next couple of days, as he was sawing, or chopping, or directing his gang to pit their weight against yet another intractable lump of wood, glimpses of Molly Hill came into his mind's eye. The bruised blue semicircles beneath her eyes. That flicker of amused intelligence as she said, 'He doesn't know everything that goes on.' The matter-of-fact way she asked him to help her up, and took his help, leaning on him heavily, trusting him with her weight.

He frowned and forced his mind back to the pressing question of how to urge, bribe, cajole the convicts into working harder. But unbidden, uncalled for, came the silent image of that poor woman's swollen ankles, her bare, bony feet. Surely she had not murdered her child? Surely that was impossible?

He told himself he would not think of her. And seemed to himself to be succeeding so well that when he asked Stokoe, some days later, if Molly Hill had had her baby yet, he was surprised to hear the words coming out of his mouth.

'Aye. And she's as ugly as her mother,' came the sullen reply.

'Is – is she well?'

Stokoe snorted. 'She bled like a stuck pig, along o' Biddy Lane.' He

124

glanced at William. 'Queer, eh, there's some mabs canna breed to save their lives, and others'll pop quicker and easier'n shellin' peas.'

William turned away.

'They've tekken her ter 'ospital, if you wanna gan down.'

What was it to Stokoe if he visited her or not?

'Get back to work, Stokoe.'

The man moved. But William could not stop himself. '*Are* you the father of her child?'

There was a note of malicious triumph in Stokoe's replying voice. 'Huh, there's 'alf the sailors on *Penrhyn* Ah reckon, queuein' up for that honour.'

The poor woman. The poor, degraded woman. William's heart contracted as he remembered again, against his will, the effort of concentration she had put into standing up; the slow, vulnerable independence with which she had moved away from him towards the tent flap. He suddenly thought of Clough in her tent – when? Two days earlier? Of Clough, without his breeches, pressed against that fragile, heavy, rounded belly. The shock of the image winded him. Dear God. For half a loaf of bread. How could He let His people come to this?

William knew that many – perhaps most – of the officers made visits like Campbell's to the women's camp. Such visits were treated as invisible. If he were to visit Molly Hill at the hospital, it would not be invisible. Because it did not fall into the usual hypocritical pattern of their behaviour, other officers would talk about it, he thought bitterly. Well let them. Why should he care?

He worked doggedly on the road and gunpowder store for a couple of days, trying to block out his thoughts with calculations about earthmoving, checking soil samples, measuring gradients. Watkin, one evening, laughed at him for his unsociability. The officers had a round, now, of jaunts and dinners and hunting parties; they lived as if the country had been created solely for their pleasure. They had fishing trips and trips out to the ships to dine with the captains; they had musical evenings with Worgan's piano; they made sorties to find natives and see how far they could induce them to be friendly, whilst jibing crudely at one another over the attractions of the naked females.

Only Reverend Johnson, it seemed to William, took his responsibilities seriously, and could be found at all hours doing his rounds of the convicts' tents and the hospital, with his Bible, his little stock of material comforts, and his vital Christian message.

But wasn't William as contemptible as those who would whisper and laugh about him if he was deflected from doing what he knew to be right by fear of their opinion? He was. He must visit Molly Hill – openly, in hospital – talk to her about her former life, convince her of the need for change, remind her of God's forgiving love. If the unthinkable were true – if she had murdered a child – what agonies of self-reproach must be generated now by a new infant in her arms? What was he doing, measuring the possible saving of her soul against his own fears of earthly mockery and contempt?

Saving souls was not actually, of course, his job; it was properly the job of Reverend Johnson. It would not be unreasonable to ask Richard if he had prayed with Molly Hill at the hospital. William would not need to visit if Richard had helped her to seize this opportune time to turn to God.

As he was returning from Point Maskeylene late in the afternoon, he caught up with Richard Johnson on the path. The sky was overcast, threatening rain, and the clergyman was heading back to the settlement.

He greeted William hurriedly and asked if he had seen Mrs Johnson.

'No – no. Not since last Sunday morning's worship.'

'Ah. She has just – she has taken it into her head to start visiting the convict women, to try to spread Christ's word among them, and I am afraid the work is not suitable.'

'Why is that?'

'Oh William – they are a very hardened type of female, many of them, with absolutely no interest in the Church, and my good wife has exposed herself to ridicule and insults on more than one occasion now. Her faith leads her into situations where, truly, angels would fear to tread – '

'She is a good woman,' William agreed, wondering whether Mary might not be a more suitable person to speak with Molly Hill than the chaplain himself.

'She *is*, but for her own protection I have forbidden her now – forbidden her absolutely – to go into the women's camp. They do not treat her with respect, and that weakens the chances any of us have of commanding their attention and turning them to Christ. I do not want her innocence to be taken advantage of. She makes my work more difficult. And it is already *so* difficult – ' He looked round almost wildly, as if his wife might be lurking behind a bush or hanging from a tree.

'I'll walk down to your tent with you,' offered William, 'to see if she's returned.'

'Thank you, I am very grateful.'

As they made their way along the narrow dusty path, the chaplain expanded on the difficulties he had encountered during the first weeks of his ministry. He had had to solemnize marriages, christenings and two funerals in utterly inappropriate surroundings; and the sick, whom he visited daily, were so tormented by physical wants that they could not fix their minds upon matters of the spirit. For some of the more extreme cases he had felt obliged to dip into his own stores of wine and food.

'Which does not trouble me; I am fortunate that I am *able* to help ease their suffering by administration of worldly comforts. Happy is the man who can afford to be charitable. But I want to read the Bible with them; we need to pray together, their time is short. Besides, my supplies are not infinite, and what is to be done when they are used up? The doctors are in despair over the diet the sick must have here. Have you seen the state of affairs at the farm?'

Mary Johnson was sitting in the shade beside their tent; she smiled sweetly at her husband as he approached, and indicated a small basket of leaves beside her chair.

'Look what I have found! These are the leaves which Surgeon White believes can be made into a useful drink for his patients. He thinks they are efficacious against the scurvy. You can take them to the hospital when you visit this evening.'

Richard nodded. 'Did you take Samuel with you on your walk, Mary? There are dangers, you know, in your wandering about unaccompanied in this wilderness.'

She laughed and stood up, offering him her chair. 'You look hot. And Mr Dawes – do sit down. Richard, I do not need to take Samuel away from his own work. The Lord is my Shepherd – I am quite safe here, I feel that He is with me.'

Richard frowned and sat in the offered chair. He began to speak, then thought better of it and glanced at William.

'You were talking about the farm,' William reminded him. 'The land by the Governor's house?'

'Yes. The seeds they planted germinated and grew like weeds for all of a week. But now the plot looks as if it has been visited by the plagues of Egypt; flattened by the rain, plundered by birds and insects

– there are a few tattered scraps of green left and nothing more. And this is the crop on which the sick must pin their hopes.'

'I have been thinking about that, Richard – ' Mary's light sweet voice broke in.

'Yes?' he said warily.

'Since the shortage of greenstuff is the cause of such distress, do you not think it our duty to cultivate a plot ourselves? Perhaps we would have better luck with a garden than they have had up at the farm. The land here is less exposed – '

'But it's autumn,' Richard pointed out. 'I don't know how anyone can expect to raise a crop in winter – '

'We must have faith,' she reminded him gently, and William added, 'This southern winter may be less cold than ours at home. It may be that crops can continue to grow.' As he spoke he remembered that Cook, in his journal, had described frost in New South Wales. He decided not to mention it; Mary Johnson was right, faith was important.

Richard spoke carefully. 'If we do make a garden, a great deal of the work will fall upon you, my dear – while I am busy with my spiritual duties – '

She nodded happily. 'You know I only want to be of service, Richard.'

He smiled and took her hand. 'Well, it will be far better than roaming off in search of edible plants, for you to be here, cultivating them, here where you are in no danger of getting lost or – or – yes. I shall set Samuel to some digging first thing in the morning. I should ask the Governor for some convict labour, if I thought he could be persuaded to look kindly on any request of mine – '

'We don't need his favours,' Mary said sternly.

'The convicts are all engaged on public works,' William pointed out, 'and they are clearing land to plant corn in the spring. No one is idle.'

'I am idle,' said Mary, 'and now I have work to do!' She and Richard smiled at one another, and William suddenly remembered why he had wanted to talk to Richard.

'I wonder whether you have prayed or spoken with a convict woman called Molly Hill – she's in the hospital now – she has a newborn child.'

Richard shook his head. 'Not unless she seems close to death. There are so many who need my help, who have a lifetime of sinning and godlessness to atone for, that I dare not let myself be distracted from them. I am fighting Satan himself for their souls while their last hours tick past. I am forced to leave the spiritual welfare of less serious cases to easier times.'

'Oh Richard, *why* – ' Mary burst out, and he stopped her with a hand on her arm.

'Because I do not want you subjected to the pestilential airs of the hospital, or the terrible sights, or for your ears to be polluted by the foul language of unrepentant sinners.'

'But I am your wife, Richard. I should be by your side, working for God – '

'And so you are. But not at the hospital, Mary.'

After a moment she nodded submissively, and he granted her a smile.

It would be impossible, William realized, to ask her to speak with Molly Hill – and as he reached this conclusion he felt a little stab of elation in his chest. There was no way round it; Richard did not have time, and Mary wasn't allowed. He must visit Molly Hill again himself.

He went late the following afternoon, on his way back to the stores with two faulty axes which he hoped to exchange for ones that had their heads more firmly fixed on. His heart was pounding as he neared the tent. It was foolish anxiety, he told himself, foolish fear of being seen and talked about by his fellow officers; nothing more than that.

He entered the hospital tent and laid the axes carefully beside the inner flap, telling himself not to forget them later. The convicts lay on the floor of the tent, in rows. The women's section was divided from the men's by the simple expedient of a sheet of sailcloth hanging between. A couple of babies were crying feebly behind it.

Balmain, one of White's assistants, was unwrapping a dirty bandage from the leg of a white-faced boy who looked no more than twelve. He glanced up at William, who could not help asking, 'Is he a convict?'

Balmain nodded, and turned his frowning attention back to the mess beneath the bandage. A woman was helping a prostrate man to a drink, and one trio of yellow-faced, toothless scurvy victims were leaning up on their elbows muttering together, but otherwise the figures in bed were still and quiet.

There were only thirty or so patients in the women's section, reflecting not only the far smaller numbers of women in the settlement, but also the fact that fewer of them seemed to be affected by the scurvy. It was a point Worgan had mentioned as being worthy of scientific study, William recalled.

He saw her straight away; she was sitting up, in much the same position as last time he'd seen her, only this time she held a bundle in her arms, a bundle that was attached to her bared left breast. He coughed so that she could become aware of his presence and cover herself, but she simply looked at him without recognition. The women were lying so close together that a private conversation was impossible; he felt himself blushing. It was difficult to look at her without seeming to stare – he knew he wasn't staring, but it must look as if he was – at her breast. He crouched beside her.

'Molly – I – you don't remember me? William Dawes.'

She frowned.

'I came to speak to you about Stokoe – only last week – ' He was taken aback that she did not remember him. 'He works for me. It doesn't matter. I'm glad your baby is safe and sound.' He glanced at the child, and coloured again, and had to avert his eyes. Her breast was as big and round as the child's head, but pale. Bluish, like the moon in winter. His heart was pounding. He heard the rustle of her movement, and looked into her face to see her watching him with an amused expression, as she slowly shifted the child's position and pulled her nightdress together.

'All right?' she said.

'Oh. Yes. Are you – are you feeling better?'

'Weak,' she said. 'Everything's – slow. You know? As if it's a bit far away. I can't quite wake myself up – ' As she spoke she laid the baby down on the blanket, and it began to wriggle and make a noise. An inhuman little bleat. She closed her eyes wearily, reminding him of the other time he had seen her do the same.

'Can I talk to you?' he said. The child's bleating was regular and angry; an indrawn breath, a bleat, an indrawn breath, a bleat.

'She wants nursing all the time. And she's heavy.' William stared at the creature. It was smaller than a cat – smaller than a loaf of bread.

'She wears me out.'

'Shall I – pick her up?'

Molly's tired eyes opened in surprise, but not refusal, William thought. He changed his position from crouching to kneeling, so as to avoid the danger of overbalancing, and cautiously wriggled his fingers under the child's weight. She weighed almost nothing – no more than a few pounds. Her head was dangerously loose; as he positioned her in the crook of his arm he had a moment's awful fear that it would drop right off. The small red mouth gasped for breath but then closed. The bleating stopped. The creature's face was very red, its eyes puckered up in wrinkles of creased skin.

'When do they open their eyes?' he asked.

Molly gave a slow breath of laughter. 'Born with 'em open. You're thinking of kittens.'

'Oh, I'm sorry.' He stared at the wrinkled face, waiting for its eyes to open.

'What d'you want to talk about?'

He glanced up at her, and saw, with a shock of pleasure, that *her* eyes were open, that they were blue-grey, watching him. 'You – you have had a terrible time.' It would be easy to talk to her. He could feel the words coming all in a rush, to flow eloquently around her, to convince and carry her along. 'All you women prisoners. Life has been very hard; herded like cattle in the transports, ill treated and – seduced – by the sailors; and then since we landed, these dreadful conditions, no homes, no comforts – ' He glanced at her to make sure she was following him. 'It would be enough to reduce a person to despair, to test the strongest faith. But now you're here; your baby is healthy – ' He glanced down at the walnut face. No eyes, still. 'It *is* healthy?'

Molly shrugged then nodded.

'And I wanted to say to you – I wanted to urge you to think of God's goodness.'

She laughed suddenly, putting him off a little.

'I know it may seem – you may think He could have found a better way of showing it, but often we don't understand. He moves – in mysterious ways. He has brought you here and given you this child. Your old way of life was – ' he hesitated – 'may have been, bad. He has given you this time of contemplation to turn – to choose to turn back to Him, to reflect on your life – to make it different – '

She laughed again. 'Contemplation? With her bleatin' half the night?'

'Yes, but – '

Molly's face was innocent. Thin, fragile, innocent. When Richard Johnson talked of hardened creatures, he did not mean such as she.

'What was your crime?'

She closed her eyes wearily. 'Thievin'. A watch. Off a captain of the guards.'

He knew it. Petty theft, not murder, not infanticide. 'Why?'

She frowned slightly, as if it was not a question she had ever asked herself. 'I'd have given it back if he'd a' come with me. I had to get summat.'

The blue circles under her eyes. He could see the shape of her bones, her skull, under the thin white flesh – so fragile, the flickering pulse at her neck. What terrors had she endured?

'You are through the worst of the storm. Whatever crimes you have committed, Christ offers you forgiveness and love; turn your back on the old life. You mustn't let yourself be degraded by men like Stokoe. You must make a new life now, for yourself and this innocent child.'

He could see she was tired, she seemed to sink back into herself. He watched her in silence for a moment. The baby was warm and still in his arms. It was asleep. With exaggerated, clumsy care he laid it down beside her, trying not to wake it. Molly did not open her eyes. He stood, waited again, still she did not look at him. He whispered, 'Goodbye,' and left.

He got all the way back to his own tent before he remembered the axes.

STEPHEN
Who's this Molly Hill, then? Where's she sprung from?

She's real enough, her name's on the passenger list of the *Lady Penrhyn*.

That's not the point, is it. She's not a name, not a Phillip or a Tench or a Dawes. She's a woman. In that first year all the parts are for men.

But William must have a woman, sooner or later. And he wouldn't take a married one; so that leaves convicts and blacks. Molly Hill appears to be what he wants. It would have been possible to choose a girl like terrified Elizabeth Hayward, thirteen years old, transported for stealing a linen gown and a bonnet – surely she would have been more innocent than Molly?
No, William wants an infanticidal prostitute.

Oh, the colonizing power of love, which knows no bounds, and sees in the most intractable and opposed territory visions of peaceful and productive dominion!

Olla?
I loved her. Wanted to make up to her for the cruelty and poverty of her earlier life; to let her into the socialist warmth of my secure and rosy world. To banish her fearsome past.

If I had succeeded? I suppose I would have obliterated her past, and therefore, what she is. Changed her, through love, into something I could no longer love. Instead of a more predictable colonial scenario: discovery and surrender, invasion, thrilling and exotic difference, rich sexual booty –
License my roving hands, and let them go,
Behind, before, above, between, below.
O my America! my new-found-land,
My kingdom, safeliest when with one man man'd –
moving on to mutual incomprehension, the difficulties of separate languages, acknowledgement of fundamental difference; clash of basic interests; war. And then the colonist's guilt; his eagerness for the colony to be equal and free; his slow comprehension that these are *his* terms, 'equal' and 'free'; that he is still imposing his terms, that he cannot understand the terms of the other. His (my) collapse into impotence.

133

Return to the original question. Molly Hill's not the official story. Dawes went to New South Wales, he built an observatory at Point Maskeylene, he surveyed and planned and helped lay out Sydney and Rose Hill at Phillip's request; then he fell out with Phillip and came home. He did not fuck a convict woman. Or if he did, it's not recorded.

Most of them did, though. There are children to prove it. David Collins, Ralph Clark, Philip Gidley-King, Surgeon White – all fathered children on convict women. Never mind their wives and children at home. A family in each hemisphere: touching. That frailty, and need, and matter-of-fact appetite for love, are so readily demonstrated, so easily accepted. Gidley-King and White took their bastard children home to England to get a decent education. Were roundly not afraid to love them. More generous, less driven, than William. Where does this pinching morality of William's come from? His religion? This white, bloodless virtue.

He needs a woman. He wants Molly Hill.

CHAPTER TEN

The charting expedition

The following morning William received an order which took him away from Sydney Cove for six days. The Governor called for an expedition to explore Broken Bay, and William and Bradley served as cartographers.

They were disappointed in their hopes of finding a sizeable river, but all the inlets of the bay were sounded and charted, and all the natives who came down to the water were solemnly greeted. On the fourth day they ran into bad weather, which continued through the night. They lit a large fire at daylight when the rain stopped, and hung their clothes around it to dry. But the clothes remained clammy to put on, with the dampness that makes your bones ache and brings on the rheumatism. The men were miserable, and given the ground the expedition had covered, there would have been no shame in rowing for Sydney as soon as they were packed up. But Phillip, stickler for duty, gave the order to explore the next cove. They rowed round into a low cold wind that made the grey water choppy and blew the seabirds, when they rose from dropping for fish, into a squawking sideways spin. As they came in towards the beach, natives splashed out through the shallows to meet the boats. The Governor, accompanied by Captain Hunter, made his way to the native huts erected under the trees a short distance from the water's edge. He nodded in his stiff way to the people who crowded round him, suffering them to feel the damp stuff of his overcoat and the braid of his jacket. He was followed by his servant Henry, carrying the familiar sack of baubles. Bradley and William brought up the rear.

This was a more substantial settlement than others they had seen; staring into one of the dark huts William realized they were crammed with women and children who returned his stare with intense curiosity. A small naked boy in the doorway dropped a shell which rolled towards William's feet. William picked it up and held it out to him, and after staring at him wide-eyed for a moment, the child suddenly stepped forward and grabbed it. Back in the safety of the doorway he examined his shell minutely then looked up at William and smiled.

'This tribe eat well,' Bradley commented quietly, pointing at the midden of crab and oyster shells at the side of the hut.

'Maybe we'll find one of their leaders here – maybe the Governor will actually – ' William felt something tugging at the back of his coat and turned to see the little boy flash a grin at him before running back into the hut. There was the sound of a woman's voice rising and falling in quick reproof. William found himself grinning stupidly at Bradley, who nodded.

'How much easier it would be if we were all children.'

But the Governor was moving stiffly on; the Indian men stood by their huts watching, William caught a couple of their glances and felt his own legs become stiff and clumsy with embarrassment.

'We are the freaks at the fair,' Bradley said under his breath. 'Wrong colour skin, strange coverings which hide our sex, hairless faces and misshapen heads – '

'Why doesn't he stop?' hissed William. 'They're all waiting for him to do something.'

As he spoke the Governor suddenly tapped Hunter on the arm and pointed into the last hut. The British party came to a halt behind him – peering over their shoulders William saw that a particularly large crayfish had attracted his attention.

In exaggerated sign language the Governor pointed to the crayfish, then to himself, then to the startled-looking woman inside the hut. She picked up her baby and moved farther back into the shadows. There was a ripple in the crowd of watching Indians and a tall male pushed his way through, entered the hut and squatted in front of the woman. Phillip went through his pantomime again, instructing Henry to take an axe from the sack. This was laid on the floor in front of the couple, while Phillip continued to point at the crayfish and himself, indicating his desire for it. The man slowly picked up the axe and fingered it, and another male stepped towards Phillip and held out his hand.

'Another axe, sir?' asked Henry, reaching into the bag.

'Mirrors will do,' Phillip replied. 'Or kerchiefs.'

A number of natives clustered round Henry and as he hesitated they pointed, in an amusingly accurate imitation of Phillip, at the crayfish, at Phillip, and at themselves.

William waited for Phillip to notice that he was being mocked, but the Governor remained oblivious; he even commented loudly to

Hunter, 'You see how like cunning children they are? By claiming part ownership of the fish, all think they can be rewarded.' William turned indignantly to Bradley, who gave a slight warning shake of his head. His eyes were glittering with amusement.

Abruptly, after a dozen or more kerchiefs and mirrors had been presented, Phillip signalled to Henry that it was enough and himself picked up the crayfish. Turning, he passed through the small knot of officers to lead them back down to the boats.

'But isn't he going to – ' William's indignation could not be held in check any longer. Bradley shrugged.

'They're friendly, and they're interested in us. It's a golden opportunity to enter into more serious communication – '

'He's not interested in that. I've told you.'

'But we could get more of their words – '

Bradley increased his pace, to close the gap between himself and Phillip's party. William was obliged to hurry to keep up with him, after waving at the little boy who still stood in the hut doorway. The child stared back gravely without moving.

'What will they make of this behaviour – ' he whispered urgently to Bradley. 'They must think us lunatics – '

Suddenly a native man who'd been walking across the beach towards them stepped up to Phillip, grabbed the crayfish from his hand, and ran up to the huts with it. Hunter turned after the man with a shout, but Phillip shook his head and climbed quietly into the boat. The others, William and Bradley included, followed him; the men took their places at the oars in unusual silence, but before they were ready to push off there was a shout from the huts and the same native, still holding the fish, came running back towards the boats waving it and shouting.

'They must have told him it's been paid for – ' William looked at Phillip for his reaction. Gravely the Governor disembarked again, followed by the officers. But on the beach he firmly rejected the proffered crayfish, with sweeping arm gestures and severe head-shaking. Calling Henry, he marched up to the huts and solemnly removed the axe and every mirror and kerchief he could see, handing them to Henry to be returned to the sack. To the Indians' looks and exclamations of surprise, Phillip shook his head in a haughty negative.

The officers stood awkwardly watching, and Phillip's displeasure seemed to extend to include them too, as he and Henry descended to the boats again.

'They must be taught the consequences of their actions,' he declared. 'As children are. They must learn the rules of fair exchange and trade; the qualities of trust and respect must be demonstrated to them, and where they fail to honour those qualities, they must be punished. If we encourage them in irrational, childish behaviour, we make a rod for our own backs.'

There was the sound of angry voices from the huts, and a couple of men came out with spears. 'Yes,' continued Phillip's dry, monotonous voice, 'they may think more carefully next time, before taking impetuous action.'

They rowed away from the angry shouting on the beach in complete silence. William could feel his own face hot with anger and embarrassment. Bradley stared impassively across the water. No one spoke to the Governor; surely Captain Hunter would remonstrate with him, surely someone would dare to point out how insulting this action had been?

But the rest of the day passed in near silence, the only conversations being practical ones about tides and currents and sounding lines; the entire party was too embarrassed to look each other in the eye. Only Phillip appeared unaffected by the mood.

They made camp that night on an empty beach. William went with four sailors to fetch water from a small stream that made a waterfall down the hillside before dissipating itself in the sand. The stream fell too close to the rock-face for them to catch it in the barrel, and they filled it painstakingly, in canteen-fulls. As William paced about waiting for them, watching the pelicans and cormorants diving in the bay, he noticed that the Governor was walking across the beach towards them.

Somebody should tackle him about the farcical events of the morning. Somebody should at least suggest to him that he had given the Indians reason to feel offended . . .

William turned and paced away from his men, briefly increasing the distance between himself and Phillip, as he was hit by a wave of panic at the thought of speaking out. That was not the thing to say, anyway; nothing would be served by simply criticizing His Excellency's actions. But if a suggestion could be made, tactfully, about how the natives *should* be treated? It's not my place, William told himself. It's not my place to discuss the natives with the Governor. But who else will? Not Captain Hunter, not Bradley, certainly not Major Ross.

It *is* your place to talk to him, he told himself as his heart began to thump more loudly in his chest. Obey your conscience, William, that's what God requires – never mind what the others do.

He forced himself to turn to face the Governor, and almost knocked him over. Phillip, who'd been striding along with his glass to his eye, scanning the top of the cliffs, recoiled with an irritated expression.

'Lieutenant Dawes. I didn't see you.'

'I'm sorry, your Excellency. I'm – I'm overseeing the men who're getting water – '

Phillip nodded curtly and raised his glass again.

'Please, your Excellency – could I ask – '

Phillip lowered the glass resignedly. Behind his head the setting sun made the sky glow; the rain clouds had all gone, the sky was a perfect dome of graduated shades of pale and darkening blue.

'It's the natives.' For a moment sheer panic drove all words out of William's head, leaving it as blank as the sky. He met Phillip's pale eyes and remembered himself. 'Will we – I hope you'll excuse my question – but I am very interested to know how you intend to proceed with the natives, sir. Is – do you think – it likely that we shall meet with their leaders soon?'

Phillip's glance flicked impatiently up to the skyline again. 'I have no idea, Mr Dawes. It seems possible that they have no leaders; certainly none have come forward.'

'But then how will we make ourselves understood to them – how will they know our intentions for the future?'

'By our actions. They will learn our intentions as children do, by our actions.'

'Our actions are – ' William could think of nothing but the stupid sack of gewgaws. 'That is, our actions – well I was wondering how we might set about – teaching them Christianity?'

'Indeed. A difficult problem.'

'I was thinking – '

'Almost impossible, I should say, while they remain in complete ignorance of our language, and we of theirs.'

'But I am making a vocabulary list – '

Phillip inclined his head slightly, icily. 'And so is Mr Collins, the Judge Advocate. But both you and he have many other duties, I believe, and are not free to devote yourselves entirely to the study of the native tongue.'

'But – ' It was in William's head to point out that these tasks could be distributed amongst other men; or that Captain Campbell, who appeared to do nothing, could be given a notebook and sent out to teach the natives English.

'I agree with you, Lieutenant Dawes.' Phillip smiled his horrible stiff smile. 'It is important that we find a way of communicating with the natives, and that we should not have to expend too much precious time upon it. It is my intention when the settlement is a little better established to bring some of them to live among us so that they can learn English.'

'To bring them – ? But will they *want* to live among us?'

'We shall have to consider ways of persuading them.' Phillip turned to look down the beach after the sailors with their barrel of water. 'I believe your men are ready.' He raised his glass to his eye again and moved off.

As darkness fell the seamen settled themselves at intervals along the beach to catch the fish that came in on the rising tide. They had made their own fire, away from the one where Henry was cooking the officers' food, and Nagle and Jones and someone else were already cooking fish and chatting and laughing in low, companionable voices. They can be easy now they're out of the Governor's company, William thought sourly.

While he waited for his food he walked past the fishermen, down towards the rocks at the end of the cove, and sat staring out over the dark velvety water. He scanned the sky, but no stars were visible yet. After a while the tall figure of Bradley came crunching over the sand to join him. They sat in silence punctuated by the light splash of pebbles as Bradley threw them into the shallows.

'He has no plans at all for the natives,' William said.

'What did you expect?'

'He's thinking he might 'persuade' some to come and live in the settlement.'

'There *are* no plans for them, William. They are not thought to be important, they can just go off and live somewhere else – inland.'

'Away from their source of food.'

Bradley laughed appreciatively. 'Quite.'

'But to Christianize, to educate, to question patiently for their knowledge of the land and its plants – '

'The Government sets no store by this,' Bradley said impatiently. 'Otherwise they would have found a berth for missionaries and teachers – '

'But the natives won't just vanish.'

Bradley shrugged. 'It's a big country.'

140

'Yes, but if the settlement grows – if they send another convict fleet –
if this really is a colony – '

Bradley skimmed a stone, making it hop four times over the calm
flat water. He did not reply.

'We can't expect to treat them as – as nothing. To ignore them. Just to
take their land – '

'And their crayfish,' Bradley interrupted.

'And – '

'Don't forget their crayfish.' Bradley mimicked Phillip to perfection.
William began to laugh.

'A crayfish is a valuable item, there must be no childishness over
crayfish here.' They were both laughing. William leant forward and
eased off his boots, then stepped down into the shallow water. It was
surprisingly warm, soothing and lovely to his feet. His anger washed
away.

'Look out for sharks.' Bradley's mocking voice sounded closer over
the water than it had done on the rock. William tilted his head up to
look for stars. There was the brilliant star, and its three fainter sisters, of
Crux Australis. And that – upside-down, yes, the belt, the arm – was
Orion. The brightest star in the sky was directly overhead; would that
be Canopus, leader of Argo? It was marked on the southern sky's
charts but he had not identified it before. He waded on through the
gently lapping water. The blue of the sky was deepening, minute by
minute, and the stars lit up against it like sparks on a chimney back.

Suddenly he heard Bradley's voice from the beach close by. 'Come
and look at this William.' He waded back, curling his toes into the
warmth of the soft sand at the bottom. Bradley was crouching over
something on the sand. William squatted beside him.

'What is it?'

Bradley snorted and whispered, 'It's stopped now, of course. Just
hold still a minute and keep your eyes on this patch of sand.'

William did as he was told, staring at the dark patch of sand just as
he had earlier stared at the sky, waiting for a star to appear. Suddenly
there was a spot of light in the sand. He leaned closer, but could make
out nothing beyond the yellow speck.

'What is it?'

'I don't know. Something like a glow-worm, I imagine. It goes out –
ah!' as he spoke the thing went dark, and they both peered to make out
the shape. But it was too dark – and it really did seem as if there was
nothing there but flat sand, until the tiny light appeared again.

'It's surprisingly bright, for such a small creature.'

'Yes.' They stared at it in silence for a while, then William tilted his head to look up at the stars again. There were hundreds now, the sky was full of them. He smiled to himself at the perversity of staring at a minute faltering speck of light on the ground, while the galaxy radiated a steady brilliance overhead. But the little light was near, the stars far, far away. The little light was close enough to touch. He looked down for it and, with half the star-spangled night sky sweeping past his eyes, overbalanced. The sky seemed to reel around him in points of light; Bradley was holding him by the shoulder, heaving him into a kneeling position.

'Are you all right?'

'Yes. Stupid – I lost my balance. Did I squash it?' His eyes searched the dark sand.

'I don't know. It's gone out, anyway.'

He was conscious of Bradley's warm hand still clasping his shoulder – suddenly conscious that they were both conscious of it, for a long moment in which he held himself utterly still, immobile. He felt his stillness communicate itself to Bradley, and Bradley got up quickly and stumbled away across the soft dark sand.

William remained on his knees, staring at the spot where the glow-worm had been. When he permitted a thought, it was that he hoped the creature would light up again. But after five minutes waiting he was getting cold. He got up stiffly and went over to the seamen's fire to warm himself. On the longboat he took a blanket aft and quickly lodged himself in the first space he could find, securely hedged in by Waterhouse and Hunter.

*

STEPHEN

This is an unnecessary complication, lad, and one that descendants of Bradley at the nth generation may not thank you for. (They may rejoice, of course; 'Great-great-great-great-grandpa's come out, and let us all be gay!') But did he have children? Yes, three. He was married to Sarah Wishart. And he and Dawes never.

But. But.

I see him. Obstinately present. That moment of need. The touch, the pause, the silence in which the question is asked and the rejection given. My poor Bradley.

How sorry I am for those who need love. Oh, how I pity them.

Brave Stephen. Stephen *mon brave*. Needing no one. And suddenly weak with grief at my lack.

Bradley, I honour you.

OLLA

Daniel is growing. His length now is fifty-five centimetres, his weight eight pounds, ten ounces. He grows steadily, like – like a marrow.

He grows, and he sleeps; at night he sleeps well, better than other children. He sleeps from seven till his feed at ten, and from eleven when I go to bed, until four when I often have to wake him. Stephen says,

'Why do you wake him, to feed? Wouldn't it be better to let him go through the night and have a big breakfast?'

'Am I looking after him, or you? Do *you* know when he needs food?'

Stephen is quiet for a while, but he cannot resist interfering.

'I thought the object was to get him into a routine vaguely resembling the rest of humanity. It's fairly antisocial to eat at 4 a.m.'

'Does it hurt you? Does it inconvenience you? Allow me to know what is best for him.'

The health visitor says, 'I hope he's a good lad and sleeps through for you. He's not noisy, is he, that's one thing to be thankful for – he's peaceable, poor little soul.' When she asks directly if he sleeps through, I say yes. Because he can.

But of course I shan't make him. Do they know him better than I do? He grows steadily, and I give him food steadily; gradually, regularly, systematically I build him up. There will be no night-time gap through my negligence, there will be no hindrance to the flow of nourishment.

There will be no interruptions, no crises, no dramas. It is all steadiness, calm, peace; his spirit must not be distracted by irrelevant emotions, because this is his time of growth. His energies must all be conserved and focused on strengthening. I make the world around him calm and beautiful and safe. No cold wind will blow on him, no discomfort graze him, no sound be too loud, or light too bright. Like a plant tended in the best greenhouse, with steady temperature, adjusted humidity, perfect light, his environment will succour him.

I play him music and read him stories.

At first I played the musical toys he has been given, the tinkling mobile that does 'Frère Jacques', the Brahms lullaby bear. And read simple little story-books about talking animals and toddlers going shopping with their mummy.

144

Then I realized – he showed me – my mistake. The patronizing nature of these things. He is not like other infants. The scope of his imagination and intellect dwarfs theirs. He requires other sustenance. Now I play him what he wishes to hear. We began with Mozart, but we have moved on to Beethoven. It is the symphonies he likes best, through them he feels the world's sorrows and the stirrings of hope. Children's books are put away. I read poetry from Stephen's shelf, Wordsworth, Tennyson, Shelley, Blake. I read him Shakespeare's plays. He does not need sheltering and pandering to, as a normal child. He does not need to have evil and passion and terror and glory diluted to sugary pastels, he does not need that deceit. He will know the world as it is, not as a nauseating lie of smiling faces and adults lisping baby-talk, and pigs and ducks who can sing. It is my task to deliver him the world as it is.

*

In January 1976 Stephen wants us to get married. I say yes. I partly do not believe it is happening. I meet his parents who are polite to me; their house is large and sparsely furnished. They ask my age and say how terribly young I am and am I really sure? While they say this they look at Stephen. He tells me after that they are concerned I may not have much in common with him. We are pulling off our clothes as he tells me, we both laugh, what we have in common is, we can't stop fucking together. Stephen has money to buy a house, he has £3,000 left by his grandmother, and savings from his teaching.

The house has a beautiful bay window at the back, looking into the garden. An old couple lived there before, all the doors and woodwork are painted brown, on the walls are large faded geometric patterns. 'We can do it up ourselves,' says Stephen. 'It'll be fun. When we get round to it.' But he is busy at school with all the changes, and after school with meetings and so on. He wants me to stop working at the geriatric home and go on courses. Get some qualifications, have an education and fulfilling work.
'I want you to have everything you've missed,' he says. 'I want to give it to you.' But he doesn't. He wants me to have what he wants me to have; what he thinks I should have. To begin with I keep my job; partly because I don't trust any of it, I am not convinced that it is real or can last, and my job is OK. £35 a week. I save the money; I still have it. It is under a floorboard in the attic. One day Stephen asks

me what I am doing with my pay. When I say I am saving it, he wants to know what for.

'In case,' I tell him. 'It may be needed.' He takes out his filing drawer then and spreads all his papers on the table, and asks me to listen carefully. He shows me his pay-slips for the last year, how much he earns. His bank account statements, his money in trust funds, the value of the house.

'Half of this is yours,' he says. 'Half of everything – the house, the bank, everything. That's what being married is. We share everything. Your name is on the mortgage – Mr and Mrs Beech.'

'But can I spend it?' I ask.

'What d'you mean?'

'Can I spend that money?'

'Of course you can,' he says. 'Both our names are on the cheque book, aren't they? Go to the bank and draw out the money; go and buy a new coat, and pay by cheque. We're married, Olla.'

'But what if I spent it all?'

He smiles as if I am a child. 'What could you spend it all on? That would be an awful lot of shoes and coats!'

'But this house,' I say. 'If there is all this money why are we not having the house decorated? We can have central heating. We can have carpets on the stairs, and a new bath. Proper cupboards in the kitchen – a freezer – a new cooker.'

He is staring at me as if I have dropped from the moon. 'Is that what you want?'

'A nice house? Yes!'

'But – '

'I want it to look lovely – pictures, ornaments, beautiful furniture – '

'But it's not important, Olla. Stuff like that isn't important.'

'Oh, I'm sorry. I should be grateful, then. It isn't an old barn. It isn't a seedy attic in a rundown hotel. It's good enough for me, eh?'

'I don't mean it like that.' He does, but is embarrassed.

'If this house is half mine, and we have some money,' I say, 'I want to make it nice.'

'Of course,' he says. 'We'll decorate it together.'

'No. You're too busy. I'll decorate it.'

He doesn't argue.

I buy books and magazines telling how to make your house beautiful, showing pictures, giving directions. It leads to more argument.

146

When I come home from work I put on overalls and work at stripping the walls and sanding the woodwork, and when he comes in he wants us to sit and talk and have a drink together, or he wants me to accompany him to a meeting, and then to the pub for a drink with his friends. At weekends he wants me to stay in bed for hours, and then to sell communistic newspapers, to go to demonstrations – even to go for walks.

'I've told you, I don't want to go for a walk. I hate walking. It's pointless.'

'It's good for you. Fresh air, exercise, it clears your head – *try* it.'

'No. I want to go to the shops and look at carpets.'

'You're obsessed with the house,' he says. 'It's an obsession. You must stop it.' He says we must get a decorator and pay him to do the house if it matters so much to me – that would be the only solution. But what he does is to get two boys from his school who need to earn some money, who can come at weekends and paint over the old wallpaper. They are not decorators.

'I don't want painted walls,' I tell him. 'I want paper, I want paper to match the curtains and carpets, I want it doing properly.'

'*Why?*' he keeps asking. 'Why does it matter? It's entirely trivial. What can it possibly matter if the walls are white or blue or covered in orange triangles?'

'You wouldn't like orange triangles.'

'OK – but anything within reason would do.'

At last he says he thinks he has a solution; I should stop work and do the house. If it means so much to me, I should do it, properly and creatively, as my work for six months. 'But who will pay me?' I say. He is exasperated. 'You don't need to be paid. What I earn is yours – '

I have £512 saved up, I have not been buying anything out of my own wages for months. It is hidden, I have it to fall back on. So I agree; and he tells me also how much I am permitted to spend, no more than £1,000. He has a lot more in the bank. I say, 'It won't be enough to do everything. Good carpets are expensive.' He looks startled. He tells me to do what I can with that much, and then we will take stock.

So I do. I am happy, then. I start as soon as he goes out to work in the morning. I visit shops and showrooms, I measure and match and select. I buy sewing machine. I do the lounge and one bedroom:

stripping, painting, papering, carpeting. I make curtains, cushions, bedspread. I buy furniture, pictures, mirrors, lamps. I select a three-piece suite, but it cost £450. So I have to ask him for more money.
'We've got a sofa already.'
'It's old.'
'But it's comfy – I bought that second-hand when I first left home.'
'It's brown. It doesn't go with anything.'
'I can't believe how much you're spending,' he says, but he agrees. I won't let him go in the rooms I am working on till they are done, I want to surprise him.

When he sees the rooms he says they are beautiful. 'Too beautiful to live in.' I ask what he means and he says he is glad he married me, because I am so different. I think he is reassuring himself that he really did choose me. The lounge *is* beautiful: pale green and white walls, in a small dappled pattern; white woodwork; moss green carpet and two gorgeous rugs in reds, greens, old gold; green and gold regency stripe curtains; the suite white, with jewel-coloured silk cushions, ruby, gold, emerald, turquoise, sapphire. An antique mirror in a gilt frame over the mantlepiece.

Some time later he explains to me that he has a difficulty with my rooms because they look opulent. 'It seems like bad taste.'
'Bad taste?'
'No, not bad taste. I don't mean that. What I mean is really screwed up, it's not rational – '
What he means in the end, is that since many people live in poverty, in ugly surroundings, it is bad taste to make your surroundings beautiful. When I ask him then how he can justify living in a pleasantly situated, expensive house instead of a dingy slum, he says, 'I know. I know. That's what I said. It's illogical, it's crap.'
'But my decorations make you feel guilty. If you lived in this house but kept the ugly old wallpaper and brown paint, you wouldn't feel guilty?'
'That's the conclusion I've come to. It's completely hypocritical.'
'So what do you want me to do?'
'Carry on. Carry on decorating. You're quite right, it's stupid having the money in the bank; if I'm guilty I should give it away, not just hoard it. And you're doing something artistic – creative – with it. You have a real eye for colour. You should do an art course – design, something like that.'

When I draw more money out of the account, for tiles for the kitchen, I note that he has written a cheque for five hundred. He has given it to a charitable group who are providing farm holidays for inner-city children. I ask him if that eases the guilt of the house and he says no, it is all dishonest anyway. His friends' houses would have been easier for him to live in, I suppose: untidy, grubby, with books and papers littered everywhere, posters stuck to the walls with drawing pins. Shabby houses that no one takes any pride in. They can *pretend* they are poor in them, but of course they aren't, they have plenty of heat and light and food. Plenty.

*

Daniel knows what he must face – but he also does not know. It's why he's mine. I am here to remind him, to lead and teach and help and unravel. He is only a baby, but his imagination must encompass all the pain of the world. He is only a baby, knowledge lies curled in him like an oak tree in an acorn. He contains it all and it will grow, but for now he does not know it consciously; does the fledgling curled in the egg know it will grow to an eagle with talons to tear, wings to soar over mountain ranges? It does not need to know, it simply grows into its predestined shape.
That's how he is. He will become vast. But I am his nourishment. I am the white of the egg, to feed him; I am the leaf-mould the acorn beds itself down in. I am his mother.

My life is fodder for him. He absorbs it as he absorbs vitamins from his dinner. I must yield myself up entirely, giving all that I know and am and have been. In being consumed by him, I move my own small understandings, risks, griefs, discoveries, into a realm beyond myself, where they are capable of making a sense my own brain cannot encompass.

I see it in bursts. It may be like music. My life, my notes – arhythmic, scattered, with passages of insistent repetition, blank gaps of silence – passed on to him, are simply the score for one instrument in the orchestra. In him, the entire orchestra will play. And my sad, seeking, tuneless notes will play again with a whole world of sound rising and falling in harmony around them, they will have their place in beauty, they will make sense; and yet they will be unchanged. No trick, no conversion; my notes remain mine. But his imagination puts them into the context which provides harmony and meaning, my song becomes part of a glorious symphony.

149

This is what Daniel is. The composer, the conductor, who brings together all the scattered notes and, by encompassing them all, makes perfection, the music of the spheres.

I feed his mind with stories. My own. The newspaper. The radio. I feed him with knowledge, so that he will suck up its pith and his mind will unfurl and start to grow, to the point where he can simply absorb from the earth, from the air, knowledge of all humanity. My efforts are like those of a mother with an ordinary baby, who teaches him to hold a spoon, to guide food to his mouth. In her lifetime he will eat things she has not dreamed of, in places she has never been. But his skill in eating began with her.

I tell him how I left my father's house.
Tadek died in the early spring.
They carry him to church in a thin, splintering wooden box; they dig into the sodden thawing earth and bury him. I leave that night. I take a sack with my blanket, bread, cheese, a knife, a screw-topped bottle I fill with milk, matches, my father's jacket and his boots. They are too big for me but stronger and warmer than my own. And it means I won't ever dare to come back. I take the clock; I think I could sell it.
I walk all night. I walk into the forest because it is easier to hide. I walk along the track, it is too thick and dark among the trees. My feet are soaked in the freezing muddy ruts. I walk as fast as I can, without stopping. Once I slip and fall, and my clothes are drenched. The track runs straight between the trees, there is a dim line of sky above it, everything else is black. No stars, no moon. Suddenly there is a big dark shape in the track; as it gets closer it interferes with the line of the sky. I stop and stare till my eyes ache with strain. It is a bus. Maybe foresters, or gypsies. The track is not fit for vehicles, maybe it is abandoned. I am afraid there may be dogs.
I force my way into the thickness of the forest but the noise is deafening, branches snapping, twigs cracking, mud squelching underfoot – and I can make no headway, the sharp lower branches of the pines stick out like turnstiles that will not turn, arms holding me back every time I try to move. A twig pokes my eye, so it smarts and closes and fills with tears. I back out to the track again. I must walk past the bus. Should I run, and get it over with, or creep? I want to run but I could slip and fall again, which would put me at their

mercy. I strain for sound. Nothing. Slowly I edge past it, it fills the track.

When I am half-way along it a man's voice suddenly says, 'Lise?' And a woman sleepily answers, 'Hush, I'm here, go back to sleep.' I freeze, then creep on; I am past it, I keep moving. Their voices were warm and gentle. I am trembling and crying, my toes are so cold I have lost their feelings. I stumble on along the track, the grey strip of sky above it lightens, a dull grey dawn is coming. I have to find a hiding place.

I force my way in between the trees, it helps me a little to be able to see. I crawl and wriggle my way beneath low branches, so that there is no tell-tale track of broken branches where I have been. I turn and scuffle the ground behind me with a stick, to hide where I have crawled. I crawl in and in, trying to keep a straight line. Once I am in the trees and have lost sight of the track, I am afraid I will not find it again; then I would be crawling between these trees until I die. This fear stops me going any deeper. I crawl beneath branches to spread my sack on the ground between two trunks, wrap myself in my blanket and lie down.

I do not sleep. The cold keeps me awake, also fear. I am straining after any sound. Once I hear singing: men's voices, they come closer then fade out of hearing, marching singing along the track. It starts to rain. The rain patters gently on to the trees, they grow so thick it hardly penetrates, only falls in persistent drops on certain spots. It fills the place with sound which I find comforting – yet it is dangerous because it muffles other sound.

It is so dim and dark I cannot tell when night is falling. I eat and drink. I want to start moving again, I'm very cold. At last the gloom is so thick I can't see my own feet. I put my blanket in the sack and crawl towards the track. It is night. I begin to walk again.

That is my first day. I move steadily by night and hide by day. I always travel straight, and when the track forks I take left and right forks alternately. The village must be as far behind me as possible. No one must see me; no one must be able to report having sighted me.

I am not sure how far he will pursue me. He will want his boots and coat back, he will want me for cooking and cleaning. He has said soon I will be earning my living, and that I can keep him in his old age. But I think he may not even bother. He may assume I will just return in a few days to take my beating. He may be glad to be rid of me. He may just be drunk.

So I walk and hide, walk and hide, and no one ever comes after me. But by the fourth day my bread and cheese is gone; the milk is long gone, I fill my bottle at streams, or puddles in the track. There is nothing in the forest to eat. I decide to walk by day, to look for sign to a village. Twice I see people approaching in the distance, and hide in the trees till they are gone. One group has a dog which begins to yap and bark excitedly in my direction; a man shouts to it to come and leave the damned squirrels alone.

In the afternoon there is a sign to a village. I follow; the track becomes a road. I examine myself, trying to tell how I will look to others. Filthy, wet and muddy. I will say I have been playing, if anyone asks me; playing football with my brother. I hide my sack in a tree which I mark by making a tear in the bark. I take the clock in my pocket, hoping to exchange it for food.

The village is small and empty. There is a baker's shop with a few loaves in the window, and one other store, with a sign for tobacco on the wall outside. I walk past the baker's, my legs are trembling with hunger. But if I exchange the clock for bread, I will have nothing left to get cheese. If I exchange it for cheese in the shop that does not sell bread – I can't think, I am so hungry. I go in the baker's and ask to buy some bread with my clock.

The woman looks at me. 'Where did you get that?'

'It's mine. I've always had it.'

She takes it off me and examines it. 'Does it work?'

'Yes.'

She puts two loaves on the counter and – I cannot help myself, I am starving – I begin to cram one in my mouth. She stares at me. 'I should call the police,' she says.

'Please – I haven't done anything wrong. Believe me, please.' I begin to get out of the shop, but she calls. 'All right. You can have a drink to wash down your bread.' She gives me a bottle of lemonade from a crate by the door.

I go straight back to the forest. I eat one whole loaf and drink half the sweet lemonade. I curse myself for not bringing more food with me. There were two sacks of potatoes in the shed at home, I should have brought potatoes – but then I would have had to make a fire.

I shouldn't have run away in spring. In autumn there would have been stuff in the fields, at harvest time there would have been more lying around.

I have to get farther away. But I have to have food. Or money. I have nothing else to sell. I should have got more for the clock. I should have asked for cash. I am afraid to go back to the village in case she has phoned the police. I head back into the forest and continue in my old direction.

But the forest comes to an end. My track is the only one, and it turns into a road; looking ahead, I can see where the trees end and give way to fields. It is getting dark.

I come out of the forest and there is nothing but fields, flat fields stretching out into the darkness all round. I keep walking, glad of the darkness which hides me a little in this exposed countryside. There is a wind, it is colder than the forest. I look in the ditch for a place to sleep but when I try it with my foot it is full of water, there is nothing to do but keep going. At last there is a light up ahead – when I get nearer I see that it is not next to the road, but away down a track. I can see the dark shape of an unlit building beside the track, between me and the house. A barn. I have to get out of the wind, even to shelter by its wall would be a relief. I hope I might get inside.

And so I do. It is silent and black inside, smelling of straw and diesel. I feel my way along the stone wall, there is a big metal thing, high and wide, strangely shaped. Then I feel the rubber of a tyre and realize it is a farm machine, or tractor. I feel my way, climb up on to its seat – and there I fall asleep.

Daniel, the story does not change. It just goes on and on. Walking from one place to the next, begging food, stealing it where I can. And the first time I think of working for it: I clean windows and chop kindling at a farmhouse and they give me a cooked meal and warm place to sleep. I stay there a couple of days, till they can't think of any other jobs for me. They give me two old shirts.

When I reach the marshes, it rains – always it is raining or else a mist hangs over the water and trees, a very white mist which the shapes of men and trees suddenly come forward in, are suddenly there, where they have not been. The mist makes everything quiet – my clothes are damp, my skin is like a frog's, cold and sticky to touch. At night it is very black, black as suffocation, the stars and moon are cloaked in cloud, blackness presses on the earth. And I am always hungry.

*

The health service women who come to the house do not understand Daniel.

I see the wisdom of this; I know it is safer for him if I am the only one to know his mission and his power. Nevertheless I cannot suppress in myself irritation at their blindness.

The physiotherapist comes weekly to check his progress and teach me new exercises. She is young and smart and very sure of herself. She wears a dogtooth-check suit with padded shoulders. She hangs the jacket over a chair and slightly pulls up the sleeves of her skinny black sweater before she touches Daniel, as if he might soil her, as if to separate her hands from the rest of herself. She stretches and bends his legs and arms without speaking, she has the look of a musician tuning an instrument. She is good at her job, I do not doubt her skill or concentration. But she never looks at his face. Never greets him, never smiles. These are small things but he would like it, it would sweeten a little the sourness of the indignities he suffers at her hands. In a petty way I look forward to the expression on her face when she sees the slack little limbs she has automatically manipulated swell and ripple with musculature; when she sees him in power, straddling the world.

The health visitor is worse. She sympathizes. She is fat, damp, sprawling. She comes in in a welter of bags and coat and hat, taking up too much space, not knowing where to put things down. She plunges at Daniel – 'Oh, the poor little lad – let's have a hold of him, come to Auntie Joyce, my chuck.' Once she's holding him she can't walk to a chair, and I have to bring one and position it for her. Her thighs hang over the sides of the seat. She is hot and breathless, with a tang of stale sweat.

'Isn't it cruel, eh?' she says, shaking her double chins over Daniel's sweet head. 'A lovely little baby like this, it breaks your heart don't it, to think he'll never run about with his little friends in the garden?' I must be civil, I understand this; the anger and impatience I suffer are nothing in comparison to the indignities Daniel endures, crushed against her enormous bosoms, bathed in her heated, foody breath. I must be cunning, a normal mother with a normal baby. We must arouse no suspicions. But I time her visit to help myself through it; she has only once stayed longer than fifteen minutes, she is always in a rush and always late, and I never offer any difficulties which might detain her.

'You're managing ever so well,' she tells me. 'You really are. I don't know how you keep so cheerful – poor little mite he is. Still, he'll be off to nursery in another year, eh, you'll find the load a bit lighter then I hope.'

I have never complained of a heavy load, nor have I appeared cheerful in her company. Nor is my son a 'poor little mite'. Wrapped in her fat ignorance she struggles into coat, hat, bag, blunders at the doorway with further cries of, 'Makes you wonder what God's up to, don't it, letting innocent little children suffer like that.' Nor does he suffer. Or, only the indignities of being alive which all must suffer. And the presence of fools such as she.

Off to nursery in another year. The social worker tells me all handicapped children go to nursery from two years of age. That's the state provision.

'He's not handicapped.'

She stares at me then laughs.

'Sorry – disabled. Although I'm told that's not the word either, any more, it's too pejorative. Differently abled, I think is the current favourite.' She shakes her head. 'All this jargon.'

I do not argue any further. It would not be wise to give any of them a hint, although at times I long to. At times I get tired of all the pretending, and of their insulting assumptions. I wonder how I must deal with this expectation of attendance at nursery. Disabled children are collected from their homes in a minibus at 8.30, taken to a special school, and kept there till 3.30. I have been invited to visit this school; I have no wish to do so.

He will not like to go away from me for seven hours a day. Especially not to be with children who howl, drool, have fits, and cannot walk. To be with young nursery assistants who will sing silly songs and wave bits of coloured cardboard in his face? It is up to me to protect him from this, although I cannot yet tell how to do the thing. He appears in this guise for his own protection, but it does not mean he must be corralled and ghettoed in a school of freaks. His heart is not yet strong enough to contain that much unnecessary sorrow. I have asked him for a solution. It will come, in time.

155

CHAPTER ELEVEN

William steals a fish

Over three weeks passed before William was able to make time to visit Molly Hill again. He wanted to take something for the baby, but could think of nothing appropriate; all he had were his books, his star charts and his clothes. His purse had never been large enough to purchase the private supplies of tea, sugar and other luxuries that most of the officers indulged in, and he was grateful, in a way, for the moral simplicity this afforded him. There was a terrible shortage of clothes amongst the convicts, and he considered giving her a night-shirt to make into baby clothes. But such a garment seemed slightly improper; he decided it would be better to ask her what she needed, and then see if it was in his power to obtain it.

He went to the women's camp first thing in the morning, leaving his work gang to start without him. The place was quiet and empty. Some of the tents had been replaced by huts, built by the convicts themselves from wattle and daub. They looked rickety and insubstantial. He passed only a couple of older female convicts on his way through. When he called Molly's name outside her tent, she opened the flap and came out, gesturing to him to be quiet.

'They're asleep.'

'Who?'

'Alicia – the baby. And Hester.' At his confused look, she added, 'I share with her. She was hurt in a fall yesterday.'

William nodded. Molly sat herself on a log which had been positioned at the side of the tent, out of the wind, and he sat beside her. She was thinner, he noticed, and she had put her hair up, which made her look older.

'Are you well?'

She shrugged. 'I'm always tired. There's nothing good to eat – it was better on the ships.'

He wondered what she meant; she must be thinking of the time before they sailed, when Phillip ordered a diet of fresh meat and vegetables for all the convicts, to strengthen them for the voyage.

'It's very quiet. Where are all the women?'

'They take them down to the beach, looking for shells. Next week I shall have to go too.'

Shells. Of course. Lime was the one ingredient for mortar that had not so far been discovered here. Phillip had a party of convicts working on a brick kiln, but they needed to crush shells for lime, since no other supplies could be found.

'I shouldn't think you will be fit to go next week – and what about Alicia?'

'I must take her with me. That's what the others do. They have to sit on the rocks with their skirts trailing in the water, feeding their babies like the savages do – '

William shook his head. 'You need to get your strength back first.'

She laughed bitterly. 'There's no choice. Unless you are old, or dying – or the favourite of some officer.' She was not looking at him. The up-swept hair made her thin neck look long.

'What happens to them?'

'Oh. They're all right. They're housekeepers. Tent-keepers, I s'pose. Bed-warmers.'

Nearly all the officers, and the captains, and the sailors, had wives at home. Well they would never consider, anyway, marrying convict women. Of course not. To be 'housekeepers' must be the height of their aspirations. How much better and fairer it would be if all the women equally served their term of punishment, and were then given their freedom. They could choose what to do with it – turn to honest ways of making a living such as sewing and washing, or work on the land, grow their own food and raise their children in healthy independence. If they were humanely treated as prisoners, if they were given decent food and adequate clothing and shelter, if they were given work appropriate to their health and abilities, then they would not need to turn to prostitution. But to be sent dragging shells along a beach, weeks after a difficult childbirth, on inadequate rations –

He checked himself. Everyone was on the same basic rations, weren't they?

'What food do you get?'

She reeled it off wearily: 'Eight pounds flour, five pounds salt pork, three pints peas, six ounces butter per week.' It didn't contain many delicacies, certainly, but it was enough to keep body and soul together. And those women who wanted more . . . traded sexual favours to get it. Their choice, William told himself, their *choice* to be officers' favourites. They are envied by the other women.

'If I were –' he hesitated, and she looked at him, which made him blush. 'If I were to ask Dr Worgan – I'm sure he would agree that you're too weak for a work gang, at present. Perhaps some other kind of work might be found.'

'All right.'

'Have you thought at all – about what I said before? If you open your heart to God, and ask for forgiveness and guidance . . .'

'Guidance,' she said. 'I haven't got much choice really, have I? Not exactly a free spirit!' She giggled, suddenly looking much younger, and William had a momentary awful vision of her freedom, of what freedom might mean to her. Was he not an innocent, with his notions of convicts' honest toil and pride in self-sufficiency? Had he not been given a graphic account of what these women did with freedom?

'The surgeon said they were sick for lack of air . . . but then they gathered themselves up from swooning on the floor and came up through the open gratings like monkeys hot for the sailors . . .' Ralph Clark's words echoed in his head. That was their freedom, the pursuit of unimaginable, unquenchable lust. The laughing woman in front of him became a she-devil, one that he was dangerously close to, who would besmirch him, drag him down . . .

'What is it?' she said.

'Nothing. I – is it true? On the *Lady Penrhyn*, did the women prisoners, when they were loosed, pursue – pursue the sailors?'

'Pursue?' she said. 'They give us food.' She was looking at him with a little crease of frown between her dark eyebrows. 'Don't you understand? We was trapped down there, in the dark often as not; nowt but stinking rations to eat, not enough blankets to go round, and some of us without even a petticoat to cover us. Some was mad, and some was sick, with children howling and drunks cursing, you'd think you was in hell. You can't sleep, you can't get out, your mind's jittering and shaking like a sick dog – and there's one way out.'

She looked at him expectantly, but he waited for her to continue. 'One way out. If a sailor takes a fancy to you, maybe, just maybe, he'll get you out. When you go up to exercise on deck, maybe he'll pull you into a corner somewhere and you won't have to go back down into that stinking dark with the other cattle. Or maybe when he comes down to visit you in that hell-hole, he'll bring you a drop of rum, as'll make it more tolerable; or a bit o' fish, or some dainty he's picked up from shore. If you didn't have them things you'd rather be dead. I would. If there wasn't no rum – '

He imagined her, in the hold. Her dead baby. He sighed, and shook his head. 'Sometimes it is not easy to see how these things work. Ralph Clark, a lieutenant on one of the transports – was shocked. He said the women were – hot – for the sailors.' He was embarrassed to feel the colour flooding his own cheeks.

'Hot?' She hooted with laughter. 'Aye, we was hot. With sweating down in that airless hole, and with children pissing and vomiting on us, and with nightmares and horrors that we'd never get out but go down like rats in a box when she sank, and with thirst, wi' burning thirst – for rum, or even for fresh water if they'd give it us. We was hot, right enough. But not for bloody men!'

William got to his feet, and paced the space between Molly's tent and her neighbour's. He could feel her laughing, quizzical eyes on him, burning into his skin.

'The sailors took advantage of you,' he said. 'The captain should have been more vigilant.'

'I told you – ' her voice was sharper, irritated. 'They give us hope. A tot of rum. An orange. You got no idea. They kept us going.'

'But it's a sin!' he shouted, turning back to face her. 'Don't you understand, a sin? In the eyes of God; the sin of fornication.' He searched her face for acknowledgement, but she lowered her eyes and her expression became both blank and stubborn, drained of vitality.

'I'm not criticizing *you*,' he pleaded, 'but surely you see how wrong it was? They bought you like – like beasts, for trifles.'

Her averted face remained set. William waited a moment, then picked up his haversack.

'I'll have a word with Dr Worgan about the shell gathering.'

She did not reply.

Worgan agreed readily that a woman who had suffered a difficult child-birth could be excused shell-gathering.

'Mind you,' he said, 'they can't be said to be working hard. Have you watched them?' William shook his head. 'They wander along the beach with their baskets – and stop at every opportunity, for a chat, or a rest, or to tend their children. Or to dodge into the bushes with the first sailor that comes along.'

William had an absurd urge to argue with Worgan; to point out that if a woman *did* dodge into the bushes, it was for an extra crust for her child, or a tot of rum, or even the forlorn and distant hope of escape into marriage. It was not because she was aflame with bestial lust, it was not because *she* was a sinner. It was the men who were the sinners. But perhaps Worgan already knew this. It dawned on William that perhaps his own innocence made him the only one fool enough to believe Ralph Clark's tales.

Worgan continued, 'The result of their days' work is often less than a sackful of shells.'

'But it is cold and wet – and the weight of a baby – '

Worgan shrugged.

'So, what should she do then?' asked William. 'What other labour is there for women? Sewing, perhaps?'

Worgan didn't know, and William discovered, through questioning other officers in a general way, that there was in fact no other women's work. There was no organized sewing work, due to the lack of materials.

He called by her tent next morning and told her she need not go shell gathering. She was preoccupied with the baby, who was screaming.

'She's hungry. I haven't enough milk for her.'

'Why?'

'I need better food,' she snapped. 'How am I to get strong on salt pork and mouldy flour? The sailors used to bring us fish, but now – '

The sailors had been banned from coming ashore because of the havoc they wrought in the women's camp.

'There isn't any better food,' he said stupidly.

'There's fish aplenty in the sea,' she said, sitting herself down and getting out her breast for the child. William watched the slack pendulous softness of her flesh. He wanted to lift and cradle it in his hands, to stroke it . . . He made himself turn away. It was the usedness of her body he ached for, the hurts and indignities it had endured – her thin bony little ankles that had been so swollen and puffy. He sat down on the floor at a distance from her, mortified by his own sudden physical reaction to her presence, and trying to disguise it with his jacket. But she was looking at the baby, not him.

'I must have summat good to eat.'

When he jerked awake, sweating, after his first hour of exhausted sleep that night, it was those words that were sounding in his head. 'I must have summat good to eat.' What was she saying? That she would find a man to get her fish? Her method of payment William could guess at only too well. He was nauseated, and, what was worse, his erect member was straining against the coarse blankets, trembling and aching with need. He turned his head to stare at the still, snoring lump of Tench's body, then eased himself over on to his side, so that his back was to Tench. As he clasped his fingers around himself the vision of her pale, soft, slack breast leapt to his mind, and a wave of heat flooded his body.

He lay motionless, wretched, as if stillness could make his body disappear. Molly must learn to live off her rations, as the others had to. The child must suck on a crust.

But he thought of dinners he had eaten; of tables laden with ham and fish and game, vegetables and sweetmeats, fruits, cheeses, wine. Of the Governor's and captains' tables, groaning under a weight of expensive delicacies from England, Rio and the Cape; of the officers' private stores of spirits, tea and sugar, of the rare and delicious eggs provided by the officers' fowls. She would not have had an egg for over a year, now. Didn't Christ himself acknowledge that the hungers of the body must be answered before the hungers of the spirit? Apart from demonstrating His miraculous powers, what else were the loaves and fishes about? People must be fed, or hunger distracts them from spiritual pursuits. Hunger must be fed. It was the same for all the convicts – their crimes were the result of hunger; their thieving, their prostitution, their seeking oblivion in drink. But no – they sought oblivion because of their *spiritual* starvation, because they did not know their lives had worth and meaning. That was why it was important to read the Bible with Stokoe, Clough and Barnes. That was why it was important to teach Molly Hill about Christ's love.

He wiped his sticky fingers on the blanket, almost crying with shame. He would get food for her. Or what right did he have to ask her to make that great effort of contrition and love, and open her heart to God?

Next evening, after the day's work, he walked down to the beach. If it was possible to obtain a fish, he would get one for Molly Hill. Darkness was falling earlier now, it was dusk by six and on a cloudy night like tonight black by seven. On the quiet water a half-dozen floating lights like fireflies hung and made reflections: the natives, fishing in their canoes where they always kept a fire alight. Perhaps they were afraid of the dark. Bradley had told him they made the fires on a small bed of clay, and cooked their catch as soon as they took it from the sea.

The evening, the beach, the quiet sound of the water brought his last encounter with Bradley forcibly to mind. On the return voyage from Broken Bay they had carried out their duties together with a minimum of words, carefully avoiding any contact. And their paths had not crossed since William had come back on shore. It was nonsense, he suddenly decided. That moment over the glow-worm on the beach: it was nothing. Nothing had been said or done that either could reproach himself with. This awkwardness, this sense of difficulty between them, was entirely inappropriate. A thousand things can happen in a day; why take one, the impression of two or three minutes at most, and make that significant enough to alter or even break a friendship? Bradley may have been feeling unwell; he may, like William himself, have had a moment of dizziness, losing his balance. He may have suffered a sudden wave of homesickness, he may even have been thinking of his wife. It would be a poor thing to sacrifice a friendship for a moment of confusion. I must see Bradley this week, he decided. I'll take a boat out to the *Sirius* – it's up to me to show him that our friendship is unaltered, that I have not taken the wrong impression from that night.

In the darkness ahead he made out some movement, splashing and muffled voices. There were sailors dragging a small boat up out of the water, whispering loudly to each other to be quiet and have a care. William hung back, trying to identify the boat; from one of the transports, most likely. Their captains were more lax than Hunter or Ball. The sailors were lifting the boat over the rocks that separated the beach from the woods. One of them stumbled and cursed loudly in the darkness. William quickened his pace and caught up with them.

'Who goes there, men?' They froze, and William repeated his question, adding, 'I have seen the boat, it's no use hiding.' He was standing with his back to the sea, staring after them into the dark woodland. They must have realized he could not see, because there was a sudden crash and flurry of movement as they dropped the boat and scattered. Silence. They had vanished among the trees and in this inky darkness he would never find them. He could at least identify the boat. He moved forwards with outstretched hands, and soon discovered the curved wooden side of an eight-oar boat. It was under the trees, and so dark he could not even make out the name. Feeling about on the floor of the boat, in the hopes of finding some personal possessions to identify the sailors, his hands encountered something wet and cold and unmistakeable – fish. His exploring fingers told him quickly that the bottom of the boat was full of fish. The sailors would be bringing them in to exchange for things the convicts had: parrots, natives' weapons, sex.

William strained his ears for any sound of the sailors. He had come down to the beach with the intention of procuring fish – he had thought of offering a part of his rations to a fisherman, in exchange for his catch. But of course it was the sailors who were used to fishing – not the convicts, not the marines. Few who were billeted on the land would have the skill or patience or even knowledge to fish.

And now – a boat full of fish. He thought of Molly Hill's pale tired face. Providence had answered his prayer. He grasped a couple of the firm cold bodies and stuffed them into his haversack. He paused again, listening for movement, then clambered back over the rocks and hurried down the beach. He would give them to her in the morning.

He woke very early, but made himself wait until the working gang of women had been herded up and marched down to the beach. He was so much looking forward to her pleasure, to her surprised smile as he gave her the fish, to her grateful relief that she need not resort to her old bad ways of fending off hunger, that he could not keep the grin off his own face. He longed to see her smile.

When the women's camp was empty he hurried to her tent. He'd got the convicts' tools with him in a bag over his shoulder; he wanted to be there to start them off on a new patch of ground this morning – he could still be there before them, it would only take a couple of minutes to give Molly the fish.

She was alone in the tent. He looked around in surprise for the baby then saw that she was asleep in the curled nest of Molly's blanket. Molly was brushing her hair.

'I've brought you something. Look.' He unfastened his haversack and drew out the sacking bundle in which he had wrapped the fish. She took it from him carefully and unwrapped it.

'Oh.' She looked up. 'Thank you.' He watched her face. He wanted her to smile. She wrapped the fish again and tucked them under some clothing on the tea-chest.

'They're last night's – '

She nodded. 'I'll cook them today.' Then she laughed. 'I didn't think you would – '

'I don't want you to – '

'To what?' She approached him. Her eyes were shining, amused. 'What *are* you carrying?'

'Oh – it's for work – the axes – '

'Well put them down, why don't you?'

Without knowing why, William obeyed. The top two buttons of her dress, he noticed, were unfastened. As if she had not quite finished dressing. Or perhaps she had just fed the child. She noticed his glance, and put her hand to her thin throat. Then her fingers were moving quickly, easily, unbuttoning all the way down. He frowned and raised his eyes to her face.

'I'm sorry – is it the baby – ?'

'No,' she said, correcting him, 'you.' She moved closer, and took his hand between hers. 'You are shy, aren't you?' Raising his hand she placed it inside her bodice, on her breast.

'I – I – ' The skin was so soft it was like petals – like something melting. She was smiling. He wrenched his hand free. 'No! Oh no, Molly – I don't want – I brought you food so that you wouldn't have to – '

'Don't you want to?' she said mildly.

'The fish is a gift – not – not – to buy – '

She moved back and sat on the tea-chest, watching him. 'I don't mind,' she said.

'It's not right. It's not what I meant.'

'Don't you like me?'

'Yes – but how can you be a – a fit mother to Alicia? If you – '

'You'll bring me more,' she said.

'I'll bring you more anyway – I promise you won't go hungry – '

She shook her head obstinately. 'Why should you? Less I give you summat for it?' She put her hand inside her bodice and scratched beneath her breast, he saw it quiver. At the base of her neck the flesh was sunken and her bones stood out. Such a combination of thinness and fleshiness . . . Her bare ankles made a lump rise in his throat.

'I don't mind it,' she said. 'I like you.' She smiled mischievously. 'Like you better'n Stokoe.'

'No.' William was filled with despair. 'I'm not like him, you mustn't think all men are – '

There was a moment's silence, then she stood up and said flatly, 'Well it's human nature, far as I'm concerned.'

'You don't understand,' William said. 'You don't understand at all – '

And because she was turning away, because he knew she *did* really understand, he knew her thin face so well, he knew those dark semi-circles under her eyes and the slight down on her cheek, he knew she must understand – he went over to her and put his hand on her shoulder. 'Molly, you don't understand – '

'I understand that,' she said, and cupped her hand around his balls.

As he stood staring at her in horror, unable to speak, she laughed. 'What are you afraid of? Come on, you'll feel better for it. Honest!' She was undoing his buttons with her free hand. He tried to speak but his mouth was dry.

'Oh, come on,' she said with weary impatience. 'What's up? *Don't* you like me?' She was pulling at his breeches, her breasts hung out of her dress and swung against her ribs as she moved and he put out his hand to stop them. That softness –

'That's better.' She was squeezing his penis.

'No – no – ' He pushed her hand away, it was terrible, this mustn't be happening – mustn't – mustn't –

'Oh yes,' she said. 'We've had shy ones before. Oh yes – ' She was fumbling with her waistband – suddenly she unfastened something and wriggled out of the dress. The skin of her belly was white and wrinkled – there were a couple of long purple lines, like welts, across it – oh, God! And dark curling hair at the top of her legs. In a sudden gesture of tenderness she put her hand on his cheek.

Oh, her poor wrinkled belly, he knelt to kiss the soft folds of skin, to wonderingly, gently stroke the purple scar – her poor dear body. Tears swam in his eyes.

She spoke softly: 'All right, then, come on now.' She was touching him and he was burying his face in the soft pearly blue-veined skin, burying his face in the milky softness of her breasts, which were so soft it seemed he'd melted into her, her flesh dissolving in soft handfuls.

'Don't cry,' she said. 'Don't cry. Here, now – that's the way, that's the way.' She was touching him – he didn't know what she was doing but he would save her sweet hurt body, its tired softness, he would never let it be hurt again, its folds its tender softness hung about him like curtains of milk, of silk, of sweetness such sweetness such sweetness tears were not enough . . . ah dear God, tears were not – so sweet a flood, light and tears. Light.

She was panting a little. She moved off him. 'There now,' she said, 'that didn't take long. Better?'

She stood up and put on her dress. Curling in upon himself like a worm exposed to the light, William buried his face in his hands and sobbed.

165

STEPHEN

I knew when I saw it, of course. As soon as I saw it, before the midwife grabbed it up and ran off with it. Knew from the way it lay and the look on her face.
And because I had expected it?
Not precisely. I had expected it to be dead.

And then I went on being surprised. Yes, that's accurate – surprised. By the discrepancy between my expectations, and events.
In expecting it to be dead I thought I had anticipated the worst. I did not imagine a worse scenario. Not that its being alive is necessarily worse. Despite the fact that it is irreparably damaged, its being alive would be considered by many to be better. It is closer to the rest of us than the dead; like us, it is alive and travelling towards death, which must be counted a plus. The demands its existence places upon others, and the likelihood of its dying soon, are a minus. As to the quality of its aliveness, what it may be supposed to extract from life – suck, suck, what it may be supposed to *suck* from life, if it were able – well, leave that aside for now.

The second surprise was Olla. Her reaction to the child. Her enthusiasm. Could not have been predicted.
Or is it just that I am blind and insensitive, and more so toward her than any other living being, due to our relationship of man and wife for sixteen years?
Undoubtedly, that is the case.

What I would have predicted would have been the opposite: that upon notification that the child was imperfect she would have closed her eyes and withdrawn. Knowing her fierce hatred for damaged goods of any kind, I would never have imagined her springing to its defence – making light of its disabilities, seeming to intend to love it.
Which expectation on my part undoubtedly reveals the shrivelling dimensions of my own imagination; because I have not been the recipient of her hope or tenderness, I arrogantly assume these qualities are outside her range. If she has pity for the child – well perhaps I should be glad.

And for yourself, Stephen? You feel hope, pity, disappointment, love? No. I think not. All well under control. After my first spontaneous shower of tears for her sake, and the surprised recognition that they

166

were to be stifled not for the usual reason – her view that pity is contemptible – but because she genuinely saw no occasion *for* pity – well, no other response to speak of.

They all go out of the window together, don't they? The more dramatic emotions. Excluded from love and hope, I am also spared pain and anger. I remain dry-eyed. The last time I wept in earnest was for the death of Campfield school. Which tears were also for my own pitiable and destructive culpability. In the end it was me, my blindness, my certainty that because I believed it must be so, it *would* be so, that killed it.
With one simple blow. I invited the papers in. To the school where Robert and I were making peaceful revolution.
Why?
Because the maths inspector was critical; a dinner-lady was making a fuss about swearing; some parents heard a rumour about drugs and took their kids away; the Education Committee were quibbling about exam results. I thought if everyone saw the idealism and optimism that were transforming our school into a brave new world, if they saw the happiness of children who *wanted* to go to school, the first fragile successes of those who'd been branded failures all their lives, if they saw the honestly good intentions of the place, and the furiously hard work of most of the staff, they would support us. I thought that honesty and decency were basic human qualities, and could be appealed to in journalists no less than in anyone else. It was a tenet of faith of the innocent that I was, that I should love and trust my brothers and sisters. I believed that if we told them the truth, they would understand the importance of what was at stake.
In the excitement also, I made love to Anna, intending no harm, knowing my intentions to Olla were good.

It was a kind of innocence, I suppose. When innocence is not just stupid but criminal.

167

CHAPTER TWELVE

A flavour he could not spit out

William avoided the observatory site for some time, concentrating his energies on the redoubt where the big guns from the *Sirius* were to be mounted for defence of the colony, and on the latest batch of requests and directives from Governor Phillip. These instructions were brought in letter form, by runner, or passed through Watkin, who attended the Governor regularly. They directed William to consider ways of fire-proofing the convicts' huts, to draw up plans for roads and bridges, to make decisions on building materials and water supplies. Watkin's presence in the tent every night was beginning to make William feel almost haunted. It was not appropriate, he knew, to reveal to Watkin his belief that the Governor's priorities were wrong – nor, indeed, his dislike of the Governor. And he absolutely shrank from the idea that Watkin or any other of the officers should find out about the incident with Molly Hill; he tried not to think of it himself.

In fact he did *not* think about it, but it haunted him – came seeping into his mind like a pervasive smell, or too-well-known musical refrain, winding itself about his thoughts so that everything was tangled with it, although he never addressed it directly. He prayed for forgiveness, but even as he did so he was avoiding addressing the sin. The knowledge that his prayers were futile made his despair deeper. He had no time, he told himself, to deal with it; to rationally consider what his next step must be. He must hurry on to blasting at the redoubt, to directing a gang how to bore for water on the plot near the Governor's house. Unbidden, visions of her soft hanging breasts, her bony white legs, the shocking dark curls beneath her belly, assaulted him. He did not think of it but was invaded, against his will, by the sight and feel of her soft milky skin with its pale blue rivers of veins and scars. Guilt was a flavour he could not spit out. He must open himself to God, he must consider what to do, he must find out how to put things right. But he could not force himself to address the matter. He should ask Richard Johnson for guidance – but that thought was terrible, he couldn't bear Richard to know what had happened.

When he woke in the morning it seemed that hope was possible; he had the sense that there must be a solution, a way of making amends, if only he could sit down for a moment and consider it. This hope lasted while he took the readings from the barometer and thermometer, recording them neatly under the steadily accumulating record of dates and figures – a tangible achievement, so many days survived and recorded, where records had never been kept before. But it began to dwindle as he set about his scattered, fragmented duties, hurrying about the camp but always, with an almost exaggerated caution, avoiding any proximity to the women's huts; avoiding any danger of seeing her before he knew how he should behave; childishly (he knew it was childish – he could do nothing else) pretending that time was not passing but was somehow suspended or frozen since that day and would remain so, without consequences, until he should choose to act.

He could not avoid Stokoe and the others for ever, and they would be missing their tots of rum. He must not add to his sins by causing a slowing down of the work. Driving himself with this thought, he went up to Point Maskeylene at the end of the week, after a morning spent siting drains. Would she have told Stokoe? Would he be watching, grinning slyly – or even calling out some foul remark? Would he ask William when he planned to visit her again?

William's tormented thoughts were interrupted when he was still half a mile short of the observatory by the sound of crying. High, gasping sobs – maybe a child? He turned off the track and into the woods, following the sound, and almost immediately spotted Barnes. He was crouched at the foot of a tree, face buried in his arms, sobbing convulsively. William was suddenly cold. He should have taken action over this before. Barnes was being bullied – he had guessed it from the start, and now it had come to this. He had failed to protect the boy. He crouched beside him.

'Barnes. What is it? What's happened?'

Barnes looked up blearily, his face was wet and red like a baby's. He tried to steady his breathing but sobs were still shaking his chest. There was a slight movement at the periphery of William's field of vision and turning quickly he saw a big man who froze as he realized he'd been spotted.

'You! Come here!' It was a convict. William had seen him before, a big, thick-necked bull of a man with long dark hair tied back like a sailor's. The man hesitated then stepped forward. A surge of rage brought William to his feet.

'What have you done to him? If you've hurt this boy I'll have you flogged – '

'I never touched 'im.'

'Don't lie to me. I've seen bullies before. And I've seen the marks on him. D'you think I'm blind? D'you think I'm stupid?' William was trembling with anger; he wanted to throw himself at the thug and pummel him with all his strength. 'How *dare* you? What gives you the right to hurt a pathetic boy like this?' Hearing a movement behind him, William turned to see that Barnes was attempting to crawl away between the trees.

'Barnes. Stop there. Don't move.' He wiped his eyes. This anger wasn't helping. 'Tell me your name.'

'McEntire. John.'

'What the devil are you doing up here?'

'I come up after the wild spinach, is all.'

'Wild spinach? Don't you know the Governor has forbidden straggling in the woods? Haven't you got work to do?'

'It's dinner hour.'

It *was* dinner hour, William had forgotten that. 'And where is the spinach? Where is the spinach that you picked?'

'I've no found any yet.' The man lied easily, contemptuously. Behind William, Barnes continued to snivel.

'Where d'you work?'

'Governor's farm.' It was on the other side of the cove.

'And you expect me to believe you took a three-mile walk up here to look for spinach?'

The man didn't reply, staring insolently into the trees above William's head. It was impossible to do anything about him here and now.

'Clear off. Get back down to the farm. And report to Sergeant Knight when you get there. I shall have you punished for this, McEntire.' William turned back to Barnes.

'All right. He's gone. Now tell me what happened.'

Barnes wiped his nose on his sleeve but did not reply. There were livid marks on his dirty neck, a trickle of dried blood by his ear.

'I know he's bullying you. He hurt you, didn't he? Tell me what he did.'

Barnes would not reply. William understood his fear only too well. If he squealed on McEntire, McEntire would find a way of getting his own back. There was no safety for a boy like Barnes here, nowhere he could hide. The memory of his own long, terrified nights at Woolwich came back to William with sickening vividness.

He gave the boy a tot of rum and helped him to his feet. His clothes were filthy, and his breeches were ripped.

'D'you have any others?'

Barnes shook his head.

'I'll see if I can get you some. You can walk? Go down to the stream and wash yourself, and wait for me at the bottom of the path. I just want to see how the others are getting on.'

Stokoe and Clough were sitting in the shade, a small pile of freshly cut branches testifying to their morning's labour. William forced himself to look directly at Stokoe, and was relieved to see that there was nothing other than the usual watchful cunning in his expression.

'Afternoon, Mr Dawes,' he said. 'We've 'ad an awful dry week of it.'

No, Molly Hill had not told him. William passed the rum bottle over to them and glanced around the site. They had clearly been doing some work, although not as much as he might have hoped. When both had taken a swig he rolled a log over and sat before them.

'I want to know about Barnes.'

They exchanged a glance.

'I want to know who's bullying him and why.'

Stokoe shrugged.

'D'you know where he is?' William persisted.

'We're better off wi'out him,' said Clough aggressively. 'He's nowt but trouble.'

'Why does he never have any food?'

Stokoe laughed shortly. 'A chub like Barnes, 'e got nowt – not a pot nor a plate nor a spoon to 'is name. They bilk him.'

'Who?'

Stokoe glanced at Clough. 'That big bastard McEntire's been cooking for a few of 'em.'

'I don't understand.'

'Them wi' no cooking pots. He teks 'is payment in victuals – he teks as much as 'e likes – '

'But is this common?'

Stokoe shrugged. 'It's not easy to come be a cooking pot, round 'ere.'

The bugle sounded for afternoon work to begin, and William waved his hand wearily at them to get on with it. They took another long draught of rum each, then Stokoe returned the near-empty bottle to William's hand. He sat for a moment with his head bowed, listening to them chipping away with their spades. What now? There was Molly Hill. Molly Hill must be seen. There was Barnes waiting at the bottom of the hill, with ripped breeches, no pot, spoon or plate, no hope. There was McEntire, who must be punished in such a way that it did not rebound on Barnes –

'Stokoe!' he called. Stokoe came back over to the log. 'Tell me,' William kept his eyes on Stokoe's boots. The sight of them reminded him that Barnes had been barefoot. They had taken his boots as well. 'Why would McEntire fight with Barnes? Why would he hit him?'

"Ow should Ah know? Ah give McEntire a wide berth, Ah'm no fond of 'is kind.' Stokoe's voice was sneering but his glance flickered to William's face to check his reaction. 'He's one o' your gentlemen of the back door, McEntire – well known fer it.'

'All right. Back to work.' William forced himself to his feet, and followed Stokoe to where he and Clough were working, digging at either side of a huge tree-stump which sat right in the path to what would be the observatory entrance.

'Try chopping some of those roots off, rather than digging them all,' he directed. 'If you can chop or saw through the ones near the surface, it will be easier to shift.' It was quicker to show than tell; taking off his jacket, he picked up an axe and attacked one thick snaking root. After a moment Stokoe picked up his axe and began to chop at another, Clough continuing to chip away with his spade. It was a relief to be working, William found. To blot out with hot red labour the press of anxieties crowding his head. The flying chips of bark and wood that hit his face were welcome; savagely, he threw his whole weight into each axe-swing, and the pale cut deepened fast. McEntire could be severely punished – flogged, put in the chain-gang – for unnatural practices. But Barnes had been used in this way before, William understood that clearly; nor was the law, under Governor Phillip's stern and rigid administration, capable of making the fine distinction between a man who bullied another in order to commit indecencies upon him, and a man who allowed himself to be used unnaturally, in return for food or other necessities. Both would appear equally guilty in the eyes of the law.

William did not notice when Clough and Stokoe stopped work; gradually it dawned on him that they had downed tools; that they were both looking at someone behind him, and making servile nodding gestures in his direction.

Panting with effort, he let the axe drop, and turned. Governor Phillip, attended at a discreet distance by two marines, was a few yards behind him.

'Mr Dawes. Carry on your work, men.' Clough and Stokoe resumed their chipping and digging. William wiped the sweat from his eyes and followed the Governor as he walked farther away from the labouring convicts.

'This is a good site, Lieutenant Dawes; a good choice of site. I am taking the opportunity this afternoon of checking for myself on labour problems. I am in the process of writing to Under-Secretary Nepean, I wish him to send us overseers for the convicts. Public works go forward very slowly because we lack responsible men to oversee the labour.'

William nodded and wiped his forehead on his sleeve again. He could feel that his face was scarlet, he wished the Governor would give him time to get his breath and have a mouthful of water before discussing labour problems. But the Governor ran on smoothly.

'I appreciate your enthusiasm to see this observatory built, Lieutenant, but I must urge you to consider the ramifications of your behaviour here.'

He must have found out about the rum. Had he met Barnes on the way up?

'For an officer to be seen stripped to the waist, labouring alongside common criminals, is a dangerous political act which could be interpreted as an open invitation to rebellion. It is an encouragement to the convicts to forget the rank which separates you from them, and thus it strikes a blow at the authority of all your fellow officers.'

William glanced back at Clough and Stokoe. They did not look as if they were about to overthrow authority.

'With respect, your Excellency, it has made them better workers. They learn by my example that the work is not in itself shameful, and they go to it with a better will.'

'They learn to imagine themselves your equals, Lieutenant Dawes, which creates the sort of expectations that lead to bloody insurrection.' Phillip's cold pale gaze was distracted for a moment by some white-crested parrots which landed squawking on a nearby tree.

'I shall not ask Captain Campbell to reprimand you, firstly because the fewer who know of this the better; secondly because I believe you have acted through youthful enthusiasm, with no proper thought for the consequences of your action. Please to put your jacket on again now, sir.' Phillip made a stiff little bow and strode off. William slowly put his jacket on. He had to go down and sort out Barnes anyway. But he would not obey the order. What would the Governor do? Punish him? Hold a court martial? Because William rolled up his sleeves and worked with convicts?

He can't manage without me, he told himself. Not unless he gets Alt off the bottle.

That night Watkin's man cooked up some fresh fish, and Surgeon White came to eat with them. There was a cold veering wind and they sat close round the fire, despite the sudden gusts of smoke that blew into their eyes. Watkin had been out exploring the inland branches of the bay, in search of the great river that still eluded them; he was full of news about the natives.

'I believe some of them are near starvation – we passed groups sitting and lying on the beaches, too listless to get up and wave to us. Their eyes are sunken and they are very emaciated.'

'Worgan told me a group of women accepted salt beef from them the other day,' said White, neatly filleting the bream on his plate and lifting its bony spine by the tail, to toss it into the fire.

Watkin looked up. 'Well it's the first time they've eaten that; in the past they have made a great pantomime of finding it sickening.'

'Hah. They're less choosy now,' said White.

'Is it because we've taken their fish?' asked William miserably, laying down his knife. He found that his own appetite for fish was sadly dulled by the memory of two large cold ones wrapped in sacking.

'I dare say,' replied Watkin. 'By hauling the seine we have taken catches which greatly exceed what they would normally catch. I guess the supply of fish is not inexhaustible.'

'Some of the savages came down to the beach the other day brandishing spears when a catch was being landed, and grabbed what they could get,' said White.

Watkin nodded. 'The Governor has asked us to post marine guards where the catch is brought to shore, to prevent a recurrence.'

'But if we're taking their *food* – ' William protested lamely. He was hungry, but it was not possible to eat the fish. She would have eaten it that night. Eaten both? Or maybe traded one for rum or clothing.

'*Their* food,' said White unpleasantly. 'This isn't an impressive country for food, is it?' He poured himself another glass of wine. 'I mean, have you looked in the hospital tents recently?'

'No.'

'Well we've got about a hundred and fifty cases of dysentery, and, oh, a hundred and eighty of scurvy.'

William did not reply, and White's tone became more harsh. 'These people have been living on salt rations for nearly eighteen months. All right, maybe they got hold of a pound of oranges at Rio, or a watermelon at the Cape. But now they're sick. You've maybe not been at sea long enough to see advanced cases of scurvy? Their gums have swollen so much you can't even see their teeth; their noses bleed, their breath stinks, their legs won't hold them up. Their skin is mottled yellow and purple. They need fresh food, and the only thing we can give them that's fresh is fish.'

'Wine's good,' interjected William.

'Yes,' White said impatiently, 'but the hospital stocks are exhausted. The Sirius sent over a couple of casks today; it'll be gone by the weekend. A drop in the ocean. There've been twenty-two deaths from scurvy so far. But that's nothing. Unless we get some fresh vegetables to grow – or unless we feed them *more* fish, more often, hundreds will die. Their punishment was transportation, not slow death by starvation. We have a duty here.'

'But if the natives will starve?' said William quietly.

White shrugged. 'Them or us. They can wander off – there'll be plenty of fish farther up the coast. They don't live in one place, like we do. They're used to it.'

Them or us. It is our business, thought William, as the representatives of a higher civilization, to ensure that it does not come to that. If our presence is the *cause* of hunger amongst the natives, then we have a duty to remedy it, no matter what the cost.

'We're talking about savages,' White said, his anger stoked by the lack of reply. 'People who haven't got the wit to cover themselves against the cold or make shelters that will keep out the rain. Their life consists of plenty followed by want. They are adapted to those circumstances.'

'But they will adapt by dying.'

'Aye, and they'll adapt to next summer's plenty by breeding,' White rejoined. 'They live like animals – what d'you expect? To starve Englishmen for their sakes?'

They sat in silence as the darkness deepened, and the shouts of a brawl up near the male convicts' tents broke out.

'It'll be a good thing when the transports are all gone,' said Watkin.

'Half this fighting is the sailors coming ashore with rum and going after the women – the captains should keep a closer eye on them.'

'Would you like my fish? I'm not hungry.' William held out his plate, knocking over the wine bottle. White swore and grabbed it. He stood.

'I'll be off to my patients. Come and have a look at the scurvy some time, William. You'll find it instructive.' William and Watkin sat blinking at the smoke in silence, then William said, 'What can we do? Until the farm begins to produce food. Or a ship arrives from England.'

Watkin nodded. 'Once the natives see the benefit of growing crops, they need never face starvation again. It will make them independent of natural shortages. He's right about that, you know – they *are* used to it. They will have suffered food shortages before our arrival. In times of plenty they feast, and in lean times they starve. Their way of life is naturally improvident.'

The spectacle of Molly Hill, and her desire for food, rose before William. The top buttons of her dress were unfastened, there were hollows at the base of her neck. He clenched his fist so that the nails cut into his palm.

Suddenly there was the sound of hurried footsteps, and a figure emerged from the darkness into the firelight.

'William? Watkin? I can't see for the smoke – ' It was Bradley. He had been out in the longboat all day, and should have gone back on board the *Sirius*. He was tired and wet and dirty.

'They have murdered one of the natives,' he told them, 'and I can't get at who it was.' William saw that he was upset to the point of tears. They sat him down and offered him William's fish, although he refused it. The story came out in fragments. The *Sirius*' longboat was fetching water to the ship, they were making their way back with the second load when they heard an outcry from the shore, from the east side of the harbour. Through his glass Bradley had made out running figures – blacks and convicts, disappearing into the trees. Since they were heavy laden and the wind was fresh from the south, it took them a half-hour to get to the shore. They were met by three convicts who were guarding a couple of native canoes. They were very excited, one of them had blood on his clothes, Bradley thought he must be injured. They told him they were from the gang at Major Ross's garden. A party of natives had landed while they were busy digging, and had run up and stolen their dinner and some of their clothes. The convicts had chased them round the cove and on to this beach, where native canoes were pulled up – and here was the evidence. In the bottom of one canoe there was a filthy old jacket and a sack with bread and beef in it.

'Where are they?' Bradley had asked. 'Where are the natives now?'

'We frighted 'em off, thieving bastards – they'll not meddle with us again!'

Bradley moved off towards the trees, since he had seen through his glass figures running in that direction. As he passed into the wood he noticed a dark swarm of insects buzzing furiously over a mess on the ground. At first he thought it was a dead possum, then he realized that whatever it was, it had no skin – no outer covering –

Bradley looked from Watkin to William. 'It was so sudden – I mean, you see injuries in battle, on ship – it's different, in the thick of things – '

'It's all right,' Watkin said gently. 'You're sure it was a native?'

Bradley shook his head, swallowing hard, although he had not touched the food on his plate. 'I wasn't sure *what* it was for a while – it was thick, you see, whitish – it looked whitish-grey, under the blood – a kind of lump – ' he sketched a shape with his hands – 'a lump . . .'

They waited in silence.

'It turned out,' he said after a while, 'well, the convicts came after me, they said they were chasing the blacks and one fell, split his head on a rock – '

'Dear God!' Watkin interrupted. 'Was it his brains?' Bradley nodded. 'They said, when they saw what had happened to him they ran back to the beach, and the other natives came back and dragged him off – dragged away the body.'

'You think they murdered him,' said William.

'It would take more than a fall to split a man's head open,' Bradley said. 'No, they caught one and they – they smashed his skull with a stone – ' He suddenly heaved himself up and moved away behind the tent. They heard him retching.

He was wiping his eyes when he came back, and almost smiling. 'My mother said I shouldn't make a soldier.' He sat down and stretched his feet out to the fire. 'Anyway, I took them back to the canoes and questioned them, and they all swore blind they hadn't killed him, and the bloodied one said that wasn't even the dead man's blood, he'd got close enough to one who was trying to pull his canoe out, to give him a punch in the face, and make his nose bleed, and they'd wrestled on the ground then the native had broken free and run off, and that's where the blood was come from. Two more came down from Ross's garden then and corroborated the whole story. What proof have I got, if I wanted to get them before a criminal court? There isn't even a body – *I* know there's a dead man, because the poor devil wouldn't be much use without that – that – ' he waved his arm, and giggled – 'but I'm damned if I'm scooping it up and taking it back for evidence – '

William waited to see if he would say any more, then offered, 'They would plead self-defence, anyway. I doubt they'd be convicted of murder.'

Bradley shook his head. 'Why would natives steal a jacket? They have no use for clothes.'

'Just to steal it,' said Watkin. 'They may not even think it wrong. They have been given rags and kerchiefs by our people. And the convicts take things from them – '

'They are hungry,' said Bradley. 'It's the food they wanted.'

The borehole William caused to be sunk on the Governor's plot struck a spring of good fresh water, sixteen feet below the surface, and the Governor was so pleased he wanted William instantly to make similar wells near the hospital and the barracks. It was true, far too many man-hours were lost carrying water supplies from the dangerously shallow Tank Stream; good supplies of fresh water near to dwellings would benefit everyone. But William had determined he would go and see Molly Hill, and now it was simply not possible in the hours of daylight (he could not see her at night; he could not, would not).

Stokoe and Clough came down to find him, the next day, as he was directing some men about the hospital bore. The marines were sinking the corner posts to the observatory, and Scott had told the convicts to work farther away from them. They had come to appeal to William over this injustice. Rather than send them back to an argument and possible fight, William set them to digging at the borehole.

'Where's Barnes?' he suddenly remembered. They shrugged, they had not seen him today. William's sense of dread about Molly Hill grew to envelop Barnes as well. He had told Watkin about McEntire's straggling and he would probably get twenty-five lashes for that, but the other matter had not been dealt with. He was responsible for Barnes, he was failing to protect him. The tall figure of Worgan emerged blinking from the hospital tent, and came over to inspect the bore.

'Got enough men working here, Lieutenant Dawes?' he laughed. 'I shall expect a Roman baths, never mind a borehole.'

William attempted to smile.

'You haven't got one you could spare, I suppose?' Worgan asked.

'A convict?'

'Yes. I'm looking for someone to guard the medical stores. I had a patient doing it, but, foolishly, I've cured him, and now he's returned to his work gang.'

'What would he have to do?'

'Very little. Sit by the door to the stores. An elderly man would do – he just needs to be able to raise the alarm if anyone unauthorized tries to enter. Since our medical supplies are irreplaceable, they must be regarded as rather precious.'

'Well, there is a man I can spare. He's not here right now, but I can send him along tomorrow.'

'Splendid. Name?'

'Stephen Barnes.'

William's spirits rose like a cork through water. It was ideal. Guarding the hospital stores, Barnes would be safe from bullying and attack because of the public nature of his duty. He would have no workmates to irritate. He was not required to do hard labour, he might even make a physical recovery during a period of stationary guard duty. William offered up a silent prayer of thanksgiving. God had not forgotten him; there would be a way out of all his difficulties. He would see Molly Hill; he would, he would go and see her on Sunday.

Next morning the camp was buzzing with the news of the murder of two convicts. When William got up to the observatory site (and yes, glory be, the corner posts *were* in, and the marines were working on the walls of the octagonal room) he found all the men discussing the incident. Stokoe, Clough and Barnes had been set to making wooden shingles for the roof of the single-room living quarters; they were working at a distance the marines had prescribed, and they were angry about it. William told Barnes to go and report to Dr Worgan. There was no sign of relief or gratitude on the boy's face; he barely seemed to understand. William worried briefly that Worgan might dismiss him for an idiot.

Stokoe claimed one of the murdered men was a friend. He regaled William with the details. Two convicts had been sent without a guard to protect them to Rushcutters' Bay to get thatch for Captain Campbell's house. Their bodies were found among the mangroves, one speared in three places and his head beaten to a pulp. The younger man was unmarked; Stokoe claimed the blacks had killed him by witchcraft. The convicts' scythes and other tools had gone. The Governor had apparently greeted news of the murder by asking what crimes the convicts had committed against the savages.

'That is not unreasonable,' William pointed out. 'We know they are not a warlike people; they have had many opportunities to attack us, if they had wished. This is in retaliation for wrongs they have suffered – '

'What wrongs?' demanded Stokoe.

'Well, the theft of their canoes and spears.' The natives trustfully left these lying about on the beach and in their caves. The spears were made from the central shaft of the yellow gum plant (which the convicts now harvested, where they found them growing, to use to stake the corners of their little vegetable plots). Scores of spears had been brought into camp; Captain Campbell alone had over thirty in his collection. The barbed heads were made of sharpened shell fixed to the shaft with resin; the shafts were decorated with patterns burnt or painted on. Each one must take several hours to make. 'And the murder of a native near Major Ross's garden.'

'There's no proof o' that,' countered Stokoe. 'And we should be protected whiles we're working. We wornt sent here to be murdered be savages. Might as well ha' been turned off in London.'

'Governor's in love wi' them savages,' volunteered Clough. 'We're not allowed near their bloody boats – a blind dog'd mek a better boat, it's no more'n a roll o' bark. An' if it's fish they're after – '

'Aye.' Stokoe slammed his knife into a nearby log. 'They stretch out their greasy black paws an' his Majesty's Governor loads 'em with fish. Lags're starving, but why should 'e care? There's plenty more where we come from, yer know.'

Fish. William's heart summersaulted and sank. He had succeeded in forgetting about her for minutes on end. He would go to her on Sunday – although he dreaded it, because none of the women would be working; they would all be hanging about the camp watching him. He would go to her on Sunday and – and find a way of making things right.

Unable to sleep on the Saturday night, he left his cot and crawled out of the tent to sit outside. The stars were shining – reminding him miserably of how he was failing in his duties as astronomer – and yet offering, as always, the comfort of their steady presence. These difficulties were small, he must get them in proportion. He must take control of events and act like a rational man. With sudden lucidity he saw that what he must do was marry Molly Hill. That was what the laws of God and man required; that was what would make their sin right.

If he married her she would be his wife, man and wife is one flesh. He quivered at the memory. The softness, the warmth of her. The other officers would laugh at him. For an officer to marry a convict. A known prostitute; Stokoe's whore. Well it was not the first time in history that correct behaviour had led to a man being mocked by his fellows. I must obey my conscience and my God, he told himself, and care less for the wagging tongues of the world.

And what other course of action was open to him, in honesty? To never see her again? After using her in that way? Or to visit her regularly, bearing gifts of food, making her his concubine? His conscience could sanction neither. It was even possible (he realized suddenly, vividly, as if waking from a gentle trance into the face of a savage, drooling enemy), it was even possible she might be with child as a result of their union. It was possible she was carrying his son! And as for the way she had behaved, the way she offered herself – so easily – in return for a morsel of food; that was not shallow immorality, that was black despair. The death of her first child – for which she *may* be responsible, for which she may blame herself – has led her into reckless despair, he thought. She considers herself damned, she no longer cares what she does. That's why she laughs and behaves wantonly. Bitter, cynical despair is gnawing at her heart, telling her she has no value, tempting her deeper into sin because she has nothing further to lose. If I abandon her now, I leave her to be sucked deeper and deeper into that quicksand. I am the man who must throw her a line, drag her into hope and contrition. I am the man who will save her, I am God's agent in this. And I have left her for near a month now, with no word or sign.

May God forgive me, he cried, and watched the fixed stars tremble and dissolve through his own hot welling tears. He would go to her tomorrow and ask her to marry him.

STEPHEN

Lucky old William; God's agent. How about a little divine intervention in my life, God? Where do we go from here?

Maybe we've entered Daniel's time. Nothing changes. No growth, no progress, no development. Just time, a great liquid bath of it. Daniel-time. No-time.

'And how's Daniel today?' I ask her despite (because of?) the fact that I can see how much she hates the question, how little she wants to reply.
She hates the question because she thinks I ought to *know* the answer. I ought to be able to recognize his ups and downs without dutifully asking after him like an aging invalid I see on monthly hospital visits. She knows it's a bland enquiry after his well-being when on the whole I wish he was dead.

Why then do I ask?
Why do anything? Why not tumble headlong into darkening silence?

Let's have this one out, Stephen. Your relationship to your son. Let's have it on the table with its arms and legs spread wide and get a good old peer inside and out, and see what makes it tick. Scissors? Scalpel? Hacksaw?

Thank you, nurse.
He is incurably handicapped. Both physically and mentally. And my wife is obsessed with his care. Fine. Given the disappointments of her life, is it not a blessing that she has turned to full-time care for a handicapped child, rather than the more common household palliatives: sherry, valium, adultery?

Yes. I'm not talking about her. If she's happy caring for him, that's good. Leave her out of it. Let's talk about him and me. Daniel and Stephen. The boys.

If he was a rabbit I'd hit him on the head with a brick.

Not good enough.

All right, try this. What if he is the physical equivalent of my spirit? As in, my fatherhood of such a child is far from accidental; is in fact, appropriate. Poetic justice.

Come on, come on – why not? If quacks are allowed to claim that

182

people can bring cancer on themselves; if the idea that people generate their own diseases merits even a second's serious consideration, then why not a child? 'He *does* take after his father, doesn't he!' I have spawned an embodiment of my inner self. I recognize myself in him: blind, pathetic, crippled.
So what? Your vanity is injured? Ludicrous suggestion. Is he doing you any harm? Isn't there space in the world for him, along with slugs and liver flukes and Tory politicians?

Of course there's room. I don't deny him room. I just don't know how to love him.

And any help I could give him would be arbitrary and inadequate, since I neither could nor would devote myself to him as Olla does. Any attempt on my part to insinuate myself with him would be an insult; the help he needs is infinite. Only total devotion will do. And for that, he has a mother. I am irrelevant, in this, as in the larger sphere.

Last night I dreamed a son. Quite suddenly, he came to me without conjuring. A mop of blond hair and an open laughing face; he was kicking a ball across the grass, shouting.
'Dad! Dad! To you!' He was running. 'Dad! *Dad!*'
Where was I?

*

William and Molly. He doesn't understand her.
Of course.
He's doing what he thinks is right.
Of course.
And he is entirely wrong.

I did what I thought was right. I married Olla. I tried to give her what she'd missed. Love, security, money. An education, a belief in human decency. What else could I have given?

A child.

Dear God. You bastard.

OK. Steady now. OK. I didn't know what else to give. And up to a point – wasn't what I gave right? She flourished in the love and security. She spent the money with glee. The education she didn't want, couldn't see the point of. And there was a contradiction in it that I couldn't digest. Feminism, equality – but she *wanted* to be at home,

183

she *wanted* to cook and clean and decorate, she *wanted* to be kept. I knew it was wrong, but she *wanted* it. Feminists seemed to assume that given the choice, a woman would go out and wield her power in the world. Olla is powerful. But she does not want to go into the world.

For which I must take the blame. For not explaining . . . not understanding . . . not allowing her to know it must be her wish rather than mine. Fuck it, I lost patience.

For which I must take the blame. She was stubborn as a mule; at school I was doing things, changing things. There were campaigns to fight, there were goals to win.

You were ashamed of her. Your old-fashioned wife. Not ashamed; incredulous. That it was ending up like that. A cliché of a husband and wife, he earns the money, she cooks the tea. A cliché, like my parents' marriage. And then Anna became an option. Liberated, talkative, sympathetic Anna; Jesus Christ Stevie, Robert's wife. Your boss's wife? You think you *don't* live clichés?

The business with Anna was wrong. A wrong thing. If Olla'd said a word; if even once she'd shown a hint of distress or anger, I'd have dropped Anna like a shot. Olla knew that. She wouldn't give me the satisfaction. And so I carried on, like a kid stuffing himself with stolen sweeties, waiting for the grown-up to shout. Not even enjoying the sickly glut. Despising myself and Anna. Pathetic, infantile.

That's when I lost her really. That's when Olla said goodbye. Not aloud, to give me satisfaction, but in her steely heart. You knew it Stephen. Christ, you above all should have known it. The man who set out to show her human decency and then betrayed her, by screwing fluffy Anna.

I couldn't even say I was sorry. She never admitted to any pain. Her defence is always to demonstrate that she cannot be hurt.

CHAPTER THIRTEEN

Trying to escape

William rose at seven, heavy-lidded after his tears; ate a morsel of bread, though he had no appetite, to give himself ballast, and carefully took his meteorological readings, acknowledging bitterly to himself that it was the one routine source of comfort in his day. Perhaps he would simply talk to her about marriage and they would agree to wait until she had served her term. That would in many ways be preferable; Governor Phillip would frown upon (may even prevent) marriage between an officer and a convict, especially since officers had been forbidden to bring their wives. Once she was a free woman, anyone could marry her. And it would give them time to atone for their sin, to rise above those animal instincts, to prepare for marriage as a holy and sanctified union. Perhaps he could ask Mary Johnson to teach her to read her Bible. What if she were feeding the baby? He did not think he could stand it, if her dress were unbuttoned, if her throat and neck were bare. He would wait till she had had time to get dressed and deal with the child. He forced himself at last to move off in the direction of the women's camp, heart thumping behind his ribs, mouth dry, fists clenched; passed through the ordeal of the women's tents almost unseeingly.

Outside her tent he paused. She was saying something – he could hear her voice – then she gave a little laugh. There was the sound of movement. Someone was with her. So much the better. He would speak to her with an audience, then there could be no question of danger or temptation. He would begin to taste the ashes of public humiliation, and enter into the possibility of redemption. He felt a little giddy, as if he might faint – as if he would fall. Quickly he pulled aside the tent flap and entered. He was confronted by the naked back of a man. Molly Hill's startled face rose over the man's shoulder. William froze, as the detail of the scene burnt itself into his memory. The man stood in the centre of the tent, he was short and stocky and his legs were braced a little apart. Curved around his dark thighs were Molly Hill's white bony legs. She was moving slowly, rising and falling, very slowly, with the movement of a nightmare. The man's breath came in controlled sighs, with silence between them; it was almost as if the two of them were not real – or they were too real – engaged in the slow balletic movement of a curious dance, intent on executing it correctly. But Molly Hill was watching William. Her lips were open. She was smiling a little and her smile was reminding him of Worgan, of Worgan's distantly smiling face above his piano. Slowly and deliberately, she winked at William. The man's left leg, William noticed, was quivering. His shoulders rounded a little then straightened as Molly Hill slowly rose, fell, rose against him. Ducking backwards in trembling haste, William got out of the tent.

He ran up to the observatory. Point Maskeleyne was deserted on a Sunday. He could not clear the image from his mind. He knew he would never be able to. Her face with its lazily dawning smile of recognition; the slow, complicit wink. Her white legs clenched around the man's thighs. The slow, controlled rising of her body, the tautening muscles in the man's buttocks and legs. That careful gasp of breath. The dark secret curve between his buttocks. William was overwhelmed by lust, a wicked fiery grief that shook him as a cat shakes a bird. He threw himself on the ground to hide, to bury his shame.

It would have been more than he deserved, he knew, for the earth to open and swallow him; to take him back into her dark womb. No, he must do the more difficult thing, at last: slowly lift his leaden limbs and rise, attempt to brush the filth from his uniform; open his eyes to the brilliant sunlight and hallucinatory image of her winking face superimposed upon it. He must pick up his aching, throbbing, defiled body, and walk with it. He set out in the opposite direction to the camp.

It would have been fitting if he had got lost, striking out through the woods without marking trees, without counting his paces, without taking a single precaution to ensure his return. But he knew again that he would not be so fortunate as to lose himself. His punishment would be that he *could* not lose himself, any more than he could bury himself; that no matter how far he wandered, into whatever areas of wilderness desolation, he could never never lose himself, but must bear the burden of his sentient, responsible, pitiful, needy self, self-consciously, to the ends of the earth and back, and never never cast it off.

STEPHEN

Is it possible, escape from self? To leap the bounds of your own
personality, jump tracks, split open the solitary confinement of your
skull and soar out into freedom? Is it possible?
For William, no. No more than it is for me. We're two of a kind, much
too firmly riveted into the iron casket of our selves to swing loose
and float free. A less secure person – a frailer, flightier, *madder* person
– might do it. In William the strong sinews of morality are racked as
is a strong body by physical torture. But weak attachments – if his
desires did not conflict with his beliefs, or if his beliefs were anyway
weak and shifting – there would be no pain, no suffering at all. In that
sense his strength imprisons him. Whereas a weaker man could act
at will – on impulse – could break out, drift, be blown to freedom.
And yet if he lost himself, what would he find? Nothing. Only the
desert. A slow, dry death.

Can a man lose himself deliberately, like Faust? Can he *choose*? No.
Because if it is done consciously, it is not being lost. It is not out of
control. The only escape from the policeman in the mind is madness.
Or mind-altering drugs. Or religion. Buddhists escape, don't they?
Isn't that the ultimate aim of meditation? Escape from self and joyful
mingling with the eternal ether? (Keep a rein on the sarcasm, Stevie.
How pathetically you betray your age, with your cautious respect for
hallucinogenic drugs, and your schoolboy cynicism for ancient
religion. Grow up.)

And exploring? Pushing back the frontiers of the known world?
Colonizing the wilderness? Embodies the desire for escape,
undoubtedly; physically *enacts* escape; yet carries with it its burden of
knowledge and self, enough to make the strange wilderness itself
like to a garden, and to remodel the new world in the image of the
old. So in the First Fleeters' eyes the strange grey-green bush with
its giant gums and barren lack of undergrowth becomes 'like a
gracious parkland'; so the weird leaping muscular-tailed kangaroo
becomes 'a large species of rabbit'; so the brave black hunters and
warriors, lords of a mythic dream-world the size of a continent,
masters of imagination and ritual, become 'wretched naked slaves,
the miserablest people on earth'. And a vast new world is recast in the
image of the old, only less satisfactory, for nothing in it is proper. The
parklands contain no real sweet grass; the kangaroos are less easy to

187

shoot and tougher to eat than rabbit; the blacks cannot be brought into servitude and do not seem to know their place.

A new world worse than the old, because it can only be seen in terms of the old. Though its birds are brightly plumed, they cannot sing. Though the sun shines bright, there is insufficient rain. Though the mountains are high and full of magic, the function of mountains is to source rivers. Dry mountains are bad mountains, there's nothing else to know.

And so the explorer, perhaps even more than anyone else, is locked in his own cage; carries its bars before his eyes, views the country through its grid. Here we may farm sheep. Here, dig for ores. Here, fields of corn, and over there a city. He does not even see the land, or traces of the massive dream ancestors that have shaped it, only how he will remake it, in the image of his own small country. He will mine it to increase the currency of his homeland. He will never escape.

And me? Am I so burdened with baggage that I'm incapable of discovering anything new too – only of discovering myself (again) in Dawes, as they found that little England in Australia? Of finding another failure?

He proceeds as lightly as he can, poor sod. His eyes and ears are open. Let him go in peace.

To Dawes. Open doors. Away.

*

It was dark as William made his way back to the camp, heading for the observatory. He had walked himself into a kind of stupor and was feeling sick with hunger. He hesitated to go down into the settlement, in amongst the smoke and fires and eyes and ears, even though hunger drove him. He wanted to be hidden. He would hide himself from everyone now. He owed nothing. He owed no confidence to anyone. No one would ever know.

She had even forgotten, he told himself. He had known from the start that she was a whore. Stokoe's whore. Every day, with a different man. It was nothing to her, nothing.

She had presented it to him with the casual logic of an equation anyone could understand. 'I need summat good to eat.' She gave herself to the men who brought it, it didn't matter who they were. If he had offered to marry her, perhaps she would have seen that that was a

188

reasonable transaction too; that in return for permanent provision of food, she would confine the gift of her body to him alone.

She would sell her self to him.

Was all it amounted to. Nothing would change in her head. She might be a faithful wife. The transaction would be the same: sex for food. Any notion of reform, of sanctity, of redemption, of any higher union than that hot wet physical spasm of bodies, would be forgotten.

Was that it? Stripped to its bones, was that marriage? He thought that maybe it was, maybe she was right. In which case he owed her nothing (having paid with the fish); and would never marry. Would never again seek to buy a woman's body, for an hour's or a lifetime's use, upon such terms.

William waited, shivering in the darkness, until the camp fell silent, then crept down to his tent. There was a chunk of bread in his haversack which he devoured before falling into a dark, sweaty sleep.

Work was the only answer. Avoiding, through choice, the company of his fellow officers, and shunning conversation with the work gangs, William worked like one possessed, covering the distance between the redoubt and the observatory four or five times a day, to urge the two works on and check the progress of each stage. The look of the camp itself was very different now, most of the convicts were hutted, their wattle and daub huts thatched with rushes from the bay. Most of the tents had come down. The observatory was nearing completion.

Its log and shingle walls enclosed an octagonal room nine foot in diameter, which was linked by a staircase down to a second room beside the outcrop. The second room, sixteen feet by twelve, with five-foot, ten-inch walls and a ridged roof rising another six foot (but not obscuring the quadrant's field of view, thanks to the higher situation of the octagonal room), was to be his living quarters, but there was also a roof shutter at the north end to provide work-space for another astronomer. Only the roof to the octagonal observation room needed working on. The roof would be a nine-foot diameter cone, made of light fir rafters, covered in painted canvas. There would be space left for a shutter to slide into one segment of the cone, and the whole roof would revolve on three cannon-ball rollers. It could thus be turned for the open shutter to permit viewing of any one section of the sky. It should preferably be painted white – though there was an absolute lack of white paint in the colony. He wrote to Maskeleyne requesting five gallons of boiled linseed oil with white lead in it, and fifty yards of

189

strongest sailcloth. The letter would go via China on the *Golden Grove*; his supplies might arrive, he calculated, in eighteen months time. In the meantime he would use the old sails and inferior supplies of paint the Governor made available to him, and pray that with renewed application they would keep the rainfall out.

Stokoe and Clough and the marines were putting the finishing touches to the building now. The marines had the more skilled labour of making and hanging doors, and fitting benches for the meteorological instruments and books, while the convicts were shingling the roof to the living quarters. There was no communication between the two parties. William sensed that the addition of a new, unknown character might destroy the precarious equilibrium of their working relations, and did not seek a replacement for Barnes. When Stokoe was off fetching more nails one day William asked Clough how Barnes was getting on at the hospital, and was rewarded with Clough's habitual sneer.

'He's found 'isself a protector, 'e has.'

'A protector?'

Clough sniggered and pretended to carry on working.

'Who's that, then?' asked William.

'Neal. James Neal. Works down brick kilns.'

William had never heard of the man, and could not think what to say next. Certainly Barnes *needed* a protector, but it showed surprising charity in a fellow convict to take on that role. 'How – how does he protect him?'

Clough laughed. 'He basted McEntire – laid him out.'

Good, thought William, and not before time. He hesitated to ask why; he had had a sudden unpleasant intuition as to what Neal got out of 'protecting' Barnes. It was the same thing, everywhere, wasn't it? The same hypocritical filth, what the weak gave the strong in return for protection, for food. The whole of human society, all its transactions and relations, came down to this sordid exchange. That he should have imagined motives of charity; that he should have imagined a man might want to help another simply because the other was less fortunate! It was no longer innocence to jump to such conclusions, it was blind stupidity. He had lived for twenty-six years and understood nothing. Understand it now, he told himself bitterly. There is no love, no honour, no charity. There are simply deals and bargains, and gratification of the basest lusts at the cheapest price.

'Does Barnes agree to this 'protection'?' he asked, so vehemently that Clough looked up, surprised.

'Aye. He were a cakey if he didna. Brickies 'av got huts wi' rooves –
that's one step up from an 'ole in a tree!'

Of course. It is always better to submit yourself to the power of one,
for enduring rewards and security, than to take your chances with
attempting to remain free, open to the predations of all. There is even a
greater bravery and honesty in prostitution, William told himself, than
in the bounds of marriage.

The opposite of all he had believed was true. Black was white, white
black. Where he had seen honesty and love, there were instead hypocrisy and lust. He walked in a world with its goodness sucked out, with
the whole frame and relief of things sucked inside out, its high points
now low, its caves and hollows become jagged peaks.

The increasing animosity of the natives was a predictable part of
this. A group of them landed near Point Maskeleyne one day and
made a raid on the hospital, stealing a goat. They never came into
the cove, were never seen in the vicinity at all any more; their rare
appearances in the whites' world now signified only trouble. Moved
almost to tears by the agitated distress he felt at this news, William was
given disturbing evidence of how far out of tune he was with his
fellows by Watkin's amused and slightly drunken commentary as they
got into their cots that night. Watkin had been to a dinner party at
Captain Campbell's.

'You missed a capital feed, William – a shark from the bay, six foot
long, and roasted to a turn. Of course, the talk was all on what the
natives are having for dinner tonight, that the goat may be tougher
than they bargained for and so on – and then – ' he broke off to laugh –
'then Campbell says to Worgan, "I might ask," he says, "I might ask
what the deuce a goat was *doing* at the hospital, sir?" and Worgan says,
very dry, "Oh, a goat is nothing, sir, to us, we are very catholic up at the
hospital. In my store room, sir, Captain Reed is keeping a kangaroo,
with which he hopes to make his fortune on his return to London. It
hops about among the wine casks and surgical instruments with a rare
intelligence. We are in high hopes of it becoming assistant surgeon
soon. Johnny White says Balmain may take lessons of it!" '

Watkin laughed again, fell back in his cot, and was snoring within
seconds. William blew out the candle. His eyes were dry and smarting,
he lay with them open, staring at the blackness inside the tent. Other
men were happy here, easy with themselves and each other. Perhaps,
he thought, I am going mad.

When he awoke in the morning a bleary-eyed Watkin suddenly

recalled that he had been given a message for William, and passed him a note from Richard Johnson. It was an invitation to dinner that night, begging him to attend as 'our friends are few and far between'. Despite his disinclination, William forced himself to go.

He was relieved to find the Johnsons were expecting no other company; pleased also to be able to compliment them on their two-roomed hut ('a miserable affair', Richard insisted, 'but at least a little more stable than a tent') and neatly fenced garden. Before darkness fell they took him round the garden, pointing out the orange tree growing from a pip from the Cape, the apple seedling, the shoots of Indian corn. Richard was in an anxious, agitated state, and launched into an explanation of his grievances before they even began their meal.

'I have had a disagreement with Governor Phillip, William, and I wanted to know whether you have heard – via any of the other officers – any word about it? As to His Excellency's opinion now, in retrospect, I mean.'

'No – I have heard nothing.'

'I am at a loss, really; perhaps I should apologize – without his support my hands are tied – '

'Apologize?' broke in Mary. 'Richard, don't you dare apologize. For wanting to build a place of worship? For expressing concern over the ungodliness of the officers? For wanting to start a Bible class? These things are your *duty.*'

Richard shuffled uncomfortably in his chair. 'That's as may be, but if I have annoyed the Governor, God's work here will suffer. I put His work before my own standing.'

With a sense of relief, William pulled out a chair and sat next to Richard. Here at least was a man he could understand.

'I've experienced difficulty with the Governor too; he objects to my working with the convicts, and I can't help but be alarmed by his dealings with the Indians – ' He checked himself. This was not what Richard had invited him to discuss. But he and Mary were nodding sympathetically.

'I almost think,' Richard said, 'that we must work out a strategy to – to *seem* to please him, so that he will look more favourably on our requests – '

William laughed bitterly. 'I've tried to do that. I've taken on all the extra work he's given me, I have been doing Mr Alt's job for weeks now, but His Excellency is never pleased. The more you do, the more he wants.'

'The cases are not the same,' broke in Mary. 'He's afraid of the power of religion, I believe, and so he wishes to reduce Richard's influence. He's not asking for more work from us but almost, it seems, trying to prevent us from working at all.'

'You are always very strong, my dear, your views are strong,' Richard said anxiously. But after a short silence he conceded, 'It may be an attack upon the Church. I am aware of that possibility.'

'Of course it's an attack upon the Church,' said his wife. 'To refuse to build a church in a Christian settlement, when storehouses, hospital, dwelling places are under construction – to set God behind all temporal needs? A church should have been the *first* building here.'

'He accuses me of interfering,' Richard said miserably to William. 'He told me to stick to visiting the sick when I pointed out to him the bad effects the immorality of the officers is having upon the men and convicts.' William reminded himself that Richard did not know about his visit to Molly Hill. No one knew. It was a secret.

'What immorality?' he asked.

'It's well known amongst people I visit,' Richard said. 'Well known, and the officers are disliked for it – for the double standards they create. Many of the officers – I dare say most – have a, a paramour, amongst the convict women.' Noticing William's blush, he said, 'There is no need for anxiety on Mary's behalf. She is a married woman and she understands the sad necessity for discussing such unsavoury topics.'

'Of course I do,' she said indignantly, and William, raising his face from his own blush, saw that there were hectic red spots on her cheeks. 'Of course I see the necessity, when there are women with child by officers who have wives and families in England – and women who are reduced to terrible, humiliating fights because they fear that one has stolen an officer's affections from another, and taken also the supply of food and drink and clothes that go along with that affection. How *dare* the Governor let this terrible traffic in human flesh continue? It is unchristian, immoral – '

'He dismisses it.' Richard turned to William again. 'It is not to be my concern. I said, "Your Excellency, as chaplain to the settlement, the souls of the settlers here *must* be my concern," and d'you know what he said? "Their souls, yes; their morals, no. If officers come to you for advice as to the care of their souls, you may raise the matter of the concubines. Otherwise, stick to the sick and those who request your assistance." '

'The other way – ' put in Mary – 'the other way to put a stop to this fornication, is to help the women to a better understanding of God's word, so that they will reject the men's advances. But His Excellency will not give permission for a women's Bible class either. I had hoped to run a small circle – a dozen or so of the women – '

William could not do any more than give a sympathetic hearing to their agitation and frustration. He hoped that they would never hear of his own guilt (what if Mary *did* start a Bible class? And if Molly attended it, and made a clean breast of her sins?) The Governor's attitude to religion was of a piece with his other behaviour, but to argue with him was, as Richard said, to lessen the chances of success for any future projects. We're trapped here, William told himself, trapped and subject to the Governor's whims as much as the convicts are; there's no court of appeal, he rules us with the power of a dictator.

Next day the final shingles were put on the roof of the rectangular room, and William sent a note to Captain Campbell requesting permission to quarter himself at the observatory. He rejected Campbell's offer of a private to be quartered with him 'for guard purposes', shrinking from the necessity of another man's proximity. It would be a pleasure (in so far as anything *could* be a pleasure to his dust-and-ashes mouth) to be away from other men. And he need not concern himself, then, with when (or if) he ate; when he stayed up to observe; when he slept. Since there was no livestock or foodstuffs at the point, he was not likely to be a target for either natives or convicts. And if he *were* going mad, it would be more comfortable to do so alone than to be made constantly aware of how ill his perceptions sat with those of other men.

To celebrate his move, he allowed himself a rare afternoon off, wandering through the woods beyond the point, making a few sketches of plants and shrubs. Farther away from the settlement, the plant the convicts had named wattle (for its supple usefulness in constructing their wattle-and-daub huts) still grew in profusion, and was now flowering. It bore hundreds of tiny golden flower heads, which glowed like little stars against the dark background of its leaves. He drew the delicate feather-shaped leaves and fluffy flower balls – it was unusual to see a plant flowering now, in the antipodean winter, and he was moved by its delicate beauty.

Blasting and excavations at the redoubt were done now, and the construction of the gun mountings was halted by a lack of bricks, which were promised for the end of the week. Work at the kilns had been severely disrupted by flooding. So William concentrated his energies on the raising and fixing of the observatory roof, paying careful attention to its smooth turning on its runners, and the pulley system by which the shutter was opened for viewing; and then on the unloading and transportation of the instruments from the *Sirius*. One by one the treasures were unpacked: the big quadrant, the frame of which would need to be leaded into a notch in the rock; the three-and-a-half-foot achromatic Dolland telescope with its special sliding support tubes; the thirty-inch night glass; the journeyman clock, and the new Ramsden sextant, the barometer and thermometers. The astronomical clock was brought ashore, carried reverently at shoulder height by two marines – rather as they had seen the people at Rio carrying statues of their popish saints, thought William. And he did feel a small flush of pride as the Timekeeper, K1, last and most precious of the instruments from England, was carried up the cleared track to the new resting place he had created for it, in the wilderness of New Holland. Captain Hunter came to look over the place and to approve the Timekeeper's new home; even though he was absent, Governor Phillip managed to sour the sweetness of the moment, as Hunter related that His Excellency had told him that if he had known the time and labour that would be consumed by construction of the observatory, he would have brought one prefabricated from England.

Alone that night, William paced his new home, making small adjustments to the positions of the instruments; listening to sounds of the timbers settling around him, testing the door and the roof shutters. It was a cloudy night, but still. He could sit here. He could look up through that open segment of roof. He could begin to carry out that work he had come here for. This was an achievement; and despite all the losses, all the mistakes, all the foulness of the preceding weeks, it was his achievement, and he would put it to good use.

It was Halley who had predicted the return of the comet that should appear above New South Wales on 7 August. His own comet (named after him because of his accurate prediction of its return in 1758) was so far the only proof of his theory that comets *did* travel in orbit, and that comets – along with all the other objects in the universe – were governed by the gravity Newton had described. The sighting of this comet from Australia would confirm the theory; it would be a great night for astronomy. William watched on every clear night. Sadly, August was an exceptionally cloudy month, with a good deal of rain, and on many nights the sky was obscured. Sometimes when it was raining he went to bed, waking again in the early hours of the morning to notice that the pattering of raindrops on the shingles had ceased; then he got up and dressed, without making a light, and went to open the shutter. The stars were brilliant and he observed numerous shooting stars, but nothing resembling a comet. He recalled Newton's theory that the sun was refuelled by comets falling into it as a result of fatal changes in their orbits; perhaps this comet had passed too close to the sun and been consumed. The image of that strange, wayward orbit, as the bearded star passed the wrong way round the sun (travelling in the opposite direction to the fixed planets) and then moved off into outer darkness, beyond the reach of the sun's life-giving warmth, struck William as an apt metaphor for life in the colony. Indeed, it was common belief among the people that comets were one of the manifestations of hell. Stocked with the souls of the damned, they flew from freezing in outer darkness to roasting heat as the comet brushed past the sun. And the colonists, flung to a terrible distance from the steadiness of mother England, froze and roasted, were in utter despair or wildest hope, knew nothing but extremes. Steadiness, regularity, temperate opinions were lost to them.

The weather worsened. The brick kilns actually fell in, under pressure of the rain, and tracks became impassable quagmires. Numbers of huts collapsed, all public work was suspended. It was more than a week after the comet's expected arrival. Anxiously William watched the sky. Was the bearded star even now moving in a fiery arc behind those clouds? Was this foul weather a result of its presence in the sky? He imagined it as the glowing head of a pagan god, its trailing hair swept back from its face by the force of the sun, whose rays combed it out. But why was it hiding from him? What must he do, how propitiate it, to make it willing to reveal itself? The sky was full of secrets. He was not worthy to understand one of them.

Night after night he watched, waiting for short breaks in the cloud, recording the positions of the planets and of the moons of Jupiter; taking lunar distances in order to more accurately determine the observatory's longitude; gazing into the blackness between stars, puzzling to know if John Michell's strange theory of invisible stars might be true. Michell had published in 1784, and had drawn upon Newton's theory of gravitation to posit the notion of massive stars whose gravity would be so powerful that it would slow down or even arrest the passage of light they emitted. A star with five hundred times the sun's diameter, and an equal density, would exert so powerful a gravitational pull as to choke off all its own light, and be invisible. It was easy to believe in these black stars, in the huge, silent, spangled sky of New South Wales. It was easy to believe that the heavens were chock-full, so great, so deep, so vast were they. If a comet passed such a star it would be sucked in. That would explain the rarity of comets, whose extended orbits led them past numerous other stars and planets; it would be almost impossible for one to stick to its course.

A straight path, between competing temptations; that was the course for a virtuous man, that was the course of Bunyan's Pilgrim. I swerved, William told himself, but I am not lost. I have dragged myself back to a right path. I have not fallen into a black star, I have not been burned up or destroyed; with God's help, I will stick to my course. Anxious about the timekeeping of the astronomical clock, he lashed it securely into its position in a niche of the solid rock so that nothing less than an earthquake could disturb its movement.

The great sky accepted his pain easily. Over weeks of nights, it floated up and away and dispersed like smoke. The sky was solace and mystery. In the track of the expected comet he found three new nebu-lae. The sky was the huge freedom enjoyed by brilliant minds like Halley and Newton and Messier and Kepler. It was worlds away from the pettiness of daily life in the colony. The story of a poor marine officer who fornicated with a whore was nothing to it. The only prob-lem was if that pitiful event loomed large enough in his own mind to displace the stars and the great black sky. That would be his own faulty vision, his own inability to see things in the right proportion. Molly Hill had loomed, blocking his view of the heavens. But now he could make her recede; now he had put her behind him.

Tonight Stephen suddenly opens the door to Daniel's room while I am reading. I stop. I can hear the television downstairs, I thought Stephen was watching it.

'Olla? What on earth are you doing?'

'I'm reading.'

'To Daniel? But – ' He comes closer, stares at the book on my lap. Too late to hide it. 'That's *King Lear*!' He stares at me in complete astonishment. I do not speak. He turns to look in the cot. 'And he's asleep. He's asleep anyway.'

'Yes. My voice soothes him. It soothes him to sleep when I read. Like a lullaby.'

'Yes – but – *King Lear*?'

'Why not?'

Suddenly Stephen laughs. 'Why not. Why not *War and Peace* in Russian, it's all the same to him as *Andy Pandy's Tea Party*.' He looks over my shoulder at the top of the page. 'Act four, scene two. Have you read all that?'

'Not all tonight.'

He puts his hand on my shoulder, he is terribly pleased for some reason. 'You've never read it before, have you, Olla?'

'You took me to see it. In Birmingham.'

'I'd forgotten, you're right. But now you *choose* it; after all that fuss about the English course at the Tech – '

'I didn't want to go to school.'

'No, but – ' He is smiling, shrugging. He looks almost as he used to. 'I'm just so glad you're reading it – through choice.'

Ah. I am again the poor girl who needs educating: doubtless he imagines it is his influence which has brought me to this. He is feeling satisfaction.

'It's better, isn't it, when you read it aloud – when you *hear* the poetry as well as seeing it on the page – '

Quietly I close the book and nod towards sleeping Daniel. 'We mustn't wake him.'

'No.' He runs downstairs while I dim Daniel's light and switch on the baby alarm. When I go down he is sitting in the big armchair, staring expectantly at me and smiling.

'So what else are you reading, on the sly? What else is Daniel treated to?' An invader, he wants to grab everything.

'Oh. Only a few things. It is not a big deal.' I cannot dent his good humour.

'You don't understand, Olla. I'm so *glad*. I'm just so pleased you're getting pleasure from books that I love – that I've always felt as if I'm forcing on you, before. I'll tell you what, shall we finish it together? Can I read it with you? Take half the parts each?'

'No. I read it on my own, to Daniel. He likes it.'

'But it's a shame to break off there. And there must be things that are – the language in places, is difficult – ' Now he wants to explain it to me.

People like Stephen want to explain. They think that everything can be explained. They wish the universe to be fitted into their own petty store of words and pitiful framework of ideas. Not only that, they want it to be explained even to stupid people, in terms that all can understand. They diminish the world to a nutshell.

'There are some words which are archaic – there are references which just don't make any sense unless you know a bit about the Elizabethan stage. You'll get so much more from it if you let me – '

Words have their own existence. He doesn't even understand that. Words are like notes played on a piano. They are sounds, and shapes. The sounds have moods. A procession of written words is an object with shape. Like a vase. Does he seek to explain a vase? A sentence has its own shape and sound and mood. Explaining it; *explaining* it – reduces it to its literal meaning. Perhaps he would like a whole world of explanations, and then there would be nothing troublesomely real in it, it would all be accounted for. Nothing would touch you unawares. Its explanation would run before it. Stupid people would be at no disadvantage.

I *shall* read *War and Peace* in Russian to Daniel. An excellent suggestion. The sound and shapes of language will fill his imagination. He soars. I rejoice that he soars above explanations.

*

Autumn 1976. There is a time then – a day? Week? Year? – when I think Stephen and I are happy. As I work on the house and Stephen finds reasons for enjoying letting me do it. He decides he is helping me, by enabling me to express my creativity through home-building. He even shows my work off to his friends who come round, talks about my imaginative use of colour, says laughingly that we will be setting up an interior design company and taking orders. That I will be studying an art course becomes one of the things that he says quite often, proudly. He can be pleased with the idea that I am an artist, that his money is sponsoring the work of an artist; simply, not with the notion that his wife is spending time and money making his house look beautiful. The first is bohemian, the second, bourgeois; the first is politically good, the second, selfish. In the first he is liberating me, in the second, exploiting.

I do not always think with this cast of bitterness, though. I take pleasure in the house. I want to make the rooms glow, I want them to hold and cradle light, so that walking into them, you feel secure. I want them to contain clear space and silence. I want this to be a place nothing will break.

And when he is proud and thinks me clever, artistic, he wants me more. He is Pygmalion, he has nurtured me from pitiable ignorance, into something that all others can see is desirable. He takes an interest in my clothes and buys me things: jewel-coloured silky blouses, scarves, an embroidered waistcoat.

I like it. I like to be admired. That he wants me makes me rapacious; before he comes in from school I take my clothes off and put on my decorator's overalls with nothing underneath. As he is telling me about his day I undo one button. He slides his hands into my overalls. Sometimes I have them off already. He tells me about being stopped by the neighbour as he is unlocking our front door, and how he has to hold his briefcase over his erection, because he has just seen me naked through the window. We laugh.

We are happy. Children playing house. When does it start to go sour?

Perhaps almost immediately, as the turning tide begins to slowly creep out again and for a while you do not notice that it has reached its furthest inland point, each wave falls not so far short of the one preceding – and some still overlap, you can't be sure. Only after a while do you realize that it has, inexorably, turned, and is pulling out to sea again. That it has left its high-tide mark. That you *were* happy.

I have finished the house. Now I learn to cook, I buy recipe books and experiment with different kinds of food. Stephen is busy: meetings, after school, with teachers, governors, union, head, pupils. In the evenings: Labour party, Militant, committees, speakers. At weekends: rallies, demonstrations, selling newspapers, pickets. A couple of times I go with him, usually I say, no thanks I'll stay at home. I don't like politics. Stephen recites his creed, 'Politics is people's lives, we must make our voice heard, together we can change things.'

Nonsense.

He wants me to understand. Long, patient explanations. He wants me to be different. It's time for me to read, go to classes, be educated. His women friends at school are in a group of consciousness raising, I should join them and think about how I am oppressed.

I tell him I am not oppressed. I am happy, I am free. I have a beautiful house, good food, I can cook or sew or shop or clean, I do not even have to work. But this is oppression, he tells me. You must have a career of your own, we can pay someone to clean, I will do cooking as well, we will go shopping together on Saturday morning. You must have a life of your own. You need to express yourself, you need a social life.

I *have* a life of my own. I am happy on my own. It is the great luxury of my life. I can be in my house, alone.

But this is no good for him. And he has a new job. They are planning a new school now, planning for everything to be different, 'child-centred'. He is always home late, always busy. He insists that he must cook as often as me, so that he is not exploiting me. He comes in late, hungry, he has forgotten, goes out again to buy soggy chips which we both hate. My shining saucepans and interesting cookbooks lie half the time unused in the kitchen, I am not allowed to cook more than three-and-a-half times a week.'Politics begins at home,' he says. 'How can I presume to set about trying to change people's lives if in my own personal life I am exploiting you?'

'You are not exploiting,' I say. 'I am happy. You give me money; I shop, I cook. I am your wife.'

'No,' he says. 'You don't understand.' He brings home leaflets and prospectuses for art courses, he wants me to choose which I will enter for. I have to have a portfolio, and he takes photos of the rooms in the house. (Twice. He gives the first set for developing to the experimental darkroom run by children at his school, and they come back weeks later, covered in murky blobs.) He helps me fill in application forms. Not surprisingly, I am not accepted on a course. He has been trying to get me in at too high a level. I must do some O levels first, I must prove I can write in English. I am enrolled at the technical college to do English language and literature, art, and Russian. ('Since you can speak it,' he says, 'it won't be difficult. It'll stop you getting rusty. Pity they don't do Polish.') I do not wish ever to speak it again.

And so I go to school, and have to struggle with *The Mayor of Casterbridge*, instead of going to the market for fresh vegetables, and polishing the windows till they shine. I see no point in studying. I think, soon I will be pregnant. I can drop it then, he'll forget this stupidity. I am waiting for a baby.

When I have a baby, it will be useful to have a car; everyone else has a car. I would like to learn to drive. He wants me to learn things. I say, I would like to learn to drive.

That is an argument. He avoids arguments, but that one he can't avoid. He hates cars. I say, you hate them but does that mean I must? Am I expected to embrace all your views, in return for the 'Mrs' in front of my name? He is angry because trapped; his position is untenable.

'Olla, cars are an abomination. They are expensive, cause pollution, waste resources, destroy the tranquillity of the countryside, they are killing public transport and then what will the poor and elderly – and children – do?'

So, I say, I must put myself on a level with the elderly and poor, in order to preserve their public transport. I have been poor, I will be elderly. But for now, I am neither. Must I pretend? Like you would have preferred to keep the house ugly and shabby, to show solidarity? I am not you, I tell him. I do not have to have your opinions.

'I've never had a car,' he says. 'I hate them.'

'You don't have to have one. Let me have one. I'll get a job to pay for it. I'd a hundred times rather do that than go to school with children.'

He does not want me to get a job, he wants me to be a student. He knows I know he can afford a car. He is a head of department, it is laughable that we do not have one. He gives in, as I know he must. He buys me a mini and I take lessons.

Driving is wonderful, I love it. I love to put my foot down and leap away from the traffic lights. I love to pull out and sail past a slow vehicle. I love starting the car and going, clearing off, and the car will go wherever I choose. I would like a faster car, though, with better acceleration. I will wait until Stephen is more accustomed to this one. I pass my driving test first time. Stephen is still quiet and sour about the car, so I volunteer to go to the women's consciousness-raising group, which he has been urging me to for months.

There are eleven of them, sitting around in somebody's front room. Two I know, friends of Stephen's. The room is dingy but very warm. They are going to talk about abortion. I would not have come if I had known this, as I have no interest in discussing abortion. There will be a demonstration of the National Abortion Campaign next Sunday and they want to know who is going and who can offer lifts. When they've sorted that out, anyone who has had an abortion is invited to speak about it. Two women speak at length. I say nothing. It is none of their business. They talk as if women were weak and helpless; they talk about needing support and counselling; they talk about emotions they can't control. One speaks of bursting into tears repeatedly for no reason, the others murmur in sympathy.

They are like self-indulgent children! They are all exposed, helpless softness; are these adult women? Have they not learned to survive? They speak as if they are at the mercy of forces and feelings they can't control, as if the world owes them a debt of kindness simply because they have breasts and wombs. Then they talk in hushed tones of backstreet abortions, young girls at the mercy of evil men who damage their insides. They say that once abortion is freely available, no questions asked, at any hospital, these practices will die out. For the first time I feel like speaking – but I hold my tongue. People survive, I want to say, people survive but you can't make it better. Evil exists. Young girls are made pregnant, and either forced to bear or abort their children. It is not good, all this making things easier. This will achieve nothing – you make people soft, and as unable to deal with hardship as yourselves.

They go on to talk about the unsympathetic nature of gynaecologists, the way they examine women like women have no feelings; the way doctors do not take female complaints seriously. I realize that they do not know how to have no feelings. They are like naked crabs. Who would listen to a crab that has run away from his shell, complaining about cold and heat and pain? They have no armour; I despise them. They talk of reclaiming their bodies, and say next week they will use a speculum. Which means, I discover, they will look in their own cunts with a tiny mirror on a stick.

When I go home I am laughing, and when I tell Stephen, he for once doesn't know what to say.

'They are taking political action, the women,' I tell him. 'They look up their own private parts!' I am not interested in reclaiming my body; it is mine. If I have to fight then I do. If a man is stronger, he will win. Looking in my cunt with a mirror is not going to change anything.

I do not tell our doctor about the London abortion and the bleeding afterwards. But when our first baby dies inside me I am frightened. What if something was damaged and I didn't know? I have to go to hospital for a 'scrape', they will clear out what is left from the pregnancy. When the nurse comes to take my temperature after I wake up, I ask her if there is any damage and she says everything is fine. When the doctor comes in the afternoon, Stephen is there. 'There is no reason why you shouldn't try again, in a few months. There's no reason why you shouldn't have a perfectly healthy baby next time,' he says. He must know.

It was hard to get the first baby out, it clung like unripe fruit to the branch. But then the second one slipped away like melting butter. I dreamed of them, bad dreams. I made myself wake up.

Stephen is very kind. He asks me what I want to do. I say, stay at home. I will make some new curtains, I will gather my strength. We must try again. Of course, he says. He will not make me go back to classes at the technical college.

For a while we are almost happy together. He is very busy at work, long meetings, hours of marking, but he is glad I am at home and dinner is ready, he is grateful and does not try to cook or to make me go out. I am happy in the house. But I want a baby to be born. At last, we have Timothy.

CHAPTER FOURTEEN

Savages

In March 1789 William was organizing the construction of a proper road from the landing place to the hospital and storehouses. The route was in turns rocky, and soft and boggy, with two steep hills to be negotiated, and a permanent bridge to be built over the Tank Stream.

Drainage was the most pressing problem, because after rain every path in the country turned to muddy swamp. This was to be, as Phillip never tired of insisting, a city with broad streets and imposing buildings. The road must not limp or hobble between intractable tree roots and jagged rocks; it must soar, straight and wide, into the heart of the settlement. It was the artery that would feed the camp and enable it to grow to city size.

But lack of materials and equipment made the job of an engineer more like that of a magician. By what sleight of hand could this be substituted for that? By what alchemy could a tolerable surface be constructed from utterly unsuitable components? What force could imagination conjure to shift rocks, since the colony's supplies of gunpowder were now so low that all must be preserved for defence?

William planned and paced and measured and drew and examined the contents of the storehouse a dozen times, while his sweating gang wrestled with those tree stumps others had left in the way because they were too impossibly difficult to uproot. Perhaps he would lay a base of logs all along the route? Rocks would be better, smashed rocks; the chain-gang could be set to work on that. But the distance involved – the sheer quantity of material needed – added to the desperate slowness with which the gang worked, meant that the road would not be ready for a year or more.

Perhaps when ships arrived from England they would have quantities of limestone, tar, and gunpowder aboard? He knew the Governor had written requesting that future fleets use limestone for ballast. But the road, really, should be ready before ships arrived from England, so that their goods could be quickly and easily unloaded. If the ships arrived while the road was under construction, he could revise his plans; since they may not arrive for months, he should proceed, as he had done with the observatory, with no regard for what might or might not come from England. Besides, in all probability the first ship to arrive would be the *Sirius* returning from her voyage to the Cape in search of supplies. And she would be carrying nothing but food. Captain Hunter and his crew (including Bradley, whom William missed sharply at times) had sailed in October, and might be expected back at any time. The colonists were on short rations till their return.

The longed-for comet had not materialized. William now observed every clear night, for as many hours as he could keep himself awake, and moved about the camp in a state of mole-like blindness to public affairs. Watkin came up to the observatory one evening a week, generally on a Monday; on the whole William avoided the others. Their self-indulgent dinners and endless carping about rights and rank and who might have given offence to whom sickened him. He thought them all lazy; but then, they were investing very little in the place. Watkin had told him that it was only the two of them, among the marine officers, who were even considering extending their term of duty beyond three years. The others were all counting the months until they could put the place behind them. They did not care about erecting buildings that would last. They did not care about constructing roads that would not wash away in the first flash flood. They did not care about making decent gardens, the produce of which could lead them to independence from the stores and a diet of imported provisions.

Sweating in the hot dark storehouse, counting barrels of linseed oil and tar, braced against touching or standing on the rats he could hear rustling on all sides – for both storehouses were plagued by them, and they were brazen enough to be seen raiding gardens in broad daylight now (would it be possible to design a rat-proof storehouse?) – William understood that his situation was unlike that of most of the officers; was, in fact, closer to that of the convicts. Because he *was* sweating. He'd begun sweating over the observatory; his energy, his muscles had helped to force that construction to rear up in the wilderness. And by expenditure of that effort, he had bought a commitment to Sydney Cove. Now, he must sweat again to ensure its survival. It was real for him. As it was for the convicts, many of them – those in his gang, certainly. Not because men like Stokoe and Clough liked the place, or chose to be there, but because their labour had changed its face. The officers had merely supervised, and that at one or two removes. Their chief physical reaction to New South Wales was not numbed exhaustion, but the prickly discomfort of heat and insects, the irritation of mud underfoot, the annoyance of running out of tea or butter. They did not care if the convicts worked hard or not, provided they caused no trouble. And therefore they didn't care if the convicts were fairly treated, which would affect only their rate of work, not their troublesomeness.

He realized that many of them did not see the colony surviving beyond five years. It had been a little adventure, simply an excursion. Since the land yielded neither instant riches nor decent hunting nor the chance of glory in battle; since the natives were not noble savages nor eager slaves, but difficult, changeable, inscrutable (and their women so coated in rank fish-oil as to offend all but the coarsest sensibilities) – well, New South Wales was of no account.

The natives *were* difficult. But in William's opinion they had every right to be angry. At the end of December Phillip had carried out his threat and kidnapped a young native man. William vividly recalled Mary Johnson bursting into the little room where he sat talking with Richard, and telling them through her tears that a black man was captive.

'They've brought him in the Governor's cutter – Lieutenant Ball and someone else, they caught him by trickery – in the middle of a friendly conversation – '

'Here – my dear – ' Richard passed her a handkerchief.

'They've tied his wrists and ankles – Richard, he was shuddering with fear, his eyes are starting out of his head. You must go down and tell them – '

'But – tell them what? If they captured him on the Governor's orders?'

'But the whole of Sydney is down there, gawping at him – and they're saying he will be kept in that hut in the Governor's garden – and that he will be manacled, manacled to a convict – '

'Come on Richard, we must go down.' William pushed back his chair.

Richard did not move. 'If the Governor has ordered his capture and constructed a hut where he will be kept, and seen fit to provide a convict guard, what use will my protests be?'

'You knew about this!' Mary suddenly turned on him, her face crimson.

'I – yes, I was present, when Lieutenant Ball discussed it with the Judge Advocate. I knew Lieutenant Ball did not relish the task of capturing a man, but he was persuaded it was for the good of the colony and – and of the natives themselves.'

'For the good? '

'What could I do?' Richard's voice also became heated. 'What could I do? My standing with the Governor could not be lower.'

'Listen,' William broke into their confrontation. 'Isn't it illegal? To hold a free man captive when he has committed no crime – doesn't it contravene Habeas Corpus?'

'Habeas Corpus will apply only to subjects of the crown,' pronounced Richard. 'A native is not a British subject.'

'All right, then. Slavery!' said William triumphantly. 'If you hold a man against his will and force him to do what he has no mind to – you enslave him. No matter whose subject he is.'

'Oh, yes, Richard!' Mary clasped her husband's arm. 'It's true. The freed slaves in England are not British subjects, they come from America – Africa – all over the place.'

The chaplain rubbed his face. 'D'you think the Governor didn't discuss the legal implications with the Judge Advocate?'

'He may not have done,' said William. 'He has been cultivating this plan for a while. And who will dare tell him he is breaking the law?'

'You!' said Mary. 'The pair of you. Won't you, Richard?'

Richard stared at her, a worried frown on his face.

'Imagine what Mr Wilberforce would say!' she pleaded. 'He sent you here as spiritual guardian to the colony. Would he condone the capture of a man against his will; that he should be kept tethered like an animal?'

'We are not in England,' Richard said at last. 'That slavery is at an end in England is indisputable.'

'Thank God,' interjected Mary.

'But it is not at an end in English colonies. Consider the West Indies, the slaves there are not freed.'

'But they *will* be. The slave trade will be abolished, Richard, you know that, you know how many good men and women are campaigning for that end.'

'But in the meantime, since we are not in England, I do not believe the Governor has done anything illegal.'

'In the eyes of God it's *wrong* – '

William excused himself and left almost unnoticed. Mary was right, he felt, whatever the legal niceties that presented Richard with difficulties. He went up to the observatory to think through the arguments clearly, and presented himself first thing the following morning at the Governor's.

But Phillip would not even see him. The marine who politely asked him the nature of his business and then announced it to the Governor came out three minutes later with a note informing William that His Excellency thanked him for his trouble but the matter of the captured native Arabanoo had been fully discussed. The Governor had pressing work to do, as did Lieutenant Dawes, he was sure.

According to Watkin, Arabanoo settled down well and displayed a kind and courteous nature and an insatiable appetite for fish and game. But he did not settle down well enough, as William took the opportunity of pointing out to Watkin, for the Governor to feel easy about removing the ball and chain that hobbled him; and from the day of his capture there was an increase in the number of attacks by blacks upon the convicts.

When William had finished in the storeroom he carefully locked the door, wiped the sweat from his face, and made his way back down to the road gang. To his surprise they were not at work, but clustered in a vociferous group around Stokoe.

'Stokoe!' he called. 'What's going on?' Stokoe detached himself from the group and came up the path to meet William.

'Them blacks, sir. They've ambushed the brick kilns gang. We're gannen after 'em.'

'Ambushed? Is anyone killed?'

'Aye, but we'll teach 'em a lesson – they're not ganna be creepin' up be'ind folks when we're done – '

'That's not your job, Stokoe. Leave fighting to the soldiers. Where have you got this from, this news?'

'John Anderson and James Neal 'ave just come in covered wi' blood – fro' Botany Bay. The others're all massacred.'

'Where are they now?'

'The guards've tekken 'em to Captain Tench – '

'Well and good. Now you get back to work.'

'We should gan after 'em – ' Stokoe normally backed down when given a direct order, but this time he stood his ground. William hesitated. If it was true, he could understand the man's anger. It was Phillip's fault, he thought bitterly – Phillip caused this by annoying the natives – and the natives took reprisals against the convicts because they could not get at Phillip or the soldiers. As he hesitated there was a cheer from the convicts farther along the path, and a detachment of marines from the barracks came into view, moving at a good speed. The convicts stepped aside to let them past, and William and Stokoe also moved back. The men's faces were already as red as their jackets in the heat.

'There you are then,' William told Stokoe. 'They will see the natives off.'

The men got back to work after a fashion, and William was left free to worry, as he took levels along the path, about what might happen if the natives really had committed a massacre; if the soldiers did find them and fire upon them. It may be the beginning of war.

The story became more clear over the succeeding days. No natives were found at the scene of the ambush, so the soldiers did not use their guns; they simply helped the seven wounded convicts back to camp, and carried in the body of the one who was dead. It emerged that the convicts were not the innocent victims of an ambush, but that they had set out from the kilns for Botany Bay, armed with sticks and knives, for the express purpose of attacking the natives in retaliation for the disappearance of one of their number earlier in the week.

In other words, it was part of the running skirmish that went on between natives and convicts, and there was no clear right or wrong on either side.

When William's incensed work gang informed him that the brick kilns men were to be flogged for the incident, he did not take it very seriously. The Governor had a habit of making last-minute reprieves, both for those sentenced to death and for floggings. If the brick kilns gang had not learned their lesson from being ambushed, flogging would not deter them. William was more concerned about the situation with the natives, which seemed to him to be sliding towards disaster. The Governor was not willing to discuss the rights and wrongs of holding Arabanoo captive; well then, maybe it would be possible to use Watkin's influence to persuade His Excellency to listen to an alternative plan, and perhaps this attack upon the brick kilns gang would focus his attention on the subject.

'For us to learn their language *must* be the first step,' he told Watkin. 'Which means the Governor must excuse a couple of officers their duties in the settlement, and charge them with setting up camp among the natives, and staying to learn all they can. By living among them, they can show themselves trustworthy and give the natives reason to believe what they say. At the moment we appear – we are – contradictory.'

Watkin listened patiently. 'And then? When two officers know their language and have gained their trust? What next?'

'Then those officers must arrange a meeting between the Governor, Major Ross, the Judge Advocate, the chaplain, and the leaders of the Ab-Origines – and interpret between the two parties.'

'And the subjects to be discussed at the meeting?'

'We must lay fairly before the natives those advantages we can offer them: how to construct better shelters, the use of clothes, bedding and cooking utensils; the art of cultivation. We must tell them about the Christian church and about their everlasting souls. We must take note of their grievances about shortages of fish.'

'All these subjects are fraught with difficulty,' Watkin pointed out reasonably. 'They want us to stop fishing, but we can't because we need the food. It will be difficult for us to convince them of the benefits of agriculture when our first year's crop has been a dismal failure – '

'I know all that. But we can begin by teaching them how to make better shelters – for the winter – then in the spring, in September, we can take them through the stages of cultivation, beginning with sowing seeds. Trust comes before any practical knowledge, and trust is what is being destroyed daily in the present state of affairs – '

'And who – which officers – would go and live among them?'

William had half-hoped that Watkin himself would volunteer, but he now realized that was improbable. Watkin liked his dinners and his wine; anyway, Watkin had responsibilities as a marine captain. Who would the Governor let go? Not William himself, because Alt was still 'indisposed'. It was difficult to think of anybody who could be spared who would have any enthusiasm or competence. Watkin suggested postponing his conversation with the Governor until they had at least come up with some officers' names to propose; otherwise the plan would founder before it began.

The entire settlement was ordered to witness the flogging of the brick kilns gang, to William's considerable surprise. He assumed up till the last minute that the Governor would reprieve them. As the crowd gathered at the punishment area, carpenters (whose skills, William reflected, were more urgently needed in the construction of huts and houses) were still erecting the posts the offenders would be tied to. Phillip brought the native Arabanoo with him, his ball and chain scraping over the rocks, and made a short pitiless speech to the assembled crowd. The purpose of these punishments, he declared, was threefold: firstly, as a deterrent against straggling from the settlement, which he had expressly prohibited; secondly, as a deterrent against attacking or annoying the natives; and thirdly, to demonstrate to a native, Arabanoo, what British justice was. The British were not afraid to punish their own people when they transgressed; these men had been wrong to attack Arabanoo's people, and must be seen to suffer for it.

This was received in sullen silence. At a signal from the Governor the flogging began. William, averting his own gaze from the spectacle, saw Arabanoo's eyes widen in horror as the cat's-tails licked into the naked backs. At first there was no sound but the whistle of the tails in the air and the thwack as they hit flesh; the crowd seemed to hold its breath. But gradually breathing became audible; the floggers began to pant with their exertions, the four tied men to gasp as air was hit out of them; the crowd to inhale and exhale heavily, as if in sympathy, in time with each lash. The sentence was a hundred each; at twenty one man began to cry out. Their skin was broken now, gobbets of bloody matter scattered over the floggers at each strike. At forty one fainted. There was a pause while he was revived with water and given a cursory examination by White, who gave an angry nod to tell the flogger he could begin again. It was at this point that Arabanoo flung himself at the Governor's feet, jabbering in his own tongue and gesturing at the prisoners, clearly begging for their release. When Phillip ignored him he moved right away and squatted with his back to the floggings. At last he was led off to his hut; William saw from the marks on his cheeks that he had been crying.

William felt like crying himself, as the men were untied and carried away, and the next four tied to the posts. The effects of this day's work were obvious: the native was sickened, he would never want his countrymen to associate freely with such barbarous people as the British. And the convicts were goaded almost beyond endurance. They must see their fellows attacked and hounded by natives and then flogged without mercy; inevitably they would vent their anger on the natives again. How is anything to be achieved, how is anything to go right, *ever*, while he governs in this crass, heavy-handed fashion, William asked himself bitterly.

His plan for Watkin to speak to Phillip appeared infantile, wildly optimistic. He was powerless, all he could do was his work.

He listened in silence to the convicts' complaints as they worked on the road. Besides the obvious reasons for their anger, one of the flogged men, James Neal, was failing to recover. They discussed his health day by day. Putrefaction had set in to his lacerated back; he had been moved up to the hospital; he stank so badly that no one would stay near him except Barnes. The doctors could do nothing for him. Barnes – of course, William recalled, Barnes was under Neal's 'protection'.

William met Surgeon White as he was coming out of the hospital, and asked after Neal.

White shook his head. 'Dead meat. He may have been diseased before the flogging; a man of that size and strength should have supported a hundred lashes with tolerable ease. I could not in all honesty say that the punishment was too severe. All the others are back at work.'

'You can do nothing for him?'

'I put a measure of opiates into his water in the evening, to ease him through the night. Barnes keeps off the flies. There's nothing more to do, William, the man will be dead in a day or two.'

And so he was. The convicts' sense of grievance led them to talk of a petition to the Judge Advocate, but then they were all distracted by the arrest of seven marines for thefts of food from the stores. If convicted, these men would be hung. It was the colony's first serious crime committed by non-convicts.

Stokoe reported gleefully to William that Barnes had been thrown out of the brickies' hut and spent the night wandering naked through the camp, crying like a baby. It was a simple matter for William to see White again and obtain permission for Barnes to sleep in the medical storeroom he spent his days guarding; a simple matter, and a relief to be able to achieve something positive.

CHAPTER FIFTEEN

Disease

It was a clear night in early April. William promised himself that tonight he would take careful readings of the distances between the stars in Crux Australis; the constellation was more brilliant now than it had been in the summer months, with its four bright stars and one lesser, and the two pointers, Alpha and Beta of Centaurus, signing its position. After that he would scan minutely a new sector of the sky to the south-east, identifying and recording every heavenly body he saw, together with its size and brightness, in the copies of the Cape astronomer's charts he had painstakingly made. He hoped to cover methodically a new sector every clear night until he had observed the entire sky, but progress was desperately slow, and there were a worrying number of inaccuracies – or discrepancies – on the Cape charts.

It was a marvellous night for observation, the first night for months that there had been a combination of new moon and no cloud. William would work through the night; his road gang could start without him in the morning.

He pulled on the ropes to open the canvas shutter with the vivid sense of satisfaction this always gave him – the sudden peeling back of a segment of the octagonal roof to reveal naked sky. The physical presence of the observatory around him was a pleasure. The earth floor in his living quarters was still uneven; but up here the clock was wedged in place on the rock, the instruments were all ranged along the wooden benches the *Sirius'* carpenter had made for him, his astronomical log and star charts stood ready. He rarely bothered to light a fire – it took too long, and besides he had seen too many blazes amongst the convicts' huts to want to risk his own wooden home; but that meant that on clear nights it was very cold, especially once the shutter was open. He put on his greatcoat over his jacket and took a quick swig of warming rum. Then, positioning notebook and pencil precisely where he wanted them, he leant over and extinguished the lamp, and sat back to wait for his eyes to adjust.

He loved this moment of pause before observation began; a punctuation like the dimming of lights in a theatre. Staring blindly and patiently into the dark room, he waited for it to resolve itself into black shapes and lighter backgrounds, till he could make out the silhouette of the telescope against the grey surrounding darkness. When at last he did allow himself to glance up at the open segment of roof, the stars were dazzling. Already, with the naked eye, he could see a strange dark nebula he had never noticed before, within the kite of Crux Australis – which was beautifully positioned in the upper centre of the open roof section. He raised the night glass. A sudden, loud voice called from outside.

'Dawes! I know you're in there, I saw your light!' Watkin Tench. William laid down his glass and sighed. Watkin was a practised observer now, spending every Monday night at the observatory; he would not hold William back from his work, but he would chatter. Besides, it was Thursday.

Silence was what William craved; silence which allowed him to become nothing but a staring, aching eye; which allowed his essence to be transported, via the tunnel of his own vision, through the telescope's hollow tube and up into the vast perfection of the heavens, leaving Sydney Cove and all its difficulties behind. His rhythm of watching with each eye then closing it, the increase then controlled diminution of strain in his ocular muscles, was as exact and familiar as a dancer's routine, and was always disrupted by Watkin's presence. With Watkin here the night would be suddenly gone in a spate of talk and tiredness, instead of paced and spanned and relished.

He was absolutely unwilling to light the lamp again. Calling out to Watkin to wait, he moved carefully from the bench to the steps, keeping his hand on the rough wooden wall, and felt his way down into his bedroom. It was very dark but he moved more easily here, knowing the unevenness of the floor by heart, and freed of the anxiety that he might break a valuable instrument.

'I'm here,' he said, opening the door on Watkin, who was illumined by starlight strongly enough to cast a shadow. 'I'm observing.'

'Well I shall fall over something if you don't make a light.'

'You're joining me? I'll lead you through.'

'No. I want to talk to you.'

'But Watkin, it's a perfect night!'

'You won't take any notice of me if you're star-gazing, you won't even hear me.'

'I'll talk to you tomorrow. How about tomorrow afternoon?'

'The stars aren't going to run away. Have you no fire? It must be nearly freezing – '

'No.' William was becoming angry. 'Go back down to camp if you want a fire. Look Watkin, three nights out of four I can't stay awake because I've been surveying from dawn till dusk; and two nights out of four it's cloudy; and two weeks out of four the moon's too bright – d'you know how many good observation nights that leaves? D'you have any idea how pitifully little I've accomplished here?' He was still standing blocking the doorway. Down through the trees behind Watkin he could see the winking fires of the settlement, and even hear men's voices singing, from the barracks, it sounded like.

'I won't stay long. It's important. Come out here where I can see you, if you won't light a lamp.'

Ungraciously, William stepped out into the starlight, pulling the door closed behind him.

'Have you got a coat on?' asked Watkin. 'Good.' He began to follow the path round the back of the observatory, heading towards the sea.

'Watkin!' William called angrily, but he was striding ahead; William had almost to run to catch up. They came out of the trees on to the cliff top, and Watkin squatted down and waited for William to join him. There were no native boats on the water tonight, only the stern lantern of the *Supply* was visible in the harbour.

'The natives,' said Watkin, chiming in with William's thoughts.

'What about them?'

'You've heard the reports that they are sick?'

'I've heard rumours,' said William. 'They're hungry, is what. I've seen a couple that looked near to starving. We've eaten all their fish – see?' He gestured to the empty black water. 'They don't even bother fishing here any more.'

'No,' said Watkin. 'They're sick. There are bodies on the beaches all around Port Jackson. They have crawled into their caves and they're dying – '

'What of?'

'Johnny White and Worgan came out with me today – ' Watkin paused.

'And?'

'Smallpox.'

William looked up at the sky, at the infinite pin-pricks of light that made up the Milky Way. Smallpox. 'There have been no cases of smallpox among us.'

'No. Not since we were at the Cape. Seventeen months ago.'

'Then where – ?'

'I don't know. But from what I've seen today, it is entirely new to them, they are dying like flies.'

William shook his head. 'There's been no pox scarring on any we have seen.'

'Quite. The only scars they bear are those self-inflicted stripes, and the scars of battle.'

'Dying like flies – ' William thought of the crowded beaches he had seen; of the laughing faces mimicking Phillip as he bartered for the crayfish; of the child with his shell. 'Is there nothing we can do?'

'I don't know. We can bring the sick into the hospital – but we can't cure them – '

'No.'

'Where has it come from? Where can it have come from?'

'Maybe from the French? From La Perouse's expedition?'

William considered. 'They've been gone a year. Unless it spread in another direction, say, to the south, from their visit, and is only just now sweeping up the coast – '

'They could be wiped out.' Watkin's voice cracked.

William waited.

'Those we saw today – ' Watkin broke off again, took a deep breath, and continued more normally. 'In one place where we landed there were three of them in a little inlet. Not long dead, White said; one of the children was still warm. They were – you have seen smallpox victims?'

William shook his head. 'Only the scars.'

'They were covered. Every inch of their body covered, in pustules; every part – lips, ears, fingers, eyelids – in raised pustules like – like – the skin of an animal, some kind of reptile. They were – *covered* in it, encased in it – ' He broke off.

'What did White have to say?'

'Not a great deal. He cannot guess how it has broken out among them, is amazed at the speed of its dissemination.'

'Does he fear for the settlement?'

'No. If anyone were going to, they'd have caught it off that sailor at the Cape. All the officers have been inoculated, and most of the convicts have had it. It's lost its power with Europeans now, *we* are not at risk – '

There was a note in Watkin's voice that puzzled William. A tension, as if he were angry with William – or possibly with himself. 'William,' he said. 'The smallpox. Where else have you heard of it breaking out among the natives?'

'North America.'

'Do you know how that came about?'

'From the whites, I suppose a sailor or a settler with the sickness. It spreads more quickly among natives, as you said; they are less hardy than we.'

'It was deliberately spread. In America.'

'Deliberately?'

'Some Indians were given blankets from the smallpox hospital.' After a short wait Watkin went on, 'They were warlike and difficult. They had killed some settlers and were refusing to sign a treaty to give up land. They would have fought – hard.'

At last William found his voice. 'What happened?'

'This. They died.'

Suddenly William's energy returned. 'How do you know? Do you *know* this, Watkin? Is it recorded?'

'I've heard it. It's known – within the army it's known, it's frowned upon, to be sure, but many regard it as a legitimate tactic in war.' He laughed sourly. 'Better than expending a squadron of recruits.'

'It's known by the government?'

Watkin hesitated. 'I don't know. Obviously no one would be prepared to admit to it officially – '

'Well it should be exposed – it should be . . . the perpetrators must be brought to justice.'

'William, consider where you are; when you are likely to return to England; and the fact that the perpetrators as you call them are probably still at Fort Pitt.'

William gazed out at the black water of the harbour. It was calm, he thought he could even see reflections of the stars in it – or maybe they were small luminous sea-creatures. He had a sudden pang of longing to be at sea again, on a little wooden island surrounded by the waters, a confined community that had only its own internal tensions and crises to resolve, and stood united *vis-à-vis* other ships, pledged to fight enemies, assist allies. The simplicity of that life, routine duties, the repetition, beckoned sweetly.

'You think – here?'

'I don't know.' Watkin shifted his position, tucking his coat under himself and sitting on it. 'I asked White today where it could have come from and he reeled off a list of impossibilities – as we have said, not from us, not from the French, not from Cook . . . and he said, not from the samples.'

'Samples?'

'Apparently he and Worgan brought, amongst their medical supplies, some glass bottles containing variolous matter.'

'Why?'

'With the idea, I think, that it may be useful as a preventative measure.'

'How?'

Watkin shrugged. 'For inoculation. It's nothing more refined than those farthing scabs they sell at fairs at home, for people to expose themselves to mild infection. He said he thought it might be useful for children born here – if they wanted to return to England, say.'

'But could it cause this severity of disease among the natives?'

'I don't know. If they have never been exposed to it before – '

'But – have they been given the stuff? Surely the Governor would never – '

'No. No. White said, it was impossible that they could have got hold of the samples. But the very fact that he mentioned it – '

'Yes.' William stood up, his knees were aching. He paced along the dark path, ten paces away from Watkin, ten paces back again. 'Well if he says it's impossible . . . Couldn't he use his samples to inoculate the Ab-Origines, in the way you describe? To treat those who are not yet infected?' As he spoke William's mind raced over the difficulties – the journeys inland and around the coast to find unaffected tribes, the attempts to explain to them that they must be made ill to save their lives . . . The settlement had neither the manpower nor the equipment for such an exercise; more importantly, they had not won the natives' trust. And was it likely, anyway, that Phillip would be willing to expend scarce resources on a medical mission?

'The samples have gone.'

It took him a while to make sense of Watkin's words.

'White says they have mislaid the samples. They were in the hospital stores, he is pretty sure, but when he looked last night he couldn't find them.'

'Someone has taken them?'

'Perhaps.'

'And given them to the natives?'

'I don't know. It's only guesswork. They may have been put some-where else; he is not certain.'

'The samples are missing, and the natives have the smallpox.'

'Yes.' Watkin stood stiffly, and brushed his coat. 'It's cold. Shall we return?' William followed close behind his dark shape.

'But who *would*? Who would do such a thing?'

'Not the doctors, obviously – '

'Well who else had access to the hospital stores?' As he asked the question, William realized he already knew the answer. Convict guards. Like Barnes.

He did not have the patience for observation that night, and was up early in the morning to set his gang to work. Once they were busy he made for the hospital.

As the wharf came into view, he saw that the Governor's cutter was alongside. Phillip, his black captive Arabanoo, Surgeon White, and Lieutenant Ball were directing the men, who were lifting out the inert bodies of two natives. They began to make their way up towards William, following the detour above the wide raw area where the road gang laboured, pickaxes ringing against stone. Phillip led the way, and hailed William from a distance.

'We could do with your road today, Mr Dawes.' William moved on down towards them, and saw that the natives were an old man and a boy. Each was wrapped in a blanket, but their faces were thick with the pustules Watkin had described; the old man was no more than a black skeleton coated in puffy blisters. As William passed him he turned his head, revealing a pink swollen mouth and throat which William saw, with horrible clarity, was also full of blisters. 'Bado.'

'Water – ' William said, to White, who was immediately behind. 'He's asking for water.'

White nodded. 'When we get him up there – we're taking them to the empty hut above the hospital. He shall have water.' Arabanoo and Ball filed past, leaving William staring after the little party. The boy's eyes had been closed as if he were dead already; his pustular face was like something from a nightmare. William hurried on to the hospital.

Barnes was sitting outside the store room staring vacantly into space. He was barefoot again, but his ugly, unfinished face was free of bruises. When he saw William he scrambled to his feet.

'Morning, Barnes.'

'Uh – thank you, sir.'

'For what?'

'For – for 'avin' me billeted 'ere. I – I can sleep safe.'

William dimly remembered that he himself had asked for Barnes to be allowed to sleep in the store-room after Neal's death. Yes, because Barnes was thrown out of the brickies' hut, and had nowhere to sleep, and was in danger of being bullied again. *He* had asked for Barnes to be allowed to sleep in the room where the smallpox samples were kept. Now a full sense of his own responsibility for the disaster struck him, bringing him out in a sudden sweat. 'Is it just you, Barnes? None of the other guards sleeps here?'

'No. Saves 'em puttin' anyone else outside, nights.'

William nodded. Balmain, passing on his way into the hospital, gave a cheery wave and 'How d'ye do?'

'Can we go into the storeroom, Barnes?' They needed somewhere private for this conversation.

'I – I – ' Barnes was stuttering stupidly with his mouth open. William felt his usual revulsion for the youth, tinged with his usual guilt; yielding to a fury with himself, for not taking his own first reaction more seriously. If Barnes had done this thing, he was utterly evil. But for William's meddling kindness, he would have been bullied to death by convicts like McEntire months ago, and would not have lived to bring a plague upon the Ab-Origines. William forced himself to speak levelly.

'I know you have a key – of course, it's your sleeping place. Let's go in now, there is something I have to ask you.'

'Uh – I can't take no one in.'

'Surgeon White has given his permission,' William lied. 'Come on now, Barnes, I'm busy.'

With stupid slowness Barnes unlocked the solid door and led the way into the small windowless room. It smelt of wine and oil of tar and vinegar and lint and poultices, a strange combination of smells that took William back to the apothecary's shop where he was sometimes sent as a child, for some of the special mixture to loosen his father's bowels. He even remembered the dreadful smell of his father's relief, which pervaded the house after he had closeted himself, grunting and straining, in his room with the chamber-pot.

'Make a light, Barnes, before I trip over something.' He had to take the tinder and strike it himself, Barnes was so slow. The stubby candle revealed a room crowded with boxes and bottles, ranging from heavy wine casks along the floor, to small stoppered glass vials on the upper shelves. Some were labelled in Latin, others bore no indication as to their contents. How could a fool like Barnes pick one lethal bottle out of this lot? 'Can you read?'

Open-mouthed, Barnes shook his head.

'And where do you sleep?'

Barnes indicated a small space beneath the bench, where a grubby blanket lay twisted into a knot.

'Your nose pressed up against the wine casks, eh? Are you never tempted to take a sip?'

Barnes shook his head again.

'Have you never taken *anything* from the stores? Not even a tiny bottle?'

There seemed to be a look of cunning in the boy's eyes; for a moment they engaged with a kind of animal intelligence.

'You *have*, haven't you?' William checked himself. He mustn't frighten Barnes by seeming eager, or curious. Barnes was backing towards the door.

'Come back. Come here, listen. I was sorry to hear about your friend James Neal. I – Surgeon White told me he was peaceful at the end.'

Barnes burst into tears, his face suddenly transformed to the mask of woe of a heartbroken child. 'They killed 'im,' he sobbed.

'It was not intentional. The same punishment was served on all, and none of the others took any injury from it.'

The boy shook his head. 'Them blacks. Them filthy blacks did for 'im.'

'How?'

'He told me. When 'e was lyin' there. 'Is back all rotten – I was pickin' maggots out of 'im – flies everywhere – ' He broke down into wordless sobbing and William stood helplessly watching him, unable to force himself close enough to put a comforting arm around his shoulder, or indeed to touch him at all. Snot and slobber ran down his pitiful slack face. As the sobs lessened William said reasonably, 'It was the Governor ordered him flogged, not the blacks.'

'Along o' them he *got* whipped. Along o' goin' after them.' He wiped his nose along his arm. 'They got witchcraft. Spells.'

'How do you know this? Who says so?'

'All the brickies knows it. Niggers look at a man an' they mutter. They put maggots in 'is back. Black bastards – they'll be sorry.'

The door was suddenly pushed open and Worgan came in.

'William, old fellow. What are you doing?'

'Just – I just needed a word with Barnes here.'

'Well come outside, will you? He's not supposed to let anyone but us in here.'

'I know, he told me.'

Worgan nodded, ushering them out and stopping behind a moment to glance around the shelves and extinguish the candle.

'Have you poisoned them?' William hissed at Barnes. The boy lifted his smeary face in shock, and half-raised an arm as if to shield himself from a blow. Then without a word he turned and ran away down the track.

William pressed the heels of his palms into his eyes until he saw shooting lights, and cursed himself for an oaf. Why blurt it out like that? Barnes knew he knew, now. He would be so petrified no one would ever get a word of sense from him. He needed to be crept up on intelligently, assured that his listener had the greatest sympathy with everything he'd done – not accused, and reduced to abject terror.

Worgan shut the door and turned the key in the lock.

'I think he may need replacing,' he said, nodding after Barnes' retreating back.

'Because he let me into the store-room?'

Worgan laughed and clapped William on the shoulder. 'I don't want to see the thriving trade in rum rivalled by one in opium, is all. The criminal brethren will set a high price on anything that buys them an hour or two's oblivion – and between you and me, we have enough opium in there to keep 'em happy for weeks. Your protégé hasn't the wit to pilfer it, but if a more cunning lag prevails upon him to be allowed in – '

'*Does* he take others in there?'

Worgan shrugged. 'Why should you be the first?'

There was a chance, then. That not Barnes, but some other convict had stolen the smallpox bottle. Perhaps he could be brought to admit that, by clever questioning. But who had a better motive than Barnes? Barnes believed the blacks had used their witchcraft to murder his protector Neal. How could I have not spoken with him before, William asked himself wretchedly. I got him the guard's position, and permission to sleep here, too, and I never even spoke to him. What was I thinking of?

'Yes,' he said quickly, seeing that Worgan was watching him quizzically. 'Yes, do get a new guard. I – I am afraid he may not be as trustworthy as I thought.'

Worgan nodded and pocketed the key.

When William returned to the road gang they were talking about the sick natives who'd been brought past.

'Why should we bring 'em in?' Stokoe was saying, wiping the sweat from his face and neck. 'Their own kin leave 'em to die on the rocks. Why're we bringing 'em in to spread disease among us?'

'It is almost certain that *we* have caused the disease among *them*,' William said. 'Don't you think we owe them a little medical assistance?'

Stokoe shrugged and lifted his pick, not meeting William's eye. Even if they have not deliberately given the natives the disease, he told himself, they would not think it wrong to have done so. There was a weight of misery inside him so heavy that he could hardly drag himself over to Adamson, who was calling on him to pronounce upon a slab of quartz they had come up against, which fractured easily but extended to depths they had not intended to dig out.

Watkin told him about the two natives later that night. The old man had died after a couple of hours and the boy had displayed no grief, simply saying 'boree' – dead – although the old man had shown great anxiety for the child. Watkin and Ball had crossed back to the cove where the man and boy were discovered, to bury another body seen there. Arabanoo had helped to bury the old man. Tentatively William raised the subject of White's samples; it crossed his mind that Watkin might be brought to question Barnes more intelligently than he himself had done. But Watkin cut him short immediately.

'It's nonsense. Wild guesswork, which will lead us nowhere. Even if the samples were stolen, why should the natives have wanted them?'

'But they like anything that's curious – you know that. And glass – ' William could suddenly see the event as clearly as if he'd witnessed it. 'They know about glass. They prize it. They use it to tip their spears now, instead of shells – you've seen the latest spears in Campbell's collection.'

In his mind's eye it unfolds with the mesmeric clarity of hallucination. A convict – Barnes – pulling the shining bottle from his pocket; offering it to the outstretched black hand, smiling stupidly to himself. Making to put it away again, teasing the native into hunger for it; relenting, passing it over. The eager black fingers clasping the glass; the bottle shaken and held up to the light, as several of them cluster round to see the contents. A quick pulling and twisting at the stopper, which maybe will not yield easily; a look between them, a quick nod, and –

smash! on a rock. The coveted chunks of glass are seized, and the fine dust inside the bottle, exploding into the air with a little mushroom-shaped puff, makes them sneeze and laugh. A poor parody of Eve's innocent, greedy curiosity in Eden; for the glass bottle gives the blacks no knowledge, no mastery. Gives nothing but sickness and death.

Watkin was fidgeting impatiently. 'Put it from your mind, William. I was overtired last night, the thing's impossible. Let it go no farther now, the fewer of us who know, the better.'

A couple of days later he passed William at work in the rain, trying to divert a stream that was suddenly coursing over the roadway, where no water had flowed before. He called to him to come up to the small-pox house.

'We have some new patients.' They were a boy and a girl, brother and sister, both emaciated and covered in pustules. White and Arabanoo were bathing the boy and putting a clean shirt on him. Matter oozed from pustules which had burst, and his thin body shivered uncontrollably. Arabanoo was talking continuously, in his gentle, chattering voice; comfort and reassurance in his tone. Watkin pointed to the black man's naked ankles.

'The Governor ordered his fetters taken off this afternoon – he has shown so much goodness in trying to help these people, and persuading them to trust us. His Excellency thinks he regards us as friends, and may now stay with us of his own free will. Every cloud, eh?'

Once William had overcome his initial revulsion at the appearance of the disease, he found himself gravitating to the smallpox hut at some point every day. The first boy, Nanbaree, was making a good recovery, and chattered to Arabanoo, who patiently tried to feed the new patients and offered them water. White said Nanbaree would live, and that he would take him into his own household and give him a Christian upbringing. Arabanoo, whom William had avoided in the past, out of shame at the ball and chain on the black man's leg, was the most gentle and attentive sick-room attendant William had ever seen.

Three days after the brother and sister were brought in, it became clear that the brother was dying. The girl crept to his side and lay by him until he was quite cold. But she did not cry or display her grief; her dignity touched William, and he told Richard and Mary Johnson about it over dinner. Hearing that the doctor was planning to adopt Nanbaree, the Johnsons decided to adopt the girl themselves. It was a perfect solution. She was already mature, maybe thirteen years of age, White judged, and there would have been a danger of giving the wrong impression to other natives, and to the convicts, had a single man taken her in. In the Johnsons' house Booron would have the kindly guardianship of Mary; she would have a surrogate mother and father.

Mary was overjoyed at the plan; she could teach Booron English, and read the Bible with her – perhaps Booron would become her first Christianized native, and help to spread God's word among her people.

'And I will help her to clean her hair – did you hear that when they combed Arabanoo's hair, he rejoiced and ate all the lice they found there!' she told William excitedly. 'I can teach her sewing, and the importance of modesty; perhaps through her it will be possible to pass on the skills of sewing to some of her compatriots, so that they can cover their nakedness!'

William nodded. Perhaps Watkin was right, perhaps even out of this devastation a little good might come. The presence of a native in the Johnsons' house would make it easy for him to study the language. In fact he could learn it as well as if he went and lived among them, but without having to neglect his daily work. He could find out about her religion and beliefs, and she would learn about white civilization. Also, she would learn here the practical skills of growing food. The Johnsons' garden was the best-tended and most productive in the settlement. She would see, indeed, she would eat, the fruits of agricultural labour.

But how many were dying, to make this possible? In the solitude of the observatory, William knelt and prayed for guidance. If the Indians had become infected through the medical samples; if the medical samples had been given to them by Barnes (or, at the very least, through the agency of Barnes passing them on to someone else); if Barnes only had access to the storeroom key because of William's intervention on his behalf; then did that not logically make William solely responsible for the epidemic?

His mind could scarcely take in such a monstrous fact. After two entirely sleepless nights he asked Richard to call at the observatory and privately told him the whole story. Richard listened intently, then put his arms around William and embraced him.

'No. No, William, no. You mustn't blame yourself. Everything you did, you did in good faith; the existence of these samples in the storeroom wasn't even known until the illness broke out. Our heavenly

Father knows you are innocent – don't torment yourself with unnecessary guilt, it is perverse, it will hamper you in your work.'

His certainty provided sweet but temporary relief.

'If anyone is to be blamed, it must be Barnes or whoever it was who *knowingly* passed that bottle on, intending to cause harm.'

Richard had a voice, William saw, for dealing with distress – a voice he undoubtedly used with the dying, or with others who confessed terrible crimes – a kindly, paternal, certain voice which allowed one to believe that he spoke with God's authority. He does, William reminded himself sharply. He does speak with God's authority, he has been ordained.

But my God, came the thought, creeping in where he did not want it, my God is more exacting. He requires me to conduct a more rigorous searching of my soul. He knows that sin is not always about intention. He demands that I find a method of atoning. Forgiveness must be earned.

The question of what to do about Barnes seemed relatively straightforward. At the very least he had abused the trust placed in him as guard; scrupulous questioning might reveal the names of other convicts who had conspired with him to infect the Indians. The Governor must be informed, so that they could be brought to trial.

Four days later the *Sirius* returned from the Cape of Good Hope after an absence of seven months. They brought 127 hundredweight of flour, along with seed wheat, barley, and salt provisions. Their voyage was a triumph; they had circumnavigated the globe, sailing always eastwards, rounding Cape Horn on their way out and Van Diemen's Land on their return. The southerly latitudes had exposed them to intolerable cold, and seas of ghostly ice floes. Their longitude readings (proved by the success of their voyage to have been accurate to the greatest nicety) were always determined by distances taken between sun and moon, or moon and fixed star – an extraordinary feat of observation and seamanship on the part of Captain Hunter and Lieutenant Bradley. At the Cape they had learned that the First Fleet's returning transports had been becalmed and struck by terrible sickness, so the skeleton crews of the *Friendship* and *Alexander* had to be put together on the *Alexander*, and the *Friendship*, crewless, was sunk. It struck William curiously that among those dead sailors there must be numbers who had fathered convict women's children; infants who would soon be taking their first steps in the colony. It was a strange twist of fate that had taken those men all the way to New South Wales, only to destroy them on the return voyage, having planted their seed at Sydney Cove.

Despite the richness of all this news, Bradley, when he came up to the observatory to speak with William, could only talk about one thing: the plague among the natives.

'As we approached the coast – the Heads – when we came into Port Jackson – we did not see a single living native!'

William had not been out in a boat for a long time. He visualized the crowds, spear-waving, or eagerly beckoning, that they had encountered on those early trips charting the harbour.

'When we tacked in closer to the shore, we could see bodies – just lying where they fell – on the beach, or beside their huts – as if there'd been a battle, a massacre – '

'I know.'

'Not a single canoe on the water – not a single fisherman or woman – it is as if they never existed – '

The outrage and horror in his face made William ashamed; had he stopped feeling like this? Had he already accepted this wholesale slaughter as unalterable fact, and moved on? Knowing how pitiful it sounded, he told Bradley the good news, the adopted native children who would be able to act as intermediaries. Bradley interrupted him.

'Intermediaries between which parties? The blacks may be wiped out.'

Watkin had extracted a promise that William should not mention the subject of the variolus samples to anyone new. Even as he'd given his word, William had mentally excepted Bradley. There was something in Bradley which warmed William and heartened him and put him on his mettle. Bradley seemed always a little ironic, watching William from depths of reserved amusement and – and – resignation, which, in itself, gave a peculiar charge to their meetings. Bradley sometimes made it possible for him to see things differently.

Bradley listened to the story of Barnes and the smallpox samples in silence. At the end he shrugged.

'It doesn't make any difference, does it, knowing who's to blame? Surely the point is, they were living quite happily without disease, before we came; a year or so of our presence in their midst has resulted in their lives' destruction.'

'No!' William urgently wanted Bradley to make the distinction. 'The point is one of blame and responsibility. If we – or members of our party – have knowingly introduced the disease among them, then we must bring the guilty people to trial. We must publicly admit our culpability, administer punishment and make reparations.'

Bradley laughed. 'What punishment? D'you think flogging poor old Barnes, or whoever it was used him as cat's paw, will solve anything? What reparations can you make to the dead?'

'That's not the point.' William could feel his face reddening at Bradley's wilful obtuseness. 'At least we could seek forgiveness – '

'So that it can be wiped clean on some great slate in the sky?' Bradley sneered. 'They're dead. It can never be forgiven.'

'Don't say that!'

'It can never be forgiven.'

They stared at each other. William was close to tears. 'Yes, but how can we live? Without forgiveness we can't live – '

'Oh yes? You are a sensitive flower, William. We live with the unspeakable, constantly, we don't even notice – '

'But to pile wrong on wrong – if we don't clear it back – Listen!' William was suddenly inspired by an image which would help Bradley to understand. 'It's like a wound. You inflict a wound, wrongly, by accident. Well, then you apologize for your action and help to clean the cut, call the surgeon to sew it up. You can't make it vanish but you encourage it to heal. Or – according to your precepts - you make a wound; you say, "Oh, it's done, nothing can change it now," you allow infection to enter and spread; it is never cleaned back and gangrene sets in and the limb – perhaps the whole life – is lost.'

Bradley shook his head. 'Behaving decently will do nothing but make the perpetrator of the crime feel better. It is too late to help the victim. We are murderous bastards, and may as well continue on our way.'

'If there was no forgiveness, we would all be damned from our first lisping lie or childish theft of a sweetmeat. There *is* forgiveness, but to obtain it sin must be admitted and repented of. We must be cleansed.'

'Internal transactions,' said Bradley. 'They serve only us. Like taking a bath when you're dirty. Sin accumulates. It spatters you – it stains you, in childhood. But as you grow older it cakes you, like a great crust of dirt, it encases you, you are burdened by its weight, your shape is moulded by it, it accretes, more and more of it, it grows tight as suffocation around you – '

'I'm not listening to this. You're mad!'

There was a silence and Bradley stood up. He was smiling and nodding. 'Maybe so,' he said. 'Goodnight.' He opened the door. 'You say your prayers, William?'

William nodded.

'Then you can pray for me.'

When he could think back over the scene, William realized he had been expecting Bradley to join forces with him against Watkin, to demand an investigation. Now he was alone. Nevertheless, his duty remained clear. He made an appointment for 14 May to see the Governor, giving himself plenty of time to rehearse his arguments. Bradley was right, a trial would not bring back any of the dead; but it was wrong to continue as if nothing had happened. That was what he must hang on to. Without that, they were nothing; conscienceless animals.

CHAPTER SIXTEEN

Misunderstandings

Visions of Barnes – snoring in the cramped, smelly medical storehouse; doing something in the brickies' hut with his friend Neal (horrible, horrible); smiling at a native and holding out that deceitfully tempting bottle – haunted William all week, and he slept badly.

Waking early on Sunday morning he walked down to the beach which lay at the base of the cliff beyond the observatory, and was surprised to see two convict women with children, clambering over the rocks which separated the beach from Sydney Cove proper. It was high tide and only a narrow strip of beach remained uncovered. He hung back in the shadow of the cliff to see where they would go, but when they reached the sand they stopped. One set her child down. A little girl who had been holding hands with the other ran to the water's edge and began to throw stones into the sea. The two women extracted hooks and lines from a sack, and cast them into the waves. William had recognized one of the women immediately. Molly Hill.

His first impulse was to turn back and get away from the beach unnoticed, but he found that his heart was suddenly hammering very hard in his chest, and that he needed to lean against a rock for a minute to get his breath. He had not spoken to her for nearly a year now and had the memory of her in tight control. But now she was handing her line to the other woman; now she was taking up the baby and bringing it out of the wind, into the shelter of the rocks; now she was walking directly towards him; now she was nodding in recognition.

'Good day, Mr Dawes. Didn't know you was here.'

'No – I – thought the beach was empty.'

'We're fishing.' The child, whom she carried on her hip, smiled at William. Her face was dirty. Molly Hill set her down on a flat rock and, crouching beside her, took out a rag and began wiping her face.

'She eats the sand,' she complained, 'and it goes right through her.' The child smiled beatifically while her mother wiped.

'Is it Alicia?'

'Aye.' A breath of laughter. 'You didn't think I'd another?'

William, unable to discover any humour in the situation, found himself without a reply. She glanced up at him and to his chagrin he felt himself blushing, lapped by hot silence. She busied herself again with the child, running her finger inside Alicia's mouth, round the rim of her gums, and then wiping the results in the rag.

'Little madam!' she said. 'Trollop!' Tickling Alicia's neck. Alicia giggled and Molly delved in her waistband and produced a small, clean white bone. The child immediately began to chew and suck contentedly on it.

'It's her teeth,' Molly explained to William. 'She wants summat in her mouth the whole time.'

William stood awkwardly silent in the face of her prattle. She glanced at him again with a slight frown, then settled herself on the rock next to Alicia.

'I'm not in the women's camp now. I'm over on t'other side.'

'Near the Governor's?' Some of the better class of women were hutted on the east side of the stream, away from the bawdiness and lax morals of the women's camp.

'Ah.' She smiled conspiratorially at his surprise, increasing his sense of awkwardness. 'I'm a reformed character now.'

William forced himself to speak. 'You – you have broken with Stokoe.'

'I have broken with Stokoe.' She nodded, and wiped a trickle of sandy snot from Alicia's nose. 'I have broken with all men.' There was an amused expression on her face; William realized that she was laughing at him. She had no right – he had acted in good faith –

Burning with indignation and embarrassingly close to tears, William stood up and turned away from her.

'I must get back to the observatory now – .'

'Wait,' she said. 'Mr Dawes – ?'

He glanced back at her to make sure she was not mocking him.

'I'll tell you, if you like.'

'About Stokoe?'

'Stokoe?' She looked puzzled. 'Oh, Stokoe – he wasn't . . .' She wiped Alicia's clean face again, and broke off, staring out towards the glittering sea. Her friend was pulling in a fish. They both watched as she unhooked it and threw it, flapping, on to the sand.

'She won't kill 'em,' Molly said. 'She's a devil for that. I don't like to see them flap.'

William settled himself against the rock again. All right; if she had something to tell him, all right, he would listen. Maybe he had been too sensitive. After all, why should she not reform? Maybe his first attempts to persuade her to change her life, after the birth of Alicia – maybe his words had borne fruit after all. More calmly now, he examined her. She was more solid than she had been last year, her neck no longer scrawny. She was wearing a ragged but clean white bonnet, with her hair coiled beneath it; she was altogether more neat and sturdy than he remembered.

'Listen,' she said suddenly. 'It were on account of Charlie Stone.'

'Stone?' William was bewildered. He had never heard of the man.

'Charlie. He died in January. He was my cousin.'

William cast his mind back to January, to conversations with Watkin and Worgan. Maybe the name had been mentioned . . .

'What did he die of?'

Molly shrugged. 'Sickliness. Hopelessness.'

'A convict?'

She nodded. 'He weren't all there. You know. Simple. More like a child, really.'

William was waiting for a story about Stokoe. But it took a while to get around to Stokoe. Afterwards, running over the tale in his mind while he carefully cleaned and polished the telescope and other instruments, William felt that he had listened to her wrongly. He had not understood that the story would be long and complicated, he had not realized that she was following a logic – and so he had been a little peremptory, wanting to guide her towards relevant material. Only now, afterwards, did he realize that everything she had said was relevant; that Stokoe was not the main part of it, although William had expected him to be. She was rendered hesitant, easily deflected by his interruptions. But she did make the shape of it clear to him at last.

The simpleton, Charlie Stone, had lived with her family for a while as a child. Molly regarded him as a younger brother, she had helped to look after him. After her mother's death Molly had gone into service, aged twelve, and Charlie had returned to his father, Molly's uncle. His father had set him to thieving, although, as Molly said, he was ill-suited to the work, by reason of his simple-mindedness.

One day when she was quietly polishing the table alone at her master's house, Charlie had burst in, covered in blood and crying. When he was upset he could not speak, and it took her a while to get the story from him. He had got into a house he thought was empty (by sliding in through the narrow larder window) and had been surprised at his thieving by a servant girl. She had run at him with a knife in her hand; they had fallen to the floor, fighting, and he had got the knife off her. He had stabbed her. 'He was that frightened,' Molly explained to William, 'he never even thought. He couldn't believe what he'd done.'

Molly burnt his bloody clothes, and taking his sack of stolen goods (into which he had even put the knife, the weapon) down to the end of the lane, she slipped it into the Thames. She bathed him, dressed him in some old clothes of her master's, and walked him home. She made him swear that he would not tell anyone – especially not his father – what had happened, and promised him that she herself would never speak of it. She convinced him that no one would be able to trace the murder to him.

On her way back to her master's house she made a diversion past the scene of the crime. It was quiet and deserted; perhaps, she told herself, Charlie made a mistake and the girl was only hurt. But next day news of the murder was on the streets; and Molly's nightmares began.

'I never thought about it when Charlie come in like that – I just wanted to clean him up and comfort him. But next day I started thinking about her, the girl – how she were just like me, doing her work, and then that – '

She began to sleepwalk and cry out in her sleep; she began to be afraid of falling asleep, and tried to keep herself awake at night. During the day she was tired and forgetful, and her mistress soon dismissed her.

'Nightmares, eh?' she said wryly to William. 'Bloody stupid. As if there wasn't enough real stuff to scare a body.'

She skated lightly over the year that followed. Charlie had been caught stealing, tried and sentenced to transportation for that crime. ('Five pair of stocking,' she told William. 'Five pair of stocking – seven years. More'n a year for each pair.') She herself had turned to petty theft, after leaving a second period of service. 'It went from bad to worse,' she said; 'the nightmares, and the difficulty getting work – so I took what I could – when I saw my way. And the odd gentleman, if I thought he'd pay me decent.'

Of course, William told himself. How else was she to survive?

When she found she was pregnant she became reckless, and that's how she got caught – taking a watch from a man's pocket before his very eyes, openly teasing him. Like Charlie, she was sentenced to transportation: her baby was born six months before the fleet sailed.

'Charlie were on the *Alexander*, next to Stokoe. That were Charlie's bad luck, and mine. Stokoe got his hooks into 'im. Charlie fell sick, very sick, he thought he'd had it. And he told Stokoe everything. About the girl he'd murdered and how I'd helped him, and how there was only me and him knew about it. He told Stokoe the lot.'

William saw the thing fall into place. Stokoe, never one to miss a chance, made himself known to Molly the night the women landed at Sydney Cove. He told her what he knew about Charlie, and offered her a deal. He would be her pimp – she would be his buttock – and in return he wouldn't blab about Charlie. Charlie was in the hospital tent, but being treated kindly by Mr Balmain. He was as well looked after as any of the sick; Molly knew because she visited him often. She believed that if it got about that he was a murderer, he would hang.

'I couldn't see him come all that way, suffering and sick as a dog, and then get turned off here. Could I?' So she agreed to Stokoe's demands. 'It didn't seem to matter much, one way nor t'other, I couldn't get worked up about it.'

'But when Charlie died . . .' William latched on to the facts rapidly now.

She nodded. 'When he died, after Christmas. Well there wasn't nothing Stokoe could threaten me with then. I were a free woman.'

'You *are* – ' he corrected her. She laughed drily.

'Aye. I am a free woman. Aside from the transportation.'

'But why didn't you tell someone?' he asked. 'Why didn't you tell me?'

'You?' she said wonderingly. 'Blab about Charlie myself, and save Stokoe the trouble?'

They were interrupted by the little girl – the daughter, William assumed, of the other woman. She ran up and presented Molly with a small pink shell.

'Very nice.'

'Will yer save it for me?'

Gravely Molly inserted it behind her waistband, where she kept Alicia's bone. The child smiled and ran away down to the water again.

'But – ' William's mind was running over the story, exploring it, trying to make facts fit.

'But?' she said, half-humorously.

'But you had a baby – '

'Two,' she said. 'Another one before her.'

'I know – what – what happened?'

235

She shrugged. 'I didn't like the ship. It were bad. You couldn't get away from them – women crying and carrying on, like a madhouse. I took to rum, as much as I could get.'

'Rum?' Of course. From the sailors. He wished he would not blush.

She told him briefly, almost nonchalantly, about the baby. She felt suffocated on the ship; felt she couldn't breathe, and that the ship's sides were closing in on her. The rum gave her courage. In one of her blacker moods she decided to kill the child and herself, to escape. She smothered the child ('Oh yes. I knew what I were doing. I held my blanket, folded up, over his face. And then I counted to two hundred.') But then she fell asleep. She didn't know why or how, only she was drunk and nothing seemed real. When she woke up she was alive and the baby was dead, and the women she was chained to were already making a hue and cry about it. She didn't know how to kill herself and so she stayed alive. Then she was pregnant again – with Alicia. Then the fleet came in to New South Wales and she became Stokoe's whore.

She smiled at William and hoisted Alicia on to her hip again, as he sat gawping at her foolishly.

'I'd better go and catch supper,' she said, nodding to her friend down by the water. 'This young article'll eat as much fish as a pelican. Won't you, my duck?' And she set off back down the beach.

Bewilderedly scraping the facts into order, William considered and examined her story. She was light and easy with him; did not behave as if there was anything she should be ashamed of or embarrassed about. Indeed, she seemed to find *his* blushes amusing. He had entirely misunderstood her. He had condemned her for a whore, while she was in fact under Stokoe's power. Even now, she could not see that William might have helped her. He did not know why she had chosen to tell him; it was not out of any desire to make amends, or set herself before him in a better light. She wanted nothing from him.

She doesn't even like me, William thought. It dawned on him slowly – with the inexorably growing, factual light of sun rising – dawned, that she did not even like him. While she – or her ankle, her foot, her soft pendulous breast – had haunted his waking and sleeping, he had been irrelevant to her. Just another man. Perhaps sent by Stokoe – she had not been sure. He could be used to provide food, and so she had used him. But she had no further use or desire for him, he had never entered into her imagination, she had never, really, *thought* of him. And now he was a listener to whom she casually told her story. Now the story no longer had any value as a secret, she told him, and wandered off down the beach. There was nothing at all between them.

He had wanted to save her and had sinned with her. He'd hoped to atone for his sin by marrying her, and had been humiliated by further evidence of her seemingly debauched nature. And now it turned out that along with his first sins he had also been blind and stupid; had guessed nothing of what bound her to Stokoe, had not begun to penetrate the hopes and fears that motivated her; had assumed, ignorantly, arrogantly assumed, that he knew what was best for her.

Whatever I touch turns to ashes, he thought. But that was too dramatic. She had not turned to ashes. She was better now; happier, leading a virtuous life, providing for her daughter. She was, as she said, a reformed character. It was a lesson in humility that was being offered to him, and as he grasped that, he began to see that it might be possible to find some relief in it. He was not responsible for Molly Hill; he was irrelevant to her. She had abandoned vice without his leading her to virtue. He was not – as Richard had assured him he was not – responsible for the smallpox outbreak. God knew more than he did; God knew the hidden purposes, and the rights and wrongs in the hearts of others like Molly Hill and Stephen Barnes, which William could never know. He should trust God. He should admit his own weakness; he should try less to grasp and shape events. He must learn he was not as important as he had thought.

On 12 May Arabanoo fell ill with smallpox. It was not surprising, as he had tended his sick and dying kinsmen for days; and yet everyone was surprised. Through his association with the whites it seemed as if he should have gained some of their immunity.

When William went to see Phillip, the Governor had just returned from visiting the sick native, and was clearly distressed. His pale face was almost grey, and the hollows under his eyes were purplish. Even when he was legitimately upset, there was something coldly inhuman about him that froze a listener's sympathy. When he spoke of his anxiety for Arabanoo he spoke almost to himself, as if embarrassed for William to witness his weakness.

'We should have kept him away from those who were infected; White should have thought of it. We should never have let him expose himself, for days on end, to the pestilential breath of the dying – I blame myself. We were his guardians and we let him into danger.'

'If he had been out on the harbour with the others, he would have been just as liable to die.' Ludicrously, William found himself defending Phillip's actions to himself.

'Well – ' Phillip tore himself away from the subject and confronted William. 'What can I do for you?'

'It is about the smallpox.'

'Yes?'

'About its origins.'

'You have a theory?'

'There were samples – of variolus matter in the stores. I'm sure you know, sir, they were brought by Surgeon White for purposes of inoculation. They may have been stolen and given to the blacks.'

'Stolen by whom?' Phillip's face betrayed no reaction.

'I don't know. Maybe the convicts who guard the hospital stores.'

'D'you have any reason to suspect a particular individual?'

Before William could speak, Phillip crossed to his desk. 'Let me read you something. This is my commission from His Majesty, in so far as it pertains to the natives.

> You are to endeavour by every possible means to open an intercourse with the natives, and to conciliate their affections, enjoining all our subjects to live in amity and kindness with them. And if any of our subjects shall wantonly destroy them or give them any unnecessary interruption in the exercise of their several occupations, it is our will and pleasure that you do cause such offenders to be brought to punishment according to the degree of the offence.

Would you say I have carried this out, so far, Mr Dawes?'

'Yes, sir.'

'And are you saying it was the intention of one – or several – of the convicts to destroy hundreds upon hundreds of the natives with this disease?'

'I'm not saying that, they may not have imagined the extent of the damage; even Surgeon White is astonished by the virulence of the epidemic – '

'Quite. So if I take the convict guards to court, I can charge them with – theft of medical supplies and – what? Murder? Or mere carelessness? How are we to prove that they even understood the implications of the bottle's contents – if indeed they stole it, which is not certain either?'

'These are things the court must decide.' William shifted his weight. Wasn't it Phillip's trick, always, to put one at a disadvantage – to make one feel foolish?

'There is one very important principle which has guided me in my dealings with the natives. It is that they must be able to see that justice is done. Now, consider the case from their point of view for a moment. If we put convicts on trial for spreading the disease amongst the blacks, the remaining blacks will understand that disease can be spread deliberately. At present, I am sure they have no such idea, and would no more blame us for their sickness than they would blame us for cold weather. By holding a trial, we set before them the notion that someone – a person – is to blame. And that person who has spread the disease must then be to blame for – what? Five hundred deaths? A thousand? What punishment could be appropriate?'

The certainty William had felt when he argued the case with Bradley was slipping from him, like clothes that were too big. He found himself naked and defenceless before Phillip's forceful logic.

'Only death. And yet we ourselves, before the outset of such a trial, freely admit that to prove intention to cause the death of even one, let alone five hundred, natives, will be impossible. Therefore we will fail to impose a death sentence. And so will seem, to our native witnesses, to take inexcusably lightly the terrible affliction which has befallen them.' He paused. 'I can see no other course than to treat this illness as – what in the main I believe it to be – a disastrous act of God. I believe we are likely to cause greater distress, both to ourselves and to the natives, by assuming (perhaps wrongly) any kind of responsibility.'

'I see,' said William.

'I haven't taken this decision lightly,' Phillip continued. 'I have lain awake at night, weighing the potential good and evil results of such a trial. And this is my conclusion.'

His tone had become a little less icy; he was trying, William realized, to be kind.

'Thank you, sir.' He wanted to apologize for being stupid and wasting Phillip's time; it was hard to see now, hard to remember why demanding a trial had seemed a good idea. William had a sudden sense of misunderstanding everything – as he had with Molly Hill. It was like going down some steps and finding the last one missing. 'I – I'm sorry,' he said lamely. But Phillip had already turned to gaze unseeingly through the window, towards the little brick hut behind the hospital, where Arabanoo lay ill. Quietly, William let himself out.

Crossing the Tank Stream, William noticed that the *Sirius'* longboat was tied to the quay. That meant Bradley might be on shore. He looked in on the hospital as he passed, and at Watkin's new hut, to see if he was there. It was most likely, he realized, that Bradley was actually waiting for him up at the observatory; it was possible he had even come to apologize for his unpleasantness of a week ago.

With this thought in mind, William hurried up the track. As he rounded the bend near the top he was delighted to see Bradley's tall skinny figure stepping out of the trees up ahead. But there was another man with Bradley: a heavy, thickset man in convict's clothes. McEntire. The two stopped with their heads together, talking. Then Bradley glanced down the track and said something to McEntire. The big man ran back into the cover of the wood, and Bradley began to walk down towards William.

'I was looking for you,' William began. 'But McEntire – you caught him roaming about up there again? He used to annoy one of the men who was building the observatory.'

'McEntire?' said Bradley casually, as if he had not heard the name before.

'Yes, that convict you were with – '

'Ah.' Bradley went on walking down the path.

'Bradley! Won't you come up to the observatory?'

'Not now,' said Bradley quickly. He was red in the face, William noticed.

'Are you well – ?' he began, but Bradley spoke over him.

'I have to get back to the boat in a hurry.' Without any further goodbye, he began to jog down the track to the settlement.

'But weren't you coming to see me?' William said, quietly because it was clear that Bradley was already out of earshot, and anyway would not stop.

William worried at the encounter as he moved on up the track. McEntire had melted away into the wood. When the two of them had first stepped on to the track – together – the way Bradley had checked to see if anyone saw them – and McEntire ran off –

William stopped walking. Bradley and McEntire?

He sat down on a stump conveniently abandoned by Stokoe and Clough. McEntire had assaulted Barnes, had used him for his gratification. But how could it be that Bradley – a decent man, an officer . . .

As he dragged himself the last hundred yards up the path, William visualized the way McEntire had stared at him, when he caught him with Barnes: insolent, contemptuous. It may not be true. There may be twenty other explanations. But why not, why not, why not, tolled in his head. Knowing Bradley's taste (you know it, he told himself angrily, why must you pretend you don't?), what was wrong with a convict? Had he himself not turned to Molly Hill, a convict?

But *McEntire*? his stunned brain repeated. McEntire? Who was – who anyone could see at a glance was – a thug, a bully, an unnatural, vicious evil man –

When he was inside his living quarters with the door safely shut, he fell to his knees. But he did not know what to pray for. Help. Guidance. Escape. He felt betrayed by Bradley. He was betrayed, it was making him cry. He felt betrayed by God. Crouching over so that his forehead rested on the dirt floor, he sobbed until his chest ached. Finally he began to pray for Bradley. I have no right to sit in judgement. He prayed for himself, for forgiveness. His prayer became wordless.

OLLA

Daniel is not well. I have been up all night with him, trying to ease his breathing, holding him, talking to him. I've filled the bath with scalding water and Vick, to make steam. I sat on the toilet and held him; when I opened the door clouds of steam rolled down the landing. But nothing much seems to help. Listening for the rattling breath to come – willing the next one on – I am back in childhood with my brother. I am back in that determined hopeless battle, where each breath is a victory.

Now the night has gone, the sky is light, and he breathes with some regularity, but snuffling and gurgling like he is drowning in phlegm. I have talked myself out. The thread of my concentration keeps his breaths coming. The insistent vacuum of my needing to hear him exhale pulls that air raggedly through the congested tunnels of his chest, throat and nose. The pressure of my attention on the atmosphere outside his mouth forces air back in again.

Stephen suggests we go to hospital for oxygen. The GP has advised this, saying we need only phone to warn before setting off. Perhaps if Daniel is still so bad tomorrow. Perhaps then. He doesn't like the hospital.
I keep him going for now. Breathe, squeeze, cough, listen, wait – wait – wait – breathe out. From time to time I become dizzy, then remember that I myself must inhale and exhale, and sometimes cannot wait as long as he.

Anxiety has leeched out of me, though, with the lightening of the sky. He will not die. This is simply how it is. Each breath is hard. Of course; what did I expect? Living is hard for him, conditions of life are hard and alien, he is here to do us a favour. This illness is his weakness. If he could choose, he would slip away and die, he would go as fast as he could. But he knows he must stay – he knows he has a job to do. And therefore he will overcome his illness. But through his illness he shows his sadness at having to be here at all, at having to be on earth.

He is rejecting me. I do what I can to make him comfortable. I use my energy and imagination to try to ameliorate his experience of life – yet still he finds it odious. My best efforts can't convince him to want to live.

Well then, I am unsuccessful. But I am still here, and still making him breathe; if he conquers this weakness and recovers, he may yet find some solace in what I can do for him. And if he chooses not to recover – if it is simply too horrible for him – well I can die too.

How calmly and unreally it is all said now. I am lying back in the old armchair beside his cot, with my head tilted back, looking up through the window at the clouds. Breathe in – silence – rasp, a little more in, a little shudder – wait – exhale. Yes. The sky is grey and the low clouds move quickly across it, slipping past in one giant woolly edged mass so that it is easy to imagine the earth itself to be spinning and the sky to be standing still overhead. Or to see that the sky is a never-ending train, an endless procession like traffic on a motorway, a constant stream like a wide river in flood (yes, that is best, the grey of the cloud is that same sullen, swollen steel grey) moving endlessly, slipping past.

Nothing matters, nothing matters. Breathe – cough, cough, gasp, hiccough, choke. I sit up, slide my hand beneath his head and raise his shoulders; after a few seconds he shudders and the airway is clear, he inhales again. I lay him down and lie back myself. The clouds slip past and nothing matters. Everything will slip past me like the clouds.

Idle slippery thoughts slide across my mind. Being alive is waiting and willing and taking the next breath. Is that repeated effort of drawing it in and pushing it out. Can be sustained and made to last longer, by me. But not extended indefinitely. I couldn't make him go on breathing for ever. I couldn't make myself. The breathing is only temporary, when all's said and done. Is only for six months, a year, twenty years, or eighty. Is only temporary. Is, therefore, a battle I can't win, so why not give in gracefully now? The clouds slip, not hurrying, but processing with smooth oiled speed as if unaware that to shift their huge bulk should require some evidence of effort.

Why all this expenditure of effort and energy on something so impermanent as life? What do I gain by breathing with him? An extra breath – an extra night – an extra year? And will it make any difference? Will it?

He is wheezing now, the air whispers and rattles uselessly in his nose and throat, and does not go into his lungs. I pick him up – no better

243

– I stand and put him over my shoulder, patting his back gently. I can feel the feeble convulsion of his chest pressed against my shoulder, it is out of rhythm, cannot tell whether it is to pull air in or push it out, heaves and labours uselessly. I walk, patting him, rubbing him, breathing slow and regular. He will hear me. He must absorb my health.

How silly and disengaged were my earlier thoughts. In general, of course, it may be true that to keep an individual breathing for the longest possible time is futile, that any breathing at all is futile. But Daniel is not anyone. (Was I forgetting that? The surface of my mind is blank and slippery, I do not get a purchase on the thoughts that pass like clouds across it.) No, Daniel is not anyone. Daniel is the one who brings help. Who will give, show, enlighten. Who will make the mystery of being alive for so many years and then dead, comprehensible. Who will bring peace and satisfaction and an end to pain, by illuminating its further ends.

As I nurture him now, so he will nurture all of us. Nurture us in what we need, to understand the point of all the breathing and not breathing. To bring a solution of power to Stephen's meddling, ignorant attempts to change other people's lives. Daniel will say, you are stupid, you clever, you rich, you poor, you well, you sick, you fat, you starved, and we will rejoice in it.

Stephen is a leveller. Communists, socialists, egalitarians. What are they all but levellers? To hold this up as a solution. You who are stupid shall be a little more educated; you who are clever, a little less educated. The rich, poorer; the poor, richer. The well sicker; the sick, more healthy. The fat, hungrier. The starving, better fed. All will be similar, levelled, equalled. And (here is the most extraordinary thing, the greatest failing of Stephen's imagination) then they will be happier. Are these happy now – the well, the clever, the rich, the fat? He thinks they will legislate for human happiness by abolishing wealth and greed. Which two things are in themselves the sole source of many people's meagre amount of joy.

It makes me tired. I do not pretend to analyse. It is not a game I have patience for, the levelling, the parcelling out, the insistence that all are equally perfectible.

It's nonsense. The work of the blind and deaf; or of those, like

Stephen, who wilfully close their organs of perception, because they cannot abide to know the truth.

The truth is Daniel. The truth is genocide and starvation. The truth is concentration camps and torturers; illness, pain. Which is impossible to legislate for or eradicate. Which indicates not perfectibility but simple earsplitting repetition. The long scream of history goes on, and doesn't pause to draw a breath.

Only Daniel knows the answer. Only a miracle can save us. Out of the weak will come strength; disguised by human imperfections stands the most perfect. Only he will be able to make clear that in difference (and in difference also from what may be imagined – as he himself is the opposite of what may have been imagined for him, our saviour) lies hope, salvation, peace, blessedness. That there must be a new vision, a new way of understanding, which will not seek to change what cannot be changed but will reveal instead an inner purpose, as words translated yield up a meaning, as unintelligible cyphers become – with a key – a message and direction. If the world is locked in frost and snow, he is the sun that, rising, will thaw it – not to change its identity, but to reveal within the petrified shapes inherent life and purpose.

To know this, he must be it. He has to be human in order to understand the simple terms into which he must translate the mystery for us. He must know the confines and rigid corridors of our brains, he must *know* the obstacles. And imprisonment gives him pain. He lies in my arms and suffers, all I can give him is my love. The eagle is trapped within the ant – in order to reveal to all the other ants a purpose written in the heavens.

The stories of hope in the Bible are right. But the Christ they worship is not the one. He has transformed nothing. He has not given us the key; he has simply offered *more* life, after death; to prolong the puzzle indefinitely. And offered the same sad answers as those that Stephen seizes upon: equality, dispersal of riches, healing the sick, loving each other. Blindly optimistic inanities: 'the lion shall lie down with the young lamb'. Never never never will it be. The lion shall *eat* the young lamb, and in its lionness, and in its lambness, devourer and devoured will be radiant with meaning.

That is the key my Daniel holds. He will save us from ourselves, he will unlock the bizarre alphabet of the world we inhabit so that we can know its inner significance.

*

Stephen did not think it would be necessary for me to make him happy. He chose me with the intention that he would make me happy. He does not expect me to make him happy.
And anyway, I can't.

In 1980 things are going very badly at his school. His new school. We have moved from Leicester to Lancashire, for him to take up a deputy-headship. We have left the flat meadows of Leicestershire with their huge ancient trees for a decaying industrial slum, where bald ugly hills press down on us from the skyline. Moors, bleak dead lands. The houses are small and mean, the shops are boarded up. The faces of public buildings are blackened with pollution, and it rains. In the air always a misty drizzle, suffocatingly low cloud pressing on our heads.
'Of course it rains,' he says brightly. 'A damp atmosphere's essential for cotton manufacture. None of this would be here, without the rain.'
What is here are vandalized mills, narrow terraced streets, a queue stretching from the counter of the small grubby post office to way down past the chip shop on the day the unemployed can cash their giro. The post office has metal grilles fitted over its windows. Outside the huge public houses litter sticks to the vomit on the pavement.

I will not live in these streets near the school. The house I choose is five miles away, on a modern estate which backs on to parkland. There are still no proper trees but on the estate there are orderly gardens. The houses are semi-detached, with garages; the road is a cul-de-sac so it is free of roaring traffic. The house is neutral inside, the vendors leave beige carpeting throughout.
'You'll enjoy getting your teeth into this, won't you Olla?' says Stephen. He is glad to see I will be occupied. Because he is busy morning noon and night. I miscarried at Easter '79; he told me the move will stop me brooding, it will do us both good.
So I decorate the new house.
The kitchen here is pleasant. Big and wide, with windows on two walls. I make it white. White tiles white ceiling white woodwork, white kitchen cupboards and surfaces, white blinds. I cannot get

246

white flooring, no one sells it. I go everywhere to try. The lightest I can get is a pale flecked grey. Stephen remarks on the kitchen, he says it is like a hospital. No, hospitals are noisy. Here it is quiet and light and safe. I like to sit at the white table when he is out. White is the colour of silence.

His school is a new comprehensive in old buildings. There is always crisis, but I think, of his and Robert's making. They have children other heads have expelled; children who bring knives and razor blades to school. The teachers from the old grammar school band together, refusing to teach certain pupils. Stephen has to teach them himself. This means he does not have enough time for his other duties.

When he tells me what is happening I listen, which is all that is required. He will rehearse the options, the pros and cons, the reasons, the political implications – endlessly, with no prompting. What should I say to him, anyway? I think what they try to do is foolish. But it will not help him to say that; no, I must listen.

Often he is at the house of Robert, the head teacher. Sometimes Robert and his wife Anna come to us. I cook good food for them, they congratulate me on it. I know about Stephen and Anna. He would like me to react but I will not give him that satisfaction. If he wishes to destroy things, let him. He's a fool.

We sit at the table, the four of us, and Stephen and Bob argue about the school. Bob is looking for political solutions, he wants to get a different person for chair of the governors, he has almost persuaded the council to provide money for a new science block and gymnasium. He says if they can hold things together and prevent any more incidents, then seeing money spent on the place will generate goodwill locally, and maybe the vandalism will lessen. But last week an old teacher gave an interview to the local paper; the headline was COMPREHENSIVE CHAOS, the subheading, 'Knives, drugs, smoking, sex – the kids at Campfield Comp know all about these, but they couldn't pass a maths GCE between them, claims former teacher Alf Clarke.'

Bob wants to exclude from school for a week the four boys caught with knives on them. Stephen disagrees. He wants to see the boys' parents, to discuss their problems. He wants to call an open meeting

247

of parents to explain how much the school needs parental support, to reassure them about the aims of the school.

'They won't come,' says Bob. 'It'll be the same six people, complete with the usual pair of nutters – ' (Anna giggles then coughs). 'They don't want to know. If they see a new gym going up, that means something. It means money's been spent on their patch, for the benefit of their kids. That's what they understand.'

'You patronizing bastard!' Anna bursts in, with righteous indignation. 'So you're going to give up on trying to involve parents?'

'They don't come to meetings. It's just not that sort of area – '

'It's not that sort of area because people in power have treated the people who live there like shit. You're the ones who're going to change that. You knew it wouldn't happen overnight – '

Stephen chips in: 'Come on Bob – there *have* been results – of course it takes time to reverse the effects of years of deprivation and oppression – '

'Time is what we haven't got – '

'Look – since we opened the library to the community, it's had people in it every day, loans have increased 30 per cent.'

'And book thefts have increased about 200 per cent.'

'That's not bad. I bet you could count on the fingers of one hand the houses around Campfield that had books in them before. If people are stealing books, maybe they're reading them. I doubt they're selling them – the cash value of a dog-eared copy of *Afro-Caribbean Legends* or *How to Make a Windfarm* isn't exactly high – '

'Yeah, but we'll have to close the damn library soon 'cos there're no books left in it. Not a positive move for our students.'

'Oh Bob.' Anna's critical tone has softened. 'I can't bear it when you talk like this. There *are* positive achievements, I mean look at the kids in the third year – '

'Yes,' says Bob sourly. 'Look at them.'

'Come on,' says Stephen. 'Be fair. They are incredibly confident and articulate. They know how to hold a debate; they organized and delivered their own petition to the education chief last week – '

'Asking for a smoking room.' Bob speaks flatly, but raises his left eyebrow just a fraction. Anna and Stephen both burst out laughing. 'Well it still shows initiative and political nous. I hope he was fucking impressed!'

'He wasn't, I can tell you.'

'Bob, seriously,' says Anna, 'they've designed a fantastic new uniform; they've written letters of support to the ANC; they make and sell their own healthy food in the tuck shop; they can take cars apart and sometimes even put them together again. They've discussed the existence of God with an Anglican bishop and argued him into a corner. They're acquiring the most amazing set of life skills. D'you think when *they're* parents, they won't come to parents' meetings? Every one of them will be there – you'll have turned the whole thing around.'

'Except we won't last that long,' says Bob.

'Oh Olla!' Anna turns to me. 'Say something. What d'you say to Stevie when he gets down like this?'

I say nothing. I shrug and smile at Anna.

'Olla's the note of sanity in my life,' says Stephen. 'She doesn't think education makes any difference to anything.' Robert and Anna laugh. What Stephen says is true, although they find it humorous.

If Stephen had married a woman like Anna she would sympathize and encourage him. Since what he hopes to accomplish is foolish and doomed to failure, why would it have been better? Anyway, he married me, and therefore chose not to be encouraged. Anna likes him. She aligns herself with him against her own Robert – as the two idealists against the pragmatist. But Bob is not pragmatic; he made the sweeping changes which have brought in the chaos on their tails. He encouraged the children to write confidential reports on the teachers' abilities, enraging the teachers; established the student council and gave it powers which led to the abolition of uniform, and children being allowed to remain in classrooms at lunchtimes (which teachers could not or would not supervise, leading to acts of vandalism which necessitated the closing down of two mobile classrooms). And so on, and so on.

Of course I listen in silence. What should I say? The whole thing is madness. Stephen follows Robert's star; he will sink with him, when Robert fails. The school is a disaster, their ideas naïve and laughable. A trickle of respectable parents are already removing their children from the school; soon it will be a flood. The children are not being taught to pass exams. What other point is there in going to school? I would not let Daniel attend such a school.

*

Something changes. In me? In Stephen? From the first he has been a

249

fool, but I did not dislike it. Or perhaps I simply did not believe it? He had so much. Work. Education. Family. Money. Energy. These were not the trappings of a complete fool.

When he talked of changing people's lives; when he went to meetings for a minimum wage, for nursery education, for wages for housework, for anti-racism – well it was just what he did. I didn't want to go with him, and he didn't badger me. It was all right. When he came home he told me things that happened, described incidents, people – I was entertained.

But now with this business at his school I am called on to do something. To help, give my support. He comes home smelling sour, smelling afraid; all the big windows in the hall have been smashed in the night, someone has it in for the school. The maths advisor is insisting that streaming in maths be restored in years three to five. Stephen says this makes a mockery of what they have been trying to do, the school is being destroyed.

Stephen is paid to go to the school, to work in his office to solve these problems, to teach the children and attend meetings. Where do I come in?

He wants me to help serve lunches; the dinner-ladies are withholding their services because a child swore at one of them and they are not satisfied he was adequately reprimanded.

'It happens all the time, in every school,' Stephen says angrily. 'But they know they can make a fuss – the press will lap it up, at Campfield. They don't need nails to crucify us, they're doing it with fucking drawing pins.'

'Who else is serving dinners?'

'A couple of parents. Some of the staff. But it's very difficult – '

'Will I be paid?'

'For Christ's sake Olla, that's not the point.'

He also wants me to come into the library for an hour after school every day, 'as a community user'. The librarian has refused to work after 4 p.m. and they have no money to employ another librarian. The theory is that the community will take responsibility for the library once they realize it is for their own use. 'People don't destroy their own property,' Stephen insists. 'Establish public ownership and you will end vandalism.'

'Don't bus shelters belong to the public?' I ask him. So, in the library, I must keep an eye open for book thieves and the person who is drawing alphabetically appropriate obscene pictures in the front and back of all the fiction. This person has begun at A ('arseholes') and is now at K ('kunt').

I do not want to go to Stephen's school and help. The school will be closed down. Stephen is a greater fool than I thought if he cannot see this coming. I imagine he and Robert will be sacked, and I ask him if our house will be secure if he can no longer pay the mortgage. This has not even occurred to him, but I know how much there is in his different accounts: £2,500 in total. Not enough to buy the house outright.
He explodes with anger at my question, saying he doesn't know, he doesn't care, it doesn't matter.

But it does. This is our house. I will not have no house. He is a pitiable fool if he throws away security for the sake of principles. When he has an easy, well-paid job – to do it badly, ruin it for the sake of stupid political ideals; that is contemptible.

I have never found him contemptible before.

I do not go to help at his school. I go to the jobcentre and find some jobs to apply for, for when we will need money. I take a job as cleaner for the council, cleaning offices and the council chamber. £1.35 an hour, I will do thirty hours a week.

When he finds out he does not say anything. Later, I hear him crying in the bathroom. I do not go in – there's nothing to say; I'm not doing anything wrong. When he has no money he'll be glad that I am earning some. I hope they will close the school down and be done with it. This is a kind of insanity which haunts him now. I think, perhaps it is as well we have no baby yet. We must be safe and secure to have a baby.

The ending of the school is protracted and ugly. Stephen becomes obsessed with the bad stories in the local paper, and announces one day that he is going to visit the editor. He is going to explain to him the aims of the school.
'They're looking for stories,' he tells me. 'And all they get are the bad ones, because *we* never speak to them. It's a propaganda war and we're idiots to pretend to be above it. We must get the press on to our side.'

251

He argues on the phone with Robert. He tells Robert that once the paper sees all the positive achievements of the school, it will stop its barrage of criticism. Robert is very angry; about the school? Or Anna? But there is no stopping Stephen. If he can get the paper to be positive about the school, he says, the tide will turn.

A reporter and photographer go to school with him. When he comes home he is more cheerful and expansive than he has been for weeks. The photographer took four reels of film. The reporter was interested in everything he saw. He interviewed six members of staff and lots of children. He seemed to understand very well the educational principles Stephen described to him. He has told Stephen he will ask his editor if next week's paper can carry a special Campfield Comprehensive supplement, to do in-depth justice to all the interesting things Stephen has shown him. Stephen talks of winning over public opinion.

The supplement on Campfield Comprehensive is not what Stephen hoped.
The interviews with teachers are carefully condensed:

* It's like teaching in a bear garden!
* Discipline has fallen apart since the head abolished corporal punishment. One member of staff has been physically threatened by a pupil. Some of them regularly carry knives.
* It's become a school for thieves. I've never seen so much new LEA equipment vanish in one school year – never.
* Standards have hit rock bottom. Children who would have been getting seven or eight O-levels at the old grammar school will be lucky to come out of here with two.

The interviews with children contain comments like:
* It's great here 'cos we don't 'ave to do any work.
* They learn yer about private parts and not getting pregnant and all that, it's dead good.
* The teachers are soft, you can doss about.
* Exams are rubbish. If yer don't want to do exams yer don't have to.

There is a more lengthy interview with one boy who claims to lead the Pithills Gang, and who boasts that his gang have beaten up fourteen grammar-school swots since September, and stopped two from coming to school altogether.

252

The photos show obscene words carved into the surface of a wooden desk; cigarette ends, cigarette papers and what look like some loose strands of tobacco, with the heading EVIDENCE OF DRUG ABUSE; two boys fighting in the middle of a crowded corridor; a classroom where children are standing on desks and chairs, throwing a sports bag between them; broken windows; the smashed wall of a mobile classroom; a page from a child's English book where every word except 'a' and 'the' is misspelt.

There is an article about the summer term outing to Blackpool, where three unsupervised children were apprehended shoplifting. There is an interview with Stephen on the subject of teaching religion in school, in which he says that he is an atheist and it is difficult to see the relevance of the Church of England to most children's lives today. This is under the heading SHOULD THIS MAN BE IN CHARGE OF YOUR CHILDREN? and it ends with the sentence, 'Mr Beech's own moral values have come under question from some of the other staff; not least, perhaps, the headmaster, who declined to speak to our reporter, and whose wife is reputed to have a close relationship with Mr Beech.'
There are photos of litter in the corridors and playground, of oily car parts spread across a classroom floor, of blobby formless abstract paintings in the art room, of a pile of ripped, dog-eared textbooks, and a close-up of a Bunsen burner with chewing gum blocking its air hole. There is a report on the four girls who have had to leave school during the past year due to pregnancy. A brief interview with the caretaker states that he has found condoms and hypodermics in the school toilets.

There is not a single good word in the supplement. The day after it is published, reporters from the *Daily Telegraph*, the *Sun*, the *Daily Mirror*, the *Daily Mail*, and radio and television attempt to gain access to the school. The Director of Education goes to see Robert and tells him the school will be closed. And Robert punches the Director of Education, and is charged with civil assault.
Parents are informed that their children will be relocated at neighbouring schools next term. A group of fourth formers (and a few parents) stage a sit-in in the hall, against the closure of the school; they paint SOS on the windows. Stephen, who still thinks the press can help him, writes an impassioned defence of everything Robert and he have done at the school and it is published in the *Guardian*.

There are a number of letters of support. Then we are invaded by reporters and there is a photo of me with the caption 'Wife of £11,000-a-year deputy head "Mr Equality" Beech works as an office cleaner.'
A group of parents who are withdrawing their children from school before the end of term because of 'bad influences' attack some of the Save our School group as they are taking food supplies in to their sit-in. One man's jaw is broken. There is an arson threat. A policeman is put on permanent duty outside the school. The first and second years write their own petition to save the school and post it to the prime minister. The local press print what they claim is a copy, riddled with spelling and grammatical mistakes.

On the night of the day that Robert appears in court, Stephen does not come home. When he gets back next day he tells me he got drunk and slept with Anna. As if I did not know. When he starts to cry, I go to bed in the spare room.

When term ends I am heartily thankful that I have my cleaning job to go to, and need not stay in the house with Stephen and his misery.

CHAPTER SEVENTEEN

Booron

'Yes. Bad thing come from that moon. We call him weere moon.'
Booron giggled. William knew her well enough by now to know that
the giggle did not mean she was being flippant.

'Is the moon always bad? Or only in this quarter?'

'Bring bad thing now. Not alway.'

'So Yennadah, that is, the moon, he can bring good fortune as well as
bad?'

She nodded, and William jotted in his notebook. He was working
under the heading 'Religious Beliefs of the Natives', his page neatly
dated 2 April 1790. He noticed that she was hugging herself.

'Are you cold, Booron? Shall I fetch you a jacket?'

She giggled and stood up. 'I go,' and she slipped into the Johnsons'
doorway. William leant back on the bench, staring up at the evening
sky. There were some patches of low misty cloud, and the usual annoyance of a haze of smoke from the settlement fires, but the stars and
moon were visible. He could hear Mary Johnson gently scolding
Booron over an imperfectly washed cooking pot and the girl's answering giggle. When she came out again he directed her to look at the sky.

'What do you see up there, in the bourra?'

She tilted her head and recited in a sing-song voice, 'Yennadah –
moon, birrong, moloo-molong, warre-wull.'

'Good, now, birrong is star.'

'Tar,' she repeated obediently. None of the natives could pronounce
the letter 's'; William found he now supplied it automatically when she
missed it from words.

'Show me what is moloo-molong?'

She pointed to the Pleiades. So they *did* have names for groups of
stars! Carefully he noted them, sifting their sounds to try if they
resembled any other native words he knew. It was likely, he thought,
that they, as much as the Greeks, might name constellations for the
shapes of creatures they resembled. When she pointed and said,

'Warre-wull?' he even corrected her: 'Worre-gal? A dog?' but she shook her head and laughed.

'Beall – no. Warre-*wull*. Is plenty many birrong.'

A great many stars. True, there was nothing in the least resembling a dog; she was pointing at the Milky Way. There was a creaking of the gate on its leather hinges and Richard let himself into the garden.

'William. Good evening, are you well?'

'Yes, thank you. Booron is giving me the names of the stars.'

Richard nodded distractedly. 'Booron, when you come in, make sure Samuel knows.' He turned back to William. 'Did Mary tell you? We are obliged to stand watch over the garden until curfew – the thieving has become so shameless. The Governor has lost all his Indian corn and on Monday night I had two marrows taken.'

'I was admiring the garden before dark – those apples have stayed on!'

Richard laughed. 'Never were three apples so coveted, eh? Mary and I have divided them a hundred times in our imagination. It would be a serious matter now, though, to lose the corn and the root vegetables. Samuel and I share the watch between us. You have heard today's word on rations?'

William shook his head. He had been surveying for the road that would be built to link Rose Hill and Sydney and had only decided at the last minute to come back into the settlement for the evening. There was a strange, desolate, holiday feeling in Sydney: desperate shortage of foodstuff and news of more successful harvests on the fertile soil of Norfolk Island had led Phillip to send 116 male and 68 female convicts, with twenty-seven children, to the island on the *Sirius*. Major Ross had been sent to govern them. The *Sirius* was instructed to proceed to China after Norfolk Island, to buy foodstuffs and bring them back to Sydney with all possible speed.

Now the *Sirius* had sailed, the convicts remaining wandered in a dazed way around their new properties; the huts and plundered gardens of the departed were reallocated among them. Short rations meant that hours of work had been reduced by about half, from sunrise to noon; public works had ground to a standstill and such lean and hungry livestock as remained (a great deal having been slaughtered and eaten by those departing for Norfolk Island) wandered freely, damaging and destroying ill-fenced gardens.

'The weekly ration now is four pounds of flour, two-and-a-half pounds of salt pork, one-and-a-half pounds of rice.'

'That's not much.' Dining out, as he did, very little – and lacking private supplies of food – William was more dependent upon the rations than most officers. Thankfully his appetite was small, but even he might feel the pinch with so limited a weekly supply. The pork had been salted nearly four years ago and was so dry that it shrunk to nothing when boiled; everyone cooked their daily morsel by toasting it on a fork over the fire and catching the drops of grease which fell, on a piece of bread or saucer of rice. The rice, also from England, was so infested it moved around the plate on its own before cooking.

'Ships from England will be here soon. They must be.'

Richard made no reply other than breathing down his nose like a horse; but as he went into the house he called back over his shoulder, 'You will stay and eat with us tonight – I insist.'

'Thank you.' Mary had already invited him but William was glad to have it repeated. It was nearly two weeks since he had had any vegetables and the presence of all these good things growing in the garden had awakened his appetite.

Booron dropped from the bench to the ground at Richard's departure and sat on her haunches now, staring out into the darkness.

'Shall we continue?' asked William.

She nodded briefly. He was aware that Mary would have chided her for not sitting properly on the bench. Oh, let her stay where she was comfortable. Her black face and hair disappeared in the darkness, leaving visible only the pale dress Mary had passed on to her. There was something very forlorn in her squatting shape.

'Do you miss your own people, Booron?'

'Moremme', she replied. 'Babunna, mamunna, wyanna.' Brother, sister, mother. As far as anyone knew, all her family had perished with the smallpox.

'Where are they now?'

The ghostly dress shifted its position, he thought she might be looking at him, but he couldn't be sure. Then a white sleeve became distinct from the mass of her body and raised itself to vertical, pointing to the heavens in a wide sweep. Yes, he thought, their souls are in the sky, hidden in the warm blackness all around her, watching her protectively, as parents should. That the stars were *her* stars, named by her people, who were themselves nestled invisibly in the blackness, gave him a strange feeling. Almost, of an intruder.

Booron stayed outside keeping watch over the garden while William and the Johnsons ate their dinner. Mary had given birth to a daughter two months earlier. Milbah Maria – they had given her an Ab-Original name, to honour her birthplace – lay sleeping peacefully in a newly made cradle beside the fireplace. Motherhood had made Mary very thin, but her energy and intensity were not at all diminished. Now she helped William to some new carrots, glancing at Richard to check he had enough, and at Milbah to make sure she had not buried her face under the covering.

'How do you find Booron, William?' she wanted to know.

'She seems thoughtful – well, almost melancholy – '

'Yes. Didn't I say so, Richard?'

Richard, his mouth full, contented himself with nodding.

'She's moody, she's brooding,' Mary said quickly, 'and it's because of her own stubbornness.'

'Why?' William asked.

'You know, don't you, how much I've tried to enlighten her with our faith.' Mary's pale thin face glowed in the lamplight. Urgency brought the tone of her voice near to tears. 'I read the Bible with her nearly every day. She knows about the Creation; about Eden and the Fall, about the birth of Christ, about His death and resurrection; she knows she has an immortal soul, she knows about heaven and hell, and life everlasting – but – but – ' Mary broke off with a gesture of despair.

'I'm beginning to wonder if her mind is not incapable of grasping the tenets of our faith,' Richard said heavily. 'Mary has used the patience of a saint but there is something entirely – resistant, in the girl's character – '

'But she's unhappy,' Mary said quickly. 'I'm sure she's wrestling with something – with some question that she doesn't understand. That's why I was asking William – '

William shook his head. 'We haven't talked about Christianity. She has – they have their own beliefs, of course – '

Richard snorted. 'Superstitious twaddle. Nothing coherent. You know she won't go to her own brother's grave? And when I asked her why, she said his ghost might grab her. But your brother was good, I say to her, your brother loved you, yes? And she nods – but she still won't come near the place.'

Mary laughed nervously and bent to adjust the baby's blanket. 'I so much want her to be baptized. When Richard baptized Milbah I explained it all to Booron, how the devil must be cast out, and the soul brought into God's family – she seemed very taken with that idea, I thought she would agree. But every time I mention it now, she gets that stubborn look on her face – she just goes silent, she won't talk about it. I have prayed and prayed for guidance – ' Her restless fingers were picking at a loose thread in the corner of the tablecloth. Richard reached across and patted her hand, stilling it with the pressure of his own.

'Patience, Mary, patience. We must have faith. We will see the darkness lifted.'

William thought of Booron at Sunday service. It was held now in the echoing new storehouse which had been built to house the long-awaited supplies from England. She always attended with Mary; she did not join in, not even clasping her hands for prayer – but she was serious and respectful, she certainly understood the importance of religious ceremony.

'It may be – we may need – her own beliefs may be the key to this, Richard. There may be some contradiction – '

'I've told you – ' Richard's voice rose irritably. 'Their beliefs are incoherent nonsense. Magic. They believe in magic. Tell him how she was cured of her belly-ache, Mary.'

Mary glanced down at her empty plate, then met William's eyes with a smile. 'She wanted to go to her own people for a cure, she was very determined about it. So Captain Hunter kindly sent the *Sirius'* boat for me, and Lieutenant Bradley and his crew took us to find some natives they had recently seen at Camp Cove.'

Lieutenant Bradley. Who took ostentatious care never to be alone with William. Who was brittle and cynical and humorous in company, and who had left now on the *Sirius* for the voyage to Norfolk Island and thence to China. Lieutenant Bradley, who was my friend, William told himself. Who is my friend. Who will one day explain and make everything clear. Mary was watching him with her large gentle eyes. He nodded, and she continued.

'Booron spoke to them in her own tongue and an old woman came forward – with grizzled hair and deep wrinkles, very dignified. She laid Booron down on the sand then she made a small cut in her head, just here – ' Mary touched her forehead – 'with a shell, and laid one end of a string against the wound. She held the other end of the string against her own gums and began to sing, rubbing the string against her mouth until she bled. She went on for a good while – till the blood was flowing freely. At last she stopped and asked Booron how she did. We helped Booron into the boat and before we were halfway back to Sydney she pronounced herself cured.'

259

Richard laughed. 'You see? Magic.'

'Booron's explanation,' Mary said patiently, 'was that through her blood flowing up the string and into her countrywoman's mouth, she was cured. But I could see perfectly well that the blood in the old lady's mouth was her own, not Booron's.'

Richard, still smiling, helped himself to more food. William was struck by the logic of the treatment.

'Our own doctors find bleeding a useful remedy. The use of leeches is much – '

'For goodness' sake!' Richard burst out. 'You cannot pretend there is a similarity between an English doctor who lets half a pint of a sick man's blood to cure him, and an old black witch who pretends her own blood is her patient's, and thereby magics a cure.'

William glanced at Mary. 'Did it work?'

She laughed. 'Strangely enough, yes.'

Suddenly there was a cry – almost a scream – from outside, and Booron herself burst through the door. She was in tears.

'What is it? Thieves?' Richard jumped from his chair and ran into the garden, shouting for Samuel. Instinctively Mary snatched Milbah up from her cot.

'Booron! Booron! Sit down – allowah! What is it?' William guided the terrified girl into a chair and gave her a sip of his port. 'Calm, now. Tell me.'

'Oh Mr Dawes! Turuga, turuga! We will be ill – galgalla will return. We will all be dead.'

Galgalla was their word for smallpox. But, 'Turuga? What is turuga?'

'A star is falling. Star falling down.'

'Show me.' Taking her by the hand he led her into the garden. Richard and Samuel could be heard calling to each other down at the bottom.

Fearfully, she pointed to the heavens. Through a thin veil of cloud the brighter stars could be seen; and the flashing movement of a shower of meteors. Shooting stars were arcing across the sky and dimming into darkness. Automatically William began to count: six; four; nine; an average of, say, half-a-dozen continuously in motion. And if this had begun before she came indoors, it had been of several minutes' duration already – fascinating.

'Turuga! Bad thing will come, bad fortune, grief to Eora!' Booron set up a wail, crouching on the ground and shielding her face from the sky, making a theatrical display of her grief. William clasped her shoulder.

'Booron! It is just meteors, a meteorite shower, nothing to be afraid of – '

But she shook her head and the real tears came. She turned away from him and crawled into the house like a whipped dog.

Richard and Samuel came back to the door, saying that there was no one there. William directed their attention to the sky.

'Shooting stars.' Richard sighed and shook his head. 'What did I tell you? Primitive superstition. She sees terrors on all sides.'

'I'd better get back to the observatory,' William said. 'It's rather bad timing to be away from my post on a night like this!'

Richard patted him on the back and went into the little house. William hesitated a moment, wondering whether to thank Mary for his dinner. He could hear her light sweet voice calming and reassuring Booron – and the black girl's subsiding gulps and snuffles. After a minute he opened the gate and quietly let himself out.

The Governor's hopes for teaching some natives English were successful in a number of cases: Booron; the boy Nanbaree whom Surgeon White had adopted; and two powerful young warriors, Bennelong and Colbee, who had been captured to replace Arabanoo. Colbee escaped after a while but Bennelong became the Governor's pet, even learning to drink wine and spirits which the other natives detested. Bennelong passed on plenty of information about his people's way of life, and their enmities and alliances with neighbouring tribes. But there was no suggestion that the British might offer them anything in return for these confidences.

Now that the British themselves were so close to starvation, it was a little hard to remember what benefits they might, in better circumstances, have been able to offer to the natives. Despite William's general belief in the importance of missionary work, he felt a degree of sympathy for Booron as she resisted Mary's attempts to convert her. He could not agree with Richard that the black girl's own beliefs were nonsensical. But he found them terribly difficult to understand. He felt he was looking for a key, or a light, which would suddenly reveal a new kind of sense. He knew he was making difficult something which must be simple. It was not just a question of translating individual words; there must come a point at which he would suddenly slip into understanding, as you can slip from air into water and move differently in that different medium. He felt sure that understanding was close.

They could not impose their beliefs on the natives any more than he had been able to impose his religion on Molly Hill – or any more than they could suddenly impose their system of farming on the land; it was different, and the difference must be taken into account. What had been clear at first was becoming less so.

One evening in the Johnson's garden he read Booron a passage from Sir Joseph Banks' journal, describing the first reactions of the New Holland Indians to a British ship. The natives Banks described were strangely apathetic:

> Under the south head were four small canoes, each containing one man, who held in his hand a long pole with which he struck fish, venturing with his little embarkation almost into the surf. These people seemed to be totally engaged in what they were about; our ship passed within a quarter of a mile of them, and yet they scarcely lifted their eyes from their employment.

A ship with huge white sails billowing in the wind, the decks crammed with white sailors and officers craning eagerly for a view of the land: a vessel twenty times the size of any boat the blacks had ever seen, moving in from the open sea, from beyond the edge of their world – yet they ignored it.

Booron shrugged.

'But why did they pretend?' asked William. 'Why did they pretend not to see the ship?'

'It is bad,' she said suddenly. 'Not for looking. Something bad, you don't go look at him. Look away.'

William laughed. 'Like a child? Covering his eyes so he won't see his nightmares?'

She shrugged again. 'Don't say hello, trouble. Keep him out.' There was a pause as she traced a pattern in the dust with her finger. Then she said, 'Whitefellers look for trouble. Go all over. They go in spirit places. They make spirits angry.'

'But how do you know? How do you know where the bad places are?'

'Mother father tell you. Everyone in tribe know that – stay away bad spirit place.'

Baby Milbah started crying and Booron went to tend her, leaving William alone in the garden. Mary was busy writing letters, and Richard down at the hospital.

William rose and wandered along the path through the Johnsons' orderly garden. Samuel had watered it in the late afternoon, and the smell of the ground hung strongly in the air. The colony's stock did not provide enough manure to fertilize one tenth of its gardens, and Richard Johnson had pioneered making use of the natives' middens. Outside their caves and huts they made piles of the shells and bones from their food – and of all other wastes. These piles went down deep and provided a well-rotted, rich source of fertilizer. Now the poverty of the soil at Sydney Cove had been proven by bitter experience, Phillip had given instructions for one gang to be permanently employed excavating these middens and bringing the contents, in old barrels, to spread on the settlement gardens. Since the devastation of the galgalla many of the dwelling areas of the natives were abandoned, so there had been no need to get into the difficulty of explaining to them why the whites needed their ordure. Richard Johnson's garden smelt pungently of fish and sweetly decaying matter.

CHAPTER EIGHTEEN

Abandoned

The terrors which the meteor shower foretold to Booron were intended not for her own people but for the British; this was the correct interpretation that William realized she, in her humility and fear, and he in his scientific arrogance, had failed to make. As new inhabitants of New South Wales, maybe the British had become, equally with the natives, subject to the whims of its savage and primitive gods. Whilst a meteor storm in England was fit matter for scientific study, perhaps here it should only be watched in superstitious terror and read as a stark omen of evils to come, so that acts of propitiation (were there any? He would ask her) could be performed.

Two days after the falling stars the *Supply,* which had accompanied the *Sirius* to Norfolk Island, came sailing up the bay alone. Her news reached shore before she did, communicated by despairing signs from those on board, and by the ready leap to fear in the hearts of those on land. The *Sirius* was wrecked.

She had been dashed against the rocks on Norfolk Island. Crew and passengers (apart from one sailor) were safe, and the major portion of the supplies on board had been ferried to the island shore. But the ship herself was so badly holed as to be – in those wild conditions – irreparable. The voyage to China for supplies was impossible.

That night Phillip called a meeting of all the officers to discuss the crisis. William, hurrying down from the observatory, where he had dined alone on a self-cooked mess of floury greens, was halted in his tracks by the appearance of a large drunken man. Augustus Alt stood swaying in the middle of the path, a bottle in each hand. As William approached he noted that the surveyor's clothes were soiled and that his pallid face was running with sweat.

'Sweet William!' he announced to the trees, as William approached, raising his bottles graciously.

'Mr Alt – are – are you all right?'

Alt stared at him contemptuously. 'I'm drunk as a lord, boy. Here – ' he thrust a bottle at William and over-balanced. William grabbed his arm in an attempt to steady him, and was himself pulled to the ground. Alt landed neatly (considering his bulk) on his arse, and again offered the unspilt bottle to William.

'No – thank you. There's a meeting at the Governor's – we're expected.' William was up and brushing futilely at the mud on his breeches. His leg hurt.

'Oh yes,' said Alt with heavy sarcasm. 'A meeting. That'll do a lot of good, I'm sure.' He took a swig from the bottle, making no move to get up.

William glanced down the track uneasily. There was no one in sight. Could he simply leave Alt here, abandon him? He was almost certainly too drunk to remember anything.

'I'll send someone to help you back to your hut, Mr Alt – I must be going now – '

'Come here, Sweet William.' Alt was beckoning with his little finger, an unpleasant smile on his bleary face. 'Come on. Closer.'

William approached him with wary disgust. Despite the coolness of the evening, Alt had his own following of flies, inhabiting a cloud of pissy stench which haloed him.

'D'you know what I'd give for that meeting at the Governor's? Eh?' William shook his head.

'Listen.' Alt's expression became more concentrated, he straightened his back. There was a loud, unmistakable noise of breaking wind. 'Ha ha! Ha ha!' He laughed as triumphantly as a five-year-old. 'A fart. That's what I'd give! Ha ha! A fart.'

Before William could get out of range, Alt made a grab for his leg.

'I'll tell you what, boy, listen. We're stranded. No ship – see? Salt pork and infested rice till June – and then we're going to die.'

William tried to pull his leg free. 'Supplies from England will arrive soon,' he said stiffly. 'Please let me go.'

'From England?' Alt looked up in mock amazement. 'From England? You *are* an innocent. They've got rid of us, lad, we're history. We've taken a thousand villains off their hands, they don't give a damn if we're here or at the bottom of the sea. They never intended to keep us supplied.'

'That's not true, Mr Alt – '

'This poxy country – ' Alt burped but did not pause – 'they sent us here to die. The other end of the earth. We've limped along – playing at house, playing at builder – eh, boy, you've built some serviceable roads. It takes a while for *all* the crops to fail, and for us to wake up and find ourselves with no ship in the bay. A one-way trip, eh?' He began to laugh. 'Ha ha, ha ha! The trap closes! Oh ho, they were clever, getting bright little fellows like you to volunteer. You thought of doing your duty! They played you like a fiddle, eh? Have you seen men starve to death? They take longer if they're young and strong.'

With a swift surreptitious kick from his other foot, William managed to free himself, and began to jog away down the hill.

'I'd have a drink,' shouted Alt after him. 'If I were you I'd have a drink. Before that runs out!'

William could still hear him laughing when he got round the next bend, out of sight. Pitiful, idle, disgusting, godless man. What was he *eating*, William asked himself bitterly. What could he be eating, that kept the bulk on that huge stinking body of his? And if he was ill, why didn't he die?

The meeting was conducted in quiet understatement; partly thanks to the absence of Ross, and partly because the very nature of the situation they confronted was so stark, a calm clipped response was the only one possible. A review of provisions in the public stores showed that, on present rations, the salt meat would last until 2 July, and rice (or peas in lieu) until 1 October. The flour ration would be halved, then it could last till 20 August. It was resolved to send the *Supply* immediately to Batavia, to charter a ship and bring it back loaded with stores. Assuming a safe voyage for the little *Supply*, and a transport waiting conveniently idle in Batavia, the round trip could be done in five to six months; the ship would arrive in September, as their own supplies finished. But if the *Supply* should meet with foul weather . . . an accident . . . sickness; if there were no ships to charter at Batavia – or a shortage of foodstuff there .. .

These things did not bear thinking of and Phillip told them briskly not to dwell on them. It was decided that *all* boats should be employed for fishing, and that all officers, civil and military, would go out on alternate nights to oversee and encourage fishing expeditions. The best marksmen among marines and convicts were to be put under the command of a trusty sergeant, with directions to range the woods in search of kangaroo, emu, pattagorang and other edible game. Phillip announced the appointment of the convict McEntire as his personal gamekeeper. He was one of the best shots in the colony, having already brought in a half-dozen kangaroos single-handed. Fish and fresh meat were then to be issued, wherever possible, in place of salt pork. The expectation of ships from England was not even mentioned and

William (his mood informed by his encounter with Alt) found himself thinking cynically that that may be *not* because their arrival was so imminent and undoubted, but rather because all hope of them had been abandoned. The First Fleet had left England in May 1787: it was now April 1790, a full three years later, and they had been led to expect ships from home within a year of their arrival. The space of three years should have seen the despatch of two English fleets to New South Wales. They had been abandoned with inadequate food, clothes, tools – how did the government expect them to survive? Alt's bleak answer tolled in his mind: they did not. The government had not intended them to survive.

That was nonsense, of course, but the mere thought of it tinged his mood enough next day for him to walk about the settlement with fresh eyes, noticing as if for the first time the appallingly ragged condition of convicts and marines alike. Less than half had shoes, or anything that could pretend to resemble shoes. The convicts wore rags tied about their bodies, pieces of sacking and holey blankets; a large proportion of the men wore nothing on their chests and backs, their shirts having been adapted into patches for their breeches, or exchanged with the females for sewing repair work which would at least cover their privates. Among the dregs of the convicts, the old and the mad, some had no more than a dirty rag tied around the waist. With their blotchy sunburnt skin and emaciated limbs, they presented a sad and wasted mirror image to those gleaming black bodies which had danced on the shores to greet their arrival. But hundreds of those blacks, of course, were gone now – dead of the smallpox. We brought death, William told himself, and now we ourselves will die.

News that the Governor had donated his private food supply to the public stores, and was going on to the same rations as everyone else, conveyed a mixed message. Certainly it was noble in the Governor to give himself an equal share in hunger with those he ruled; but perhaps there was some secret knowledge behind his sacrifice – perhaps some guilt at the fate he had brought them to. Perhaps he knew more about the government's plans for them than he had ever revealed . . .

Although the suspicion was unfounded, William knew from conversational sources as exalted as George Worgan and as lowly as Annie, his convict washerwoman, that many shared it. There was a general feeling that Phillip was in some way to blame for their predicament, and his selfless donation of food made his guilt seem all the more likely. Hunger and frustration are making us mad, William told him-

self; and as if evidence of the fact were needed, poor Lieutenant
Maxwell rowed himself back and forth across the bay for two whole
days and nights, until he was overpowered and brought in by fishermen. White sedated him and pronounced him incurably insane, and he
was confined to a hut.

William wondered how Bradley and the *Sirius'* crew, trapped on
Norfolk Island, were passing the time. Our sentence is the same as the
convicts', he realized. The island was reputedly more fertile than
the land at Sydney; perhaps they were all busy farming. Molly Hill, he
had heard, was among those women sent to Norfolk Island.

Hunger brought a listlessness which he did not want to give in to.
Public works were all but stopped, and not even the Governor had
much heart for planning new roads and farms. How long will it take
the wilderness to reclaim this spot? William found himself thinking.
How long before my road to the hospital is overgrown with trees and
grass again? If we all died here, in ten years it would be reverting to its
former appearance. Then he thought with fascinated horror of his
observatory, abandoned; of the telescope and night glass standing
unused in the little shrine of the observation room, with weeds growing between its planks; of what Booron would tell her people of the
white man's stars. The absence of public work meant that William
actually had time on his hands. Along with the other officers, he was
supposedly out fishing alternate nights. In fact it was enough for him
simply to meet three of the returning boats and check their catch; his
presence in a small boat would have been an unnecessary encum-
brance. He was able, therefore, to spend a portion of nearly every night
observing.

In the daylight he unearthed his flora and fauna notebook and began
to make detailed drawings again, of the plants in the woods around the
observatory. And he visited Booron often, continuing his investigation
into her language and beliefs.

There was some discussion about whether the captive natives
should be returned to their own people, since staying with the whites
might doom them to starvation. But the Governor was against the idea,
fearing that reports of hunger among the British might encourage a
native attack. Bennelong, the Governor's current favourite, was given
fresh fish and Indian corn over and above the ration, but still seemed
discontented with his diet and did in fact escape soon after. Mary
would not hear of parting with Booron, and pointed out to William

that there was no evidence that the free natives might not starve – when fish was short, they had even fewer resources than the whites.

William and Booron sat companionably either side of the Johnsons' warm hearth, now the weather was cooler, and he noted down sentences and different word endings, getting glimmerings of the structure of her language and finding that its verb endings changed according to the verb's subject, much as Latin did. Because they were such excellent mimics, she and the other Indians had picked up English quickly, which meant that their language remained a mystery to the British; a mystery which was not felt, generally, to be in need of solution.

Booron was in a strange position, as the native who had been among them longest and had the best grasp of English, and yet was only a female. The young boy Nanbaree, adopted by White, showed far less aptitude, and Booron's relationship to him was that of protector. Sometimes she was taken on expeditions, when it was thought useful to have someone who could translate for the natives, and then she took on almost the role of ambassador. But still in the Johnsons' house she was principally a maidservant, washing, sweeping, gardening, and nursing little Milbah.

They were quiet, muted, waiting days, the days of April and May. Despite the fear of starvation, there was a peace to them, and a humility that came with them, which William gradually began to appreciate. They were no longer conquering the Cove, carving it into shape, slicing roads and blasting redoubts and boring wells; they were simply surviving here, like castaways, lightly. And through his renewed observation of stars and plants, and his halting conversations with Booron, the place itself – what it was, rather than what they might make of it – began to impress itself gently upon his mind.

STEPHEN

A woman coming out of the house at 5.20 as I park the car; she's neat and young, short-haired. Carries a business-like shoulder bag.

'Good evening Mr Beech.'

I have never seen her before in my life.

'I'm Daniel's physiotherapist. I usually come in the morning – '

I nod and pass her, but she puts a gloved hand on my arm.

'If you've got a minute – ' She glances back at the house, then leads me out of the gate again, on to the pavement. She moves to stand beside a car – hers, I suppose. It's already dark, the streetlights are shining.

'What is it?'

'I hope you won't think I'm interfering – ' her face is serious, very young – 'but I'm concerned about your wife.'

My wife?

'It's – I think she's quite depressed. I don't know if you've noticed – '

Noticed. What should I notice? That Olla has a mission; a child; a purpose. That Olla is fulfilled.

I'm not responding or making encouraging noises. Miss Physiotherapist sighs and puts her heavy shoulder bag on the bonnet of her car.

'Sometimes it's hard to notice change if you live with a person every day – but I see her once a week and . . .'

'And? She's changed?'

'I think – I mean, she seems very withdrawn. And, and, she never smiles.'

I have to restrain a ghostly impulse to laugh. That's my Olla.

'Because I deal with children like Daniel all the time – well, I'm getting to know the signs of strain, in their parents – I really think Mrs Beech needs a little break.'

'A break?'

'I think, maybe, she spends too much time with Daniel.' Her words are rushing now, she's embarrassed. 'I mean, you see, I know how easily it can happen, but the thing is, does she ever go out? She's losing confidence, socially – '

'How do you know?' The question is more combative in tone than I intended, she flinches and takes out her car keys.

'I'm not trying to interfere, honestly Mr Beech – but it is part of my job to be aware of the mother as well as the child – and I just thought you – well you might not have realized – '

'You usually call in the mornings? Why are you here this evening?'
She glances down at the car keys. 'I swapped Daniel's visit with
someone else's.' Because she wanted to speak to me. She's timed her
visit and waited. Probably asked Olla what time I get in. She's gone to
these lengths. To tell me – what? That my wife is depressed. I rest my
weight against her car door.
'Well. I'm grateful to you for taking the trouble – '
'That's all right. No trouble.'
'But I'm not sure there's much I can do.'
She looks up at me quickly, a flash of incredulity. 'She's exhausted –
she needs a break from Daniel. To go out. Maybe to have a rest in the
evening while you cook dinner and put him to bed. I don't know if
you can imagine the strain of looking after a baby like Daniel
twenty-four hours a day – '
I realize I'm staring at her rudely. I make myself glance back to the
house, to break the stare. The young woman's voice becomes colder
now, less hesitant, less embarrassed. She has pigeon-holed me. Male
chauvinist pig.
'You're going to work, Mr Beech, you're in a different environment,
meeting different people, eight hours a day. But your wife's at home
all the time dealing with Daniel, worrying about him – it wouldn't be
good for anyone. If you can't give her some help now, she may become
quite ill. And then you'd have to look after Daniel on your own.' Her
voice is hard with dislike and the triumph of her logic. 'I mean even at
night, she's waiting for him to wake up – she never gets a proper
night's sleep. Couldn't you wake up with him on Fridays and
Saturdays for example, when you're not at work?'
'Has she complained to you?' Dumb question that feeds her
contempt, but it's squeezed out of me by sheer amazement. I know
she hasn't. Olla never complains. How does this woman presume to
know?
'She doesn't need to complain – how long d'you think anyone can go
without a good night's sleep? She can't even go to the toilet in peace,
he might wake up and cry – she's never off duty. Can you imagine
what that must be like?'
Silence.
She jangles her keys, swings her bag off the bonnet, opens the car
door. 'I'm just very concerned for your wife's welfare, I think she
needs your help.' She forces herself to smile. 'Why don't you hire a

baby-sitter and take her out for the evening. Even women need *some* time off, you know.'

She hops into her car and slams the door triumphantly; drives off without another glance. I stand on the pavement gaping after her. But Olla doesn't want. She doesn't want. My help. With Daniel. She doesn't trust me. She doesn't *like* me. She wants him to herself.

And if it's true? If she's making herself ill. Well, it's a free country. Don't people up and down it have the right to make themselves ill with an excess of whatever takes their fancy? Cigarettes, alcohol, heroin, sweeties, work. They all kill you in the end. Why not motherhood? Why shouldn't she be allowed to overdose on motherhood, if that's what she wants?

She wouldn't *let* me help her. Is the reply I should have given to Miss Righteously Indignant. She doesn't want my fucking help, she'd rather die. Stick that in your feminist pipe and smoke it. She wouldn't take my help if I gave it her on a silver plate.

The incident lingers unpleasantly. The mutual incomprehension. The distance I have moved from a world where a man and woman might share domestic duties; or even from the sit-com cosy world of a husband returning from work flourishing theatre tickets and a bunch of flowers. Imagine taking Olla out. Impossible. She does not want to go. She does not want anything that will separate her from Daniel.

There is a world. Where men take women out for candle-lit dinners. Or even for a walk to the pub. Where one person has a lie-in and the other brings breakfast in bed to share. Where people are kind to each other. Good God. A world of aliens.

Once I dreamt she stroked my cheek as she crept back into bed late at night. But when I woke she was still in Daniel's room.

CHAPTER NINETEEN

The sky is falling

The Second Fleet arrived from England in June 1790; the *Lady Juliana*, the *Justinian*, and three other transports, bearing news of the wreck of the *Guardian*, which had been despatched to New South Wales with supplies back in 1788. So the settlers at Sydney Cove had not been forgotten; the purpose of their venture was endorsed. The excitement of news from Europe – the revolution in France! – of letters, replenished food supplies, clothes, and other necessaries and luxuries, was tarnished by the appalling condition of the convicts landed from these ships. Many had died on the voyage and others died in the very act of disembarkation. The hospital was quickly filled to overflowing, and emergency tents set up to house the sick, starving, scorbutic, and enfeebled. Phillip accused the masters to their faces of greed and cruelty and wrote strong letters back to England. Surgeon White was enraged; on several transports the convicts had been offered no fresh air or exercise for the entire voyage, and had avoided reporting the deaths of their neighbours in order to be able to take their rations.

William received two letters from his father, anxiously questioning the state of food supplies in the colony (alarming reports on this score having already reached England) and expressing concern over William's opportunities for promotion if he remained in New South Wales. The fussy, affectionate, unselfconscious tone of the letters brought his father close in memory, but did not stir any homesickness. There was also a friendly note from Maskeylene, along with the new night glass, sextant and other goods William had requested for the observatory.

Back on full rations, the convicts were set to public works again, and the roof of the new storehouse was quickly finished, plus work on the quay and landing stage at Rose Hill.

They were back where they had been before: the settlement full of people and activity, a half-dozen ships in the bay, energetic discussions over future plans; digging, building and sawing on all sides . . . And yet they were not quite back in the same place. It was clear, now, that without regular supplies from England the settlement would die. No one but the Governor believed his own optimistic projections that the colony would be self-supporting in ten years. Empty desert as the land was, there was no prospect of the settlement becoming a centre for trade – there was nothing here *to* trade.

But on the other hand, the convicts were beginning to adapt to the place; the shrivelled constraints and complexities of their lives, exposed to open air and space, seemed to fall away. There was the example of Molly Hill. A number of convicts in quick succession claimed that their terms had expired (many who were sentenced to seven years having served three or more on the hulks before the fleet even set sail). Phillip could not verify their claims since no records of either their crimes or their sentences had ever been given him, but there was no reason to disbelieve them. Those who wished to settle were given land, with tools to clear it and seed to plant, and the promise of food from the public stores until they were self-sufficient. Those who did not wish to settle, unless they could afford a passage home, had to continue with public works, to earn their keep from the stores.

William had the task of measuring out plots for the settlers. Their industry and determination was impressive. They hutted themselves and their families, chopped and burnt the trees, dug and turned the land (no ploughs having been sent out from England), and planted wheat and Indian corn. Within eighteen months the first of them, James Ruse, had taken himself off the stores, and was expecting to be able to support his wife as well the following year.

Looking back, in the silent dreamy hours of the early morning, William's mind wandered from the moons of Jupiter which he was observing, to the future of the colony. He recalled his first thoughts on arriving at Sydney Cove; they were strangely unreal, now; they seemed almost fantastical. Even those things which he had hoped for which *had* come true were not as he had expected. Many of the convicts had reformed; had shown themselves capable of working for an honest living – but yet that self-conscious reformation he had envisaged, that deliberate turning from their earlier crimes, the renunciation of sin, the seeking of forgiveness in honest toil – none of that had happened. It was almost as if no deliberate or conscious choices had been made; simply, things had drifted, undergone subtle adjustments. There was still thieving and pilfering, but not as a way of life – perhaps because there were not enough valuable possessions here (nor enough demand

274

for them) to support such an industry. The only item of real value was food, and all were short of that.

And the natives – his plans to convert and educate the natives had come down to talks with Booron, and to an increased – rather than diminishing – sense of the gulf between their worlds; to an uncertainty about what might be best for her.

The observatory was built, certainly, and he had made some (sadly limited) progress in the area of astronomical observation. That was a clear achievement.

But the nightmare: the nightmare he had had on his first night on land – the fear of being nothing. What had happened to that nightmare? Slowly, but with growing clarity, he saw that it was no longer a thing to fear. There were purposes – God's purposes – working themselves out. When he had tried to force things to happen, they went wrong, did not turn out as he intended. The spectacle of Barnes holding out the smallpox sample bottle to an eager, smiling Indian floated before his eyes. Then Molly Hill, winking over a man's naked back. It was important to learn. To wait. To understand. To *be* nothing, perhaps. To be willing to be nothing, sometimes, to have that humility, to wait for God's intentions to be made plain. It was important to understand that he understood very little.

Governor Phillip had not changed. He had the same set of plans and ambitions he had brought with him when he stepped on to the land three years ago. Recognition of the distance he had come made William a little giddy; he was moving into unknown territory, more unknown than the land had been when he first examined it through his glass from the decks of the *Sirius*. Because then, he knew where he was going. Now, he was off the path.

His work took him mainly to Rose Hill (or Parramatta, as the natives called the area), the settlement higher up the bay, where more fertile farmland had been found. Storehouses, a quay, barracks, roads, were all needed at Rose Hill. It was difficult to make a regular time to talk with Booron, but he continued to visit the Johnsons' house every time he was in Sydney.

Booron felt her separation from her people keenly; linked in with that, he recognized, was an intense nostalgia for her own childhood, for the days of innocent happiness before the galgalla. When prompted by external events, she sometimes talked to him about beliefs which had, to William, the logic of dreams; which were rooted in such another way of seeing the world that he had to listen to them with an empty head, leaving himself behind.

One afternoon William found her squatting behind the Johnsons' gate, her face in her hands. She was so wrapped in her misery she did not even greet him, but when he asked the cause of her grief, she told him without artifice or embarrassment. Mr Johnson and Mr Tench went over the water, in the boat, to Kayumy. They met up with Eora, her people, on the beach, and found one woman holding her screaming baby closely over the fire. When they tried to prevent her, the woman snatched the child away and ran off with it. The baby, Mr Johnson said, was white. The other women had explained by signs that she was trying to blacken it with smoke, to make it a proper colour. Mr Johnson came home very angry.

William guessed that Richard Johnson's anger might have been directed more at the white sailor or convict who had taken advantage of the poor native woman than at her treatment of the tell-tale white child. He patted Booron's shoulder.

'You musn't grieve, Booron. I'll speak to Captain Tench. Maybe, if the mother cannot reconcile herself to the white baby, it could be brought into the settlement. I am sure there are women here who would look after it.'

Booron raised her face and looked at him with a flat contempt that shocked him.

'Booron? What is it? Why are you so angry?'

She looked down again at her bare toes, flexing and tensing in the dirt. Despite all the Johnsons' efforts she absolutely refused shoes.

'What's the matter?'

She opened her mouth to speak then closed it again. He crouched beside her, so that he would catch whatever she said.

'Booron?'

She shook her head miserably, and muttered, 'Eora all gone. All gone, all gone. White baby coming.'

William waited to see if she would say anything else, but after a moment she looked up with a sad little smile, and scrambled to her feet. 'I go help make dinner now.'

Watkin came up to the observatory, as he usually did, the following Monday evening – and straight away volunteered the story of the native blackening her baby.

'It's not the only one, either,' he added. 'A fellow who's farming up at Parramatta told me he saw a woman caking her pale child in mud at the lagoon, plastering it with thick black mud.'

'Booron was very distressed about it.'

'But how is it to be prevented? I have seen them offer their women to our men a few times now; and with the ratio of men to women that we have, there will always be some fellow eager to take advantage of them.'

'Bradley's told me about them offering their women. But is it genuine, or an elaborate mark of courtesy?'

'I think it's genuine. They are not very concerned with chastity or fidelity, if the tales Bennelong told are anything to go by. I don't think they see anything wrong in a woman sharing her charms with several admirers. Bennelong was always on the look-out for new conquests – and he told me without any rancour that his former wife has gone to live with Colbee now.'

William considered in silence the thought that Richard Johnson had recently voiced to him: that they should consider seeking a native husband for Booron. How would the Johnsons deal with such a casual interpretation of marriage?

'Here,' he said, pouring Watkin a dish of tea from the kettle on the stove.

'What are all these leaves floating about? For goodness sake, it's a waste bringing you decent tea. Is this how you usually drink it?'

'I don't, usually.'

'You live like a barbarian, William. Would you like my spare teapot? Or do you really have no tea?'

William shook his head. 'A Second Lieutenant's pay doesn't run to such luxuries, Watkin. I enjoy it all the more when I come to visit you. Tell me, what is Bennelong's attitude to his wife's children?'

'Ah,' said Watkin. 'That is interesting. He makes no distinction between those he has sired and those sired by other men, indeed I believe he does not even know which ones are truly his. When I asked him which were his sons he gave me a long rigmarole about siring a child by dreaming a significant dream. He says his spirit makes the children, and the spirit can pass into the woman during a dance, or eating – even, in sleep.'

'They do not believe children are a result of sexual relations?'

Watkin laughed. 'Who knows? Maybe they don't. Or maybe they think *we* don't know, and they want to save us from the shock!' His face became more serious. 'It may simply be that they have a poetic version for polite conversation. I mean, it's more romantic to imagine a child being created through some sort of spiritual union, than through the sordid physical coupling which we know only too well has produced that unfortunate child of Biddy Lowe's.'

'Biddy Lowe has had a child?'

Watkin stamped his feet in exasperation. 'Where do you *live*, William? How can you not know what the whole of Sydney has been gossiping about for the past week?'

Biddy Lowe was a convict woman with a badly scarred face – the result, Stokoe had once said, of an angry rival throwing scalding porridge at her. Her behaviour was coquettish and wanton, perhaps as a result of her disfigurement. She had propositioned almost every man in the settlement, if rumour was to be believed, and most took delight in rejecting her. She had spoken once to William and he had formed the sad conclusion that she was insane. Even William had been unable to avoid hearing occasional Biddy Lowe jokes among the marines or the convicts, about how low a man would have to sink to lie with her, about some wit who offered to pay her if she would put a bag over her head, and so on.

'Is the father known?'

'Guess.'

William could not guess; Watkin's delighted face suggested it must be someone more important than a convict. For a terrible moment he wondered if it could be the Governor. No, no, impossible.

'The surveyor!'

'Alt?'

'Yes. That fat drunken pig has sired a little replica of himself upon poor Biddy Lowe – doesn't deny it, his name is on the birth certificate.'

William thought of Alt's oppressive smell, and felt nauseated. He forced his attention back to the original subject.

'Booron was very angry. It was not pity for the child–'

'Angry with the mother? For submitting to a white man?'

'I don't know. I'll ask her again. She said – ' He hesitated. ' "Eora all gone." I don't know what she meant.'

*

STEPHEN

Where are William's bad dreams? He has anxieties, yes. Fears. Griefs. But nightmares? Real nightmares, places beyond hope and reason – does he have them?

Not really. Every time he's knocked off his perch, he climbs right back again. What is he, a wobbly man? Springing back to an eternal position of upright hope? He doesn't know what horror is. Which is strange given what he sees: men killed in battle, public hangings, death by starvation and scurvy and smallpox. You'd think he would know about horror, but he remains obstinately clean.
Bradley, now; I think Bradley might know about horror. Bradley might have nightmares. But something keeps William safe. I thought it was innocence but it's not; I think now it must be faith. Not necessarily religious (though the belief in God helps) – no, faith in man. In some ultimate human court of appeal, some ultimate notion of decency. That confidence dispels doubt, deprives horror of a place.

It may, of course, simply be his age. I didn't have nightmares at twenty-eight.
No. Never had any until much later. *Now*. Now I have them.

Daniel. Come down, Daniel, to the lions' den.
Thanks Dad, I've already been. They only got me brain.

Are there lions in there? In the space between my wife's hips, in the black hole of generation? Of course there are lions, and beasts and devils of every description – do you doubt it, when you actually inspect the range of deformities that are spewed out in the name of offspring? Do you doubt it, when the social worker takes us to the special school Daniel will attend, and you are brought face to face with abominations, with bedlam creatures, with a legless child who shrieks and bites her arms till they bleed, who has to be restrained in her chair by two strong nurses, in whose grasp she writhes and convulses like a trapped snake?

In the special school the teachers are calm and friendly. They smile at us and the other offsprings of darkness, and speak in gentle voices. They talk of children realizing their potential, and quality of life, and social skills. They are kind to us. They do not pity us because our child is nothing strange, to them; and they do not know that I am a

279

child-murderer, a hater of cripples, a piece of shite. They have not thought about picking up a cushion and putting it over the inadequate breathing apparatus of a child who's destined never to feed or excrete without help. They think of attainment targets and exercise programmes, they think life is sacred. They mention Christy Brown. They are on the side of goodness and light. They are blessed with faith, and I have none. Who can teach me to be like them? Who can help me?

And Olla was calm, polite, collected – even charming. Displayed no signs of stress. Daniel will go to the special nursery when he is two, he will be looked after by these faith-ful women. Olla is showing no objections to relinquishing his daytime care to them. She is far too cunning for that.

Is Miss Physio mad? 'Your wife is losing confidence socially.' I think not. But then must question, perhaps, my own competence to judge such a matter. Am I able to judge if she is normal? Is our life normal?

Miss Physio has got on to the GP. He phones me at work. He wants me to persuade Olla to make contact with a 'respite carer' who would have Daniel one weekend in four. Would she agree to that? Never. He suggests I try to 'take her out of herself'.
An extraordinary proposition.

They are ganging up on me. They think I am a bastard.
I am. What other role is available?
I tell him Olla is well. We have been together to see the nursery. We are going out one night next week, I'll find a baby-sitter for Daniel.

Will I? Will she? Who am I protecting? Her, or myself, from them?

*

After some careful thought, William asked Richard to ask Mary to have a word with Booron about the origin of babies. He was anxious that she should know it lay within her own power to determine the skin colour of any child she herself might have.

When he next visited, Mary told him she had had 'a little talk' with Booron, but was clearly frustrated by the girl's unresponsiveness.

'She is so sullen these days, William. I speak to her and it is as if – I don't know, she doesn't take it in. I think Richard may be right and we should try to find a husband for her, from among her own people. I think she may be pining for their company.'

Richard developed the idea. 'We could build her a hut in the garden, and they would live there; he would have his freedom, go off fishing and so on during the day, and Booron could help Mary here, as they are both accustomed to. It is more natural, when all's said and done, for the girl to have a mate; and marriage will remove other thoughts and temptations from her mind. Mary's right, you know, she has become very moody, it's difficult to get to the bottom of it.' He sighed. 'I only wish religion could be a comfort to her. If she would open her mind to God, and take strength from the teachings of the Church, she would find her way more easily. She needs the moral guidance of Christ's teachings – she is lost and wandering. I have taken over the task of her spiritual education from Mary, but I have not made any impression upon her so far. Will you try, William? She speaks more easily with you, she seems to trust you. She will make a poor companion for little Milbah, growing up, if she is not a Christian.'

The Johnsons were invited to dinner at the Governor's, an unusual enough occurrence to put them into a flurry, although Richard was gloomily aware of why they had been asked.

'Poor attendance at Sunday service will only be remedied by building a church to shelter us from the elements. If His Excellency thinks he can stem the decline in congregation by giving me dinner, rather than committing resources to the building of God's house, he is much mistaken.'

Milbah was to be entrusted to Booron's care for the evening, and William said he would stay with them and see if he could steer Booron's thoughts towards Baptism. She seemed to be in a quiet and serious mood, and might therefore be more receptive than usual to the subject.

When they were settled either side of the fire, with little Milbah sleeping comfortably in her cot, William began. 'You have heard Reverend Johnson speak of heaven, Booron?'

'Heaven.' She nodded. Her straggling black hair had grown long enough now for Mary to plait it and fix it up at the nape of her neck, which emphasized the graceful tilt of her head. 'Where you come from.'

William was startled. They had spoken of England several times. She knew better than that.

'No. *Heaven*, where God lives, with the angels and souls of the faithful.'

She frowned, staring down into the fire.

'You told me before, Booron, that the souls of *your* dead go up into the sky.'

'True. But now the heaven fallen, all mix up living people, gromedah, bowwan, mahn.' They were words for shadows and spirits, he knew that without recourse to his notebook.

'What do you mean, the heaven is fallen?'

'The lid of the bourra.'

'The sky?'

She nodded. 'The lid of sky is fallen.'

He fumbled after a meaning. 'You mean the falling stars we saw here once? The meteor shower? That is nothing to do with *heaven*, Booron – '

She nodded obstinately and he bit back his words.

'The sky is fallen. I tell you now what small child know.' She glanced at him, and he nodded. She checked Milbah to make sure she was still sleeping peacefully, and William leant forward to put another section of branch on the fire. The wood crackled and spat loudly as it burned, as if conducting a fierce argument with the fire.

'The bourra, sky, it held up by a prop, at each one edge of earth.' She raised her hands, pale palms outstretched, in a mime of Atlas supporting the world. 'Like a gum tree only plenty bigger, great big prop them hold up heaven. Each prop have a guard, do him repair, keep him good and strong. That way, all the prop hold up heaven, and sun can come up every morning bring warm and light to earth. But word come that Booroowee prop is rotten – '.

'East? The prop in the east?'

She nodded. 'Where the sun comes rising. Dawn-side. That prop go for fall down; wet, broken, no good that prop. Old man keeper of that prop got to fix it, quick, before it break and heaven fall down. All the people, many, many Eora, Darak, Tharwal, all people bring gift for old man, rug made from possum, plenty axe head, goong-un, cannadial, doo-ull – spears – for to make old man in Booroowee repair him prop. But – ' she pursed her lips and shrugged.

'He didn't repair it?'

'I tell you. If the sky fall down, all ghost come in from Booroowee, all mahn, all spirit of the dead come tumble into earth, all mix up anyhow.'

'But not *us*, Booron. We have come from England.'

282

'From far.'

'But on *earth*, not from the sky. We come from a far country on earth.'

'White men come from Booroowee, east, where prop fall down. White men come floating on islands.'

'But we came in ships, you know that. You have been out to the *Supply*, you have seen her.'

She shook her head. 'There came many island floating over the wave. On island grow tree, with branch, and white men run up and down tree like possum without tail. Them island have big white wing like bird, them island come from heaven, bring dead men back to earth.'

He held out his hand.

'Touch me. Am I not flesh and blood, like you? Is little Milbah not alive, like an Eora baby?'

She made no attempt to touch his proffered hand, and her face became opaque and sullen.

'Booron? This is a story, yes? A story to frighten children.'

She shrugged. They sat in silence. At last William broke it.

'I'm sorry. I shouldn't have interrupted.'

She continued to stare into the fire in silence but he thought he detected a softening in her expression.

'Tell me what they are like, the mahn, your spirits of the dead. What do they look like?'

'White,' Booron said simply. 'They are white.'

William rubbed his face with his hands.

'And what happens at the end of the story?'

'Heaven fall down, the sky is broken – all mix up him dead and live, white and black all mix up. Dead spirit lost their place in heaven, they crowding many many, more and more come fill up Eora land. Every spirit know its place, fish in stream, bird in air, root in earth. Spirits of the dead take land off living. Chop tree, break earth, make place for white spirit. Now black feller die, him jump up white feller. All Eora gone – gone.' She spoke hurriedly, as if afraid he might interrupt and when he was silent at the end she giggled.

William thought carefully before he began to speak.

'You know white children are born to white mothers – like Milbah. And we die. You know white people have died here – Reverend Johnson buries them; sick people from the hospital.' Her eyes showed that she was following what he said, but she made no reply.

'We live and die as your people do. We are not spirits. God, who is

283

the heavenly father of all peoples, black and white, looks after the spirits of the dead – in heaven, in happiness. They have no need to come back to earth.'

Her eyes flickered and she turned her gaze back to the fire.

'This is a story, Booron. You don't believe the sky can fall.'

After a while she said slowly, 'You can have bad dream. In the night, bad dream, bad thing come. One time no trouble, creep up near by fire, curl up tight, bad dream go move on, bad dream – ' she opened her hands suddenly, in a pantomime of 'empty' – 'pass you by. But other time, trouble. Him catch you. Then, bad dream live with you long long time, bad dream not moving on, bad dream bring plenty grief.'

William looked at Milbah's fair, sleeping face. Her little pink lips were turned out like a kiss. She was not having a bad dream.

He wanted Booron to know he was sorry for treating her like a child. But she was staring at the fire as if she had forgotten he was there. She was very still, her black face in profile now illumined as the firelight flickered up, now melting back into darkness. Like Patience on a monument, William thought, she was waiting for the bad dream to pass by.

'Would you like to go back to living with the Eora?' The question surprised himself, but she did not seem to find it odd. She remained motionless for a while, then shrugged.

'The Johnton give me plenty food.'

'But you are lonely. You miss your old way of life. And you are old enough to marry – .'

She turned her head to face him. 'Them the Johnton word.' It sounded like an accusation.

'But they only want you to be happy.'

She shrugged, then picked up the sleeping baby, and silently left the room.

When he went out ten minutes later to see what she was doing, he found her standing in the open doorway with Milbah in her arms. The moon was shining brightly and the garden was silvered with it. She was crooning an unintelligible song. As he spoke, he was already regretting it.

'If you married you would have a child of your own. A black child.'

Booron closed her eyes, not faltering in her singing. William waited a minute or more but she continued to ignore him, and he had no choice but to go back to the fireside.

Long after the Johnsons' return, after his solitary walk back up to the observatory, after he had checked his instruments and gazed at the now cloudy sky, William lay in bed unable to sleep. There was a child's story in England, he seemed to remember, about the sky falling down. A chicken thought it was falling and she wanted to tell the king . . . maybe it was one of Aesop's fables. The chicken, he recalled, was eaten by a fox at the end. And did Booron think the souls of the dead were balanced on the lid of the sky, like dinner on a plate?

No. It *sounded* literal, that was because of the language, and because she often tried to avoid the letter 's'. She had been present when Campbell and Ralph Clark were imitating Bennelong, one time, and laughing at the way he said 't' for 's'. She would not lay herself open to mockery of that kind, she was very proud. William recalled the dignity of her grief when her brother died of smallpox. She crept close to him and lay by him until he was quite cold; only then did she suffer herself to be drawn away, and then she neither cried nor made any other display of her feeling.

If the Greeks, William told himself, can describe the sun as a chariot drawn by horses across the sky, then I'm sure the Ab-Origines have every right to describe the sky as a lid held up by props, and for me to think none the worse of their intelligence for that.

He wanted to know if it was an old story, though, the invasion of the dead from the east – or if it had sprung up as a response to the British arrival. He wanted to know, really, how much store she set by it. The question why had the Johnsons given their daughter an Ab-Original name popped suddenly and insistently into his head, where it was as irritating as a pebble in his boot. Milbah Maria. Blackfeller die, him jump up whitefeller.

Booron was waiting for something to happen, she was waiting for things to change. For the bad dream to pass by. She did not, herself, want to make anything happen. That was why she feared returning to live with the Eora. Maybe. He did not know.

STEPHEN

'To rise from Generation free.' A stray line from Blake. Which has
been haunting me.
Daniel? Yes, and Booron. And children. And genocide.

Who has the most, strongest, healthiest children, gets the future.
Obviously. The biggest empire – the richest colony – is the future.
I see blond Aryan youths in lederhosen and SS armbands singing
'Tomorrow Belongs to Me'. Children in the gas chambers: the
ultimate solution. That's *them* out of the future. That's cleared us a bit
of space. Soldiers raping and impregnating enemy women, to
people the future in their own image. Tomorrow belongs to me. If
your children are not your own . . . resemble someone else . . . are in
fact your enemy – the future will defeat you. Invalidate you. Spit on
you. Of course Booron weeps at the betrayal of the birth of white Eora
children. At that ultimate invasion.

But 'to rise from Generation free'. What was Blake celebrating there?
Getting off the conveyor belt? Being absolved from a stake in that
never-ending, breeding future? What's the freedom? What Olla and I
have, presumably, in Daniel. The freedom not to believe in the
future. If children are hope, progress, ambition made flesh; if on
the grand scale of evolution (which on the whole our twentieth-
century Western minds don't dissociate from the notion of progress,
bizarrely, since the dodo and dinosaur certainly did, and we will too
when insects, or whatever's more viable than us when we screw up,
take over) – if on that grand scale people like to believe that they are
better than their parents, and their children better than them, then our
child is a wet fish. A slap in the face with. The antithesis of child: a
reversion, a throwback, a retrograde step, a link back to the mindless
soup of protoplasm we thought we'd crawled out of, rather than a
leap forward to the perfection of mind and body the dream of 'future'
holds.

And if the future is not evolution to a better state –
but is in fact a brain-damaged cripple – What then? We *are* 'from
Generation free'.
It's the end of the line, there'll be no descendants.

Oh no, no more than if we were childless – although childlessness is a
cleaner, more attractive proposition; a straight abstention on the
future rather than a 'no' vote.

A positive act of responsibility, facing up to the fact that three score years and ten are it, rather than sheltering behind the ability to chuck a few eggs and sperm into the surging river of continuity and hoping that the stock of humanity will thereby be improved.

'From Generation free' then a freedom? An honesty? No more hiding in that soft-focus future of equality and brotherly love and peace? Is that what he means? I need to look at the poem.

> *To Tirzah*
> What'er is born of Mortal birth
> Must be consumed with the Earth
> To rise from Generation free:
> Then what have I to do with thee?
>
> The sexes sprung from shame and pride,
> Blow'd in the morn; in evening died;
> But mercy chang'd death into sleep;
> The sexes rose to work and weep.
>
> Thou, Mother of my mortal part,
> With cruelty didst mould my heart,
> And with false self-deceiving tears
> Didst bind my nostrils, eyes and ears:
>
> Didst close my tongue in senseless clay,
> And me to mortal life betray.
> The Death of Jesus set me free:
> Then what have I to do with thee?

Ah, how badly remembered. I am humbled.
'Thou, Mother of my mortal part/With cruelty didst mould my heart . . . Didst close my tongue in senseless clay,/And me to mortal life betray.'
It *is* Daniel. Betrayed to mortal life. And if only there were any other kind, poor dumb little sod. Like Ariel's, like Caliban's, that I could let you loose to fly to. If only there was heaven.

Cruelty. Yes. The mother is cruel; she keeps him alive. Olla doesn't believe in progress, no dismissing her as a sucker for evolution to a brighter future. She's never bought that line.
Then what?
Survival. She simply devotes herself to his daily survival. To keep

him alive (though it be for less purpose than keeping a cauliflower alive – much less, since the cauliflower is growing to be eaten or to produce seeds) satisfies her. It is the base pulse of nature. Survive. The first genetically programmed instruction. To the first slimy blob in a pond that called itself a living cell. Survive. Reproduce. Survive.

Fuck the future, fuck progress, fuck wisdom, happiness, love: survive. Reproduce. Survive. Cling on to life, by your nails, by your teeth. Grow some if you haven't got any, and cling on. Because if you drop off you're gone, a dodo.

Survival's the same, isn't it? As 'Tomorrow Belongs to Me'. Only stripped of the gloss of ideological and sentimental aspirations, stripped of the crap about progress and a better world, stripped of politics both evil and well-intentioned.
And the ones who rise from generation free are dead, aren't they, in the grand scale? Dead and rotting underground. Weep for the Eora, Booron. Fight to have black babies. Hang on to those self-deceiving tears, boy, and that tongue of senseless clay. It's all we've got.

CHAPTER TWENTY

A whale at Manly

Relations between the settlers and the natives changed dramatically over the next few days, thanks to a whale which became stranded in the bay and was washed up on the beach at Manly. Over two hundred natives gathered to feast upon it, more than had been seen since before the smallpox. Bennelong was spotted among them and Phillip went over to pay his respects to his favourite. Bennelong was friendly but wary, unsurprisingly, after the length of time he had spent as the Governor's captive. However, he accepted bread and wine (which he always politely referred to as 'The King'), and generous chunks of whale flesh were hacked off and ceremoniously passed along to the Governor's boat.

As Phillip approached unarmed, into the crowd of natives, to present Bennelong with a hatchet he had requested, a lone black took fright and threw his spear. It struck deep in the Governor's shoulder and he had to be helped back to his boat, bleeding profusely.

It was an extraordinary stroke of luck, William realized when he thought about the incident, that no one else had been hurt. The other natives were clearly shocked by the action, and melted quickly away into the woods. The English, intent on getting the Governor to safety, scrambled for the boats and pushed off with all speed. Of the four armed marines accompanying Phillip, only one's musket would fire, and his shot fell harmlessly short of the culprit.

Once it was clear that Phillip would make a good recovery, the usefulness of the incident to the English became apparent. The natives were full of anxiety and regret. Bennelong sent a message via some fishermen in the bay, expressing hope that the Governor was recovering and assuring him that his assailant would be punished. Another party of natives told some marines that Wileemarin, the spear thrower, had run away, and that Bennelong and Colbee would visit Phillip in Sydney to apologize in person for the outrage. Phillip, satisfied that Wileemarin had acted out of fear rather than malice, did not propose any reprisals.

So the way was suddenly open for friendship, on the novel basis of the whites being the wronged party. Phillip requested the return of his dirk, which had been dropped at the scene of his attack; and Bennelong, agreeing, put in a dignified appeal for the return of spears and fishgigs stolen from his people by the convicts.

William was very pleased to be one of the party entrusted with returning these items to Bennelong. He went with Watkin, and Richard Johnson and Booron accompanied them. Booron had been following developments with keen interest, and was clearly delighted that Bennelong and the Governor were to have a friendly meeting.

'We might ask Bennelong about trying to find a husband for her,' Richard confided to William.

William saw that Booron had overheard him, and that she deliberately looked away. Perhaps she did not like them speaking about her. Perhaps she wished to choose her own husband; although that did not seem to be the natives' custom, from all that they had heard.

It was a beautiful clear spring morning and the bay sparkled in the sunlight. Three pelicans came gliding out of the distance, from the direction of Parramatta, heading for the sea. When Booron saw them she began to chant.

'Gnoo-roo-me ta-twa na-twa ra-twa. Gnoo-roo-me ta-twa na-twa, ra-twa, tarra wow, tarra wow.' When she saw William opening his notebook she laughed. He was leafing through for the word for pelican, and she called it out to him before he found it: 'Carranga bo murray'.

'But you call it another name in the song? What does the song mean?'

She laughed again and shook her head.

'It not meaning much. For luck – when carranga bo murray fly over your head – children learn them word for luck.'

'Teach me.'

She repeated the chant slowly for him, giggling at his mistakes, waiting patiently as he wrote. Two of the pelicans had soared on out of sight, but one was coming down to fish. William marvelled again at its huge wingspan. They watched the heavy descent and splash, the ruffled rearranging of feathers. The short feathers of its head gave it a spiky, rakish look. Booron laughed and clapped her hands.

'Lucky, lucky bird for me!'

They could smell the whale carcass before Manly came in sight. Richard Johnson held his handkerchief over his mouth, and wondered aloud if they might not take some dreadful illness, from breathing such polluted air. But everyone else remained cheerful. As they rounded the head they could see numbers of pelicans riding on the waves, diving for fish, tossing them in their gigantic beaks to get them the right way round to swallow.

'Good fishing,' commented Booron. 'Plenty good fishing here.' The sandy beach was dotted with groups of natives sitting and lying around fires. At the far end of the beach the putrefying remains of the whale stood like a ruined building, with a hoard of scavenging screaming gulls wheeling round it and darting in for scraps. The exposed ribs, arching heavenward, reminded William of a ship under construction at Portsmouth docks.

Bennelong himself came down to meet them, and greeted Booron kindly. Watkin directed the stolen spears and weapons to be unloaded on the beach, and with astonishing efficiency numbers of natives selected and carried off each their own property. Bennelong called through the crowd for someone who was hanging back shyly, and after some hesitation a smiling, plump woman came forward. Bennelong proudly introduced her as Barangaroo, his wife. Three of the fishgigs turned out to be hers, but there was still a pile of items left unclaimed. Two men carried them higher up the beach, out of reach of the tide, and left them there.

'You see how honest they are,' Watkin commented to William. 'They take only what belongs to themselves. How long before those are harvested again by sailors or convicts?'

Bennelong said he was ready to be taken across to Sydney to visit the Governor, but Barangaroo immediately began to argue with him. The conversation was too fast for William to follow, but she was clearly warning him not to trust the British, and pleading with him not to go. Bennelong, embarrassed, shrugged and laughed and nodded to Watkin, and Barangaroo became really furious. It was Booron who suddenly interrupted her tirade, with an apologetic, cautious offer. Barangaroo hesitated, then shrugged and walked away.

'What did you say?' Watkin wanted to know.

'She afraid Bennelong not come back. I tell her we wait here – we wait here and he go Governor. We not leave until he come.'

'Good – well done. An excellent solution. Would you like to stay, Booron?'

She nodded.

'And you, Richard, will you play hostage?'

Richard agreed, asking them to be sure to return by nightfall; and

William also stayed. They stood on the beach with Barangaroo and the others, and watched Watkin, Bennelong and the boat's crew moving off across the water. Richard spoke confidentially to Booron.

'Tell Barangaroo what life is like in Sydney. Maybe she could be induced to visit us there, and make friends.' Booron went over to the group by the fire.

William and Richard walked a little way down the beach toward the whale carcass, but the smell was so overpowering it drove them back. The Ab-Origines paid them very little attention now the boat was gone; they were obviously glutted with days of feasting, and lay lazily chatting beside their fires. Booron and Barangaroo were deep in conversation, William saw, when they turned to walk back in that direction. He did not want to intrude on the girl's first free association with her people in nearly two years, and steered Richard up the beach towards the scrub that marked the beginning of the woodland. They sat against a rock there, looking over the beach and out to sea. There was something wonderfully restful in the notion of being a hostage, of having no other duty than to remain here on this beach all day. Richard was relating the sad tale of a convict who had recently collapsed and died of starvation. He had made some enquiries about where the man's rations had gone, and discovered that he was selling them for money towards his fare back to England. When White had opened the corpse's stomach, it was found to be completely empty.

'The willpower of some of these people is extraordinary,' Richard commented. 'My influence is very circumscribed, but Mary and I have been considering the children . . .' For a moment William thought he meant Milbah.

'No, the convict children and children of the marines. They are running wild.'

It was true, there was a gang of youngsters – no more than six or seven years old – who roamed the settlement with extraordinary confidence. Twenty-seven children had been sent with their parents to Norfolk Island in March, but their departure had the effect of making those who remained in Sydney more bold and lawless. They knew no restraint except the bounds of the settlement, and though they were employed running errands and minding livestock or younger brothers and sisters, they had the time to cause considerable mischief, catching lizards and snakes which they let loose in each others' huts, chasing one another in and out of the work gangs and using very foul language.

'Every woman convict who is capable has borne one or more children since our arrival, and we have had an addition of, what, is it thirteen youngsters with the last fleet? The group of young villains racing about the camp now will become a wild mob as these babies grow older. There is no provision for them.'

'What would you like to do?'

'Mary and I want to set up a Sunday school, so that they will at least receive some instruction in the Bible and our Lord's teachings. But really there should be a weekday teacher for them. The advantages of removing them from a criminal background in England are lost if we present them with no alternative influence here. The Governor – ' Richard sighed, and William found himself smiling. He could predict Phillip's reaction.

'The Governor thinks it an excellent idea but regrets that there are not yet sufficient resources available to devote to the building of a school.' Richard smiled wryly. 'It must take its place in the queue, behind the church.' He settled his back more comfortably against the rock, took out his notebook, and began to plan his Sunday sermon.

William looked at the small groups of natives, trying to work out if they were in families, or grouped according to some other system. Two children, catching his eye, came wandering over to within ten yards of them and stood staring and smiling shyly. When William greeted them in their own language and showed them he could count to four, they laughed and ran away – returning a few minutes later with three more youngsters. Soon he was surrounded by a crowd of them, reciting words and chants for him and giggling at his efforts at pronunciation. He glanced over their heads from time to time and saw with satisfaction that Booron was now repairing the returned fishgigs with Barangaroo – and now pushing out and climbing into one of their tiny canoes with her. He watched her trying to steady herself, and heard the two women's shrieks of laughter as she almost upset the canoe. She must have been fishing before she came into the settlement; she was missing the little finger of her left hand, which was said to be removed from women in order to make holding the fishing line easier for them. But he guessed it would take frequent practice to kneel in that uncomfortable way in a canoe, a knee braced against either side, and keep your balance.

In the heat of noon he and Richard retreated to the shade of the trees to rest. But the air was humming with flies and mosquitoes, which swarmed around William in particular. Richard was soon asleep.

William spent half an hour irritably rearranging his jacket to cover his hands, his face, his neck, but gave up when he was bitten for the sixth time. He caught a mosquito with a slap to his neck and was rewarded with a splatter of blood across his shirt sleeve. He scrambled to his feet and saw Booron was standing alone by the water's edge, drawing patterns in the sand with her toe. Barangaroo was by the fire with the other Ab-Origines, tucking into a chunk of whale meat. William smoothed his crumpled clothes and went to join Booron by the water.

'You are getting on well with Barangaroo?'

But Booron kicked at the sand and did not reply.

'Would she like to visit the settlement? I'm sure Mary would make her welcome.'

'She not want come to camp.' Booron spoke sulkily. 'Her people angry. Too much white feller at Parramatta, her people got no food.'

'Let's walk along a bit.' William turned to walk along the tide line, away from the stinking whale. 'Does she come from Parramatta?'

Booron nodded. 'Parramatta is hunting place. Plenty opossum at Parramatta – and flying fox. But whitefeller chop down trees.'

They certainly were chopping down trees. Rose Hill was the best farming region they had found, the plan was to get 100 acres planted with wheat this year. And to station half the marine force there, to protect settlers from the natives.

'She should come and see the Governor, Booron. She should come with Bennelong and they should explain their grievances to him. After all, he has sent back all this fishing tackle – '

She did not reply. He wondered if it was remotely possible that Phillip would agree to leave their hunting areas alone. Not at Rose Hill, no, plans and building there were too advanced; but if other, untouched areas could be specified now – even Phillip must see the good sense of allowing them some areas where they would not be disturbed. Of making some partition of the land, until they were ready of their own free will to join the British way of life.

'I like not go back.' Booron spoke abruptly.

'Not go back?'

'To Johnton.'

He gawped at her.

'I go live with my people now.'

After a moment he walked slowly on, and she kept pace beside him. She did not want to live in the settlement. Why was he surprised? He fumbled after the argument she had given him once before: 'You have plenty of food at the Johnsons'.'

She smiled, and gestured at the whale carcass. 'I go fishing. I like go boat. I dig roots. Plenty food.'

'But not in winter. When the weather is cold and you have no warm bed to sleep in – '

She shrugged. It was true, he thought. Material comforts were not enough; would not be enough for anyone.

'Mary is very fond of you. And the baby – won't you miss little Milbah?'

She scowled. 'Plenty baby here.'

'The Johnsons thought you might like to marry – one of your own people – that he might live with you in Sydney.'

'No.'

They walked on again in silence, Booron stopping now and then to pick up a shell and run her thumb around its rim. He realized she was still looking for materials to repair the spears.

'If you stayed . . .' William hesitated. No, it was worth saying, it might make some sense to her. 'If you stayed, you might be able to help your people – to understand better the ways of the British. Now you can read – there are many things to learn.'

But she was looking at him blankly. What might she teach them? Not about God, two years of living in the chaplain's house had not brought her that far.

'Better for me here.' She glanced round at Johnson's sleeping figure. 'You can tell Mr Johnton for me?'

'But he's going to be very upset, Booron. I can't just – you'll have to come back to Sydney tonight. To get your things – to say goodbye to Mrs. Johnson and Milbah.'

'I got no thing.'

She had, she had a Bible Richard had given her, and a star chart William had drawn for her while he was trying to learn her words for the constellations. She had been delighted by it, and he had taught her to write her name on the back of it. She had clothes and ribbons of Mary's, a blanket, a cup, knife and spoon of her own. But he could see that she would not bring these things here. She was still wearing a dress of Mary's, the baggy white one with pale blue flowers. He thought, with a distressing confusion of bodily feelings, that it would be very shocking to see her without it, even though every other woman on the beach was naked.

'You have helped me a lot, Booron, you have taught me many words. I shall be sorry to lose you.' She glanced quickly at him and laughed.

'Difficult word.' He nodded, and laughed with her.

But he knew how strongly Richard would feel the defeat if Booron returned to her people still unconverted. He must be given the chance to make one last attempt.

'Come back for a short while. Come back to the settlement for a week – '

She was shaking her head; there was something frantic, almost panic-stricken, in her expression.

'What is it? Tell me.'

'If I go back to Johnton – I not come here again.'

She was an outsider here as well of course. Perhaps they would only hold the door open for so long.

'You would come back and visit us? Wouldn't you, Booron?' She shrugged and giggled. Maybe she would not. Maybe she had been very unhappy in the settlement. He was ashamed that he did not know. She had seemed so open and straightforward a few months ago. Now, although he knew more of her language – and she more of his – than any other black and white in the settlement, now her thoughts were as impenetrable as the interior of the country.

'I will speak to Mr Johnson.'

Richard was as angry and upset as William had expected. He and his wife were genuinely fond of the girl, a fondness which had been much increased by seeing how kindly she cared for their daughter Milbah.

'Mary needs her – Milbah is used to her, how on earth can I replace her? And she will give up all the comforts of civilized life – to live – like this – and eat rotten whale meat?'

William tried to argue Booron's case, but Richard was adamant that she should come back and explain in person to Mary why she was leaving. She received the news in sullen silence, then sat ostentatiously alone near the water's edge, waiting for the return of Bennelong's boat.

On the journey back she would not speak at all, and hid herself away in her tiny lean-to bedroom when they reached the Johnsons'. Richard told Mary as she was lighting the candles. She sat down abruptly and her large dark eyes swam with tears. She blinked them back though, twisting her neck blindly as if she were trying to get her head out of a painful position.

'I would be afraid for her,' she said softly. 'She's seen – she knows, the peace that God's love can bring. If she turns her back on it now, she will be lost for all her life.' She was silent a moment, running her finger-nail along a scratch in the table top. Then she looked up at Richard. 'And the way that they live – you know what Watkin told us. About the beatings.'

William sank down on to his haunches, where he was leaning against the wall. But she turned to him.

'They steal their wives from other tribes – the men beat the women on the head until they bleed, William, it's true. They drag them off without any consent – '

'But we met Bennelong's wife today,' William said. 'She was telling him he mustn't come to Sydney. She looked well able to defend herself – in fact, *he* seemed more afraid of her.' He forced a little laugh. But he had heard these stories too. And other things. That when a mother died, if the child was young, the father crushed it with a stone, upon the mother's body. In some ways they were savages, yes.

But Arabanoo had wept to see a flogging. Cruelty meant something different to them. William found his own eyes filling with tears too. He moved to sit at the table.

'It must be her choice, Mary. You have shown her great love and kindness, but it's natural for her to want to be with her own people. You have done everything you could. Maybe she *will* turn to God one day; maybe when she has a child of her own, and remembers Milbah's baptism; maybe as she gets older . . . But she's free, we can't keep her here against her will.'

'Milbah will miss her terribly!'

'Mary, that's not a reason for her to stay. Milbah has us; we can find a good, quiet girl amongst the convicts' children to mind her. William's right, we must let her go.' Richard's opinion swung round behind William's, and he knew the battle was over. Mary sat in stubborn silence a while longer, with tears rolling down her cheeks; but when Richard said, 'Let us pray,' she knelt beside him and William, and bowed her head submissively.

William slept the night in the Johnsons' dining-room and woke soon after sunrise. Booron was already up; as he went into the garden she was coming along the path to the gate, with two buckets of water for the household.

'They have agreed, Booron. The Johnsons say you can go.' He held open the gate for her. Booron frowned and set down her buckets. She nodded. 'I wait, now.'

'You wait?'

297

'I wait a while now. I think – I don't go down there today.'

'But you wanted to – you wanted to stay yesterday.'

She shrugged. 'Another day. I go one day.' She laughed. 'Plenty more word to learn, eh? I go bath Milbah.'

OLLA

Daniel has recovered a little; but Stephen is asking me to go out with
him. It is a test, a trick, I know I must play along with it. He suspects
me. He has been asking careful questions: did you go out today, Olla?
Have you spoken to anyone this week? How are you sleeping? You
have not eaten much tonight, have a little more.

I think he has spoken to the doctor; the doctor has told him what to
ask. I know their game: they seek to prove that I am unfit. Unwell,
unable to cope. If they can prove it they can whisk Daniel out of my
care, and get him where they want him.

I must be cunning. I tell Daniel: it is necessary to do as Stephen
wishes, to foil their attempt. I invent for Stephen a long, convoluted
conversation I have had with the social worker, concerning a problem
family whose mother is drug addict, teenage son is out of control,
baby is failing to thrive. This shows I talk to someone. It is also useful
to remind him that there are real problems in the world, before he
spends more time imagining problems for me. And I agree to go out.
'We haven't been out since Daniel was born!' he says brightly. 'What
would you like to do?'
I would like not to go out. Therefore it is not easy to select what to
do. I ask him to make suggestions. He offers cinema, theatre, meal,
concert. The meal is certainly out, he will watch how much I eat and
we will struggle for conversation. I don't care which of the others.
No, Olla, you are not thinking; the concert will bring you home
earlier than either of the others. Cinema, theatre, can last until 10.30.
The Hallé concerts are over by 9.30. One hour less away.

Stephen organizes babysitting: a woman from his office, I have met
her before, she has teenage children of her own. 'You couldn't ask
for anyone more competent,' he says.
'She will not bring her children?'
'Lord, no, they'll be at home with their dad.'
Of course.

I tell Daniel I will be leaving him. We will have to leave the house at
6.30, to have time to drive into Manchester and park; but we should
be home by ten. It is only three-and-a-half hours. He is sad but he
understands why I must do it. I must do everything to appear normal.
He is sad, and so much at the mercy . . . I am frightened. I plan to feed
him early, in case he brings back his tea and chokes. But then I

realize that if he is fed early he may be hungry and wake again before ten, then she would have to feed him. She won't know how to feed him, she will spoon too much into him or drown him with a bottle. I cannot decide what to do for the best. In the end I feed him half an hour early, and leave no food or drink for her to give him. He is sleeping when she arrives, a plump woman smelling of chemical deodorant. Daniel does not like her. She peeps into his cot and says isn't he sweet. Then asks where is his bottle.

'It's all right,' I say. 'He has been fed. He will not need a bottle.'

'But if he wakes,' she says. 'If he wakes he'll need a bottle for comfort, won't he?'

'I – I think he will not wake.'

Stephen interferes. 'It might be sensible to leave one, Olla – just in case.'

The last thing I wanted to do. But I must be cunning. I must not create difficulty. Quickly I make up a half-bottle of milk. My fingers are clumsy, I knock it over as I go to put the teat on it and it falls, splashing my skirt. Stephen calls, 'Are you ready? We really ought to be going.'

She comes into the kitchen and sees the mess. 'Oh, your poor skirt. Run upstairs quickly and change – never mind this, I'll make up the bottle – I've done enough in my time!' I do not want her to make up the bottle. She may use the wrong quantities, there may be germs on her fingers, she may touch the teat. As I am quickly flicking through the wardrobe for a clean skirt which will go with the red and white blouse (there is nothing – nothing – the black with the broken zip will have to do) Stephen is calling me again, and I am crying. Ridiculous. I make myself stop. Hold my breath and pin up the zip. The black skirt seems to hang a little strangely, I have not worn it since I had Daniel. I dab under my eye with a tissue, trying not to smudge the make-up. I see Stephen in the mirror behind me.

'Are you alright?'

'Yes. Just something in my eye.' I must say goodbye to Daniel. But Stephen guides me by the elbow through the hall. 'Come on,' he says, 'he's fast asleep.'

I know he is not fast asleep; he simply has his eyes closed, he hears me walking past his door and not coming in; he follows me with his mind of reproach as my heels clatter down the path and into the car; his sorrow grows as the engine starts, he has heard my explanation but still my departure is a treachery.

I reach for the door handle, and Stephen jerks on the brake. 'What are you doing? What have you forgotten now?' He will find fault with my behaviour. There is no use doing this to placate him, if I do it badly, make stupid mistakes.
'Nothing. I'm sorry. Nothing.'

The Free Trade Hall is full, the stairs are crowded and we move up slowly, in a mass. When we are halfway up I realize that I can run neither forwards nor backwards – if something were wrong, I could not escape.
I have not been in such a crowd for a long time. Stephen is looking at me. He smiles.
'It's as bad as corridors in a school, this.'
My heart is beating very fast; I am glad when we reach our door.

We have seats above the orchestra, to the side; they are coming on stage already and the hall is full. Below, and across the stage, and over to our left in the balconies – hundreds and hundreds of people, faces, as many as swarms and swarms of bees.

They are tuning up, the sounds are repetitive and discordant. Then the clapping, spreading across the whole auditorium – the conductor comes on stage.

I have been here before; I have seen this before. Why is it frightening? There is a glaze across the hall, which serves to distance and yet brighten all the faces; they tremble luminously, like a mirage. They are able to detach themselves from their seats and float towards me. They are clapping, clapping, a woman soloist in a sequined jacket, the light strikes off it in pointed blades.

Stephen claps, a benign smile on his face. He has noticed nothing wrong. Silence. And the music begins.

For a while it is like a kind of sleep. My concentration is lulled, I hear but do not hear it, I hear without listening. I am suspended above the sound with all the other glassy floating heads; I float. Daniel is calling me. He is awake but he will not cry because he knows she has mixed his bottle badly, she has screwed on the teat with her fingers that scraped tinned rabbit into her cat's bowl then cleared out its litter tray (oh, god. No.) He will not cry but he suffers. He suffers the pain of everyone who is left alone; who is betrayed, abandoned, left with no help. The crushing pain of the world presses on his fragile chest.

Suddenly the music. Suddenly the music becomes solid. It was there before, I heard it unthinkingly buoying me up on its surface like a sea. Suddenly it becomes solid shapes. Suddenly it rears up: dark blue and purple icicles, sharp, stilettoing their way across the uplifted faces – with red globes rolling and scuttling between them like severed heads. A dark movement, flapping like a bird, a dark green pair of wings comes through the roof. On the stage they are throwing off silver razors which fly up in the air and catch the light, then twist and fall, circling, slicing. There are more dark shapes behind the icicles. Bigger, bulkier, closer together. I can't make them out but they're moving nearer; they are black, they are draped in black like headless faceless nuns their suffocating blackness moves roaringly in, they will stop all breath, they blot out the glinting razor lights –

Stephen suddenly jumps and pushes me.
'Olla! What are you – ?' I hear his voice but the black shapes have filled my eyes, I turn my head from side to side to glimpse him, as a horse with blinkers.
'Can you stand?' he whispers. 'I'm sorry . . .' I hear him mutter, 'not well. Could you excuse – ' He rises and pulls me after him, the row of people has reared up like horses on hind legs to tunnel us through. Above their heads the sounds collide and thunderous raindrops fall, they are hot as blood, I shield my face.
He pulls me through the door and shuts it. The sound and shapes are trapped. Trapped on the other side.
'Sit down. Here. Put your head between your knees.' He kneels beside me. There is a tall attendant watching.
'I'm all right now. Those people – let them out!'
He stares at me as if I am mad. I hear Daniel. He is calling me now, he begins to cry. Of course, I must go to him. I pull myself up against the wall.
'Which people? Out of where?' No, he mustn't be distracted from taking me home. They can get out, the audience. They don't matter. We must hurry.
We begin to go downstairs. Perhaps those solid sounds are messages. A thing they need to know. They need to know the end is near. Daniel is perhaps preparing them . . . perhaps through my presence

in the concert hall. Perhaps I was a channel, a conductor for his knowledge.

This is difficult, my mind is heavy, I need to be on my own and concentrate, and Stephen talks talks talks.
'I knew you were too tired. You're overdoing it Olla, you're stretched to the limit, you've got to rest. I'm taking you to the doctor in the morning – you hear? And we're getting some help in for – '
I look at him and he falters, pretends to be busy holding open the door for me, does not resume till we are down the steps and in the darkening street. 'Well, some help around the house, a cleaner.'

I have messed it up. He has evidence now for his theory that I am unwell. I have managed very badly.
'What did you see?' he asks. 'In the hall? You looked as if you'd seen a ghost.'
He didn't see it. He didn't see the stabbing glinting suffocating coming-on of death. You are lost here Olla, be cunning. Try to remain cunning.
'I don't know. I felt – I felt a little sick. I expect, something I ate.'
We walk in silence to the car. When we are in he says,
'Why d'you want to pretend you're all right? When it's obvious that you're not? You need help, Olla – Daniel is too much for you.'
Strong. Cunning. Cunning. Strong.
'I pretend nothing. As you say, why should I? I am quite well. You take me out to a crowded, hot, noisy place; I feel a little faint, and you take that for a cue to criticize me. *You*, who admits to nothing; you who have had a nervous collapse while insisting, "I'm all right, I'm all right." '
He is silenced by this, and when he replies the strength has gone from his argument. So long as I can maintain a display of rational behaviour, I am safe from further consequences.
'It's precisely because I know the sort of state you can get into that I worry about you, Olla. I know those feelings of panic and anxiety, I want to be sure you get treatment if you need it.'
'I am fine, Stephen, I promise you. Only not used to crowds any more. I am very fine and well.' I lean my head against his shoulder as he drives, he likes this, and we drive for a while in silence.
'Shall we stop for a quiet drink then?' he says. 'It's still very early.'
'No!' I speak before I have thought, the word jumps out. I cannot tell where it has come from, but my mind sees a picture of Daniel, his

throat is slit. They raise him and pour him like a jug, for the blood to flow out. But I know it is not true. I am rational. 'No,' I repeat more gently. 'I am a little tired, I think maybe it was enough excitement – for one night.'

'Of course,' he says. He is not happy. But it is not my job to make him happy.

CHAPTER TWENTY-ONE

Ten heads in bags

Saturday 11 December dawned hot and clear. William was already on the boat heading down the Parramatta River towards Sydney. The men rowed in silence, some still half-asleep, and the bush responded to their quiet intrusion with its own ragged alarm calls: the clumsy, slow lift-off and flight of a flock of cranes which had been poking disdainfully about in the mud; the agitated shrieks of scores of rose-breasted cockatoos in a nearby gum tree; the sudden thudding motion of a band of kangaroos which had been nibbling invisibly upon the undergrowth. Mist clung to the surface of the river and was divided by the boat's passage. In places where the river flowed more swiftly or the banks were unusually low or bare, it had already lifted, and fish were leaping, splashing and ringing the surface like boiling water in an iron pot. Having started at five, they would be in Sydney by eight-thirty, before the heat became intolerable. Right now it was cool and sweet on the water.

The water-lilies which grew in the shallows at the side of the river were in flower: beautiful five-petalled fringed yellow flowers, like stars. Their tubers, William knew from Booron, were an important source of food for her people. Leaning back and staring at the soft mist and grey-green foliage on the banks, he was flooded with restorative curiosity and hope – like a familiar and welcome tide, lapping right in to shore, covering the dry rage and exhaustion of recent labours. He had been at Rose Hill all week. He hated staying there, because there could be no pretence that he might even snatch an hour during the night for observation – all the instruments were down at Sydney. At Rose Hill he was nothing but surveyor and engineer, juggling measurements and distances and the impossibility of making all lots equally convenient to water supplies; dealing with Phillip's grandiose plans for a treasury and a public library (with Grecian frontage, no less) alongside the erratic quality of bricks being produced at the Rose Hill kiln; and the sudden instruction (Phillip again) that every new hut and hovel should have a chimney; which, unless the building of all were carefully supervised, would lead to as many fires and disasters as had been generated by the previous lack of chimneys.

Most of all, though, Parramatta (as the whole area was more often called now) made him uncomfortable because the Eora absolutely did not want them there. Booron had given him messages on the subject, which he had passed on via Watkin to the Governor; but their only effect was that Phillip strengthened the military presence at Rose Hill. The British desperately needed an agricultural success story and Rose Hill seemed the only spot that might produce it. The Governor was prepared, if necessary, to fight the blacks for the land. One soldier had already vanished from guard duty, presumed murdered; and a raiding party of natives had attempted to set fire to the Parramatta stores. William, Phillip's instrument, surveyed and divided the land to the best of his ability; all the time with a nagging sense of anxiety, which was fast becoming guilt. The thing was being wrongly done.

When he reached Sydney William made straight for the Johnsons'; he would break his fast with them. Booron was in the garden watering the melons and cucumbers which were just beginning to show as small, shiny, dark green fruits among the tangle of hairy leaves and yellow flowers. She stood very erect, one of Mary's dresses hanging shapelessly from her angular shoulders. Something in her posture distanced her from her occupation, as if she were not really watering the plants – or only doing so on sufferance.

She greeted William without surprise, as if she had known he was coming. It made him feel right to be there. He stopped to ask her how she did, but she nodded her head towards the house.

'Trouble.'

'Why?'

'Eora attack that bad man, very bad man belong him Governor.'

'Who – is he dead?'

She shook her head. 'Mr Johnton been down to hospital.'

Richard called from the house, 'Who are you talking to Booron? That's not William, is it?'

'Yes, Richard, I have escaped from Rose Hill – ' William entered the cool of the little hallway, and turned back to say something else to Booron. But she had resumed her watering, moving down the garden, and did not see him.

'William! Come on in – '

William let himself into the small dining-room. The Johnsons were at table over the remains of breakfast, and Milbah was waving her fists contentedly at the ceiling from her cradle beside the empty hearth. Richard pulled out a chair.

'Have you breakfasted? We're late, that's to say, I'm late – Mary, call Booron to boil more water for the tea.'

'Thank you, yes. I'm glad to see you well – Mary – and young madam – ' He crouched beside the cradle briefly, and Milbah's gaze swivelled to him, her eyes as grey as an English sky.

'What's happened?'

Richard sighed. 'They've attacked another convict. But I'm afraid they picked the wrong man this time.'

'Who?'

'His Excellency's gamekeeper. McEntire.'

A vision of McEntire rose before William: his big thug's body, his strangely sleek, tied-back hair; his insolent expression. The memory was so powerful he could even hear Barnes shuffling and whimpering behind him. He blinked and took the cup of tea Mary offered, bending his face into the steam. 'Thank you.'

'The Governor's furious,' said Richard. 'Wants to teach them a lesson.'

'It was unprovoked – apparently,' Mary added. 'That's the pity of it, he was going towards them quite unarmed.'

'Is that his story?' William asked angrily. 'D'you know he used to steal weaker convicts' food, under pretence of cooking it for them? He's a bully and – and worse. I've never understood the Governor's trusting him.'

Richard was looking at him quizzically. 'Well he may have his faults, but I'm sure even you wouldn't wish his present fate upon him. There's a spear lodged in his side which Surgeon White says cannot be extracted – he's in excruciating pain.' He suddenly glanced at Mary, and reached across and patted her hand. 'I'm sorry my dear, don't stay and listen to all this again.'

'No.' Folding her napkin, she rose. 'But William's right. All the Indians hate him. Bennelong once threw back a brace of ducks the Governor sent him because McEntire had shot them.' She picked up Milbah and left the room. Richard leant back in his seat and gave William the story.

McEntire and two other convicts, supervised by Sergeant Flowers, had been out in the woods on a hunting expedition. They stopped overnight in a small hut constructed for this purpose, some four miles from the settlement. Their intention was to get up before dawn, and shoot kangaroo. Sergeant Flowers was woken after midnight by rust-ling noises outside. He roused the others; peering out into the moon-light they could see two natives with spears approaching the hut, and three others behind. McEntire was not in the least alarmed; he told Flowers he knew them, and went calmly out of the hut to meet them. As he walked towards the natives he spoke to them in their own tongue and they retreated slowly into the darkness of the trees. He followed them a hundred yards or so, talking to them familiarly all the way. Then with no warning, one of the natives jumped on to a fallen tree. He jumped from shadow into moonlight, the sergeant said he suddenly *appeared* up there, spear poised – and hurled it at McEntire.

Flowers and the other men ran out of the hut with their guns but the natives had already melted into the blackness of the woods. McEntire was screaming with pain; when they went to help him they found they could not pull the spear out, and his shirt was already soaked through with blood. Rolling on the ground in agony, he cried that he was a dead man and begged them not to leave him. After some hard exertion (causing the wounded man to lose consciousness for a while) they broke the spear off at about twelve inches from his body.

He was still unable to walk, and blood pouring from the wound, but he insisted that he would crawl back to Sydney.

'He is a man of uncommon strength,' Richard added. 'I think you or I would have given up on the spot.'

They arrived back at the settlement on Friday afternoon. Doctors White and Worgan examined the wound and pronounced it mortal. And so Richard was called – 'There being nothing more to do for the poor body, some thought is suddenly given to the everlasting soul,' the chaplain added drily.

'So he can speak?'

Richard nodded.

'I guess he had killed a native, out there on one of his hunting expeditions.'

'He says not. He says he once fired over the heads of some who were throwing stones at him from the bushes, but he has never killed anyone. He knows his attacker.'

'And he knows their language.' William suddenly recalled this detail of the story. 'Why? What is his connection with them?'

Richard shrugged, losing interest. 'All I know is, the Governor is convinced of his innocence and is planning to punish his attacker. The

Indian is clean-shaven, so he's been with whites recently. And he has a blemished left eye.'

William was quiet a moment, visualizing the scene. 'He only attacked McEntire,' he said suddenly. 'They could have hit Flowers and the others from their hiding place in the trees. But they only went for McEntire. That's the strongest argument in favour of their having a score to settle. He has injured them in some way – depend upon it.'

In the course of the day William heard rumours from a number of sources. From Booron, that McEntire had stolen Eora children and that the black youth with the crooked left eye was Pemulwi, a great warrior from the Botany Bay tribes, who had vowed to drive the whites from the land. From a couple of convicts on the road gang, that McEntire had never properly divulged the nature of his crimes in England; that they were unspeakable crimes against young boys. From a marine on guard duty at the hospital he heard that the natives had made one cowardly attack too many – always hanging about in the woods for stragglers, always attacking lone men then running away; that it was time to show them whose firepower was superior, and teach the murderous savages a lesson.

He messed with Watkin and Worgan that night; both were unusually subdued. Worgan confirmed that Colbee and other natives had visited the hospital and knew the attacker's name, but showed no signs of being willing to bring him in, despite the Governor's earnest requests.

'The spear must come out if the man is to have any chance – I asked Colbee how *they* get them out. He claims instant death will follow any attempt at extraction.' Worgan took a swig of wine. 'Since he cannot live with the thing in him, he may as well die quickly having it taken out. Johnny and I will remove it in the morning.'

On Monday William was woken by Watkin's servant. William had been up most of the night observing, and was snatching a couple of hours' sleep during the heat of the morning, when there was a knocking and shouting at the door.

'Captain Tench's compliments, sir, and will you come down and see the orders for the day.'

William scrambled into his uniform in confusion. The orders must be extraordinary if they included directions for himself. He had been excused all regular duties as a marine officer for nearly two years now, to free him to perform Alt's work. He never needed to look at orders for the day.

He hurried down to the posting board by Campbell's hut, groggy

309

from lack of sleep and his sudden waking. The midday heat was vicious, and the camp lay deserted about him – all had retired to shade and rest. When he finally stood, swaying, before the board, the whiteness of the paper and blackness of the ink danced before his eyes, and took long seconds to resolve into words he could read.

> Several tribes of the natives still continuing to throw spears at any man they meet unarmed, by which several have been killed, or dangerously wounded; – the Governor, in order to deter the natives from such practices in future, has ordered out a party to search for the man who wounded the convict McEntire, in so dangerous a manner on Friday last, though no offence was offered on his part, in order to make a signal example of that tribe. At the same time, the Governor strictly forbids, under penalty of the severest punishment, any soldier, or other person, not expressly ordered out for that purpose, ever to fire on any native except in his own defence; or to molest him in any shape, or to bring away any spears, or other articles, which they may find belonging to those people. The natives will be made severe examples of whenever any man is wounded by them, but this will be done in a manner which may satisfy them, that it is a punishment inflicted on them for their own bad conduct, and of which they cannot be made sensible, if they are not treated with kindness, while they continue peaceable and quiet.
>
> A party, consisting of 2 captains, 2 subalterns, and 40 privates, with a proper number of non-commissioned officers, from the garrison, with three days provisions, etc, are to be ready to march tomorrow morning at day-light, in order to bring in 6 of those natives who reside near the head of Botany Bay; or, if that should be found impracticable, to put that number to death.

Beneath appeared the names of those instructed to make up the party: Captain Watkin Tench, Captain William Hill, Lieutenant William Dawes, Lieutenant John Poulden . . . etc. Signed, Governor Arthur Phillip.

'To bring in six of those natives . . . or, if that should be found impracticable, to put that number to death.'

For McEntire? Six innocent natives, for a convict thug?

William turned his head one way and then the other, trying to drain some of the blinding sunlight out of it and get some sense back in. 'To make a signal example of that tribe.' He was to go out with a party of armed soldiers and shoot six innocent natives, to make an example? Surely not.

While he stood, obstinately swaying in the heat, he was halloed from farther up the hill.

'William. I want to speak to you. William!' Watkin, calling from his hut. Slowly William stumbled up the path and into the black shade of Tench's doorway.

'All right, old man? Come in, sit down.'

He sat on a straight-backed chair in the dim room, and stared at Watkin, sun-induced coloured blobs still sliding across his vision. Watkin's man set a tot of rum and a glass of water on the table before him.

'Now listen, before you say anything at all, listen to me.' Watkin's face was drawn and worried. He leant forward on his elbows, fixing William's eyes.

'Firstly, your name is on that list because I chose you. The Governor put me in charge of the party and told me to choose my men. I know you have been excused ordinary marine duties. This is an extraordinary duty, and I need you.'

'To shoot innocent men.'

Watkin gripped William's arm. 'Listen. I have been talking and arguing with him since four o'clock this morning. He sent for me before it was light, gave me a set of orders to read which called for the capture of two natives, and for *ten* to be put to death. Their heads were to be chopped off on the spot and brought back, for which purpose hatchets and bags would be furnished. He had been up all night; he was beside himself.'

William found himself staring at Watkin with fascination. Ten heads chopped off with hatchets. Heads carried home in bags. The Governor was mad.

'He went over all his thoughts and reasons twice – more – there's something in this incident which has pushed him to breaking point. I mean – ' Watkin checked himself – 'I don't mean that his arguments are unreasonable. He points out that a total of seventeen unarmed whites have been attacked and killed by natives since our arrival, and no reprisals ever taken. We have always assumed (and I think rightly) the killings to be either self-defence, or retaliation for some offence offered them by the convicts, or pure fear and misunderstanding – as when he himself was attacked. But he says the story in McEntire's case was clear, Sergeant Flowers is a witness, it was a premeditated attack on an unarmed man, and must be punished. Must be *seen* to be punished. He spent the whole previous afternoon trying to persuade Bennelong and Colbee to bring the aggressor in. But neither shows any sign of stirring in the direction of Botany Bay. So the responsibility for carrying out retaliation falls back squarely upon the settlement. Oh – and the two prisoners brought back were to be publicly executed in the presence of as many natives as could be assembled.'

'But the case of McEntire is *exactly* like the other attacks; he *has* provoked them. They hate him. Booron says he steals children.'

Watkin loosed William's arm and sat back in his chair. 'The Governor says not. The Governor says McEntire is innocent. And it is time to teach the natives a lesson.'

'What did you say to him?'

'He asked me what I thought – '

'Of ten heads in bags – '

Watkin burst out laughing, and William found himself laughing too, hysterically. It was beyond belief, did Phillip think they were maniacs? Murderers? Axe-men?

'It's not funny.' Watkin was struggling for breath, wiping his eyes. 'I've never seen him like that, William. I've never heard him ask for advice, much less take it. Anyway. I suggested – very tentatively – capturing six rather than killing ten. Capturing six, a couple of whom perhaps might be publicly executed by way of example, and the others held with threats of a similar fate – and at length graciously pardoned.'

'And?'

'You've read the orders. He agreed immediately – clasped me by the hands and thanked me for my good sense – but told me that if we couldn't capture six, we must shoot 'em. No more talk of bags and hatchets, though, thank God. Then he did me the kindness to put me in charge of the whole circus, and instructed me to choose my men.'

William drank his rum and water. 'Well. It's still an impossibility.'

'What do you mean?'

'It's impossible. By what right do we go out, without a declaration of war, and attack a peaceable tribe; capture six of their number and execute two? I've heard McEntire knows his attacker – the most we could do would be to arrest *him* and try him for murder, with due course of law. We can't go out and pretend to put things right by murdering innocent men ourselves.'

'It's an order, William. We don't have to think about that.' Watkin frowned and rubbed his hand across his eyes. He leant forward again on the table. 'Before you say another word, consider the situation. The convicts see their people attacked and no reprisals made. They see Bennelong and Colbee feast on the fat of the land and sleep in a brick house while they labour like slaves for starvation rations and sleep in hollow trees and mud huts. Phillip isn't a fool, he's a politician. He knows – better than you or me – when, and why, action must be taken. Maybe he even knows how many lives will be *saved*, by such an action; the bubbling angers and dissatisfactions of convicts must be balanced against the soldiers', who feel they are treated as harshly as the convicts; soldiers against natives; natives, against convicts; and to crown it all, the majority of the officers are a squabbling, idle, second-rate crew – '

'Watkin, I – '

'No. Listen to me. Why d'you think he asked me to lead the expedition? Eh?'

William was lost for a reply.

'Why me and not Campbell, or Captain Meredith, or – '

'Because you're a better soldier.'

'Rubbish. Because he knows – better than you think – every officer's attitude to the blacks. He knows who would be only too keen to see a little action, get some target practice shooting at black backsides.'

William stared at him in amazement. Watkin thumped his fist on the table in exasperation. 'Sometimes I think you're blind and deaf. He *could* appoint an officer who'd turn it into a massacre. But he has chosen me. Why me?'

When William did not answer, Watkin continued. 'Because he knows full well how abhorrent I find the command. He knows that six is the absolute maximum I will capture, he knows that it is extremely unlikely I will shoot six. He knows that my enactment of the orders will be to the letter and not one jot over.'

'And you have chosen me – '

'For the same reason.' Watkin patted him encouragingly on the shoulder. 'I can trust you to be decent.'

'Watkin, I can't go.'

'You must.'

'I can't go.'

'It's an order.'

'And I am going to disobey it.'

When the arguing stopped, Watkin went away. William noticed that he washed his face to conceal the signs of crying. He said he was going to see about ammunition and supplies. He left William with paper, pen and ink, to write to Captain Campbell.

William's hand moved across the paper slowly, making words and a dark smudge of sweat. When he had finished his letter he read it.

Dear Captain Campbell,

It is with great regret that I must inform you of my inability to carry out my orders posted this day, 13 December, to accompany Captain Tench on a punitive raid against the natives.

I cannot disobey my conscience, sir.

It seemed short, but there was nothing else to say. He added a salutation and signed it, fanned it to dry the ink and called Tench's man to deliver it to Campbell. When it was gone he folded his arms on the table and rested his head on them, closing his eyes. The soft blackness was a relief. It was done. It didn't matter what happened now. It was done.

But within a minute, it seemed – five at the most – Tench's man was back, panting with hurry.

'Mr Dawes – sir – Captain Campbell wants to see you in his quarters immediately.'

Rehearsing his arguments again with Campbell, William was struck by the man's concern and decency. He had always held Campbell in contempt. He was idle, a glutton, a man who dabbled in New South Wales rather than living in it, subsisting on his vast supplies of foodstuffs from England, building up a large collection of parrots, exotic birds, and native weapons which soldiers brought in for him, without ever so much as venturing into the woods himself. He had done no more than eat, sign orders, and occasionally sit as magistrate ever since arriving in Sydney. But now he paced the room, clasping and unclasping his hands behind his back, quite forgetting to point out his latest ornithological beauties. He put all the arguments Tench had put, and then spent some time simply urging William to save his skin.

'If you can find it in yourself to change your mind now, Lieutenant Dawes – even at this late stage – and agree to obey the order, I give you my word of honour no one shall ever hear of this incident. Consider your future – consider your father. It is with the greatest regret that I should be forced to put you under arrest, you are a good officer, one of the best. I – it breaks my heart to see you throw away such a promising career in this way, I assure you, sir.'

William felt ashamed to be causing such distress to this courteous, sweating man; but it could not be helped. At last there was a silence, and Campbell broke it with, 'You leave me no alternative but to pass your letter on to the Governor.'

'Thank you, sir.'

William dragged himself back from Campbell's hut to Tench's; it was too far to walk up to the observatory, and he wouldn't be allowed to spend the night up there anyway. With a shock he realized that he would almost certainly spend the night in the lock-up.

But the day continued to surprise him by repeating itself. No sooner was he settled back in his seat at Tench's, with a cup of tea in front of him (he was hungry, he realized; he had eaten nothing all day, it was late afternoon), than the summons came to wait on the Governor 'at your earliest convenience'. He took a couple of scalding mouthfuls of tea and hurried across to the mansion, noting that there was a suspicious-looking dip in the road about four yards short of the Tank Stream bridge, and that he must get the men to have a look at it before that whole section subsided. He was shown straight in to Phillip, who had the letter before him on the table.

'Lieutenant Dawes. I am obliged to you. Your conscience, sir. How does it instruct you?'

'That I must not take up arms against innocent men.'

'Never?'

'No sir. Not without a declaration of war.'

'Even if you are ordered to by your commander.'

'No sir.'

'You are a soldier.

'Yes sir.'

'Then your duty is to your commanding officer. He has the unfortunate responsibility of being your conscience. He clears you of that burden.'

Campbell's argument, more elegantly put. Phillip did not have the air of a man who'd been up all night, beside himself, as Watkin had suggested. He was pale but utterly in command, precise as ever.

'Sir, as I am to be judged before my Maker as an individual soul, so I must take individual responsibility for my conscience, and yield that responsibility to no man. I am able to obey my commanding officer only if I judge his commands to be honourable.'

Phillip flushed. 'You are insolent, Mr Dawes.'

Trying to concentrate on every word he spoke, William closed his eyes and said slowly, 'I am very sorry if you think so sir, it is absolutely not my desire or intention to give offence.'

'No,' said Phillip. 'Your only desire is to show everyone else how virtuous you are. What would happen if men like you ran the world, Mr Dawes? With your precious consciences? What would ever get done? Affairs of state could wait, I suppose; criminals and revolutionists and insurrection would wait, I dare say, for you to wrestle with your conscience before taking – or not taking – action.'

This interview was unlike the previous two. Watkin and Campbell had pitied him, William realized. Whereas Phillip – Phillip hated him.

Phillip crossed to the window and stood staring out for two minutes by the clock. William watched its pendulum's regular swing, and felt the sweat trickling down the back of his neck. He was still standing to attention.

At last Phillip spoke softly, without turning: 'Before I take this letter as your final word on the subject, I recommend you to discuss this order, and your conscience, with the person best fitted for that discussion: Reverend Johnson. Notify Captain Campbell of your intentions, after you have spoken with the chaplain. I suggest you attend him now – you will find him at the hospital with Mr McEntire.'

CHAPTER TWENTY-TWO

The sin of pride

As William made his way to the hospital a degree of energy returned to him. Phillip's contempt stung him. Everything that Phillip had asked, he had done. Single-handedly he was responsible for more of the physical construction of this settlement than any other man. He had made Phillip's buildings and roads a reality, he had engineered what the Governor had only dreamed. He had obeyed Phillip in all the important requests – maybe he had bent the rules a little here and there, in giving the convicts rum, for example, and working with them – but he had done so only in order to achieve the ends Phillip also desired, more speedily. Though he disagreed with the Governor in his treatment of the natives, he had bowed to the Governor's superior power and wisdom; he had allowed himself to be the Governor's tool. Every day that he worked at Rose Hill, he did so against the grain of his own conscience. Out of obedience to his commanding officer.

But this was nothing to Phillip. William's concerns were no more than the irritating buzzing of a fly. He was not to be listened to, not to be heard. He was to be brushed aside contemptuously.

The injustice filled William with thick red resentment, so that his chest felt tight, his heart pounding inside it as if it would burst out. Phillip was wrong. Others would see that. The natives, for a start. How would Bennelong and Colbee react to the murder of their friends and brothers? What would Booron say? It was *not* his duty to obey.

The hospital smelt strongly of oil of tar, which they had been burning to clear it of the other smells. McEntire lay still in his cot, eyes staring from a shockingly hollow face, his grey skin slimy with sweat. Richard was reading from the Bible; he looked up as William entered.

'I'm sorry.' William nodded at the dying man. 'I must have a few words with you, Richard.'

The chaplain nodded, closed the Bible and laid it on the cot beside McEntire, who clasped his fingers around it convulsively. McEntire's breath was harsh and short, as if he had been running; as if he could not get enough air, and was afraid of drowning.

William led Richard outside the hospital, to sit on a tree stump on the shady side of the building. 'I'm sorry – this won't take long. The Governor sent me. You've heard the orders for the day?'

Richard nodded. 'I've spoken to Watkin.'

William shrugged. 'The Governor advises me to discuss my conscience with you.'

Richard studied his fingernails. 'I think you should go.'

'Why?'

Richard spoke slowly. 'I think you should beware of the sin of pride.' It was not what William expected to hear. Richard looked at him and continued. 'Conscience – is a difficult thing. Our degree of freedom of action . . . is difficult to determine.'

William waited. Was Richard suggesting, as Phillip had done, that his vanity made him want to *appear* virtuous? *Was* he proud? There was suddenly no ground under his feet.

'I have prayed,' said Richard. 'As I am sure you have. But only you can find out the answer to this. God has his own purposes, which, you will allow, are hidden from us. When a train of events leads towards a certain eventuality – as with this attack upon McEntire . . . the question you must ask yourself, the question you must really examine and cross-examine your heart for, is, "What do I seek to gain by refusing the order?" '

'What do I seek to gain?' repeated William incredulously. 'Nothing. Disgrace. Court martial.'

Richard shook his head. 'Look beyond, William. Is your action not tinged with pride? Do you not seek a status for your soul – for your conscience – which you deny to others? Consider the practicalities of the affair. If you refuse to go, you will be replaced by another officer. Your refusal will not cancel the expedition, all it will mean is that Watkin has to work with a man he trusts less, thus risking a bloodier outcome to the event. The practical results will all be bad; you will be put under arrest and prevented from playing any part in public affairs henceforth, and the punitive expedition will be carried out without your restraining influence. So it is not *practical* good which you are promoting by your disobedience (which, incidentally, in an officer must be cause for very great concern for the bad example it sets the troops). Therefore it is personal good: the ease of your own conscience; your ability to say, "My hands are clean, though my brother's hands are dirty." As a Christian, I have to ask myself whether this is pride.'

'But – ' William fumbled after the clear facts in the case. 'The order is to go and capture or kill six innocent men. What about Christ's teachings? What about "Thou shalt not kill"?'

Richard shook his head. 'It's not that simple, is it?'

'Surely it is. Surely it is simple.'

'Ask yourself for whom you act. You will not save any lives by refusing to go; rather the contrary. Will you have that on your conscience?'

William looked up at a couple of cockatoos flying past. He suddenly wanted to go down to the shore and bathe his sweating feet. 'Do you really think I should go?' he asked.

'Yes, I do. I'm going back to McEntire now – ' He rose and patted William on the shoulder. 'I will be praying for you.'

When he had gone William made his way down towards the Tank Stream. Was he proud? Setting himself up above others? Even if he wasn't, other people would think he was . . . But that was no reason for going – fear of what others would think. Surely he was beyond that.

But no one agreed with him. Watkin, Campbell, Phillip, Richard – all thought him wrong. Wasn't it pride, to insist he knew better? He suddenly thought of Bradley. What would Bradley have done? Bradley still marooned on Norfolk Island. For a moment hope flared, until he got a real sense of Bradley – the man, his flat voice and glittering, amused eyes. Bradley would not disobey an order. Bradley would be too mistrustful of his own motives; Bradley was more humble. (And, William added before he could help it, more disappointed. Bradley did not indulge in the luxury of a conscience.)

Indulge. William flicked a pebble into the water with his toe. It was answered, then. He must admit of the possibility that five other honest men (no, four; he would not do Phillip that honour) knew better how he should behave, than he himself could know. He must be – humble.

He walked up to Tench's, to get the man to take a note to Captain Campbell. And how would he explain to Booron that he had gone to hunt her countrymen, in order to protect them? How could he make that sound like sense? As he walked tears sprang to his eyes and he cried, out of nothing more, he felt, than utter weariness.

Watkin embraced him warmly when he heard of William's change of heart; then announced that they would forget the matter entirely. The party set out at four the following morning, in order to cover as much ground as possible before the heat of the day. They marched in the silence Watkin had ordered, although the element of surprise was clearly not their strongest asset. The whole of Sydney, and therefore all the Ab-Origines within a hundred miles, must know of their departure.

Two captains, two lieutenants, two surgeons, three sergeants, three corporals and forty men, carrying weapons and three days' provisions – marching through the deserted scrub, wading through boggy marshland, as if to a battle . . . the whole enterprise had an air of unreality. The peninsula at the northern head of Botany Bay was reached by 9 a.m., but the shores and waters of the bay were deserted, the silence and glittering emptiness of the land making mock of their hot blistered feet and sweat-soaked, aching shoulders. Watkin called a halt and ordered the men to rest in what shade they could find. The impracticality of attempting to cover ground in temperatures in the high nineties was blindingly obvious, and after consultation with the scouts and all the officers of the party, Watkin decided that they would make camp until nightfall, then move, under cover of darkness, to the known site of a village some twelve miles distant.

Some of the men went down to the shady trees by the water's edge to fish and bathe, but William unrolled his bedding and slept again. He felt bruised and exposed, as if his innards had been poked about in public; he wanted only to curl up and hide. He was laughable; inconstant, pitiable, proud, dishonourable. His mind skittered away from what Booron would think when she heard Richard telling Mary the news. The blackness of sleep in the smothering heat was the only escape.

At dusk rations were issued, but no tell-tale fires were lit for cooking; camp was struck and they moved off with surprising speed, for such a cumbersome body of men. The first obstacle was a river to ford. They had to wait nearly an hour beside it for the ebb of the tide. Tench decided that they needed to travel as light as possible, so left a sergeant and six men with all the knapsacks and provisions. Fearful for the firearms, he ordered the men to tie their cartouche boxes fast on top of their heads, to keep their powder dry. In single file they waded into the water. The sudden cool strength of the current against his calves brought William to himself, and as he waded deeper he became intensely aware of his surroundings, as if he had just woken from a deep sleep. The crunching, slightly shifting gravel of the river-bed underfoot; the cool force of the water pulling at him; the still warmth of the balmy night air around his head; the intermittent whispers and grunts of the men as they moved cautiously through the dark water, and the little splashing sounds they made. The incessant background noise of frogs, coming and going, closer and farther, as the men moved and frightened those nearby. The overcast sky, faintly illumined by a full but misted-over moon, giving every assistance to the secrecy of their operation in the close darkness . . . Suddenly he was thrillingly excited, every sense alert, attuned precisely to the mood of the men around him. On the other side of the river they adjusted their clothes and firearms and moved swiftly along to the west, following the course of the river. The elation of swift and energetic action after months – indeed, three years – of military inactivity, was like a drug. They were soldiers, moving swiftly under cover of darkness, towards the enemy.

After an hour and a half they came to a wide creek bed which looked more or less dry. Tench halted the men and consulted with a scout, who said that the creek was not easy to cross, but that if they could cross here, they would certainly save time. The sky would begin to lighten soon after four-thirty, and the whole point of their attack would be lost if made in daylight. Tench gave the order to cross. For a while there was no sound but footfalls in the mud, squelching down and sucking up again. Then the leaders of the party, William amongst them, got near to the middle. The thick clinging mud was no longer ankle-deep, but knee-deep – knee-deep and sinking, clinging on with the tenacity of a drowning man to their legs, so that lifting each foot became agonizingly hard work, requiring the use of every muscle and sinew. With each leg's slow, exhausting haul from the mud, William told himself it must become shallower at the next step – but it did not; it was no longer possible to raise the leg above the surface, only to push it with excruciating slowness forward through the dense mud, which was now above his thighs.

'I'm sinking!' Caution, silence, secrecy, were shattered by the frightened cry of Sergeant Knight.

'God help us – I'm sinking!' – a voice closer behind William, and then a scream as a man attempting to plunge forwards lost his balance and fell. There were gasps and grunts of effort as two others moved with terrible slowness towards him and heaved him up, choking, out of the mud.

Turning his torso, William was able to make out the dark figures of men at the back of the party, who had not got bogged, turning back and running along the bank to a safer crossing place. Sergeant Knight was not only stuck but sinking, the whole bottom half of his body had disappeared from sight; he was only a couple of yards in front of William.

'Captain Tench!' William called. 'All men behind me should turn back. It is too deep ahead.'

'Yes!' called Watkin, who was about as far in as William, but farther upstream. 'Turn back!' Now the silence was broken there were curses and groans and exclamations on all sides, cries for help, and shouted advice. William tried to move closer to Knight, calling to him that he was coming. A soldier who was farther across than Knight bellowed to the men who had already made the opposite shore, by going round: 'Throw us boughs! Cut boughs from the trees and throw them to us!'

'Well done, man!' bellowed Watkin. 'Do as he says!'

Branches and boughs were hacked off and flung out to the stranded men, who grabbed them and began to flail and haul themselves through the mud towards the opposite shore. Moving with nightmarish and exhausting slowness, William arrived close to Knight, whose teeth were chattering.

'My legs won't move, Mr Dawes.'

'All right, we'll find a way . . . A branch over here, if you please!' Two boughs were passed back to them, by men on their way out, and Greenly, a huge ox of a man, came lurching towards them through the mud. William on one side and Greenly on the other grasped Knight, now buried up to his chest, by a shoulder apiece, and tried to heave him upwards. It was pulling against dead weight, no give at all.

'Here,' gasped Greenly, 'wedge a branch under each arm at least, to keep yerself up – '

'Use a rope!' called Watkin, who, though struggling to approach, was still fifteen yards off. 'We have ropes to bind our captives. Can you catch, William?' He flung the coiled rope and William caught it and passed one end of it under Knight's armpits. The mud was now up to his own waist, he could no longer move forwards but slowly leaned from one side to the other through the mud – every movement taking an age. At last the rope was secure and he passed the coiled end to Greenly, who hurled it on to men nearer the bank. When five of them were ready to pull, William and Greenly heaved at Knight's shoulders again. Knight gasped with pain as the rope tightened – and slowly, very slowly, his weight began to drag up through the mud – though it seemed to William that in lifting Knight he was wedging himself ever more firmly down into the slime. At last with a great sucking slurp, Knight plunged forwards a move.

'I've got him, sir, you take care of yourself.' Greenly moved forwards with Knight, half-heaving, half-dragging him free. Grasping the bough they had left, William hauled and hauled and was at last rewarded by the impossibly slow lifting of his own lead-heavy feet from the depths. Crawling up and spreading his weight to lie across the bough, he wriggled forward, coughing and gasping as the evil-smelling slime splattered near his face, edging towards the helping hands of men waiting, safely only up to their knees, nearer to shore.

At last they were all on shore, many, like William, shaking and trembling with exhaustion. Several had lost boots and weapons. Tench ordered all weapons to be wiped, and asked for a count of those which might still be judged serviceable: less than half.

'We must move on quickly or all this is for nothing – ' Tench crouched beside William, who was scraping mud from his breeches with the blunt side of his knife.

'Of course.'

Dazed and shaking, the men were assembled and urged on, at a run, towards the village. Arriving there in the grey light about half an hour before sunrise, Tench formed them into three divisions and ordered each to approach and enter the village from a different side. William's party moved almost silently between trees and into the clearing; at their head, he motioned them to be still and strained to hear any sound from the huts. There were no live embers in the fires; as he ducked his head into the open end of the first hut he already knew with a surge of disappointment that it would be empty. The place was deserted. No men, no women, no children, nor even any remains of food or fish-bones beside the fireplaces. And looking round the bay, which lay exposed to view on the other side of the huts, illumined by that cold grey light preceding dawn, not a canoe or native was to be seen.

William told the men they could rest and they slumped to the ground thankfully; he stood watching them, struggling with his own conflicting emotions. Disappointment – which was felt by every man jack of them, after the exhausting labours of the night, to find that their attempt was futile. And relief, huge swirling giddying relief, that the expedition was an absolute failure, that no Ab-Origines were captured or killed, and that they would return empty-handed to Phillip. Perhaps Watkin had known all along that they would fail – perhaps that was why he had agreed to lead the expedition –

No. Watkin had pushed himself to the limit, as William had, to get here before sunrise; he had hoped for success.

Watkin and a scout broke in on William's thoughts with a practical difficulty. If they wanted to cross back over the estuary – the first estuary they had forded – they must do so within the next two hours, or else have to wait another twelve for the tide to ebb. And all the food had been left, with the baggage, on the other side.

The exhausted men, who had been staring at the bay and talking longingly of washing themselves and their clothes clean of mud, staggered to their feet and were urged into a half-march, half-run. There were a few who were past the limits of their physical endurance and simply could not keep up. They were left to follow at their own speed, with a covering guard of stronger fellows who relieved them of their muskets. They retraced their way to the creek of mud, crossing well inland of their previous attempt, and at last reached the deepening river and forded it. They made their camp on the other side, where they rested throughout the heat of the day.

William had hoped that they might return to Sydney that night, but Watkin clearly felt that more of an effort should be made to carry out orders. He had the troops roused at 1 a.m. They set off inland this time, with the intention of arriving at the western, inland end of the bay, where natives were often found fishing around dawn.

The terrain was rocky with low, prickly shrubs; difficult and treacherous in the dark. Men whose boots had been lost or worn through by yesterday's efforts were incapable of keeping up, and again a baggage camp was made, leaving the barefoot soldiers in charge of provisions. There were no trees here, though, to offer shade after sunrise; and the whole party was short of water. More rum than water had been brought along, on the assumption that they could refill canteens en route. But they had not passed a single fresh-water stream, and now the only liquid they carried was a pint of rum per man. William instructed the sergeant he left with the baggage camp to erect some kind of shelter before sunrise. Watching the exhausted, raw-footed men slumping gratefully to the ground, he doubted it would be done. It would be impossible to drive tent poles or pegs into the rocky ground; the only thing in favour of the terrain was that its openness precluded a surprise attack by natives – the soldiers would see them fifty yards off.

Attack by natives. Yes. Taking part in soldiers' action had made him again a soldier, and the natives his enemy. They had already injured him – caused the blisters on his feet, the sore stiffness in his limbs, the blinding headache which made darkness pulse as he walked. He was suffering, because of them. They must be punished for it.

With an almost amused detachment he could see himself becoming the plaything of events; it took intense and focused effort to make himself catch up with Watkin and speak.

'We should turn back. It's dangerous to go farther without water.'

'Well we're heading towards water, aren't we? Cook took in water at Botany Bay, and so did the French – so did we, come to that, in those first couple of days.'

'But we took it in from the southerly side – we won't get round there today.'

'We should get to the westernmost end of the bay – there's a river – '

'It's tidal. I've been up it seven miles. It's salt.'

'A bay this size, there must be streams feeding in – '

Worgan, moving heavily beside Watkin, spoke. 'Medical advice, men. Get them to the bay, but if we find no water, they must rest for the heat of the day then head direct for Sydney. The rum will keep them going in the dark but we'll have them collapsing like ninepins in sunlight.'

They came towards the shore of the bay in pearly dawn light, the water was grey with slow-moving, unbreaking waves like ripples in lead. Directly ahead of them and completely alone, a native stood waist-deep, far out in the water, fishing. Silently, a halt was ordered and a couple of scouts sent forward; returning, they confirmed that the rest of the bay was entirely empty, no boats, no fires, no natives. Just this lone, unconcerned figure.

'I'm going to ignore him,' Watkin told William. 'Don't you think? I mean – ' he shrugged. 'There's one of him. Seizing or shooting him at that distance from land will not be easy – and there's absolutely no point, if there are no others to witness and take a lesson from the event. I think we just ignore him.'

William nodded. For forty armed men to plunge into the bay after a single unarmed fisherman would be ludicrous.

Watkin passed the order to wheel about and make for the shore half a mile farther west, giving the pretext that he believed a stream lay in that direction. As the party began to move away, the black fisherman started wading in to shore.

'He's seen us.' The men watched his movement through the cool water with envy – and some amazement at his courage. The Ab-Origines were usually afraid of the soldiers' red coats, they never approached them. Watkin ordered that no one should fire; smiling at William he added, 'His confidence is his protection. Who could raise arms against such fearlessness? He walks into the teeth of forty muskets.'

'Wahay! Captin Tench! Doctor Wogun! Halloo!'

'He knows us!'

Now they all stopped stock-still, and watched the thin black figure move out of the water and up on to the shore.

'It's Colbee! It's Colbee from Sydney!' Some of the men began to laugh.

And laughable it was, William thought to himself. They had left this man, who claimed to know Pemulwi, McEntire's attacker, in Sydney. Because Colbee *would* not bring him in, the forty of them had sweated and struggled through the last forty-eight hours, to reach the bay and capture natives, and here they found no native but Colbee, innocently fishing.

'Where is Pemulwi? Have you seen him?'

'No Captin. Pemulwi gone, many many mile, redcoat cannot go in that country.'

'And you have come here – ?'

Colbee laughed and indicated the bay. 'Fishing. Take look round. Catch fish, plenty good fish here.'

It was obvious that he had come to warn the natives here, William thought. It is he who has cleared the area. Wise, brave man.

The party settled in the shade of some trees, to rest out the heat of the day. Colbee yielded the information that there was no fresh water to be had on this side of the bay, and so the decision was made to return to Sydney in the afternoon.

Colbee lit a fire and warmed his fish, offering to share it with Tench and the other officers. Conscious of the hungry men around them, Watkin refused, and Colbee ate alone, chattering with extraordinary energy and light-heartedness between mouthfuls. Yesterday he went to the hospital to see Surgeon White cut off a woman's leg. The woman cried, she screamed, like this — . She rolled on the table and four men had to hold her down; she was shuddering, like this! He enacted the whole drama, without viciousness, yet contriving to make it humorous. William found his weary, cracked face breaking into the unaccustomed shape of a smile. He listened with half an ear, considering the complexities of Colbee's behaviour. Colbee had come into an area of war – he must know that – risking his own life, to warn his fellows of the impending attack. And now he was laughing and chattering with the enemy, performing, clowning for them. Everything he did he did easily, lightly, without the sweating weight of intention of the Europeans. He laughed and told tales for them but they had no idea what he thought of them.

With hardly a pause Colbee moved on to his visit to the Governor. He had told the Governor he was coming to Botany Bay. The Governor did not want him to – the Governor had offered him *anything*. Between peels of laughter Colbee listed a blanket, a hatchet, a jacket, a hat like Captin Campbell, a house like Bennelong's, anything he desired, if only he would not go to Botany Bay. William slowly grasped what was being said. Having despatched Tench and his army to kill natives at Botany Bay, Phillip was beside himself with fear that his favourite might get himself killed there. Any native at Botany Bay was fair game for the soldiers. Indeed, under any captain other than Tench, that lone fisherman would have been seized or shot . . . on Phillip's orders. Colbee's story got better. Upon his refusal to take any of the offered bribes, Phillip had ordered a feast; Colbee sat down and ate one of the fish the English call a 'light horseman', five pounds of beef and bread, and vegetables from the Governor's garden. Two weeks' ration at a sitting!

'Governor Phillip say, "You like lie down now, Colbee? Have good sleep with belly full – " ' He caught precisely Phillip's ingratiating, indulgent expression. What fools we must seem to him, William thought, shaking his head in weary disbelief. What idiots.

Colbee had gleefully rejected the suggestion of sleep, and set off immediately on his way to Botany Bay. With satisfaction William considered Phillip's anxiety; hoped that he would have lain awake all night imagining Colbee hurt, wounded, dead, by his own order: one of the meagre two natives he had managed to befriend (and that by capturing and petting them like animals) now murdered by his own troops. The fear of it must at least be enough to bring him to his senses; when they returned empty-handed, Phillip must feel nothing but relief.

The march back was long, tedious, thirsty. Three men collapsed and had to be carried the last five miles. But all the way, William was conscious of a growing strength. Phillip had been afraid that they might shoot Colbee. His actions proved that he knew his own order to be ignominiously wrong. Fear of the sin of pride had forced William into taking part in this expedition, but now he knew that his initial refusal was justified. To take arms against innocent men was wrong.

He knew it now; it was the same absolute knowledge as the physical knowledge of his aching limbs and burning throat. It was not open to question ever again. He did not have to obey Phillip.

When they arrived in Sydney Cove, Tench took the other officers with him to report to Phillip. There was no glimmer of a reaction in the Governor's face as the sighting of Colbee was described. He did not mention his own attempts to keep Colbee in the settlement. He received their report in silence, thanked them and gravely dismissed them. As they were filing from his room at the end, he said to William, 'So, Mr Dawes, you played your part. You got the better of that conscience after all.'

William's throat convulsed so that he thought he would not be able to speak at all. He managed to croak, 'I was persuaded into going, sir, and I regret that weakness. I am determined never to follow such an order again.' He felt his face flood crimson, and, raising his eyes to Phillip's, saw the man's face harden with contemptuous dislike.

Shaking with exhaustion, William made his way slowly to the sanctuary of his observatory.

CHAPTER TWENTY-THREE

Freedom

William slept all night and part of the following morning. He woke to bright sunshine, hot stillness underlined by the constant chirrup of the crickets in the woods outside his door. He sat in the shade of the open doorway with his water bottle and a lump of bread, nibbling and swigging and staring out into the trees. The long sleep had made him feel weightless – almost as if he floated – yet also made the surroundings, and his situation, crystal clear. He could see it, pristine, vivid, uncoloured by conflicting demands and expectations. He felt clean.

He would never follow an order he disagreed with again. From that small fact unfolded a clear picture of what would and would not happen. It reminded him of the passion, which had been spread among the seamen on his first ship by a French sailor, for making pictures with dominoes. When the ship was becalmed they would spend hours arranging rows and spirals of upended dominoes on the deck; then, when they were satisfied it was perfect, one man would lightly tap the first domino of the design. And with a ripple that ran along the lines of dominoes like a living thing, they would fall flat, opening out the black line to make a pattern which brought whistles of admiration and applause from the gathered crowd. One touch: that's all it took. He had pushed that little domino, and now a new pattern, unfolding of its own accord, lay before him.

If he would not obey orders, he could not be in the marine service. Therefore he must return to England, with the other marines whose three-year turn of duty was over, as soon as a boat came out for them. He would resign his commission.

If he would not obey orders, he was free. He could choose what he would do. He did not have to obey a commanding officer; he did not even have to please his father. He did not have to achieve high rank. He did not have to make his fortune.

He could return to New South Wales as a free man. A settler, say. Use his back pay to buy a return passage and a small plot of land. Maybe, if Maskeylene was pleased with the charts and notes he had made, he might secure a retainer from the Board of Longitude, to maintain the New South Wales observatory and meteorological records. If he were a Board of Longitude appointee, he would owe the Governor nothing. He would not have to blast out rocks with gunpowder, or order men to dig foundations. He would not have to divide and fence and clear lands to which the Indians laid claim. He would be free to disagree with the Governor; publicly, if he chose. He could define his own relations with the Indians, and speak out – and lead others to speak out – when they were unjustly treated. He would be free to act as his conscience directed. He would be free to do God's work. Not as the Johnsons did it – their roles already defined and prescribed by Richard's title, Chaplain to the Fleet, in the pay and under the command of the Governor. No. William could put himself outside that. He could buy freedom of conscience, at no more than the cost of resigning from a service which chafed him at every turn.

The sun, rising higher in the sky, drove back the small shadow of the observatory door, and shone directly on to his outstretched legs. The intensifying heat corresponded with a welling feeling in his heart and body that he struggled to put a name to, then suddenly realized was happiness. Yes, he was happy.

It did not appear to be necessary to inform anyone of his decision. He realized that word of his statement to the Governor must have travelled right around the camp.

He went to see the Johnsons the following afternoon. Mary, Milbah and Booron were sitting in the garden, under the shade of a piece of sailcloth which Samuel had rigged up over four poles. The two women were both sewing. Mary rose to greet him, and clasped his hands warmly between her own.

'It's right,' she said. 'I know you're right. But we're so afraid you're going to leave – ' He sat beside her on a little wooden stool; Booron did not look up from her needlework.

'I'll have to go to England,' he agreed. 'But I'll be back. I have to go to England to leave the service.' He leaned over to tickle Milbah's chubby feet.

'I've had an idea,' said Mary, picking up her sewing and putting it down again. 'It might be perfect. You know we were talking – Richard and I – about setting up a school? For all the children, convicts' and marines' – well, when you come back, you could run it. You'd make a wonderful schoolmaster, wouldn't he, Booron?'

Booron's eyes flickered up from her work and down again. She said nothing.

'Because listen, William,' Mary hurried on, with a quick smile and light hand on his shoulder, 'we've already got the Governor's agreement for it. He's asked Mr Alt to find a site for a school building, and they're going to begin it in the autumn. By the time you came back from England, everything would be ready.'

So Alt was working again, was he? William wondered how long it would last; he had designed and planned a number of perfectly competent buildings, over the three years, but his efforts were always interrupted by fresh bouts of his mysterious 'illness'.

'Thank you for the thought, Mary – it may be a possibility. But if the appointment's within the Governor's gift, I don't think he would consider me. Nor would I want – really – to be responsible to him again.' Mary sewed for a few minutes in silence, staring intently at her work – she was embroidering a delicate little garment for Milbah.

'There are ways round that,' she said. 'The Society for the Propagation of Christian Knowledge, for example. They are very keen to see the convicts converted. They could send out a teacher, salary to be paid from their own funds. That would make you independent of the Governor.'

Richard appeared at the gate and Mary got up to meet him. He was red-faced and tired-looking. He waved at William, and indicated that he was going in to change. Mary followed him into the house, talking. William glanced at Booron. She was concentrating on her hemming. After Mary's pale face, her dark skin was lustrous, beautiful. He made himself look away.

'Is it difficult, the sewing?' It was a large piece of rather coarse fabric, maybe a sheet.

'I don't like. It hurts the eyes.'

'Well rest for a minute. You heard about the expedition?'

She nodded.

'Colbee was very brave.'

Booron rubbed her eyes. 'They will go again. The soldiers.'

'Maybe. But I'm not going again.'

'You go home your people.'

'Yes. But I'll come back.'

She shrugged. 'I go my people also. I think they make war.'

'War?'

'Bennelong, he fights Camraigal, Botany Bay tribe. He tell Governor, send redcoats again to Botany Bay. He want for beat Camraigal. Old wars, between Bennelong people and Camraigal.'

'But the Governor only wants to punish McEntire's attacker. He doesn't want a war.'

She smiled. 'They no catch Pemulwi. Pemulwi cannot be kill, he pass like the wind. Redcoats cannot see him. He burn field up Parramatta; he kill whitefellers in the woods. Pemulwi is powerful warrior, cannot be kill by redcoats.' She glanced behind her quickly, Richard and Mary were coming out of the house. She picked up her sewing again.

Richard set down the chair he was carrying and sat on it heavily. 'I've been at the post-mortem,' he announced.

'Of – ?'

'McEntire. Surgeon White opened him to examine the wound. The spear penetrated seven-and-a-half inches, passing between two ribs into the left lobe of the lungs. Barbs of stone and shell remained lodged in the flesh after the spear was extracted, and putrefaction spread from these points. His lung was entirely decayed.'

There was a silence, Mary concentrating very hard on her sewing.

'Terrible work,' Richard said, 'in this heat. I don't know how the doctors stand it. The smell – ' He recollected himself. 'I'm sorry, Mary. In the midst of life we are in death.' He clasped his hands and closed his eyes. 'I pray you look on the soul of our departed brother McEntire with kindness, Father. And forgive us all our trespasses, as we forgive them that trespass against us, for Thine is the Kingdom, the Power and the Glory, for ever and ever.'

'Amen,' said Mary. 'Shall Booron fetch you a drink, Richard? William?'

Booron went into the house.

'Did he confess before he died?' asked William.

'No. He was very frightened. He said he had nothing to confess, but he was terrified.' Richard shook his head. 'He took a long time to die.'

There was a silence; Booron came out with a jug of water, then went indoors again.

'So your thoughts will be turning to home now. You have finished with us here.'

William was hurt by the bitterness of Richard's tone. 'You still think I'm wrong? You still think I'm acting out of pride?'

Mary laid down her sewing and looked expectantly at her husband.

'I don't know,' he said finally.

'Oh Richard, you do know!' she cried. 'You know he's right, his conscience *must* be his guide. Why are you always looking for compromise?'

In the shocked silence that followed, William saw that the colour had drained completely from her pale face, leaving it the yellowish-white of old ivory. Richard was staring at her in amazement.

'Mary?' he said. She sat down and bowed her head, fighting to keep back the tears.

'I'm sorry.'

'But what do you mean?'

'Nothing.' She cleared her throat. 'Nothing. I'm sorry.'

'You think I compromise with God's work?'

'No.' She looked up, she was almost laughing. 'Oh no, you have done more good here – than anyone – '

'Yes.' William grasped the subject eagerly. 'Richard, you're the nearest thing the settlement has to a saint. You know that – look! Whose garden is it that escapes pilfering, when they've even stripped the Governor's bare? Yours, because the convicts know how often you take its produce to the sick – they *know* your goodness – '

Richard's red face took on a deeper shade. 'Any Christian would do that; we have a duty to be charitable. Unto those that have not, shall be given, and from those that have, shall be taken away.'

Mary laughed, wiping the tears from her eyes. 'But the fact remains, my dear, that you are the only Christian in the settlement who does give his own food and drink to the convicts.' She left her seat and knelt beside him, clasping his hand. 'I'm sorry, my dear. I think I'm overtired.'

William was as relieved as they that a rift had been averted. But how she bends to him, he thought sadly. And at what cost to her is peace maintained between them. Booron would never submit to a man in such a way. Nor even would Molly Hill, despite Stokoe's use of her – there was always a part of her that remained independent. Is it a necessary part of marriage? he wondered. That the wife must bend herself to her husband's opinions – even, confine herself to the limits of his courage, if he is less brave than she? Is such submissiveness essential for a couple to live in harmony?

Richard patted Mary's shoulder, and after a moment she excused herself and went into the house.

'I'm just afraid,' Richard said quietly when she was gone. 'I suppose it's selfish. I'm afraid to see the moderating influences being removed.

333

You know Watkin has now decided against a second turn of duty, and is also leaving?'

William nodded. 'But I have every intention of returning. And anyway, we're not gone yet. Who knows how long it'll be before the next fleet docks? What I want to do before I go is to really make a study of Booron's people. Systematically, from how they educate their children, to how they bury their dead; from politics and war to celebrating a marriage. I want to build up a set of notebooks that will help us to understand, really, how best to help them – all our efforts so far have been no more than blundering in the dark. We have to understand how they see the world before we can hope to show them the relevance of our faith.'

Richard frowned. 'I don't know how much you'll find. More, maybe, than I give them credit for. But the point is, William, it suits the Governor to treat them as children. He will not necessarily welcome such discoveries as you may make – '

'No. I'm sure he won't. But the more evidence I can lay before him – or better still his masters in London – that the natives are not children, but adults like ourselves, with their own complicated society and beliefs – then the more chance there is that he will be forced to treat them as equals.'

'I'll give you some letters to take to London,' Richard said slowly. 'I'll give you a letter to Wilberforce.'

At the end of February the Dutch ship the *Waaksamheid* finally brought the crew of the wrecked *Sirius* back from their enforced stay on Norfolk Island. Phillip had chartered the Dutch ship to take them back to England; now they returned to Sydney Cove simply to put their affairs in order, receive letters and messages for England, and make their farewells.

The Governor gave a dinner for Captain Hunter and the *Sirius'* officers, to which William (as an officer who had sailed with them) was invited. Watkin was also invited; the Johnsons were not.

'I shan't go,' William told Watkin. 'It would be ridiculous for me to sit at the Governor's table. He can't stand me.'

'Say what you like about him, he never allows these private quarrels to interfere with the smooth running of public life.'

'But that's precisely what I have against him. The hypocrisy of it. As if the anger we both feel can be comfortably cloaked by a polite smile and a plateful of food – '

Watkin shrugged. 'You should go for Hunter's and Bradley's sakes, if not His Ex's – it's in their honour, after all.'

But that was difficult. William turned it over in his mind all day, and still felt, at the end, that he should not go. To meet Bradley again after so long, in such a public setting, would be a strain, and he could visit Hunter privately to pay his respects. He wanted to present the captain anyway with copies of his two latest star charts, which might be of some use to Hunter for navigation during the voyage home – or which he might be willing to verify or correct. Hunter would not feel slighted by William's absence from a dinner; he would probably not even notice. In the end he sent a polite note declining, citing the need to spend the evening in the observatory as an excuse for his absence.

It was a fine clear night and William was quickly absorbed in his work. When someone knocked on the door around ten o'clock he was surprised. Watkin was the only person who ever joined him in observing, and Watkin was generally the last to leave a dinner party.

'Hello?' he called, fumbling for a light.

'It's me. Bradley.'

It took William a while to get the lamp lit. When at last he did, its flickering light revealed Bradley already in the doorway to the observation room; he had found his way through the dark living quarters and up the stairs. He was even thinner than before, and tired-looking. In the uncertain light his eyes were deep hollows.

'Hello.'

'I thought you were at the Governor's – '

'I left early.' There was a silence and he shrugged. 'It was singularly joyless – John Hunter is furious that Phillip left us stranded on the island for so long. We could have been rescued by a ship of the second fleet seven months ago.'

William nodded.

'And I wanted to see you.'

'Yes. Of course. Have a chair – d'you want a drink or something?'

Bradley shook his head, and sat. 'I'm interrupting you.'

'No. It doesn't matter. How was it, on Norfolk Island?'

'Terrible. Major Ross is insane. He wanted John to put the *Sirius'* crew under his command. In the end I moved away from the whole nasty stew of bickering and pulling rank and expecting daily rescue – I built myself a shelter a few miles from the barracks, and got on with clearing and planting a patch of land. Working on my own.'

William nodded. 'It's easier, working on your own.' There was a silence. William officiously trimmed the flickering lamp.

'And now we're off to England. Thank God,' said Bradley.

'Yes. I asked permission to leave on the *Waaksamheid* too, but I was refused.'

'Why?'

William made his voice measured and toneless as Phillip's: ' "The Governor sees no reason to make an exception of Lieutenant Dawes. He will serve his three-year term with the other marines and leave when they do." No matter that three years is already up.'

'No, I meant, why d'you want to leave?'

'You haven't heard?'

'I know you fell out with him over the expedition to bag natives – ' Bradley grinned, and William found himself smiling. 'But I don't see why you want to leave.'

'I don't want to take orders any more. I'm going to leave the service.'

'You don't have to do that. Now you've stood up to him, I don't think he'll trouble you again. You don't have to sacrifice your career. They need men like you here – '

William shook his head. 'I'll come back. But I'd rather be free. I want to be able to oppose him. At present he's a dictator, everyone in the colony is bound to obey him by lines of duty and command. I want to be outside that. His policy towards the natives – I want to be able to question it, publicly – '

Bradley smiled. 'God bless you!' His eyes were shining – with amusement? It was hard to tell if he was being ironic. William laughed and waved his arm.

'No need to mock me – I know your views on God. Listen. He's leading the colony blindly into war. The Indians are aligning themselves behind Pemulwi. Everything Phillip does is calculated to enrage them. That business over McEnt– '

'Entire. Yes.' Bradley evenly filled William's pause. McEntire. William had forgotten about Bradley and McEntire, in the heat of the conversation. There had been nothing else in his head when he first looked up in the guttering light and saw Bradley leaning in the doorway. But as they'd talked, it had receded; vanished.

'McEntire,' Bradley repeated harshly. 'Of course you know I had an association with him.' He stood up and walked across to the Dolland telescope, pretending to inspect it. Suddenly he laughed. 'I sometimes wonder if you are real. If it is possible for a man to be so innocent, so unaware – '

'But I'm not – ' William wanted to tell him about Molly Hill – to tell him quickly, before he went any farther. But Bradley turned on him in a fury.

'You *are*. Don't pretend there's no difference between us. The difference is, my desire is punishable by death. My love knows it will find nothing but revulsion in the heart of its object. In loving, I must hate myself.'

'But McEntire – '

Bradley grinned. He spoke jeeringly. 'Is foul. McEntire *was* foul. And so, by association, am I. Don't you find?'

'I – I don't find – ' William's sentence stammered into silence.

'You don't find,' sneered Bradley. 'You don't find. *Me*. Yet I exist. I exist with McEntire. In the dirt. That's real. I exist *here*.' He thumped himself on the chest, and his voice cracked. 'I am outside your world.'

William stood uncertainly, but Bradley shook his head. He seemed to be crying.

'Keep away,' he gasped. 'Keep away from me.'

William watched him helplessly for a minute.

'Please. What can I do?'

'Oh,' Bradley gained control of himself and turned to face William. 'Nothing. I know my due. My pleasure lies in pain. I find it. It finds me.' His face convulsed. 'I consume it like a starving man.'

There was a silence. William was cold, he could not help shivering. He was afraid. Not of Bradley, but of the vision Bradley opened up. Of the world Bradley inhabited. Bradley was watching him, the ghost of a smile came into his face.

'You mustn't worry,' he said. 'I don't want you to have bad dreams.' He moved back to his chair by the bench, and sat. He spoke simply now, the horrible taunting tone had gone. 'I would give anything – my life – ' he shrugged – 'to make you happy.' He placed his fists on the bench and pressed the knuckles together, William watched the skin whiten. In between the irregular shivers that shook his body, he could feel his own heart beating, too hard, in his chest. It hurt. Bradley was looking at his fists; after a while he spoke again, quite calmly.

'Which is ridiculous, of course. Your happiness is entirely independent of me. Your happiness lies in doing what you know to be right.' He glanced at William. 'I wonder if you know what a luxury that is.'

There was a long silence. At last William broke it. 'Is there anything – ?'

'You can do?' Bradley met his eyes and smiled. 'Oh William.' He laughed. 'Live your life. Sort out the natives. Serve your God.' He rose to his feet. 'Be good.'

With a quick movement, he was out of the door and clattering down the steps. William heard the outer observatory door open and quickly close. He was gone.

William lit a fire and sat near it, with a blanket wrapped round his shoulders, trying to get warm. His mind was in two parts; at the front there was a turmoil of feelings he could not address. At the back, there was a calm observer who had seemed to stand outside himself all evening, watching and nodding at the scene between himself and Bradley. The observer had even known what Bradley would say. It understood Bradley's wanting William to stay in New South Wales; it understood that in so doing William would, in a way, be acting for Bradley – doing what Bradley could not do; that though Bradley cherished no ideals, or dreams of doing good, he had an interest in William's, and wished them to succeed. That in serving God William would, to a degree, be acting for Bradley's soul. But the distant observer was swamped by a wave of despair. I knew. I knew everything, before he told me. And I pretended to myself I didn't. I love him. I caused him pain.

But there was no way out. There was no *way* – dear God there was no way – forward or back or around. The despair became rage with God; who had dared – chosen – to make life like this. Who seemed to take pleasure in his creatures' distress, who seemed to delight in cruelty.

When it began to get light William took off his blanket and put on his jacket, and went outside. He walked up the hill to the cliff-top, and down the narrow path to the beach. It was where Molly Hill had talked to him. There was no one about today; just sky, sea, rocks. There was nothing he could do.

There was nothing *to* do but carry on.

Olla

Today I take Daniel for a hospital test. Stephen wants to come with me, it is pointless. I tell him don't be ridiculous. They will not tell us anything we don't already know. And if they *do*, don't you think I will inform you?

'But you always have to deal with the hospital and doctors – you're very tired. I should take him, and you should have a day off. Go out somewhere.'

The man is a fool. Leave Daniel to him? Imagine he can defend Daniel against the doctors? I don't bother to reply, I continue to pack Daniel's food for the day. Stephen is persistent, it is time-consuming. He says he has arranged to have the day off work. How did he know in advance? He has been looking in the drawer where I keep Daniel's medical records and appointments. When I accuse him of snooping he is enraged.

'Is it snooping for a man to know what's wrong with his own son?'

'There's nothing wrong,' I say. I keep my voice calm. Daniel does not like shouting.

'You shut me out at every turn, Olla,' Stephen shouts. 'You block me out. Why?'

I glance at my watch, 8.15. Daniel's appointment is 9.30. I should leave by 8.45. I switch on the kettle. Keep my voice calm. 'Stephen, I'm not blocking you out. D'you want a cup of tea?' I put bags in the pot. 'Listen, you've got your job, haven't you? You have to go off every morning at 8 o'clock, you have work to do, responsibilities. Daniel is *my* work. I don't come to your work and say you are blocking me out – '

'But this is my *home*. My *son*.'

'Don't you think I am looking after him? If I wanted you to come to the hospital I would ask. I can be trusted, surely, to understand what a doctor says? Why take away my responsibility?'

'But it's wretched. I could give you some moral support at least – '

'That's why I don't want you to come. You find it wretched. I find it perfectly all right. I do not need "support". If you came, *you* would need it. Why should I take your misery to the hospital, when I am quite content alone?'

He stares at me. I pour the tea and push his mug towards him. I glance at my watch again: 8.23. Daniel needs changing. Stephen abruptly leaves the room. I listen to see where he is going. He goes into the hall, I hear the rattle of car keys being taken off the hook. I stand up and open my mouth to call to him – I told him yesterday, I need the car today. I need the car to take Daniel to his appointment. The front door slams. I close my mouth. Daniel whimpers, he will be upset now. I hear the car being revved. Better to let him take it than cause further dispute. He is a selfish idiot; cannot think to give me the one thing I need, the car – wants only to inflict his own oppressive presence on me. He is less than no help. I go to phone for a taxi.

The arrangements I made were good, did not trouble him. I asked for the car, that's all. But he has to interfere, make his own arrangements, change everything. And for what? To make life more difficult for Daniel and me. I waited twenty-five minutes for a taxi to come home from the hospital last time. That's why I wanted the car. And I am late, I must rush, and Daniel is distressed.

At the hospital we wait with other mothers and children. Some of them are hideous. There is one propped in a pushchair who twitches constantly, arching his back and twisting his face into the seat-back. His eye opens and closes, he makes gargling, rasping noises in his throat. I sit at the back, in the empty row. One of them is making a noise, not crying, just wailing in a vacant, pointless way. A nurse comes out and asks the mother if she'd like her to take him away for a bit.
'Sure!' says the woman loudly. 'Take him away for as long as you like, love.' She laughs and looks round, and some of the others titter.

There is a toddler, a girl, in front of us. She is banging her head against the back of the seat and moaning. Her mother tells her be quiet, and she kneels on her chair and turns to face us. She keeps on rocking back and forth. Her eyeballs are rolled up into the top of her head, they flicker as she rocks. Her mother keeps hold of her by the ankle and continues to read her magazine. There is a notice on the wall about a support group for parents of children with cerebral palsy.

Support. A word for Stephen and his kind. What Stephen thinks he would like to give me. What do they get from a support group, these pathetic guardians of damaged goods? You see the bigger ones in wheelchairs – eyes staring, necks awry, hands and feet twitching; straining to make hoarse ugly cries, lurching with the effort.

340

It is pure sentiment to keep them alive. Impractical, unrooted sentiment – like Stephen's. Animals do not keep sickly young alive, they abandon them, and strengthen the herd. They know better than to waste energy prolonging the lives of invalid creatures. Creatures that are not valid. Invalids. What can be the point? If you cannot live then you must die. I would clear the room of ugliness.

A woman holding a small baby comes and sits next to me, although there are plenty of empty seats.

'Hello,' she says, 'have you been before? It's my first time.'

'Yes,' I say.

'What's wrong with yours?' she says, peering to look.

'Nothing.'

She is embarrassed. 'Oh – I'm sorry – I thought we were all – ' There is a silence then she starts again. 'Mine's Down's syndrome, poor little mite. She's only three months old.' As if her age has anything to do with it. She holds the baby out for me to see, it is pink with a snub nose. 'Madeleine,' she says, 'd'you like it?'

I nod.

'I do,' she says, 'but we chose it before they diagnosed – you know – the Down's – and now my husband wants to change it because he says what'll they call her for short, "Mad", and that's not funny is it?'

'No.'

She looks around. 'What you here for then?' she asks suddenly.

'Tests.'

'Oh.' She is trying to think of something else to say.

'I must go and change Daniel,' I tell her, and take him to the bathroom. He does not need changing, I changed him before I came out. When I take him back I sit in the front row, I am left in peace until it is our turn to go in.

A different consultant. Asian, with spectacles. He is reading the notes. The nurse is putting files away. We sit and wait in silence. At last the man looks up.

'Well,' he says, 'how are we getting along?'

'Fine, thank you.' He nods at the nurse who closes the drawer and comes towards me.

'Just give him to nurse, please, and we'll have a look. Now – ' The nurse takes Daniel off me, lays him on a changing mat on a trolley, begins to strip his clothes.

'I – '

'It's all right Mrs Beech. Now, if you can tell me a little about him.'
She is not gentle enough. She only unbuttons the top of his jacket,
then pulls it off over his head. He doesn't like that, she'll upset him.
'Mrs Beech?'
'What? What do you want to know?'
'Well, feeding. How's he feeding?'
'Fine, he eats well.'
'No problems with chewing?'
'No – I – I purée his food.'
'I see. And is he still using a bottle?'
'Yes.'
'Sleeping? What's his routine, is he waking at night?'
I answer all the questions; he should know the answers already if he's
ever seen a child Daniel's age. I told him, nothing's wrong.
'And how are you?'
'Me? Fine.'
'You're not too tired? Feeling a bit peaky? Are you getting out at all?
Have your periods started again?'
'I go out every day. I'm fine. My husband and I went to the Hallé the
other night.' I am pleased I got that in.
'Very good.' He consults the notes again. 'That's the ticket, then.' He
crosses to Daniel who is naked and defenceless on the mat. He will be
cold, it is not warm in here. I go closer but the doctor waves me back.
'Please sit down, Mrs Beech. I won't be long.'
What is he going to do? Some harm – some damage – while I just sit
here politely, five feet away, unable to raise a finger? He holds
Daniel's feet and pushes them in so that his knees bend. He prods the
stomach, listens to the heart, turns Daniel over and listens at the back.
Raises him up to sitting position by pulling his arms and lets him go –
'No!'
'It's all right,' he says, 'no harm done.' He has caught Daniel's head
with his hand at the last second. 'I need to see what he can do, Mrs
Beech. I won't hurt him, I assure you.' He raises Daniel's hands and
drops them so they fall to the mat with a little thud. That will hurt
him. He will be bruised. He pushes his finger at Daniel's fist.
'Will he grip your finger, Mrs Beech?'
'Yes, he grips it.'
'With which hand?'
'Both. Either.'
He clasps and unclasps Daniel's fingers for a while, trying to make

them close over his big finger. Of course Daniel will not clasp his
finger. Why should he? He does not like the man.
'What exercises are you doing with him?' They must be in the notes; I
tell him anyway.
'And the physiotherapist calls regularly?'
'Every week.'
'You have been doing the exercises each day?'
'Yes. Of course. From two to four every afternoon.'
'Two hours a day?' He sounds astonished, and glances at me.
Something is in his mind. I must be cunning, more cunning. They are
up to something.
'Nurse, will you – ' He gets the nurse to hold Daniel while he tests for
reflexes. She spreads a grey-ish towel on her knee, and sits him on it.
How many other naked babies have sat there today? Hasn't she
heard of germs and hygiene? They are slacker every time I visit this
place.
'Is he raising his head at all? Does he make any attempt to raise it,
when you lie him on his stomach?'
'No. Not really.'
The doctor nods and tells the nurse to dress him.
'It's all right, I'll do that – '
'Please sit down, Mrs Beech. I'd like a little chat.'

He talks about Daniel. The muscle tone, he says, is very poor,
especially considering the amount he has been exercised. He must
be making almost no voluntary movements whatsoever. He waits to
see if I will speak but I want to know what he's driving at first. He
continues; they had hoped Daniel might be able to hold his head up
by now. He thinks it would be useful to have Daniel in hospital for a
few days – for three days – for a brain scan, and more exhaustive
physical tests. He can have more detailed sight and hearing tests at
the same time, they will bring all the specialists together to assess the
best way forward –

Three days in hospital. 'I can stay with him?'
'Really, I don't think you should, Mrs Beech. I wouldn't encourage it.
I think you yourself have worked very hard looking after him for
the past year. I am sure you could enjoy a little break, knowing he is
in good hands – ' He is watching me. Exactly like Stephen. To see if I
will make a fuss, object to leaving Daniel. If I do, they will decide I am
unwell; they will find an excuse to separate us for longer.

I am filled with such scalding rage I cannot speak. Because I am a good mother, because I want to stay with my child and look after him – they imagine I am mentally unbalanced. Creatures like that one in the waiting room, who are only too glad to hand their offspring to perfect strangers, who are glad to be rid of their children – they are regarded as normal.

But I must be cunning. I must be calm and cunning. 'I will discuss it with my husband,' I say. 'I'm sure that he'll know best.'
There is a little wrinkle of frown above the bridge of the doctor's spectacles. He turns the pages of notes. 'Ah – what does your husband do?'
'He works in the Education Offices.'
'I see. Very good. My secretary will give you a date.' He begins to scribble on the notes. 'We'll get the physio in as well and have a think about pushchairs and bath-seats and so on – have they given you many gadgets yet?'
'Gadgets?'
'Well for example, there's a bath-seat that you can strap him into so you don't have to support him all the time. He's becoming quite heavy, don't you find?'
I don't find him heavy, no.
'Is he too fat?' I ask. 'His stomach – '
The doctor stops writing and looks at me. 'He's not fat at all, Mrs Beech. I would say you are controlling his diet extremely well. His stomach appears flabby and distended because of the poor muscle tone – everything that's in there simply bulges out, without a nice firm band of muscle to hold it flat. Don't imagine he's fat.'
The man is disgusting, does he talk to all his patients like this? I take Daniel from the nurse, adjust his jacket and untwist the leg of his baby-gro so he will not be uncomfortable. 'Goodbye.'
'Ah. Mrs Beech.' He does not look up.
'Yes?'
'Will you ask your husband to give me a call? The number's on your appointment card. Goodbye.'

What is this? Why? Something he wants to discuss with Stephen and not me? Then I realize there is nothing at all in writing. My husband can forget to call him. It's easy. He's forgotten already.
The secretary books Daniel in for 19 December, four weeks away.
When we get home in our taxi, the car is outside. Stephen is not at

work. Do I have to face him hanging around for the rest of the day now? Am I to have *no* peace? He is not anywhere downstairs; I leave Daniel in the kitchen and go up to the toilet. He's in his room, the door is shut. I leave him there. He is the one who slammed the door, and left me to go to the hospital with no car. He is the one who should apologize. I hope he stays in there all day.

CHAPTER TWENTY-FIVE

Sailing home

HMS *Gorgon* finally sailed for England on 18 December 1791, five days after the New South Wales marine battalion was embarked. The weather was very hot and calm; they weighed anchor and left the cove at 7 p.m., to tack slowly down the bay and make the most of the light land breeze that would bear them out through the Heads in the early morning. William watched Sydney Cove recede in the clear evening light. Already it was different; he felt the thrill of being aboard ship again; pleasure in the vast slow movements of sails overhead, and in the height of the deck itself. Already the bay looked smaller. There were three fishing boats out, but no native canoes at all, nor was there a single Indian visible on any of the beaches or cliffs of Port Jackson, nor smoke from any native fires.

Over the slow months of the voyage home, the contradictions of New South Wales shimmered in William's head. There was the report on him that Governor Phillip had entrusted to Captain Parker. The Governor had coldly informed William that his report was unfavourable, due to William's insubordination, but that a full apology and change of heart would still be acceptable. Since he was leaving the Marines, the Governor's bad report did not matter. But when he visualized the wide straight road at Parramatta; when he thought of the hospital's borehole and drains; when he remembered the redoubt with its thick walls, its sentry post and gun mountings, he could not prevent a feeling of rage at the injustice which forgot so much of his work so easily.

He and the Governor had come to a final, bitter clash over the instruments at the observatory. Setting up the observatory was, in William's mind, one of the few clear achievements of his stay, and he assumed it was a permanent fixture. But the Governor announced that since the Board of Longitude had made him personally responsible for the instruments, and since William's departure would leave no one in the colony who was fit or trained to use them, the instruments must travel home with William. In vain William pointed out that a new astronomer might be appointed at any time; that the instruments would come to less harm in the security of the observatory than in being transported back halfway across the globe. No, he must endure the final humiliation of dismantling his own workplace, and overseeing its pointless return to London. It would be a fine irony if he did secure Board of Longitude support to continue astronomical work in New South Wales; then Phillip would be able to watch him unloading the instruments and setting them up all over again.

Augustus Alt had visited him before he left the observatory. Alt had moved into a new brick house near the Deputy-Governor's, and Biddy Lowe was his housekeeper. He wanted details of the Rose Hill projects William was working on, so that he could oversee their completion. As he handed over drawings and ground maps, William realized that Alt would simply step into his shoes. He would not be missed. Perhaps if he had not been there – if there had been no one other than Alt for the Governor to turn to for surveying – Alt would have been sober more often. Maybe William's hard work had enabled Alt to be irresponsible. Sometimes William had to pray, to find the strength to resist a terrible sense of pointlessness. What had he achieved? What was it worth? And how did it weigh in the balance against the miseries he had caused? Molly Hill (but only I was made miserable by that, he reminded himself); the posting of Barnes to the hospital storeroom; Bradley.

But prayer always led him up again. What was important was finding a way forward. Learning. Finding out how to make better things possible. Not imposing. Not achieving: that was Phillip's role. What was necessary was to remove his own importance from the picture.

He had five notebooks of detailed information on Eora life and language. There was still a great deal he did not know; it would be a life's work, to move slowly closer into understanding with them. Mary had suggested he start a school for Eora children, with the thought that it would be easier to convert them and explain British ideas to them when they were young. But Booron had been puzzled by the notion when he spoke with her. She could see no reason why her people would want to bring their children to a British school, and he tended to agree with her.

If he went back simply as a settler, he would have no power. The natives trusted him, it might even be possible for him to speak with Pemulwi and other leaders. But what power would he have to negotiate with them? As a mere settler, what power would he have to ameliorate the evil consequences of the Governor's rash decisions? A military captain, someone in Watkin's position, had vastly more power – as when he had persuaded the Governor that only six, rather than ten, natives should be hunted down.

Perhaps it would be nothing but futility to return?

But then he thought of the place.

The baked, sun-filled mornings, the shadowy grey-green woods streaked with brilliant birds; the natives' fires dotting the shore at night.

He thought of the luminous stars, and night-time choruses of frogs and insects; the smoky eucalypt scent of the air. He thought of the ancient power of the land, and the raw newness of the settlement. The honest lives that reformed convicts were sweating to build and grow, on their farms. He thought of the Eora and of the dangers facing them. He thought of Booron.

He would go back. In a role which Phillip, or Phillip's successor, could not manipulate. He would find a way to serve the people and the place. If looking and listening and praying and searching could find a way to serve, then he would find it. He would be free, and he would give his lifetime to that labour.

STEPHEN

Leave him there. Sailing before the wind into his future, heart full of hope.

He never returned to New South Wales. Among other letters entrusted to him was one from Richard Johnson to his patron Wilberforce. The great man's anti-slaving bill (which sought to outlaw trading in slaves, and pave the way for the abolition of slavery itself in British colonies) had just been defeated in the Lords. But the tide was clearly turning against slavery. British ex-slaves, freed since Mansfield's famous judgement in 1772, were a *cause célèbre* amongst right-thinking people. In the very year in which the First Fleet had set sail for New South Wales, 400 freed black slaves had sailed for Freetown, Sierra Leone, where a settlement had been established by Granville Sharpe and his supporters. (Yes, they too sailed from Portsmouth in 1787. There were even tales of the ex-slaves refusing to board their ship, for fear it might take them off to Botany Bay and more years of servitude.)

Wilberforce persuaded William to accept an appointment to Sierra Leone. The settlement there was struggling, the original freed slaves had been decimated by hunger, disease and hostile neighbours. Money and support were forthcoming from England, Wilberforce and his Clapham friends had already formed the Sierra Leone Company, to send more liberated slaves out there. They needed a Governor in Freetown who would devote himself to the principles of its establishment and to the practicalities of its survival. There would be scope for William to use power wisely; to transform lives. He set sail again after little more than a month in England. He served two terms as Governor of Sierra Leone. On his first leave in 1794 he married Judith Rutter, who bore him a son. Were they happy? Did he love her? Did she submit to him? Who knows?

When he came back from Sierra Leone he worked teaching maths at Christ's Hospital, and gave evidence to the House of Lords Committee on the Slave Trade. He was always short of money. Judith died, and in 1811 he married again – Grace Gilbert. Grace. I think he found happiness with Grace. He went with her to Antigua in 1813, to establish schools for slaves' children. And there in 1836, aged seventy-four, he died. His son William Rutter Dawes was brought up by old Benjamin, and became a famous astronomer.

349

You can't leave him there. Just sailing into the future – his story cut off –

Bloody hell, Stephen, don't we all get cut off? He *died* teaching slaves' children. Not feasting on oysters or snoring in a brandy-sodden haze by the fire, or with popping eyes gasping for breath trying to fuck a nubile fourteen-year-old. Not beating his houseboy or robbing the poor. The story's got to end somewhere. He refused to obey Governor Phillip's orders, he asserted the rights of the Blacks. He was a good man. How much clearer can you get?

No.
You want to carry on to the bitter end?
Yeah.
Sierra Leone. Antigua. The lot?
Yes, I want to *know*.
You won't find out any more than you know already. He stuck to his principles. He kept trying. He kept hoping. He learned to listen. And I don't know anything about Sierra Leone. I know nothing about Antigua. All I know is the kindly summary Gillen gives Dawes in *Founders of Australia*:

> Dawes became Governor of Sierra Leone . . . He became associated with Wilberforce in efforts to limit slavery, and in 1813 he went to Antigua to establish schools for slaves' children, under the auspices of the Church Missionary Society. Like so many of the most worthy of public servants he was never given proper recognition, nor given financial compensation equal to the value of his work.

There is something childish in your persistence, Stephen, in this expectation of an answer. Like the little red engine (James? Or was it Thomas the Tank Engine?) huffing and puffing as he forced himself up the hill – 'I know I can do it. I know I can do it. I know I can do it.'

Like the last crazed months of school, when the enterprise was springing leaks left right and centre, and Stephen was the one dashing from a teacherless class to an irate parent to a knife-wielding fifteen-year-old to an icily insulting science inspector – dashing from leak to leak, plugging and plugging; leaving home earlier in the morning, returning later at night, knowing that if only he could run faster, work harder, plug quicker – the whole thing might stay afloat – that it was all up to him, that he must save the world.

If I go on. Overturn every step and stone of Dawes' life, if I keep trying, work harder (I know I can do it) – won't there be an answer?

To what? What was the question? Olla? Daniel? My life?
He doesn't even know.
Dawes is finished. His story is told.

*

Saturday afternoon, most unwisely, I go to Manchester Central Library. Social sciences, catalogues. Call up books on Sierra Leone. I know it will be bad.

Sierra Leone. Not joyful exodus to a promised land, for the liberated black slaves of Britain; no, forcible repatriation of terrified people on a slaving coast where they ran every risk of being sold into slavery again. Abominable conditions aboard the transports, fever raging before they even set sail. (Fifty dead in Portsmouth, of cold and sickness, and thirty-five dead during the month-long voyage. Arthur Phillip only lost twenty-five in a voyage of eight months.) Bitter, angry, ill-treated people. Blacks who had fought with the British in North America, risking their lives for the promise of their freedom; who were then left to beg in the streets of London. Who were asked to sign a declaration that they would never attempt to return from Sierra Leone to be a burden on the British. Dispatched with pitifully inadequate supplies, to suffer disease, starvation, internecine quarrels, and raids by French slavers. Freetown was in the middle of a fever-infested swamp. Within three years, 300 were dead. Only the arrival of a new contingent of freed American negroes from Nova Scotia in 1792 enabled the place to survive at all. The second wave were healthier, more organized, had their own ideas about government . . . That was when William arrived. The English Christianized, educated, and governed them. Then waited 169 years to give them independence.

Serve you right, Stephen. What the fuck d'you expect? Honest philanthropy? Pure motives? That the Sierra Leone Company was formed out of love for the oppressed? Didn't someone stand to make a quick buck, paid by the government £14 per head to remove niggers from the land? D'you expect anyone ever to have done the right thing for the right reasons?

351

I told you *leave* him. Leave William to steer his own course through the shit. He was doing OK. He went on to Antigua. Set up schools for slaves' children. Limited enough, maybe, in its ambition, to even be pure.

Though not without sinister consequences: alienation of people from their roots, cultural imperialism, the imposition of Christianity, the fostering of talents and hopes which could never be fulfilled and would therefore lead to greater frustration, anger and violence . . . And thence to vicious retaliation and suppression . . .

Fuck it, he'd have done better to tie his hands together and gag himself, wouldn't he, than offer to educate slaves' children? Imperialist lackey, he'd have done less harm if he'd set out honestly to whip them, rather than pretending to be their whitey friend.

He was a good man. He was a good man. He was a good man.

He was a good man. And what good did it do?
Pathetic really, isn't it? I crouched against the stacks in a dark corner of the library, I was trying to read and I couldn't clear my eyes of tears. It was C. L. R. James:
'Those who see in abolition (of slavery) the gradually awakening conscience of mankind should spend a few minutes asking themselves why it is man's conscience, which had slept peacefully for so many centuries, should awake just at the time that men began to see the unprofitableness of slavery as a method of production in the West Indian colonies.'

Fucking sucker again Stephen. Fucking stupid sucker.

It was raining when I came out of the throbbing fluorescent library. A black December afternoon. I couldn't breathe very well. Maybe the rain – and my nose was blocked. The Christmas shopping traffic was going home in solid lines of noise and sharp light. I got down the steps to the pavement and I couldn't breathe at all, my lungs seized up.

Buried alive, just my head poking out. A fine and pertinent image for mankind, thanks Mr Beckett. Happy Days are here again. But I lack Winnie's phlegmatism. Panic. Fall over, gasping dryly. Lie twitching in a puddle for a bit while the headlights flicker over me and on, then manage to pull a breath in. Crawl up to sit on the bottom step. Breathe in. Out. In. Thank god for breath.

I don't want to lose him, William Dawes. In the midden of the world's history. If he's impossible, the faeces, the dung, the piss the shit the crap is over my head. I'm snuffed. My nostrils bunged with dirt. There's nothing left.

Run while you can, Stephen. Run, I should. Run.

The woman in the travel agents' stares and presses a button. A man in a suit comes out from the inner office and inspects me.
'I want a plane ticket.'
They glance at each other and she says, 'Do you have any form of payment on you, sir?'
I feel for my wallet. My mac is wet through to the inside, I notice, with black streaks where I've fallen. I wipe the rain out of my eyes and realize that my hand is very muddy too. I am shaking. They must think I am drunk. I try to be very calm and unthreatening, in case they refuse to serve me.
'I could pay by Access. Or a cheque.' I lay my cards and cheque book on the counter.
They glance at each other again and then the man shrugs and goes back into his office. The woman says, 'When would you like to travel, sir?' and glances at her computer screen. She seems surprised by what is there. 'Did you say your destination?'
'No. Australia.'
She nods and presses some keys. 'When?'
'Today.'
She looks up quickly.
'I mean, as soon as possible.' I am thinking now. 'I've had a shock – a relative of mine – is ill.'
'Ah.' She relaxes and smiles. 'I'm very sorry, sir. We'll get you there as quick as we can, don't you worry.' She flicks through a few screens of information, reels off some times and prices, offers – to my astonishment – several cities –
'No. Sydney. Only Sydney.'
– and finds me a seat. Day after tomorrow. I have to get a visa from the Australian Consulate in Manchester. Then fly – 6 p.m. from Ringway.

*

The plane is bad. Full to the gills, sweatily hot but also strangely cold.

353

The circulation in my feet has stopped. The noise is appalling; the engines, the whispering chatter of hundreds of headsets, the violent clatter of food tins from the galley I am one row behind. I have drunk as much alcohol as they will serve me, in an attempt to induce sleep, but the only effect is a severe headache and mild nausea. There are little, fluttering, experimental waves of panic rising beneath my ribs. I want to get off. I want to open the door and step out. I want to get off the plane. I might burst into tears. There are sixteen hours of flying time left.

Olla didn't turn a hair. As if I'd said, I'm going to town to buy some shoes. She didn't so much as blink. As if I went to Australia twice a week. She just carried on feeding the child, she didn't even look at me.

Be calm. Close eyes. Consider. Where am I going to and why?

I am going to Australia, in search of William Dawes, dead since 1836.

And what do you hope to find? A sense of his life? A moment of his optimism?

Bad question. Start again. Where am I going *from* and why? From my wife and child, house, job and country. (Oh, and car. Mustn't forget the car.) From my life.

Ah.
Were you expecting that? You knew you were going from your life? Well depends if you mean 'my life' as, 'the kind of life I've been leading', or 'my life' as opposed to 'my death'.

Obviously. Well?

Well from my life. Which could equally well be, to another kind of life, or death.

'Another kind of life'? What precisely did you have in mind? Cattle rancher? Mining engineer? Flying fucking doctor? You loser. Get real, Stephen. Get real.

My hands are slick with sweat. The man on my left farts continuously in his sleep. They are bringing round more food. What the hell will I do when I get there? What the hell am I going to do?

It doesn't matter.

Yes. Almost as reassuring as the thought of the plane coming down to land. It doesn't matter. When I get there I can get off this plane. Go to a hotel. Have a bath. It doesn't matter what I do. Because no one on earth cares.

*

Sydney, Sydney Cove, is a city.
Of course.
Skyscrapers, buses, a monorail, crowds of business people and shoppers. Shady gullies of racing traffic between high glassy buildings. Fast. Rich. Loud. A city. There will be nothing here.

I come out at the harbour-front where the ferries dock. The great white sea-shell tit of the opera house to the right. Harbour Bridge to the left. Water (muddied and oily with use, but none the less blue) ahead. I take the ferry to Manly.

And then I can see it. The shores are still green, more or less, despite the litter of real estate. There are still beaches; crescents of pale sand where white wavelets froth; there are islands, Garden Island, Prison Island. Back under the bridge and away upstream lies Parramatta; and ahead the coves, the Heads, the Pacific. The shape of the harbour lies open and familiar as the outlines of Bradley's map, framed above my desk at home. I grip the rail of the shuddering ferry and gulp down its diesel fumes, staring round at the rise of land on the north shore; back to where Harbour Bridge springs from the city side, which must have been Point Maskeylene; to the opera house on Bennelong Point, where the black man's brick hut was built, to Bradley Point, Farm Cove, Dinner Cove, and all the rest. It is the same place.

Manly is ice-creams, silly hats, rude T-shirts, the December heat becoming fierce. Holiday-makers are dwarfed by the giant flatness of the Pacific. A little sense of tawdriness, like Scarborough on a hot June day. Phillip named it Manly because the natives were so. And then I lost it. It is simply a holiday resort.

In the evening in my sweetly air-conditioned room, I take stock. This isn't what I came for. I am tired and unreal but I can make a decision. With surprising ease, with oiled smoothness – just as I was able to get on the plane. Nothing is very difficult, there's no connection. I glide without friction, I barely touch the sides of it – life. Slipping like shit through loose bowels.

355

Get out into the country, Stephen. Find bush, wilderness, desert. Find a place that will be – that will contain – something real.

*

He's bought a map. He's hired a car. White Toyota Corolla with air-conditioning. Feels rather sharp and flash. Even Stephen can learn to love cars in the end! I drive north out of Sydney heading for Bathurst, glittering in the sun, with the air-conditioning and the radio on, like the beginning of a road movie.

I'm slipping through scenery, mountains, farmland, slipping through flat industrial sites and towns where there's nothing but a petrol station and pub. Wide glittering roads; the foreign strangeness of road signs – yellow and black, distances in kilometres. Gum trees like parodies of gum trees; coloured birds. (Noticed that even in Sydney. Just flying about – green and red and yellow birds. A little, pleasurable, shock.) But mainly the light. *Huge* light. Brilliant clear dry light, blue sky out of a child's paint box. Light which, coming out of English December, is a blow to the head, an assault on the eyes, a permanent state of dazed unbalance. I bought sunglasses at a petrol station but don't much want to wear them. Feels like this assault of light upon the brain might be something. Be worth something – achieve (illumine?) something. If my head can open up enough to let it in.

On the second day there's a long straight road through nothing, that feels as if I'm getting near to what I wanted. Barrier Highway, it's called. There's dead kangaroos on the verge, there's road houses with nothing between, for 100 k and more. There's monstrous lorries pulling rows of containers behind them. There's not a lot of traffic, and the whole flat land wriggles in the sun and glows. It is entirely alien. I have driven 1,060 kilometres – light and giddy with shimmering tiredness, moving towards the centre, away from the civilized edges. Moving in towards the heart.

In the evening I pull into a town called Wilcannia. I see my first Blacks. Aborigines. Real Australians. Whatever. Still the same ludicrous not-knowing what to call them, as for Dawes. 'Aborigine' an insult – but since Eora are wiped out (and anyway I'm out of their region) what's the ethnic name? Pitjantjatjara?
Their name is beside the point.

No it isn't. No one's name is beside the point. In naming you define your relationship to the named.

Look, the point is what I see. Bright yellow early evening street carved with black shadows from high sandstone buildings (pseudo-classical, the post office even has Greek pillars for Christ's sake); the odd slow vehicle, a battered old farm truck with scrawny throw-back dogs snarling over the tailgate; and three Blacks squatting on the pavement in the shade, backs against the wall. With a near-empty two-litre flagon between them. One has his eyes closed. The other two watch dully, unmoving. All have bare feet. Their clothes are jumble sale; dirt-brown trousers undone at the hem. One has a too-tight T shirt, the others ragged shirts. They squat there, silent, unblinking. One unscrews the flagon. He raises it to his lips, gulps a couple of mouthfuls, and passes it to the next.

At the hotel the man behind the desk asks if I've got a locking petrol cap. Yes; why?

'The boongs. They siphon out yer petrol.' It takes me a while to work out what he means; that this is *his* name for the original owners of his country. First committed to writing by Judge Advocate David Collins in his 1790 Eora/English vocabulary: 'boong' = 'arse'. When I go back down to buy a drink I ask him, what for? What for do they siphon out petrol? To put in their own cars?

He laughs. 'No. It's the kids – the youth. They sniff it.'

Sniff it?

'Yeah. They sniff it. Gives 'em some kind of a buzz.'

Sniff *petrol*?

He is vastly entertained by my incredulity. 'Sure. They sniff it. Some of 'em walk about with a can on a string round their necks. They sniff it all the time. It rots their brains.'

Then what?

He shrugs. 'They go blind. Fall over. Fucking stupid bastards, eh?'

I can't get the smell of petrol out of my head now. The sickening clinging stink of it. Jesus wept. To lose yourself for whatever momentary relief of escape you can once or ever get from *that* . . .

I calm myself to sleep by reading the map. The names. Mount Hopeless, Mount Deception, Killalpaninna Mission (ruins), Moon Desert. Mulumulu Lake, Warrawenia Lake, Lake Muck and Salt Lake. Wagga-Wagga, Murrumburrah, Woodstock. Warrumbungle, Wee

Waa, Gloucester. Duck Creek opal field. Lake Uloowaranie. Moomba oil and gas field. Phosphate Hill mine, Woomera, Maralinga (prohibited). Pitjantjatjara, Yungkutatjara and Ngaanatjara Lands. Utopia (Angarapa), Mount Beauty, Walhalla; Mount Hope, Coffin Bay. Denial Bay, Anxious Bay, Avoid Bay, Wreck Bay. Great Sandy Desert. Mount Warning.

Olla.
Olla?
If I could try again.
Olla. Still you know a little – kind of leaping on to her name. My heart or tongue, a little leap. Olla.

Press on. (In his motor car, naturally, tankful of four-star.) Press on, north, into the country. There's a compulsion to this eating of distance. I'll keep moving now, movement is what's needed. Something's opening up. The land? My head?

In the middle of the morning I take a right turn off the main road, to continue heading north. The map calls it 'major route, unsealed'. It's a red dirt track, rutted by wheels, unfenced at the sides – just a ditch and low, erratic trees. No farms, no animals, no vehicles. Just a red track through nothingness. I am coming to the right place.
(What has he been right about, ever? A catalogue of disasters, Stephen, you're a fucking joke.)

But I'm here. I'm *here*. Doing 80 k on a red dirt track, trailing a cloud of dust thick enough to hide whatever's behind. Up ahead an eagle's taking off. And there's a big red kangaroo moving fast in the bush beside me as if he's racing the car, he keeps up 50 k for over a mile then heads away into the scrub. The stunted grey bushes shimmer in the sunglare. I am coming to the place. The windscreen's coated in red dust; I squirt it again and use the wipers, there are curtains of dried mud tears down the sides. Its hot and getting hotter, no air-conditioning today. I won't use it, I want to feel real heat, thirty-five degrees and rising. Windows closed against the dust; my hands slippery on the steering wheel. The dust still gets in through the ventilation, baking dust coats the insides of my lungs. My shirt's stuck to my back, the sweat stings when it trickles into my eyes. I'm hot hot hot.

The track ahead's straight as a die and empty. It's ridged, crosswise, so the car bumps regularly – I take the speed up, 100 k, 110, their impact is lessened. Blue sky red earth grey leaves the world is bright, glassy, molten. Speed, space, distance, oh I can shake you off Stevie, I can can shake you off!

I'm Toad! I'm Toad, I'm Toad, the terror of the road. I'm singing: big, loud, rousing songs, at the top of my dust-caked voice –

> Heart of oak are our ships,
> Jolly tars are our men,
> We'll always be ready,
> Steady boys, steady,
> We'll fight and we'll conquer again and again!

> The people's flag is deepest red;
> It shrouded oft our martyred dead,
> And 'ere their limbs grew stiff and cold,
> Their hearts' blood dyed its every fold.
> Then raise the scarlet standard high!
> Within its shade we'll live or die.
> Tho' cowards flinch and traitors sneer,
> We'll keep the red flag flying here.

> Bring me my bow of burning gold:
> Bring me my arrows of desire;
> Bring me my spear, oh, clouds unfold!
> Bring me my chariot of fire –
> I will not cease, from mental fight,
> Nor shall my sword –

Suddenly the land to my right is fenced. And there's a sign. An official-looking, printed, black on white sign. I stop to read: ABORIGINAL LANDS. NO ENTRY WITHOUR PERMIT. NO ALCOHOL. Same grey-green scrub, same empty skyline, same country. Aboriginal lands.

There's a shifting in my head. As if the wobble heat lays on the land has got into my skull; maybe I'm heat-hazed. I see and don't see – one of those pictures that changes if you move, or if you close one eye. With the right eye the clown's face is sad, with the left suddenly it's smiling. That's what I see. Except I don't even have to move, I'm seeing two things at once, and there's a shimmer to them. What? A trick of the light. Defect of the vision. My mind is split.

I'm looking at low scrappy bushes and sand-coloured rocks, and I'm appalled. Are Aborigines corralled here like rare species in a game reserve? Do visitors gather at the fence to watch them feed? Is this apartheid or what?

But I'm thinking, with the shimmer that transforms the picture utterly, yes. It's the only way. Draw a line to keep the whites out. Ban the drink. Keep the sacred places private.

No. This must be a fucking joke, what sort of a sop is this? Steal a continent, then fence a strip of desert and say, 'That's yours?'

But then yes. If it had been done from the start – if some division of land had been made to put boundaries around the whites' insatiable greed – Weren't the blacks saying it, way back then: that the Brits could have Sydney but they wanted to keep their hunting grounds up at Parramatta? Share. But no, even when they had retreated to the most barren and inhospitable deserts, cattle farmers and mining companies drove them off again.

This is too little, too late, Stephen.

But William would be glad. Aboriginal lands. No alcohol. No entry without permit. Even after two hundred years. 'What is now proved was once only imagined.'

The Blacks didn't need to imagine. They knew the land was theirs. But William imagined it into a white brain – in the face of 'Terra Nullis'; in the face of British law which gave Aborigines no rights, which permitted them to be hunted and despatched like vermin.

But he achieved nothing, Stephen.

He imagined. Here. And in England, Africa, West Indies. He *imagined* – against the current of his time – black people to have rights.

Of course he didn't achieve. You expect one man to change the world? You expect *one man* to change the world, Stephen? How many centuries does it take for a trickle of water to wear a groove through rock? You poor silly arrogant sod. You are a leaf on the tree, a speck in the dark, a jot, a dot, a quark.

*

My skin's prickling and burning – have to turn on the air-con. Swallow the cooler air in gulps. Slowly, I drive on.

There's a big space in my head. There's a space, there's light. Where the pressure was before. Like someone's drilled a hole to let out all the steam. Sweet space and light.

Bit of a wobble there. Wave of something. Tiredness, maybe. OK? I think so, yes. Check the map. Heading for Wanaaring, then left for Milparinka, Pooles Monument, Sturt National Park. Spend the night there. The unsealed roads shave about 150 k off the journey.

At last I come to a left turn, with a signpost for White Cliffs, then another left fork about 30 k up the road. I leave the empty-looking, fenced Aboriginal lands behind. I'm heading towards Yancannia Range, wrinkle of hills which dances like a mirage in front of me. The track gets more stony, there's a huge lizard (baby dinosaur, looks like) sunning himself at the side, that doesn't move even when I slow right down. A couple of piles of rubble. Homes of the farmers who used to shop in Wilcannia? In some places mines – little winding ghosts of tracks leading over a ridge and out of sight, to abandoned holes in the ground, and heaps of dirt. Even if they found opals and gold – the land just shrugged them off. I've got the whole empty horizon to myself, the whole hot stony alien world.

A sudden subliminal change on the dashboard. Red light. Before I can work out what, a juddering – crack like a pistol shot! The engine dies. Suddenly, hard, so that I stop – don't even roll to a halt, I stop. A cloud of steam.

I prise open the bonnet, burning my fingers. Something's bust. The engine stinks of burning. It's smoking hot. It's steaming.

I get back in the car. Twiddle the key. And realize that without the engine not even the air-con will work.

I'm in the middle of fucking nowhere. The sun directly overhead. If I had planned it I couldn't have done better.

I sit in the car as it heats up. There are no more trees ahead than there were behind. There are spindly two-foot-high bushes with sparse narrow grey leaves. I even know why they're narrow. To reduce the surface area and thus limit loss of moisture by evaporation.

My hands on the map make dark fingerprints of sweat. There's nothing back the direction I've come from. Nothing for miles. Ahead – a couple of homesteads marked, maybe 20 k on. But if they're like the others I've passed, they'll be abandoned. Won't there be water? A rain butt, a borehole? No, of course not – that'll be the first thing to collapse. It's maybe 70 k to the main road. Where I might conceivably meet a vehicle. About 35 miles. Possible to walk it in a night.

The car is unbearably hot. I open the doors. It feels hotter than outside. But the roof does provide shade. You know what to do Stevie: stay in the car; conserve energy and liquid, and walk after dark.
I drag my open suitcase off the back seat, it sprawls to the ground, scattering clothes. What a pillock you'll look if someone does drive along in ten minutes' time. Crawl on to the back seat, curl up my knees to fit myself on to its length. Like a chicken in a roasting tin.

Shit, no. Crawl out again, sit on the baking ground with the towel over my head. How can I make myself do nothing for six hours?

Impossible. If you've got to be in the sun (where else can I be?) you might as well start walking towards the main road. You're not conserving liquid any more by sitting here sweating than you would be in walking. Doing nothing is worse. Lying in a metal box cooking. For Christ's fucking sake.

I've got half a litre of fizzy water, a can of lemonade, and a packet of cheesy biscuits. Can't find the lemonade. It may have rolled under the front seats. Or down the sides at the back. Stifling stink of hot plastic and rented car air-freshener makes me gag. Not there. I know there was a can of lemonade. I didn't drink it yesterday. It's gone.

Water. In the radiator. And window-squirters.

There's a sledgehammer in my head now banging out the strokes of heat like a blacksmith on his anvil clang clang clang. I burn my hand again on the radiator cap. Wrap it in a T-shirt. Wrench it off. Foul reek of burnt metal. Ah. And sight of daylight. The radiator is not only empty but cracked from stem to stern, I can see the ground through it. Ha ha, Stevie. The car's revenge.

There's a couple of inches of liquid in the bottom of the window squirter bottle. OK. That and the mineral water. And the towel over my head.
I start to walk along the track. The time on my wrist is 14.02.

Right to walk. Better than sitting still. Arms're burning though. Should have put on long-sleeve shirt. Lobsters die a horrid death.

Yes Stephen, thank you. Head aches. Not clanging now; shimmering, a constant pain like one of those things they make quiver, playing music. A kind of metal strip. Well a string would do. Violin string, anything.

If I piss I could save it in the bottle and drink it. But I don't need to piss. I forgot the biscuits. Could have eaten them tonight in the cool. Maybe get dew. Do you? In the desert? See the stars, eh? William's stars. An adventure. Walk the desert at night.

15.00 Drink the window-cleaning water. At least I don't have to carry the sticky bottle any farther. Tastes of soap and dust and something a bit chemical. Only a couple of mouthfuls. Hardly worth bothering. Leaves a bad taste. Very bad. Throat burning. Have to take a swig of mineral water to wash it down.

15.27 Giddy and nauseous. Sit down. Ground burns me through trousers. Try to stand. Vomit.

Vomit copiously.

Shit shit and shit. All that liquid. All that fucking liquid wasted. The bastard fucking window washer. Emptied my stomach. Better keep going.

The track forks. No signs, no indication of anything. Both look equally unused. Start to laboriously unfold map, the heat is coming off the path and socking me in the jaw. Realize no point since I don't know where I am. OK. Eeny meeny miny mo. The left-hand track.

15.58 Hotter and hotter. Left side of my face burning now – sun getting round towel. Arms blistering. Lips feel big, tongue too. Feet bad, swollen. Belly ache. Recall Tench's account of a day so hot that fruit-bats dropped dead from the trees, and flying birds from the sky. No birds here to drop. No trees.

17.17 Heat less fierce. Sun nasty, vicious on L side of face, but losing power. Feet very bad. Wet inside shoes, raw. Throat parched. Stomach deliriously light and queasy. Allow brief rest.

Drink four mouthfuls water which takes level down to bottom of label. No more tonight. Consider removing shoes, but what's the point. Arms very painful. Also back centre of neck which towel seems to have left exposed. Sun rapidly descending. I am hungry.

If I chose the wrong track I've been walking along it for two hours now. Succumb to urge to examine map – the tracks do fork, but they all meet the road in the end. Some just take a bit longer. Oh fine, well, there's all the time in the world isn't there Stevie? But I should have come to a homestead, if that was an official fork in the track. And I never.

Getting dark. 19.03. Bless the cooling air. Possibility of comfort makes me want to curl up and sleep. Get up before you seize up. Got to make the most of the night.
It *is* a track. It's small but it's a track, so it must go somewhere – somewhere someone wants or once wanted to go. But I should have got to something by now. What if it leads to an abandoned farm and stops?
Well what're the choices? If you go all the way back, maybe the other one dies too. Then you've wasted time *and* got no farther forward. (As opposed to simply getting no farther forward.)
Choice is, go on or back. Both directions equally unknown. OK, I'll go on. It's less fucking disappointing.

Night. Walking again. Stars're bright. Keep eyes fixed on tyre rut. It's uneven. Nearly fell a bit back. Animals about. Kangaroos. Couple of dogs – dingoes I suppose – at the carcase of something. Maybe a car killed it? Someone using this road. Animals oddly noisy – thumps and rustles. Expect it to be a person. Bad stomach cramps. Doubled me up a couple of times. Too empty. Those fucking biscuits in the car how stupid can you get. It's got cold quick. Surprisingly quick.

Olla doesn't know where I am.
Olla doesn't? *You* don't, you hopeless joke.
It'll be all right. I'll get back. I'll do you a deal.
Who? Me?
There's only you, Stevie. Who d'you think I'll do a deal with? Fucking God? I promise I'll go back. It'll be different. Now I know.
Yes?
Now I know. I don't have to change the world. I'll go back to teaching. If you let me get back. Back to the classroom. Imagining. Trying, at least. On a small canvas. Limited enough (as you said), maybe to be pure.
And Olla?
That too. Keep trying. Don't give up. In the very act of trying – you prove – what? Something. That you're alive. That you still think, maybe . . . that her name still . . .

That's the deal?
Yeah. Now let me get back.
Wish I could, kid. Wish I could.

Cold. Very cold. I'm shaking.
Fell over. Stopping to rest.

04.00 Teeth chattering. Going on a bit. Keep dropping bottle. Hands
too cold. It won't wedge under my arm any more. Might as well
drink it now. It's not enough anyway. Legs sluggish.

Dawn. All very. Pretty for a moment. Yellowish sky. Bushes dark.
Stars still. Funny really. If you do die. Didn't think you could, did
you. Escape. Get lost. Ironic. Should sit and look at this. Beautiful.
Make the most of your last.
Can't. Panicking.
You don't give up, do you Stevie? Wanting to be alive. Even though
rationally –

Smudge of cloud over there, moving. Strange. Like a small tornado.
Against the clear sky. Coming towards me?

Keep your eyes on the ground. No stopping. Will to live is stronger.
Primordial instinct.
Even Daniel.
Battling on. Doesn't want to die.

Daniel.
Boy?
Is it you? Hobbling through the desert? Waiting for the sun to scorch
you again?
Ill-equipped – crippled? Too dumb to cry for help?

Oh shit. Wanting to stay alive, as much as I bloody do?

Oh child.
Have to stop. Sit. On this rut. Oh child. To make me waste precious
bodily fluid in a tear.

I'm sorry.
Daniel. I'm sorry.

The results of Daniel's three days of tests show a much greater degree of brain activity than the consultant expected.

Of course.

The consultant – Dr Ahmed, the little bespectacled Asian – is excited. He wants to show me coloured pictures of Daniel's brain, and graphs with irregular patterns of waves across them. He wants to know what Daniel responds to at home; how I can tell when he likes a piece of music, for example? He talks about the amazing channels of communication opened up by computer technology for physically handicapped children. He mentions (as has Stephen's mother; Mrs Brown next door; teachers at Stephen's school; the newsagent; the health visitor; complete strangers who stop us in the street to poke their noses in) Christy Brown. He looks at me differently. He mentions faith, and miracles.

I am unsure how to proceed. Was it Daniel's intention to start making his powers known so early? Is there any danger for him, in doctors guessing at his potential? I think not. They are unlikely to imagine – to be able to conceive of – the extent of his powers, and so have no reason for wishing to harm him. On the contrary, Dr Ahmed is so delighted by this freakish reversal of their expectations that he seems disposed to lavish time and money on finding ways to assist Daniel's development.
But is this the thing to do?
Must he not develop secretly, with no assistance but mine? Is it possible they may divert or even disengage his powers, by their interference?

And yet look how often he has been sick. He has succumbed to illness repeatedly in the last few months, and I know the reason as well as he does. The world's cruelty and pain oppresses him, smothers him, until he wilfully draws illness into himself, to battle internally, teasing himself with the longed-for possibility of peace and escape through death; blocking out the bigger distress of the world with close-up physical struggles of his own. This despair, this seeking refuge in disease, is despite my efforts and my love. All that I can do only, at best, counterbalances the evil. And as he grows older, can perceive and encompass more of the world – will it not be necessary for him to have other help than mine? He is strong, he will be strong;

all-powerful. But to grow up beating and beating against all distress will sap his energies and test him to the utmost. If help can be offered; if they will ease the transition from helpless infant to all-powerful one – then I should agree. It must be in his interests for me to agree. And if he is to become a subject of scientific attention, and have a computer with controls attached to fingers or toes, to assist communication, isn't that better than the nursery assistant with her rattles and coloured cardboard (a threat which I have not yet found a convincing way to avoid).
He will be *choosing* what to communicate; he is as capable of guarding his secret as I am.

Yes. Surely, this must be the clinching argument. He has *allowed* his brain activity to become known to them. It was his choice to reveal it. Therefore, he desires their help. He is making this known to me. It detracts nothing from what I alone can give to him. But it eases his path to power. And allows him insight into the closed world of these clever men. It is the best thing he could have done. In allowing himself to become their subject, he penetrates their world of knowledge. I must help him, simply, to take the best of everything they offer. I must be with him to protect him from any abuses; I myself must understand and be familiar with whatever tools and equipment they offer him. I am his guardian. This is the first step; the secret is not revealed, but is too great to be kept concealed entirely.

And maybe he will conquer them by wonder. It was wonder I saw, on Dr Ahmed's face. Wonder at Daniel, my son.

Stephen, knowing nothing of this, has gone. Perhaps it would not have interested him. He left on Sunday for Australia. I am glad not to have him in the house, his presence oppresses Daniel. He has gone for a month, to do 'on-the-spot researches' for his book. Why he has really gone is a mystery to me; the book will come to nothing, as I am sure he knows.

I think it possible he may not return. When men leave their wives, the reasons one hears are clearly defined. They leave for another woman. For several other women. Or men. For excitement, freedom, to avoid responsibility. To break out. I do not believe any of these is the cause of Stephen's departure. He has no energy for any of these

367

things. He is not looking for a new life; he has been hardly present in this one.

There is a freezing white fog outside, the garden is completely obscured. It is oddly radiant. The school Christmas holidays last three weeks; I do not know whether he has informed the office he will be absent for the first week of January term. I don't even know the time he is supposed to arrive back.

Maybe he hasn't gone to Australia. Maybe this is his way of disappearing; the way some people do by leaving their clothes and wallet on the beach, wading into the sea and pretending that they've drowned. To start again. But if he seeks a new identity, I cannot imagine he will find one. I cannot think of one he could adopt. What could dinosaurs have become, if they had avoided extinction? A plesiosaurus, for example; it is not an adaptable shape, it would not have fitted in to a new world order.

He is well-insured. Uncharacteristically, he told me that and showed me the papers, just before he left. Daniel and I would not be short of money. But I would just like him to know about Daniel. I would like to see *him* wonder.

When Daniel is asleep I go through Stephen's room. He has tidied. The surface of the desk is clear. I turn the radiator off. There is anyway enough heat from the rest of the house to prevent dampness. The top drawer of his desk is the usual mess of writing implements, Sellotape, drawing pins, cheque-book stubs. In the second drawer stationery. In the third drawer a fat brown envelope. I examine it: his book on William Dawes. There is no letter in it. Underneath the envelope, some pages stapled together, headed 'Chapter 24?' Nothing else. The wordprocessor is unplugged, the library books have all gone. He has not left a message.

I check Daniel, he is sleeping sweetly. I sit at Stephen's desk. Why is this chapter out of the envelope? I begin to read.

CHAPTER TWENTY-FOUR

A special place

September 1791. Booron had several times expressed a wish to visit Parramatta, and Richard Johnson brought her with him on the boat, one Saturday when he was coming to officiate at two marriages and a number of baptisms. William met them and conducted them along the great road from the landing place to the Governor's new house, the road was almost completed now, providing a clear view along the straight mile of its length. He was proud of its construction and nodded at Richard's compliments, noting with satisfaction Booron's wide-eyed, silent gazing at the view. They entered the Governor's garden in order to look over the great natural crescent of land lying below it, which had that month been planted with eight thousand vines – a sight, as Richard said, to gladden the heart.

Leaving Richard to go about his business, William led Booron round the new storehouse and barrack, the nine covered saw-pits where work could be continued in all weathers, the new blacksmith's shop, and the two long thatched sheds which formed the hospital. She was not talkative; William guessed that she was inhibited by the open stares she attracted, a barefoot native woman dressed in European clothes. Down in the Cove most people knew that she lived with the Johnsons but here in Parramatta she was an oddity. He felt awkward and embarrassed on her behalf, and was relieved when they set out away from the main settlement, towards the woodlands which were currently being cleared.

It was a mild sunny early spring day, with a stiffish breeze from the south; ahead of them, plumes of dark smoke rose diagonally against the blue sky.

'It looks strange, doesn't it?' he said, smiling, looking for a point of contact. But she shook her head and scowled, and so they walked on to the edge of the clearing in silence.

Work was proceeding at an impressive rate; within six weeks, five hundred convicts had burnt and cleared two hundred acres of wilderness. In the blackened expanse small clusters of men dug and hacked at recalcitrant stumps, dragging their booty to flickering fires. Their sooty skin and ragged filthy clothing made them appear appropriate denizens of this charred landscape; here and there the wind whipped up eddies of flying cinders, and twirled thin streamers of smoke from smouldering logs, so that the whole surface of the land seemed to be shifting, fragmenting off into the sky.

'They should be ready within the week to turn the earth,' William said, staring at the toiling, ant-like figures, 'and plant seed before the end of September – which will ripen over the summer months and be harvested in January. Next time you visit here it will be unrecognisable – a sea of green shoots.' He turned to her with a smile. But she was crying. Quite silently, her wide open eyes welled with tears that overflowed and rolled down the soft black curve of her cheeks.

'Booron? What is it? Don't cry – '

Silently she turned and walked away into the trees that bordered the cleared land.

'Booron!' She did not look back. After a minute's hesitation William followed her, she was already hidden by the trees.

'Booron!' He quickened his pace. The smell of smoke and soot was, if anything, stronger in the trees: it hung there sheltered from the wind which rattled the higher branches of the tall red-gums. It was a swathe of forest Phillip had initially ordered to be left to provide Parramatta with timber and firewood – but many were now arguing that it should be cleared. Escaped convicts lived in the woods, and made incessant raids on tools and supplies; natives also used the woods as cover, they had already attacked one settler's house and destroyed the crops with fire.

'Booron!' He broke into a run, following the direction he had seen her take. There was no sign of her. Without doubt she would find her own way back; but he was unsettled by her tears. Besides, it was stupid for the time to be wasted. Over their last few meetings in Sydney Cove he had begun to glean from her stories about the stars and moon, a sequence of stories he would like to complete. It now appeared that there were stories to explain the presence of every star in the sky. She had promised to tell him about the morning star, Mullyan the eagle-hawk, and his wife Moodai the possum.

Any day now there would be a boat to take the marines back to England; his opportunities to hear and record her stories were strictly limited.

'Booron!' He leant against a tree to catch his breath and listen. But the rustling of leaves overhead made it difficult to hear if there was any movement on the ground. When she stepped silently out of the trees only a few feet away, he jumped, his heart suddenly hammering in his chest. Her face was set and scowling, but the tears were gone.

'You kill the land. No trees, no animals. All kill.'

'It's not *me* – ' No, that was contemptible. As one of Phillip's party he was still as responsible as the rest of them. Not until he had left the service could he make such a disclaimer. 'But Booron, new plants will grow there. Crops, good food to eat. And now the trees are cleared, healthful air can circulate – it will be better for the land.'

'No.'

'But your people burn the woods – at Port Jackson – all along the coast – '

'Not like this. Eora set fire to hunt animal, burn off tall grass, make new shoot come. Not to make land dead and empty.' Her voice wavered. 'So big! So much place burnt away.'

'New shoots *will* grow – maize, wheat, where there was nothing – '

'Something. Look here. *Some*thing.' Angrily she struck the tree beside her.

'But the settlement depends on the food that can be grown here – '

'Food in the woods. Plenty food in the trees.'

'The odd kangaroo or emu – it's not enough, Booron. Without fish *your* people wouldn't survive.'

'Food. Plenty possum in trees, bring him down with smoke. Eels we catch in hollow sticks. Goanna, blue-tongue, many creature. Ants, fine grubs, honey from high trees. We dig yams, roots; pick figs, currant, apple berries, lillypilly, sweet nectar from the bush.'

He knew, she knew he knew. He had made lists and drawings of edible plants and even insects, as a result of questioning her. Certainly there was more to eat than met the untutored European eye, but nowhere near sufficient quantities to support the settlement. The naturally occurring foodstuffs were enough only for small, seasonally moving bands of people – the Eora themselves. Not whites.

'You know we have to grow enough food for hundreds of people. We have to clear this wilderness – '

'Look. You will walk?'

He nodded, following her with relief. He was a poor apologist for Phillip's land clearances. If the Eora chose not to join the European way of life – if they preferred to fish and hunt, rather than grow crops, didn't they have the right to live as their forefathers had done? Some of them clearly wished to have nothing to do with the whites and it was easy to see why. All too often, those who came into the settlement suffered through the contact. First it had been the smallpox; now most of the blacks whose faces were familiar in Sydney Cove were covered in venereal sores – even the children. And Bennelong – and a few of the others – had developed quite a taste for rum.

Booron led him through the tranche of preserved forest to the untouched land at the western extremity of Parramatta's clearances. She moved quietly and at a good speed. William followed, noticing again how gracefully she walked – the way she held herself very erect, as if she balanced something on top of her head. She moved lightly but without hesitation; fearlessly. Maybe she knew these woods of old. With a pang he realized that he still knew almost nothing of the life she had led before she was brought into the settlement.

Eventually they came to a place where the trees opened out into a natural clearing. The gentle spring sunshine, here unhindered by trees, had warmed the ground; ahead, there were low bushes of that type the convicts used for wattling, covered in masses of tiny golden flowers. Small blue and yellow butterflies hovered above them.

'Sit,' commanded Booron.

William sat on the dry colourless grass, his body relaxing in the warmth. Around the clearing the tall pale-barked gums made an almost perfect circle. Booron sat down a few feet distant; she was watching him. She didn't seem to be angry any more. He smiled.

'Special place,' she said.

He nodded.

'You see it?'

He could still hear the stiff rustling and soughing of the wind in the trees, but it was no longer overhead. They were on an island of silence lapped by its noise. The space was light and warm and open, protectively framed – cradled, almost – by the surrounding trees. It reminded him suddenly of a place in England, which he had visited as a boy – a place . . .

He struggled for the memory. Near Oxford. His father had taken him to Oxford to visit an aged cousin, an historian at the university – it was in the summer. One long hot day they had driven out of the city in the historian's curricle, down narrow dusty country tracks to the foot of a small and steeply sloping hill, where the historian was engaged upon excavations. Wittenham. The name came back to him. Benjamin preferred to rest at the bottom, but William and his old cousin had toiled up to the deep ditch which encircled the top of the hillock. Here three men were digging, under the historian's directions, making a pile of stones, bones and other fragments for his inspection.

While the old cousin looked through their day's discoveries, William went on up to the top of the little hill. Its slopes were wooded, mainly oak and beech, with a few dark holly trees thrown in – but the top was cleared. From the top there were long views, between and over tree tops, of the gentle undulating Oxfordshire countryside. Underfoot the ground was riddled with rabbit holes, the grass nibbled short and dotted with their pellets.

He sat in a clear patch, with the sun prickling his skin; a slight breeze moved across the big-leaved trees with an expectant sigh, then fell away. In the stillness then he gradually became aware of the power of the place.

It was a heady, rising, expanding sensation – as if, by being there, he had become part of something greater. There was a power which lifted and opened him to all the world. It was making him a part of everything, it was a spirit that opened and embraced, so that he soared above himself yet was securely held. It was belonging, it was understanding. It was escape from his own bounds.

Sometimes afterwards in church, when the whole congregation was in voice, singing as one, an inkling of that memory touched him and he wondered if it was the same: and if it was God?

God is love.

Was it love that had opened him wide as the world and made him one with it? Was it God he had been embraced by, become part of, on top of the ancient hill-fort?

As he surfaced from the memory, Booron was watching him; he felt embarrassed by her scrutiny.

'It is a powerful place. Is it old?' he said foolishly, scrambling to his feet.

'Sit down. I tell you story.'

He sat.

'Every place have story, dreaming. This place, this place, this place – ' she indicated with her hands – 'each one have different story. But you – ' the arms spread wide, the hands quickly down-turned, flattening – 'burn. Kill. Make same.'

'No – '

No. No one would destroy this place; a place like this could not be destroyed.

'One story,' she said firmly. 'In old time many many people come through this country, tribe of dog, pigeon, black swan, blue-tongue lizard, many people each tribe name for a creature. They make ceremony and move on. Every day, two days, these people move on to new Bora. Until the poor widow Millindooloonubbah come staggering into camp crying. *You all left me to travel alone with my large family of children. How could the little feet of my children keep up with you?* Nobody help those children, nobody stay to help that mother. Each time she come to camp with her children, the tribes move on. There is nothing left in water-hole but mud. *My thirsty children cry to me and I can only give them mud.* At each water-hole one child is dead. A woman goes to her with water. *Too late! Too late! Why should a mother live when her children are dead?* But she take one mouthful water. It gives her strength to cry to all the tribes: *You were in such haste to get here! Now you will stay!* Then all the tribe close by her turn to trees – ' Booron paused, raising her right arm theatrically to indicate the circle of trees around them. 'And every other tribe become his namesake, black swan, emu, duck and all the rest. They lose the power to speak. Then Millindooloonubbah lay down here and die.'

William looked up at the tops of the gums, dipping and swaying in the wind. He could hear Millindooloonubbah wailing for her lost children. His heart ached with the dumb guilt and restless sorrow of the trees as they stood, branches tossing, rooted to the spot for ever.

Booron squatted upon her haunches. She was watching him with her clear brown eyes, a single wrinkle of frown between her brows.

'You understand?'

An opening of heart and mind. He was part of this. He got to his feet, lifting his face blindly to the curved blue sky. The ancient clearing held the sunlight. It held the two of them at its centre. It held the difference between them.

'Yes. I understand.'

She nodded, satisfied.

He reached out to take her hands and pull her up. She started to rise then her face lit up with teasing laughter, and she braced her weight against him. William felt his own face breaking open into an answering grin of delight. Rocking on his heels, he pitted his weight against hers. Her hands were strong and hot and dry in his. He did not want to let go.

Anyone looking for Booron in the journals of the First Fleeters will find that she was more commonly known as Abaroo ('from our mistake in pronunciation', Watkin Tench). As with William Dawes and all the other historical characters, I have aimed to be faithful to the recorded facts of her life. Since her people were wiped out, no one can tell what stories she may have known; those she relates here are from other New South Wales tribes. The Eora words which appear here were recorded by the settlement's Judge Advocate, David Collins, and first published in 1798.

I am indebted to the many other writers and historians whose work I have drawn on, and two in particular who fired my imagination: M. Barnard Eldershaw in *Phillip of Australia*, and Keith Willey's *When the Sky Fell Down*.

Mollie Gillen's excellent *The Founders of Australia* gives a brief biography of everyone who sailed with the First Fleet, including the convicts' crimes (where known), and their eventual fate in New South Wales. In one or two places I have used a novelist's license with the facts.

Thank you to everyone who helped me with the research for this book.

J.R.